Books by J. D. Evans

MAGES OF THE WHEEL SERIES

Prequel (Summer 2020)
Reign & Ruin
Storm & Shield
Siren & Scion
Ice & Ivy (Winter 2020)

MAGES OF THE WHEEL BOOK THREE

Siren & Scion

J. D. EVANS

Published by Whippoorwill Press LLC 2020

North Carolina, United States

ISBN: 978-1-951607-05-0

Cover Art—Tatiana Anor; https://www.artstation.com/tanyaanor

Cover Design—Eric. C. Wilder; https://www.ericcwilder.com/

Interior formatting & Design—Terry Roy

Editing—Michelle Morgan; https://www.fictionedit.com

To those who cannot see their own bright, glorious light,
because the darkness is so deep.

I see you.

Poem of the Wheel
3rd

Our light shines brightest in
the darkness
Mercy birthed of pain
For they are the kindest
Who can rise again
From wounds inflicted
Over lifetimes
In love from pain reflected
We surface from abime

ONE

AMARA WAITED ON THE steps of the palace as Djar parked her personal carriage and saw to the horse. It was a lovely day, and she had considered riding, but wanted every opportunity she could take to prove that what she wanted to ask of the Sultana, yet again, was not above her station at all. The carriage spoke more to her standing as a successful merchant, so she had chosen it.

The change in seasons showed in the budding trees and the promise of flowers on plants that preferred the warmth of spring and summer to the cool temperatures of winter. While Amara could appreciate an artistically constructed flower arrangement, she knew too little of plants themselves to predict the pace of spring by their rhythms. The open spaces at the palace were beginning to look more like the gardens they were as leaves made appearances on bushes that had, through the winter, been more skeletal sculptures than greenery.

The mud had worsened, of course, as snow in the mountains melted and rain was just a bit more frequent than it was at any other time of Turn. Which was to say, still infrequent. However, the mud was enough to cause Amara the necessity of boots and utilitarian clothing, which she despised. Especially considering that her reason for seeking an audience with the Sultana certainly would have been better served by her most opulent brocades.

As Djar finished watering the horse and wiping its legs of mud, Amara observed three young women exit the garden to the west of the courtyard. They were vaguely familiar, daughters of Viziers, no doubt, just into their womanhood and on the hunt after a winter of forced isolation. Amara smiled to herself as their attention was collectively caught by Djar. He was a fine specimen of a man, broad-shouldered and slim-hipped, with the easy economy of movement she had only ever seen in men accustomed to fighting brutally. Everything about him pronounced him a warrior, from his posture to the way his gaze swept his surroundings with habitual frequency. In Narfour, trade with the many nations of the Sun Sea made foreigners as common as grains of wheat. The Merchant Pier and surrounding districts were a bright rainbow of humanity. But that bright rainbow rarely made its way to the palace, and so the girls had stopped upon the threshold of the garden and courtyard, staring wide-eyed and whispering, as Djar strode with all the lazy awareness of a lion to where Amara waited for him.

"Do not swagger quite so obviously. Their eyes might boggle from their heads and then how will they find husbands?" Amara tsked. Djar grinned, the bright white of his teeth against the matte black of his skin only amplifying the stark beauty of his broad face. "I would leave you to your amusement with them, but I cannot today."

"They are *nehar*," he said with a dismissive shrug.

"Nothing is forbidden, in the right context." Amara dismissed the idea that he was below anyone, though the divide between the nobility of Tamar and the merchant class could be cavernous, depending on which family one was discussing.

"*It would be wrong of me to ruin their prospects of a happy marriage. What husband would want a woman who was constantly pining away for another?*" he said in Meneian. His grin made a reappearance and Amara returned it with an approving smile.

She might have spoken to him about his pride, but was interrupted by the arrival of a guard escort of four mounted men through the main palace gate. They were followed by a plodding gaggle of disheveled, filthy refugees, whom they herded toward the arena. Amara watched their passage with both sympathy and concern. When she had arrived in Narfour many Turns ago as a girl from Menei, she had been in no better state than these. The Blight in Sarkum was driving them in ever greater numbers into Tamar, and places in the eastern valley had already reported cases of the Blight wiping out their own spring crops. Soon Sarkum refugees would be joined by those from Tamar. The situation was becoming dire, and explosive. A second camp had already been set up at the far north end of the city, and a third, which these people were likely destined for, was planned in the valley. Resentment was building, and fear.

"I saw them on our way up the palace road," Djar said, turning to face the arena. "Coming down the mountain from the pass. It is the fourth such group this quarter."

"I'm afraid you've lost your admirers." Amara nodded to indicate the three women, who had turned their unrewarded attention to the gate. The last of the refugees were ushered into the arena and the guard commander, Bashir Ayan, dismounted at the rear of the group. That he was personally conducting some of the refugee runs was worrisome. It meant the guard force remained taxed, despite the men the Sultana had pulled from the City Watch to augment them.

Djar made a low sound of recognition. He and Bashir got along well enough, in the way that rivals often did. A guarded friendliness and mutual respect.

She approved of the girls' physical taste in men, at the least. Bashir had always caught her eye. But earth mages never held any appeal to her beyond their often very pleasing looks. They were too steady, predictable, and intractable. All traits she found tedious.

"It is just as well," Djar said in lyrically accented Tamaran, "I cannot abide the witlessness of Narfour's nobility."

To that, Amara heartily agreed. She watched Bashir for a moment longer, contemplating the refugees and the direness of the spreading Blight. It was not her place to question the Sultana on her plan of action. She knew that the Sehzade, as Vizier of Agriculture, had turned a great deal of attention to researching the Blight and coming up with countermeasures. But the devastating plant disease gave no quarter and was spreading with a rapidity that defied explanation.

As the guard commander turned his back to Amara, she moved toward the entrance of the palace, only to see a woman exit at a jog. Amara stared, watching her progress across the broad half-circle of the landing, down the sandstone steps, then as she broke into a sprint across the gravel of the courtyard. Amara was not tall by any standards, but this woman made her look so. Her hair was unbound, a wild nimbus of chestnut curls, and she wore the oddest clothes Amara had ever seen in Tamar. Her salvar were tight-fitting, wrapped at the lower legs, and her caftan barely long enough to cover her backside. She wore swords on her back as well, two of them, a most unusual adornment for a woman of Tamar.

"She's returned, then," Djar said, revealing he knew more than Amara. She turned an accusing glare on him. He knew better than to harbor knowledge that she did not.

"Attiyeh Charah," he said, naming the First House Charah that had been named to the Circle only a quarter ago. Amara knew of her, of course, and that she had recently been sent to the Republic—for what purpose Amara did not know. She had never seen her before.

"I expected someone more...distinguished."

Djar laughed. Amara continued to wallow in shock as the diminutive woman called Bashir's name. He stiffened and glanced over his shoulder, then down. Surprise, confusion, then joy suffused an expression that had been nothing but exhaustion a moment before. Charah Attiyeh leapt into his embrace.

"Did you know about…" Amara indicated the two of them, who were doing nothing at all to hide their obvious affection. "…that?"

"Knew. But did not care." Djar shrugged. "She is a good match for him, I think. There is more fire in her than you might imagine, from her stature."

"And lightning, so I hear." Amara dismissed the entire situation and started up the stairs. It would not do to let curiosity over another mage make her late to an appointment she'd been maneuvering to get for nearly a season. "Kiya can speak of nothing else. Ever since they appointed Attiyeh Charah as Lieutenant Commander she has begun to talk of entering the force as well. She speaks of watching her spar until I can bear it no more. Do you wish to spar her as well?"

"I have no interest in enraging her lover," Djar said. A peerless fighter, Djar was not a mage, and so was at a deadly disadvantage in Tamar. Though to be fair, a mage would have to be a very quick spell-worker to damage Djar before he'd left them with fewer appendages than they had begun with.

"Were I you," Amara said as they passed beneath the columned arches of the entrance to the palace, "I would be more concerned about enraging *her*."

They were met in the entrance hall by Samira, the Sultana's faithful and ever-present head maiden-in-waiting, who greeted them with a formal, gracious bow. "Mistress Mutar, it is always such a pleasure to see you," Samira said in her fire-warmed voice. Amara knew she did not mean a word of it.

Samira was quite protective of the Sultana and by proxy her cousin, whom Amara had set her sights on some number of Turns ago. She had never met another fire mage as subdued and repressed as Samira. Especially considering she was a gifted Sival, whose magic was not quite as repressed as her emotion. The woman would be a sight to see were she ever unleashed. Perhaps in the throes of passion? Amara had occasionally dabbled in a trio or quartet for trysting, but never found it as enjoyable as one on one. However, seeing other women in their pleasure had been a most interesting diversion, and she occasionally thought such a thing would be just what poor Samira needed. A bit of release from the tension and sorrow that seemed to hang about her like a shroud.

"Master Djar." Samira inclined her head in respect. Though Djar was not Amara's servant, he often stepped into the role. Samira would have outranked him by vast degrees if he were a servant, but she never treated him as such, or any servants for that matter. Amara liked her for that reason, even if they remained in unspoken disagreement about Amara's desire for a betrothal to the Sehzade.

"Are you lonely today, Samira?" Djar rumbled in his lion-voiced purr. It was a private joke between them that Amara did not know the origin of. She did know that Djar, who was rarely rebuffed when he chose to make an advance, had once pursued Samira. He had never told Amara what Samira had said when she rejected him, but they had remained in good spirits around each other. Every time they met he asked the same question, and every time she gave the same answer.

"Not today, Djar." She gave him a warm and genuine smile. Perhaps Djar did not see the sadness in it, but water always saw truth most easily in fire, and Amara could see ghosts in all of Samira's expressions.

"The Sultana and Sehzade are ready for you, Mistress," Samira said, her clasped hands held primly in front of her caftan. They followed Samira across the marble tiles of the entrance hall, between the repeated arches that separated the central walk from the outer edges, where cushioned benches lined the walls. The hall was by no means bustling on this day. Amara had seen it filled with ten times the number that occupied it now. There were only a handful of nobles, scattered in small groups, chatting idly as they waited for meetings with Viziers or with other court officials.

They passed through the soaring gilded archway at the far end of the central hall and into the Sultan's receiving hall. Amara did not mind the pace Samira set for them, a kind of quick saunter, that allowed her to admire, yet again, the opulence of everything that surrounded her. The first time Amara had set foot in the palace she vowed she would live in it. Only then would she feel she had truly and forever shed her past and be rid of the frightened, broken little girl that still existed within her.

Weakness. Amara could sometimes forgive it in others but despised it in herself.

Samira stopped in front of the open archway to the room the Sultana had chosen to receive them. It was surrounded above and to the sides by open, geometric lattice painted in gold, the solid panels to either side of the door and near the floor were white, with the Sabri crest carved in relief. Samira entered the room and bowed. Amara followed, with Djar just behind, and bowed as well.

"Mistress Mutar," the Sultana said as Amara straightened. She was seated on one of the curved benches that circled the walls, and the Sehzade sat beside her. While Amara was quite confident that she and the Sultana shared a mutual respect, her relationship—if she would even bother to use that word—with the Sehzade was quite different.

It was because Ihsan was a water mage that Amara had first conceived of the idea to work her way into his circles. Water was a sensual element, one which imbued its children with the desire for connection, physical, emotional, intellectual. Second House mages most often ended up with others of their same House, because the only other House with similar tendencies was the Fifth, and fire and water rarely mixed well.

Yet if she had not already known he was a Second House mage, she would never have guessed it. Instead of being open, warm, and engaging, he was closed, cold, and critical. She still wasn't certain the man understood that she existed. Not, perhaps, out of haughtiness, but rather because he so obviously despised his cousin's court and its machinations, and would rather be hiding away in his own home. Amara did not know what he did there; most of the women at court agreed that the most eligible bachelor in the city was a recluse, and wasn't it a shame. Some speculated he hid himself away because he was ashamed of the scars that swept his neck and face.

Amara suspected Ihsan was not trying to hide his physical scars from the world, but something much deeper. Besides, she did not want him for his beauty or his affection, or frankly cared much at all what he preferred as his pastimes. She wanted the position a marriage to him would afford her, the affirmation that she had finally, and completely, risen from the nightmare of her beginnings, and could never be forced to return.

"Efendim, I am greatly honored by your willingness to see me during such trying times. I observed the arrival of another group of refugees as I entered the palace," Amara said.

"Your request was in fact well timed, as I have a matter to discuss with you as well. Samira," the Sultana said to her handmaiden, "you may show them in."

Amara continued to smile, but did not care for the change in the focus of their meeting. Of course the Sultana was aware of the reason Amara asked to meet with her. This was the third time she had approached the Sultana about a marriage. It was unusual for a woman to seek a man's hand in marriage and especially a prince's, even in progressive Narfour, but Amara had vowed to pilot her own destiny from the moment she fled Menei. She would not be frightened away because what she wanted was unorthodox.

"I would like for you to meet someone. Or rather, two some-ones." The Sultana rose as Samira reappeared, a man and a woman in her wake. The woman Amara recognized as the petite First House Charah she had seen moments before in the courtyard. The man was a relation of hers, Amara decided, as they entered and he bowed. The two shared the same smile and eye shape, though his were dark and hers marked with the storm of her magic. In every other respect they were opposites. He was tall and handsome and had taken care to dress himself in colors and tailoring that suited him well. She was short and plain, dressed in the strange modified clothing Amara had noted earlier. She needed a comb and yards of ribbon to tame the wild mess of her hair.

The man bowed to the Sultana, the woman did not, but peered curiously at Amara and smiled. Amara returned it without feeling, looking instead to the Sultana.

"Mistress Amara Mutar, Charah of the Second House and Master Merchant. I would like to introduce Aysel Attiyeh, Lieutenant Commander of the Palace Guard, Agent of the Agassi, and First of the Circle. As well as her brother, Master Mathei Attiyeh, Agent of the Agassi, Master of the Library, and Deval of the Sixth House."

Amara took a beat to consider the Sultana's phrasing. The Sultana was well aware Amara had no intention of joining her Circle of Chara'a, and while Amara's power was no secret, she limited the use of her magic to small spells that made her daily life convenient. The rest she would have severed away from her like a dead limb if she could. It was a matter of necessity that she had risen to where she was without the use of her magic. And it would stay that way.

The siblings looked at Amara as any sane person would look at a stranger just introduced as a Charah. Despite the fact the woman before her was an equal in magic power, she stared at Amara as though she were awe-inspired. Amara normally accepted such looks with pleasure, but this one made her skin crawl. And the other, while she applauded his sense of fashion, was a death mage. Amara could not very well imagine associating with someone from the Sixth House, despite the Sultana's wish to integrate them back into Tamar.

"It is a great pleasure to meet you both," Amara said, sweetly. "I have heard only a little of your exploits since your arrival from Sarkum. From thieves and refugees to Charah and Master. I must admit to a bit of jealousy at the speed of your rise to notoriety." She smiled. Aysel and Mathei both smiled back.

Aysel gave her brother a knowing look and he took a step closer to Amara, his gaze traveling the length of her clothes.

"I have heard, from my small but growing network of acquaintances, that anybody with any taste at all buys only from you." The intense look of greed in his dark eyes endeared him to her immediately, despite her misgivings about his power.

"My client list is quite full, but I might be able to make an exception for an up-and-coming young man of your…stature." She shifted her stance to emphasize her shape. He was handsome and rangy, exactly the sort of distraction she had been in need of lately. Behind him his sister's eyes widened and a laugh was suppressed behind puffed cheeks. Mathei returned her smile, but his gaze slid sideways to fix briefly on Djar, then back to her.

Amara inclined her head in understanding. In Menei men who preferred men were derogatorily called "blade chasers" and were extinguished swiftly upon being revealed. Tamar was much more tolerant in comparison, death was rarely the penalty, but social status often took a serious blow. Amara never understood the fuss—having grown up in the harems and brothels of Menei had exposed her to preferences far more sinister. How could she fault someone for finding the same qualities attractive that she did?

"Well, we will have to set an appointment for coffee and to discuss outfitting you in a more complimentary fashion. It seems we might share a similar appreciation for beauty in all its forms." It would not cost her much time to engage with him, and earn herself another stream of information from the palace. Her circle of friends would welcome him, they always appreciated a new, handsome face.

The breathtaking joy that overtook his countenance was worth any strain it might put on her schedule. Amara did not know how Sarkum treated men such as Mathei, but perhaps he was not accustomed to being accepted as he was.

"I apologize for the interruption, Sultana Efendim." Mathei bowed to the Sultana. She gave him an indulgent smile, then looked at Amara, her expression smoothing once more to impassivity.

"We both know why you've requested this audience, and I would like to begin by telling you my answer remains no."

Amara inclined her head in acknowledgment. She had not expected the Sultana to simply turn her beloved cousin over just because Amara had asked more than once. It would take negotiation, and in that vein she had carefully planned her verbal maneuvers. Her skill at negotiation had already gotten her this far.

"Since we have last examined the subject, I have added a second vessel to my trade fleet. My monetary worth is now equal to that of the Grand Vizier." Amara folded her hands in front of her.

"Is it a fleet if it is only two ships?" Aysel asked mildly. Her brother elbowed her and gave her a scathing look of censure.

"How many ships do you have, Attiyeh Charah?" Amara said acidly. Aysel raised an eyebrow in challenge.

"Your accomplishments are many, Mistress Mutar, and I have been nothing but impressed with your acumen and tenacity," the Sultana said. "But I am afraid none of them qualify you to marry the Sehzade."

"Because I am not noble born?" Amara said, some of her certainty trickling away, pushed out by temper. The one thing she could never change. And yet the examples of women who qualified by accident of birth were silly and indulged. They could not stand beside a prince and be thought of as anything but ornament. Amara would only improve people's opinions of Ihsan by her drive and accomplishments.

"Because I am rebuilding Tamar in the image of the Old Sultanate. Chara'a have historically chosen to serve the people, are in fact beholden to them by the very nature of their power. I will not allow someone in line for the throne, allow someone to marry my cousin, who does not have the people foremost in their heart."

Her cousin, an acknowledged recluse who did little in the palace beyond scoff at those who chose to play in politics. Yet Amara had to prove herself worthy. She held back a glare that she wished to level at Ihsan, and sighed. "How might I accomplish this, Efendim?"

"It has been rumored, since my father was a child, that there are enclaves of descendants of the mages that fled the Sundering War scattered to the far reaches of the Old Sultanate borders. As far as the Republic, according to some accounts. It is my hope that we may find Third House mages among them who might be capable of dealing with the Blight. Attiyeh Charah has a certain…affinity for collecting information," the Sultana said, and Aysel shifted her feet, looking uncomfortable.

A spy then. Amara heard rumors to that effect. In fact she had heard that the woman was practically kin of the Agassi's, the Sultana's betrothed, brought from Sarkum for her *affinity*.

"I delegated the task of researching the rumors to her, and combing the histories for mention of them to her brother." The Sultana nodded to Aysel, who took a step closer to the dais.

"There are clans of people that the Republic refers to as Suloi, or roadborn, who I believe are descended of those that fled the war." Aysel folded her hands behind her back as she spoke, looking between the Sultana and Amara. "They are nomadic, and difficult to track down. They hide their camps. But I was able to find a few to speak to within the city of Haenna. They are hunted—for persecution and as slaves. The Republic does not condone magic, but its wealthy are apparently happy to abuse magically gifted Suloi for convenience." Aysel paused, her face drawn and sadness overtaking it. "The ones I spoke with were broken and frightened, with very little magic."

"Did you find any Third House mages?" Amara asked, genuinely curious. While some death mages, as obviated by the Agassi and Mathei, had survived the Sundering, the Third House was not so enduring. Amara knew very little of that history, but it seemed to imply that while the other Houses might survive an Unbalance in the Wheel, Creation could not.

Aysel shook her head. "As I understand it, their clans are broken up by House or at least by descent. I was unable to find anyone who could direct me to any clans with creation magic. But my Republic Trade is passing at best and frankly, coercion is not my strength."

She gave Amara a pointed look. No. Amara did not need to know much more of the woman than what she had seen to guess that her strength lay in other areas. Even with some distance between them Amara could sense the storm in her, see it playing across the depths of her pupils. That would not encourage words and confidence in even the most brazen of people.

Aysel continued, "I was able to identify the city of Haenna as the hub of trade in Suloi slaves."

Amara also did not need to know much more to see where this was leading, and everything in her balked. She was multilingual, as most people in Menei were by necessity, and of course, coercion and negotiation were the foundation of all she had achieved. Her gaze flitted to the Sultana, who confirmed her suspicions with a nod.

"I am in need of someone to go to the Republic who is capable of hiding their ties to Narfour. You are Meneian by birth and appearance, are a self-made merchant capable of operating in a strange environment"—she smiled—"who is intelligent and adaptable. You have experience with merchants and shady dealers alike, and apparently," she added dryly, "now have a fleet. I have heard you speak Republic Trade as one born to it, among other languages."

"I heard about someone who might be able to help you," Aysel said, storms flashing more brightly across her irises as she spoke. "An abolitionist based in Haenna. I know very little else about him, only rumors."

The entire scheme was preposterous. She was not beholden to the Sultana in any way, she did not know why the woman thought she could flick her fingers and send Amara off on a wild boar hunt. "Go to the Republic, at risk of my life, and pretend to be someone else. To what end?"

The Sultana smiled faintly. "You will go under the guise of establishing trades with Republic suppliers for Menei. Find the Suloi. If there are Third House mages among them, bring as many as are willing back with you. The abolitionist may be of use to you in this, otherwise I trust you will find a way."

The Sultana looked at Ihsan, who leaned indecorously against the back of the bench they shared, one arm stretched out away from him, his countenance melancholy. He nodded once, and his gaze flashed to Amara's, its demeanor changing from melancholy to obstinacy.

"Prove to me you are capable of handling tasks of this magnitude, that you can put Tamar first," the Sultana said, resigned, "and I will promise you a betrothal to the Sehzade."

Amara smiled to suppress an upwelling of bitter laughter. One corner of the Sultana's mouth lifted in a knowing smile and Amara would have liked to slap it off her face but that she respected the woman's brutal tactics too much. Outmaneuver Sultana Sabri indeed. The woman had not carved a place for herself in the world of men by being dull-witted. They were sisters, in ambition at least.

With a sigh, Amara looked to Mathei and smiled sadly. "It seems our coffee will have to be postponed."

TWO

AMARA STOOD BEFORE HER mirror, watching the reflection of Djar as he paced by the windows. She squeezed the water gently from her hair, contemplating all that needed to be done to prepare for a trip of such length. When she had started as an apprentice, she had made many of the voyages to Menei, but the Republic was much farther, and she did not know how long she would be gone. It made planning for the upkeep of the shop and packing for the voyage much more complex. There were orders for two seasons out, and one of her Guild-appointed apprentices had recently taken a promotion to a tailor, leaving her shorthanded already.

A knock came from downstairs, and Amara reached to her dressing stand, picking up a silk entari, which she pulled around herself as she nodded to Djar. He turned from the window and hurried to the stairs. After a moment, the time it would take him to reach the back door, she heard two voices, one of them feminine in answer to Djar's rumbling greeting.

People only came to the back door of the shop for a handful of specific, usually unpleasant reasons. Amara hurried down, not bothering to dress now that she knew their guest was a woman. She was standing just inside the back door as Djar closed it when Amara reached the bottom of the stairs, and looked up at the sound of Amara's bare feet on the stone. The woman stood huddled and hugging herself.

"Welcome. Are you cold?" Amara asked, gesturing to the small brazier she always kept lit to balance her magic. The woman shook her head. Her greying, light-brown hair was coming loose from the twist she kept it in, and her eyes were red from crying, her hands shaking. Amara took them in her own and led her to a couch she kept in the shop for weary husbands to occupy while she assisted their wives. The woman collapsed onto the couch, continuing to shake her head, as if it would help her to form the words.

"Djar, would you please bring us some coffee?" Amara suspected the woman might calm in his absence. He left without a word, to the small kitchen that was the only domestic room that occupied the lower level of Amara's home. The rest of the space was her shop, half of it storage and sewing space, the rest her storefront. They sat now in the back half, surrounded by bolts of fabric and several maiden forms fitted with caftans in various stages of completion. It was Amara's favorite place in the house, surrounded by the potential and beauty of all the uncut fabric, the vision of each creation coming slowly to fruition before her eyes. Perhaps that was why she had allowed the rumors to spread that if someone was in need, to come to the back door. They would enter into the space that was the truest reflection of her.

"Has something happened? Are you hurt?" Amara asked, in her softest voice. She did not need to use magic to soothe, though she could, when something as simple as a warm and gentle tone would do.

"Not me. Not me." The woman swallowed, then took a deep breath. "My girl. She's with Havva. All cut up." The woman took another shaking breath. Amara took a more thorough look at her. She was wearing linen and cotton salvar and caftan, without entari, the

clothing of a servant. The three cloth belts at her hips, stained and
in disrepair, were embroidered with lilies. The lilies were the symbol
adopted by the poorest brothel in Narfour, and all who worked there,
whether dancer, prostitute, or wine maid wore clothing marked with
it. This woman was too old for the worst work of the brothel, but her
daughter might not be. Amara had been inside the Lily on a few occa-
sions, and over Turns had come to understand that it attracted men,
and women, with odd tastes for pleasure. This was not the first time
she had heard of it going awry.

"If she is with Havva she is in the best place she can be," Amara
said, gently, squeezing the woman's hands. If whoever had hurt the
girl had cut her face, her time at the brothel would be over. That
might seem like a blessing in the short term, or to those who did
not understand that there were few other prospects beyond that work
once one had been indentured to it. But Amara knew better. "Tell me
about her." She had found work for other such women, which was why
people came to the back door of the shop. Because Amara understood
that victims did not only need sympathy and charity. They needed
lives, ropes to lift them out of the darkness of the impossibility of their
lots. Sometimes, she could give them that. A set of clothes to make
them presentable, a recommendation to one of the many merchants
or other tradesmen she dealt with, a place to sleep until they could get
their feet under them again.

"She's Fourth House, like her *ba*." The woman sniffed and wiped
at her reddened nose with a dirty caftan sleeve. It was not unusual
for the poorest of the Fourth House's daughters to end up in the
brothel. Their House's tendency to bestow attractiveness predisposed
them to it.

Djar reappeared bearing a wood-inlaid tray with Amara's favorite
gold and blue painted ibrik and demitasse set atop it. He placed the
tray on the low table by the couch and poured coffee into the cups,

filling the room with the bitter scent of coffee cut with the warmth of cardamom. The woman looked up at Djar as he poured the coffee and handed her a cup, her face filled with the distrust Amara had seen on countless faces, once they were removed from the lie of the brothel. He did not return her gaze, only gave them each coffee then returned to the kitchen. He was every bit a lion, but could be a kitten when mercy dictated.

"The man…he…well she was his favorite. He always asked for her. And she fancied he cared about her." The woman took a drink of the coffee, her silence telling the rest of the story. Amara knew it. The young ones thought when they were someone's favorite, it meant they were cared for. It was never true, in Amara's experience. "She told him she was going to test at the University tomorrow. The Sultana has a scholarship, for gifted mages from the poor quarters."

The girl had told him her hopes and dreams, and all he saw was the prospect of losing his favorite toy. So he'd tried to ruin it. Cold rage washed down Amara's throat and she set her cup down on the tray. "I see," she said. "And your daughter. Is she all right?"

"Her face." The woman shook her head. A face. A face should not be worth what it was.

"But her hands? Her voice? Her legs? Can she work? Can she cast?" Amara pushed, a bit impatiently. The woman took a deep breath.

"Havva says she'll recover, but she'll bear the scars. But she's scared, and she won't speak. All she does is cry."

"A day will come when she stops. And when she does, come find me, and I will make her clothes fit for a student of the University, and go with her to her testing," Amara said. The woman stared at her.

"She won't want to go now, not all cut up and ruined," she protested, as if this were something obvious and practical.

Amara stood. "She is not ruined. Do not ever say that again. Do as I say, and bring her to me when she is well enough. You understand?"

"Yes, Mistress," the woman said in a near whisper, her eyes wide.

"Djar," Amara commanded. He appeared in the doorway of the kitchen. "Fetch the twins."

He bared his teeth, his eyes lighting with the promise of violence, and headed for the back door.

"And you," Amara said as she looked at the woman again, "will tell me who this man is that hurt your daughter, and where he might be found."

THREE

CASSIAN BROWSED THROUGH THE tables of the gambling house. He had time for a round or two to help settle his nerves before the auction that evening. He'd stepped into the gambling house on his way to collect Peio from the poor choices he had made that afternoon, and decided to see if Luck had time for him. Peio could wait, likely on whatever taverna stoop he'd passed out on.

Though the city guard in Haenna was beginning to crack down on gambling, they were not nearly so rabid about it as the capital, and so games could still be found. Gambling houses were also the best places for Cassian to obtain information when he was in the market for it, social standing being forgotten once you crossed the threshold. Sailors gambled against politicians, merchants against slaves. Today he had all the information he needed, though rumors were always handy to have stashed in the back of his mind. He happened to have a handful of spare coins, and was hearing the whisper of Luck's suggestion. Today could be a good day, if he chose the right game.

If the auction went well, he wouldn't be in the city for many days, giving all the debtors time to lose interest in him. His last five coins lay heavy against his hip as he identified those tables where dice were being thrown. Most were using ivory dice, only one was using the more humble clay dice that Cassian preferred. He stopped at that table to watch the game unfold.

The first man was a servant, perhaps one that had bought his way out of slavery, by the look of him. A smaller man that bore the swirling neck tattoos that marked men of the Northern tribes. They occasionally harried Republic forces to and from the Northern territories, and when they lost, were taken as slaves. He had pale skin and hair and strong features, though eyes that might once have been filled with pride and warrior spirit were quiet and resigned now. It was a look Cassian had grown accustomed to in recent years, if not comfortable with.

The Northerner's opponent was a rarity, a whipcord fellow dressed in the style of the desert nations that bordered the Sun Sea. Loose, billowy trousers tucked into knee-high boots, a shirt of the same, wrapped beneath a chest-high circuit of darker brown fabric that likely concealed knives and valuables. The burnished brown of his skin marked him, even more than his dress, as Meneian. They were uncommon in Haenna. Their tradesmen usually continued around the horn to the Republic's capital, Corsyra.

The small crowd circled around the two men, jostling and arguing as they placed bets against the game. The Republic had outlawed gambling, and the punishment for observing was just as severe as it was for actually playing, but people continued with it anyway. While the guards often overlooked the law in Haenna, ignoring gambling houses and the street games that popped up spontaneously, they sometimes— out of boredom, Cassian suspected—could be roused to break up games that had gotten too rambunctious. When he'd started gambling as a teenager the crowds had been habitually rowdy and loud, often breaking into brawls. Now they tended to be more subdued and quiet, so as not to give the guards reason to be interested.

The game they played now was the highest of a tallied score out of three rolls, and the Northerner tossed his first set. Cassian watched the two men, both silent as they traded the dice back and forth. A man stationed behind the Northerner had a tally sheet upon which he ticked each of their scores.

"I'll play winner," Cassian said. The Northerner looked up at him and nodded acknowledgment; the Meneian did not spare him even a glance. They tossed their last set, and the Meneian won by several points. The Northerner shook his head. During the distracted shuffle as money changed hands, Cassian tucked a hand into his pocket and palmed two dice. When the Northerner rose from his chair, Cassian gave him a friendly slap on the back.

"Best of luck. Hasn't been beat all morning," the man grumbled as he shouldered his way away from the table. Cassian spun the empty chair around and sat, folding his arms across the back of it and assessing his new opponent. Luck rarely favored any one man for too long, which was why Cassian always had insurance. He grinned at the man across from him.

"I thought you might be getting tired of winning," Cassian said amicably. The Meneian shrugged one slim shoulder. He looked young, but Meneians were often gifted with the lingering appearance of youth. His face was fine-boned, his features somewhat androgynous, and his hair was hidden beneath a length of fabric wrapped around his head, the tail of which hung down near his face, to be used to protect it in the event of one of the sandstorms that were rumored to often sweep the high desert in Menei.

"Bet," the tally-maker prompted, gruffly. Cassian reached into the leather bag at his waist and withdrew four of his remaining coins. He placed the coins on the table, a paltry collection next to the stacks that had accumulated on the Meneian's side. The Meneian slid four coins next to Cassian's then picked up the dice and handed them to Cassian to examine. Cassian gave a show of hefting them and inspecting their markings, before handing them back.

The Meneian tossed them casually onto the table. A six and a five. Cassian tucked his two hidden dice against his palm. Not time for them yet. Winning early meant early suspicion.

The first match was over quickly, in Cassian's favor, the second as well. He aimed his gaze at the pier, though a wall blocked his view, to where the great statue of Luck stood to wish the sailors well. Or laugh at their folly. He was in her favor this day. A third game would set him up with enough to finance his upcoming jaunt into the wilderness.

"Make it interesting?" The Meneian fixed Cassian with a solemn, dark-eyed stare. His accent was not heavy, but added rhythmic gravity to an otherwise bland statement. He jerked his chin to indicate Cassian's pile of money. The man had suffered through two games of small worth for him, considering Cassian's small bets. He supposed he owed him at least one game with enough money to catch his interest. The weight of the dice in his left hand, as yet unused, reassured him. Cassian pushed the pile of money toward his opponent, studying him again as he did. He'd never known any Meneians personally, though he had seen a few in his life, and knew some of the labyrinthian history of the country.

The small crowd around their table began chattering again, setting new bets. The Meneian slid an equal pile of coins toward Cassian's and Cassian retrieved the dice, switching them in his hand as he dragged them over the table toward him. He'd made his dice himself, experimented for weeks to get the right balance. He scooped them toward the edge of the table and allowed the real dice to fall into his right hand, leaving his dice on the table. The Meneian nodded when Cassian raised an eyebrow in question.

He tossed them at a sharp angle, so they tumbled off the table and onto the floor.

"One and four," the Meneian read off, and the tally-maker marked it on his sheet. Surprised at the impossibly low roll, Cassian leaned out of his chair and retrieved the dice, switching them once more as he handed the real ones to his opponent. The Meneian's next toss scored a double four. Interesting. He hadn't scored a single roll in the previous games that outscored Cassian. The Meneian looked at him blandly.

Cassian threw with the real dice for his next roll, to prevent suspicions. Two and three. The tally-maker marked it, and the Meneian retrieved the dice. Cassian watched his movements, and his face, but saw nothing that concerned him. Still, a sense that something was off made him sit straighter in the chair. The weighted dice had never failed him before.

Sweat beaded on his brow, the crowd seemed to be getting louder, the room smaller. He just never knew when to quit, while he was ahead, he cursed himself silently. The Meneian's throw scored a three and four. Cassian wiped his hand across his mouth and repeated his switch of the dice. The silent Meneian watched him, but nothing indicated he noticed the switch.

Cassian looked at the tidy stacks of coins, and out of habit glanced toward the pier once more. He threw his last cast, aiming only one die off the table that time. Three and three. A very unlucky roll.

He snagged the single die off the table and grabbed the second from the floor. These were the same dice that had won him six games only three days prior. How were they not working now? His pulse picked up, and the beads of sweat became a trickle down his temple. Cassian palmed the weighted dice once more, depositing the real ones on the table for the Meneian.

The Meneian stacked one die on top of the other and lifted them into his hand. As he shook them he held Cassian's gaze with what Cassian could only call righteous calm, as though this were all a great scheme of revenge and Cassian the target. He tossed the dice, and they landed only a hair's breadth from the edge of the table on Cassian's side, taunting him. Two sixes. Cassian's breath left him in a rush.

The Meneian stood. "Unfortunate." He swept his winnings into a stiff-sided leather bag and the crowd bellyached. As they shifted away, someone darted to the Meneian's side. Cast from an identical mold, in height, build, face, and clothes, Cassian thought he was looking at a mirror image for a moment. The second one whispered in the first's ear. He stopped the motion of packing away his winnings, his gaze settling on Cassian with enough weight to pin him. The other slunk back into the crowd.

"A cheater?" the Meneian said loudly, a light both sinister and amused flashing in his gaze. The crowd turned to stare, as if as one. Cassian didn't dare pocket his dice at that exact moment, with all eyes on him, but he needed to offload them quickly or—

"What's that?" a voice snarled from inside the crowd. They hastily parted, revealing one of the gambling house's enforcers. Thick arms folded over his chest, a pistol slung against one hip, a knife against the other, and a scowl of recognition. Cassian cursed under his breath, his hand tightening around the dice. He met the man's gaze as the Meneian ducked from between the two of them, leaving only the table as Cassian's shield.

"Cassian," the brute said. "I should have guessed." They were well acquainted, since Cassian owed the man's boss several games' worth of money. He grit his teeth. Could he get out of the chair, through the crowd, and out the door before the man got to him? The establishment owner, Sophus, had never kept his enforcers around the place during the day before, it was the only reason Cassian had chosen to chance a game. If only his damned dice hadn't failed him.

"You're up early, Gallus." Cassian stood, turning his chair carefully the right way 'round, but keeping his hand on the back of it. Gallus raised his brow. He could not raise only one eyebrow, because the two had endeavored to become one dark streak over his forehead. It gave him the look of a mindless brute. Which was exactly what he was.

"Seems we have a rat," he replied, making his way around the table. No one wanted Gallus' attention, it was usually accompanied by physical pain of one sort or another. The crowd cleared out of his path. Cassian turned as Gallus came toward him, sliding the chair to keep it between them. Gallus' meaty arms unfolded, his hand heading for his knife. Cassian had one scar from that knife, he didn't want another. "Let's see those hands, eh?"

Cassian shoved the chair at Gallus and lunged around the table, keeping it between them, and dropped the dice as he went.

Gallus let out a roaring laugh and upended the table toward Cassian. It tripped him, and he fell on his side. The crowd helpfully scattered out of Gallus' way, forcing Cassian to scramble and crawl until he could gain his feet again.

He lunged for the single window in the entire, square, squat building. Its shutters were thrown open for the spring air, and Cassian dove for it as Gallus grabbed for his shirt and caught him.

Cassian was halfway out of the window when Gallus tried to retrieve him back through it, slamming the back of Cassian's head against the outside frame as he did so.

Cassian braced himself with his elbows against the outside of the window and kicked, futilely, against Gallus' chest, then twisted around as Gallus tugged and aimed his next kick at the enforcer's face.

Gallus' grip broke when Cassian's boot connected with his shoulder instead of his face, because he might be stone-stupid for conversation but he was quick-witted in a fight. Cassian fell out of the window, landing on his neck and shoulders in the street, and slid the rest of the way to the ground with a groan.

He rolled, stumbling to his feet, his head pounding, his neck aching. Gallus appeared in the doorway to the gambling house, and Cassian turned and ran north. The gambling house was on a narrow side street that fed the main road running north from the pier into the city, or south, to the warehouses where tradesmen stored their goods. He needed to head south if he was going to make it to the auction, but did not intend to lead Gallus there.

Cassian despised running on even a good day; it always signaled things were not going his way. Unfortunately for him, Gallus, despite his lumbering size, was also fast, and as Cassian rounded the corner, Gallus barreled into him like an angry bull, sending them both tumbling to the ground. Cassian's head slammed against the stones and lights burst in his vision as Gallus flipped him onto his back and punched him square in the face. Pain radiated across his cheek and jaw, and he could only grab at Gallus' fists as the man got up and hauled Cassian to his feet.

"Sophus wants to see you," Gallus sneered, and turned back toward the gambling house, swinging Cassian in front of him and shoving him forward as he drew his pistol and aimed it at Cassian's back. Cassian stumbled, regained his balance, and wiped the blood from his chin and split lip as he glanced over his shoulder at Gallus. The bruiser gestured with his gun, and Cassian turned forward again, pinching at his nose to make certain it wasn't broken. He'd heard it pop under the assault of Gallus' fist, but his jaw had taken the majority of the force.

"We could talk about this." Cassian released his grip on his nose and looked back again. He didn't have any money to give to Sophus, and he wasn't interested in being beaten to bits of bone and sinew. He'd seen some of Gallus' delicate work on other gamblers who owed.

"Could, but I don't like the sound of your voice." Gallus jabbed his pistol into Cassian's back.

Cassian cast furtive glances about him as they walked. The street was a mix of homes and small public spaces, little parks cast in shade from the buildings, a fountain here, a taverna there. Nowhere for him to run. But at the base of the stairs leading into the back of a taverna stood a stack of barrels, and the metal barrel rings from others tipped against them. Cassian altered his stride, moving slightly left, away from the middle of the street and toward the taverna stairs.

He counted his steps as he approached. There was an alley just beyond the taverna that would put him out on another side street to escape Gallus. The man would not be happy, if Cassian failed to strike true. Five more strides. Four more.

Three.

Two.

Cassian lengthened his final stride, swung around and grabbed a barrel ring as he went, slinging it across his body in an arc. The iron ring slammed into Gallus' head, sending him sprawling into the street. Cassian grabbed Gallus' pistol from where it had fallen from his grasp, and ran, glancing back only once to see Gallus just managing to get to his hands and knees.

"Some other time!" Cassian shouted over his shoulder. He dodged into the maze of homes, alleys, and businesses that filled the ring of the city that separated the Basilica and the upper crust from the outskirts and the poor.

FOUR

THE TWO SAILORS WHO had volunteered to escort Amara murmured to each other as the three of them stood on the edge of the northern pier. She'd been in Haenna two small turns and had pieced together rumors about the sight that she surveyed now. However, this was the first time she'd been able to make time to see it for herself.

This part of the city was ugly, dominated by factories, smoke, the deafening clatter of hammers and workmen yelling orders to each other. It stunk of hot metal and fouled water, greasy smoke and sawdust. The crank and clink of heavy pulleys and chains underpinned everything, as giant cranes lifted a mast into place on a ship.

Amara counted fifty ships in the still, oil-slicked harbor. Some were floating at anchor, with workmen scurrying about their decks conducting finishing work. Others were half-built skeletons. Several sprawling warehouses squatted near the water, with rail systems disappearing into the sea, where she suspected more ships were being started.

"What do you think?" Amara asked the two sailors.

"War galleons for certain, Mistress," the first said, then spat a red-tinted projectile onto the stones near her feet. Amara chastised him with a glare, and he cleared his throat and mumbled an apology.

"Sixty cannons, I'd say." He lifted a hand to count as he said it, his finger bobbing, one eye closed. Then he nodded to agree with his assessment. "More small arms, obviously."

"Obviously," Amara said beneath her breath.

"Wheel preserve us all if that's meant for Narfour," the second man said. "They'll line up at the coast and bombard it from the bay. And us with nothing but fishing boats and merchant carracks."

Amara tightened her mental grip on her magic, though it simmered in the presence of her apprehension. Even a trickle of power was too much here, in the land of the enemy. A land that intended to enslave or silence magic. A land that could build, with such speed, a fleet for war. That speed was a product of their advanced manufacturing capabilities. Something Tamar lacked. Machines of complexity were eschewed there because of Tamar's reliance on magic and steadfast belief that the Wheel dictated the capabilities of humans, not humans themselves.

Tamar was a land gifted and trapped by their magic, something she had not fully realized because she had cloistered herself there after leaving Menei. The most dangerous of the Republic's machines were guns. They were everywhere in Haenna. Amara had seen so many, casually belted on every man and near-man whom she passed. Carriage drivers had guns with them on their vehicles, stashed in the benches. The guards that patrolled the city wore them along with their swords.

Guns were unheard of in Tamar. Amara could not recall ever seeing one since arriving in Narfour, outside of Meneian merchants and their guards.

"Return to the ship. Warn the captain to pay mind that he and the crew look as innocuous as possible." That Amara had chosen to employ a man as merchant ship captain who was more suited, by history and disposition, to piracy than diplomacy would serve her well in more ways than one on this expedition.

"Mistress." The sailor frowned as he noticed all the looks directed their way. Haenna was not a port often utilized by Meneians, it seemed. And if they ever did find their way to Haenna, they clearly did not make the trek to this part of the city. Tamar was not chock-full of Meneians, but there were enough that Amara felt comfortable. Unremarkable. Here, she and her people were candles in the dark. Everyone looked. Everyone stared, whispered. Judged. As though their skin were an attribute to measure them by. "Let us take you out of the pier, at least."

"No need," Amara said, when she caught sight of Djar as he separated away from the shadow of a building and strode toward them. The sailors acknowledged Djar with nods. They headed south, toward the merchant pier, where they had docked their rowboat. The ship was moored in the outer reaches of the bay.

"Will you be wanting one of those?" Djar looked over his shoulder to watch as the galleon passed the buildings and moved out to open water and several of its compatriots anchored farther out. "To augment your fleet?"

"I think not," Amara said primly. Neither one of them mentioned that she'd hardly be able to climb aboard a ship that size, that towered over the water. Heights had been her enemy since she was a child, regardless if it were water or stone below her feet. "They are building instruments of war," she said as Djar pointed them toward the villa they had secured in a quiet part of the seaside trade city. The wealthy had homes in the city, but most spent their time at their country estates. The less prestigious were easily bribed for the use of their domiciles while they were away.

"Everything is an instrument of war, when one wants war." Djar gave the shipyard one last backward glance. His brow furrowed, likely asking himself the same question that circled her own thoughts. How many did they intend to build? When did they plan to sail them? There was little more to be gleaned, for now. And there were more pressing matters.

"You have news for me?" Amara asked.

Djar grunted an affirmative. "Bek confirmed the auction is tonight. You'll need this to get us in." He held his hand out and Amara plucked a clay token from his palm.

Bek's sticky fingers never ceased to prove useful. The token was stamped with the profile portrait that was ubiquitous throughout the city, celebrated in busts, business signs, and carved into temple entrances. Not always the same faces, though she had determined they were always men of import. She had yet to see a woman in profile, which did not surprise her. Menei and the Odokan put weapons in the hands of their women, and Tamar made them merchants and now, rulers. But that was not the way in the Republic.

Though, solemn statues of their many goddesses were scattered about at shrines. A rather garish portrayal of a comely, bare-breasted woman graced the main merchant pier, her laughing countenance gazing out to the sea. While Amara did not hold to the belief that breasts were something to be hidden away like the family fortune, there was a time and place to employ them, and it seemed odd to place her nearly naked among the sailors and dockworkers. Perhaps she was the patron goddess of brothels? Amara had seen no less than a dozen passersby kiss her outstretched palm, and three adolescent boys laughingly jump upon her pedestal to clasp her stone breast.

Meneians worshiped deities as well, but Amara's mother had taught her the turn of the Wheel. It seemed odd to assign so much gravitas to a person. Even if they did claim divine birth. Divine birth from what? The stars? It simply did not make sense. Were people not fickle? Then gods must be too. Amara turned her eyes from the statue and her mind from the subject.

"Are Bek and Kiya at the Fountain House?" Every home in Haenna had an auspicious name. At least those in the nearest circles to the Basilica and its Assembly. The one they had paid to use was the Casa delle Fontane, which Bek had shortened to Fountain House. Amara had chosen it for its namesake. Though there was no shortage of water in Haenna.

Djar sighed in impatience. "No. They are investigating, or so they say. They know to be at the proper place when the sun has set though. Or I'll have their hides as shield-skin."

"Charming." Amara glanced about them; the leering was petering out. But only temporarily. She shuddered with the feeling of being watched. Their continued appraisal, furtive though some of it was, felt like crawling insects up the back of her neck and arms. "And our quarry?"

Djar shook his head. "Nothing yet, but this auction will have Suloi from the most recently decimated clan. He is as likely to be there as anywhere else we've searched."

Amara frowned. The underground trade of slaves had been much easier to ferret out than the man who worked against it, and news of another clan razed by the Consul's mage hunters had lit the network up with news of an auction of captured Suloi. The night auction offered them their best, and final chance of contacting the abolitionist Aysel had uncovered, or at least afford Amara the chance to speak with some of the Suloi. Even if it meant purchasing them or stealing them herself.

"Two turns since we arrived and nothing to show for it," she said. "Except that ridiculous rendering of him on those arrest orders posted about." She could hardly believe someone's only purpose in life was to sketch dubious likenesses of criminals and post them about the city. Most of the posters of this so-called thief had been vandalized. Eye patches drawn on with charcoal, a beard, mustache, hair as long as a woman's…in one he even sported a hook for a hand and in another vulpine ears. He either had friends in the city with little to do, or he was his own industrious artist. She wondered whether he did it to mask his face, or to taunt the authorities. It would be interesting to meet the man, if she could only find him.

"He'll be there, or an agent of his." Djar swiveled a sharp gaze around them. Always watching for danger. Soon he wouldn't have to anymore. Soon she'd have all the safety they would ever need. This one last endeavor was the final hurdle.

"Yes. But we'll still have to discover which he is in a vast crowd."

They crossed the long, wide bridge that connected the shipyard island to the rest of Haenna. The city was built across a cluster of land fingers and small islands that clung to the coast of the Republic, connected by canals and bridges. The bridges were a wonder. Each a feat of engineering and art, all the more impressive in that they were not built with the use of magic. Mathematical and precise in their construction, they were topped with beautiful brass and stonework. Some had ornate iron railings, others elaborate stone ramparts topped with statues. Some were even completely covered by wooden toppers. Several were large enough to accommodate shops and apartments. And almost all were wide enough that she did not have to look over the edges. Those that had open railings or were narrower were not so far above the water that she was dizzied by the height. A fact she appreciated a great deal.

Djar smiled, catlike, as he looked down at her. "No man you have sought has ever escaped you."

She returned his smile with one more subdued. "This is a different circumstance."

"Then it is well that you compel the truth," Djar rumbled.

Amara stopped smiling and looked away from him. They walked along a path that wound its way between colorful, multi-storied apartments and one of the smaller canals in Haenna. The long, thin boats piloted by men with a single long oar standing at the bow. She'd ridden a few, as it was a much easier mode of transport than walking, or the more grating experience of bouncing over cobbles in a carriage.

"We'll return to the Fountain House, see if the twins have returned from their *investigating*, then find this auction," Amara said.

The Fountain House was near the city center, close to the oppressive presence of the Basilica. The Assembly met there, populated by senators that were supposedly elected, but who passed the position on to their heirs. A complicated and nonsensical method they claimed was fair to all.

Amara had now spent time in three very different nations and had decided that a Seventh spoke on the Wheel was more plausible than a government that was fair to all. But oh how the citizens, at least those who lived in comfort, lauded the ingenuity of it. Amara had been subjected to long, one-sided conversations about how the Republic had brought so many peoples into the modern age. Why, one man had proclaimed, we tamed those Northern barbarians! Built them homes and roads and gave them proper religion! Meanwhile, behind him, a Northern woman scrubbed the steps of a taverna on her hands and knees in rags; someone spit on her on their way in. Certainly *she* appreciated being brought into the modern age.

It was a city of contrasts. Soaring marvels of architecture and art. Beautiful sculptures cast in marble and bronze. Sparkling, bright buildings with ornate cornices and lovely ironwork. Amara saw lust-inducing fabrics on the women of wealth, jewelry that would buy an entire forge. Poets read their work on street corners, and plays were enacted in empty spaces. Glassblowers created breathtaking, multi-hued works of art in shops that lined the narrow streets. It was a city that spoke to her love of art and beauty. If she were capable of shutting out that darkness that moved, like shadows in the dark, just beyond notice.

Slaves, who toiled to build and repair, who hauled trash and water. The poor, who begged in between the glassblowers and the poets. The stares that followed her and her people everywhere they went. This was not a Balanced city. It tipped so heavily in favor of the wealthy, who were so far out of touch with their reality they did not realize the precariousness of their situation. A land built on the backs of slaves was a land with no foundation at all.

Afternoon slowed to evening as they walked, the light warming and deepening to cast everything in golden tones. The Fountain House sat nestled inside a formidable stone wall, to keep the undesirables from seeing or getting too close. Gardens surrounded the house inside the wall, so those within could pretend there was no wall, and that they actually lived in the city they occupied. It acted as screen and filter, so they were less likely to see things that might burst their illusion that all was well.

When Djar and Amara arrived in the interior courtyard they were greeted only by the sounds of birds flitting through the many trees and vines, and the clatter of the cook as she prepared the evening meal. Amara peeked around the open doorway of the kitchen.

"Taliba, have you seen the twins?" she addressed the short, plump woman as she prepared a pile of vegetables. Taliba slapped her hands against her apron and wedged them against her hips with a frown. "Those two"—she shook a finger at Amara—"stole half the bread I made this morning when they left and haven't been back. As well they shouldn't. When I get my hands on them…" She lifted a wooden spoon and slapped it against the counter.

Amara turned to Djar, who frowned. "I am certain they are safe," he said. "They know not to take unnecessary risks."

Everything felt like an unnecessary risk in this city, where they were too noticeable. Too different.

"Let us hope so," Amara said.

FIVE

HEN NIGHT FELL, CASSIAN finally made his roundabout way to the pier and the alleyways that constituted the night market. The metallic taste of blood lingered from his split lip. One eye was nearly swollen shut and he couldn't see out of it, and his head ached abysmally, almost too much to focus on what he was doing. The streets and canals of Haenna, the second largest city in the Republic, were labyrinthine on a scale only moderately outdone by Corsyra herself. Even on his best days, despite nearly thirty years spent in the city, he had to concentrate absolutely on where he was going. They were dangerous at any time of day, and especially deadly at night.

His pistol and knife deterred most of the petty criminals, pickpockets and muggers, but his main protection was Peio. Even the most brutal of cutthroats steered clear of a man sporting more weapons than digits. The favor was returned though, Cassian was just as much protection for Peio. A lone, clanless Suloi wandering about the city was very likely to end up tossed into a wagon. They were friends of nearly a decade. Not that either of them felt particularly friendly, at the moment.

"You stink," Cassian growled when Peio staggered sideways into him and the sour smell of alcohol and sweat filled his nose.

"If we had any money to pay for a bath, I wouldn't." Peio righted himself, though wove in place a bit, still suffering from his afternoon spent in the company of a vat of watered wine. Cassian usually did not judge or mind his friend's self-medication, but tonight they were both useless, and in his misery he wanted someone to blame.

"I told you they cheated, it wasn't my fault." Cassian ducked into a side alley when a trio of men at the outlet of the street eyed them with too much interest.

"It is never your fault," Peio intoned. "*The path does not force us to walk it.*"

"Spare me your bloody Wanderer and his unbearable Suloi wisdom." He was having the damnedest time seeing straight, his depth perception completely altered by his injured eye. It was not the first time he'd sported a black eye, but it would draw unwanted attention at the auction.

The auction was a sometimes event of the night market, called such not because it operated at night, but because its illicit goods fell under the proprietorship of the goddess Laelia, patroness of all things lost and stolen and twin sister to the moon goddess Satia. The Night Sisters, thieves and pirates called them.

Cassian cursed as he tripped over a pile of garbage in the dark and frightened away a cat in the process. Peio hissed at it then laughed.

A few steps later Peio broke away from Cassian, fumbling a charcoal stick out of one of his belt pouches. "I always miss these alley ones," he mumbled as he leaned an arm against the brick wall of a taverna and began sketching on one of the guard posters plastered all over the city.

"It doesn't look anything like me anyway, would you stop?" Cassian batted his friend's hands away from the poorly drawn likeness and shoved him out of the alley.

"I'll never be a great artist like you if I don't practice," Peio mocked.

The city center had lamps lining all the streets and slaves to light them. Not the pier, and certainly not the poor districts, where they would make the most difference. But who cared about poor people tripping about in the dark or being murdered on their way home? Certainly not the Assembly.

Cassian wedged his way between a pile of detritus and the mouth of the alley, emerging on one of the larger side streets that led to the pier. He patted the pistol slung low on his hip, fingers playing over the ornate metalwork. It had been his father's, a gift from a Meneian merchant who had stumbled into the wrong warehouse once and been mistaken for a slave. Cassian would always prefer guns to swords, they required much less skill, but the benefit of a sword was that one did not have to stand around for long seconds reloading before having a usable weapon. Though, a pistol made a handy bludgeon, when desperate moments demanded.

Peio scratched with both hands at his scalp, his face scrunched as he surveyed the street before them. The side street eventually led to the outer edge of the night market. Sprawling from the pier and along the deepest alleys and narrow side streets of Haenna's warehouse district, the night market specialized in items outlawed, stolen, or taboo. The people that browsed the tiny stalls were generally a malignant lot. Occasionally Cassian caught sight of a nervous face, someone at the end of their rope and at the market for the first time. There were old folk cures that could be obtained from charlatan sellers, items the Republic had outlawed because their use was dangerous or simply full of false hope. It was not unusual to find women and children in the market, desperately searching for something to cure a loved one or themselves.

The booths were all small, makeshift tables or crates stacked and covered with cloth to showcase wares, all designed to be quickly and easily disassembled if the guard took any interest in patrolling by.

They had only done so once that Cassian could remember, when Consul Stephanus had visited Haenna's Assembly after the death of Consul Tiberius. It had been imperative that Haenna appear to be a city under the control of law and order, and for the span of days that Stephanus had resided at the Assembly, it had been. Cassian had never seen the streets so clean or the guards so disciplined. But that had been years ago, and the city was well back to its disheveled self.

The market was the only lit area of the pier at this time of night. Oil lamps hung from poles set into barrels, and hooked to roof lines, set upon tables, so that in Cassian's blurry vision dozens of balls of light wavered and made his uninjured eye ache with the strain of trying to focus. He ignored the upper market. On occasion he browsed it, not for wares, but for rumors.

"I need more red sap," Peio mused, squinting toward the tables in the darkest corners of the market. Red sap was the poison the Suloi used to coat their weapons, though they were the only ones who could use it. Even handling it could kill you. Suloi hunters spent a lifetime building up a resistance to it. It wasn't sap at all, but venom from a basilisk, the fat, docile rock lizards that were multitudinous in the northern mountains but rare in the south. Some Suloi kept the things as pets. Cassian grimaced. He'd seen them for sale in the market but refused to allow Peio to keep one in their home.

"Not tonight. We're running late already."

"And that probably isn't your fault either," Peio said.

Cassian didn't answer, intent on his destination and too irritated to speak without snapping, They were not the only ones headed for the auction, the alleys and side streets were nearly deserted compared to the usual bustle. Everyone went to the auctions, if not to buy, then to gawk.

There were far more interesting things to be seen at the auction than at the market itself. Eannean beauties, Meneian warriors, Northmen still wearing paint and furs, very occasionally a plainsman from the far eastern steppes, and tonight, Suloi. The auction was always packed when word of Suloi slaves came to Haenna. Slavery was not illegal in the Republic, but Suloi were. Magic was. A fact that Cassian found both darkly amusing and enraging. Of all the peoples the Republic enslaved, the Suloi were the least threat. They kept to themselves and the wilderness and were not numerous enough, even before Stephanus' eradication campaign, to pose threat to anyone. The supposed crime of their magic was only propaganda used by Stephanus to legitimize his new war. His lust for an Empire.

The auction was hosted under the warehouse district, in the catacombs that spread out from beneath the city center. Part of Old Haenna. The catacombs ran all throughout the city, but sections were defunct, abandoned when Haenna grew so large that the Assembly funded the building of an entirely new network of aqueducts and underground sewers that bisected or destroyed the final resting places of the dead. But not to worry, they were only the tombs of the lower classes. Sewer pipes for the gold-flecked shit of the wealthy were far more important.

"Look." Peio grabbed Cassian's sleeve. When Cassian stopped, Peio pointed toward the cemetery that butted up against the warehouses. That was the main entrance to the catacombs. For the buyers. The gawkers used a long-defunct sewer outlet tunnel. The cemetery had stairs that led into the crypt where the auction was held. It took Cassian a moment to focus in the dark and past the shuffle of people to see what Peio wanted him to. While Meneians were not an unheard of sight in Corsyra, or even in the cages in the auction house, he couldn't recall ever seeing them entering the auction as buyers. But there were two of them doing so now.

"Are those the ones you played at dice?" Peio asked.

They were too far away to make out completely, but one was tall, and the other, if he wasn't mistaken, was a woman.

"No." Cassian did not like coincidences, and four Meneians in one day was a coincidence.

"I don't like it," Peio said under his breath, looking behind him as though he suspected someone was sneaking up on them. "Never seen any at the auction before. Any that weren't in cages anyway. They aren't after you are they?" His voice dropped even lower at the last.

Cassian shook his head. No one in Haenna knew what he was beyond his parents' disappointment of a son. There was no way a foreigner did. Still. Cassian flipped the hood of his shirt up and did the same for Peio. He tugged a piece of black cloth from the larger pouch at his waist, frowning at the empty one next to it, which had contained his coins. Lean times for this run out of the city. How had that Meneian known he was cheating, and more importantly, how had he won despite the fact?

Cassian narrowed his eyes as he shook the cloth out and tied it around his nose and mouth. Save the black eye and swollen face, he looked too much like his mother to go into the auction uncovered. Too recognizable to some.

Peio did the same, lifting a cloth he kept tied around his neck. Auctions attracted all kinds beyond the slavers bound for Menei or over-land caravans headed for the Spice Road. The wealthy of Haenna loved Suloi, for the small conveniences they could provide. Servants and slaves of those wealthy households would also be browsing the wares, and Cassian and Peio had to stay anonymous if they intended to continue their work. Most who shopped the auctions wore masks, and no one thought twice about it. Cassian was too familiar with the upper-class families to be fooled, however. He could often recognize them by the way they walked, the cant of a head, the movement of a hand. He'd spent his entire youth learning their tics.

Cassian led the way into the alley that wound to the stairs that would take them to the crypt drainage pipe. There had once been a massive iron grate across the gaping maw of the outlet, but it had rusted away from the stone. That had been the secret back entrance for years, until someone industrious removed the grate entirely. Now it was simply the entrance for the less well-heeled auction buyers.

The stone tunnel led into a destroyed section of the catacombs that had been, over the years, refashioned into a makeshift auction house. People milled about in the tunnel, shifting in slow tides toward the broken-open wall that marked the beginning of the catacombs. This tunnel was tall enough for someone of average height to stand in, and wide enough for groups of three or four to congregate.

The two of them wove their way through the crowd, at points having to scramble half up the curve of stonework to edge their way around other people. They were not a polite lot, those who traded in the lives of others. Cassian nudged his way past two men having a last smoke before they entered. Pipes were not allowed in the auction, the smoke had nowhere to go and obscured the merchandise. The tunnel was not lit, but the wide, open space beyond it was. Oil lamps, or, if Lucaius was showing off, the mage lights some Suloi could conjure.

The secondary benefit of the cloth over his mouth was that it filtered the complex stench of the space. Even though it was a wide, open room, nearly the size of the Assembly hall, there was very little air movement. The old, grown-in waste smell of the sewers permeated the very stones that surrounded them, the musty, molded odor of decay that came from the emptied tombs, the burning, ammonia stench of piss because no one could be bothered to trek all the way back out to relieve their bladders.

And there were the slaves. Housed in cages along the walls, so that buyers could browse the *wares* before they went up on the block for sale. Some were packed four or five to a cell meant for one or two. Most were unwashed and covered in their own filth. The worst off were fresh from a battle, often wounded and festering, as likely to die moments after purchase as they were to murder their purchaser. One such lay in a cage to himself, on his side on the soaked straw tossed in for his comfort, one hand clutching the bars near his head. The other hand curved protectively over a wound on his ribs that had soaked that side with blood. His eyes were bloodshot with the fever that ravaged him, his skin pale grey. The hatred in those eyes burned as hot as the fever as he looked at the people that examined him. As if he were potential livestock for their pens.

Cassian didn't pass too close to the man's cage. He'd had a Northerner try to claw his eyes out of their sockets once, a shield maiden, in fact. The men liked to lunge and grab for more sensitive parts. There were tales told about one who had actually been successful, ripping the cock and balls right off a merchant and laughing while the man bled out. Stories only. He and Peio weren't there for Northerners anyway. They could not save everyone.

Regret clutched his throat, as it always did at an auction. He tried to tame the guilt with a story he'd told himself many times. Northerners were not cursed with magic. They were often treated well, and often had the opportunity to buy their lives back. Suloi never did and were bought just as often for experimentation around their piddling magic as they were for work. They needed him more.

The crowd meandered in a generally clockwise flow around the circular room, the auction block nothing more than a wooden platform built in the middle of the room. Thugs that served as guards stood at each of the four corners, ready to keep the crowd back and the prisoners where they belonged. Two auctioneers chatted on the platform as buyers browsed the cages. People still trickled in from the stairs that led up and into the cemetery, directly across from the sewer Cassian had used as entrance. He glanced periodically as people came down the stairs, taking stock of the new arrivals, to see if he needed to actively avoid anyone who might recognize him.

"I don't see them," Peio said, looking without looking, a talent fostered by a people who made avoiding eye contact an art form. Cassian nodded. The Meneians.

He tucked himself into a gaggle of five merchants, who were gathered at a cage two down from the wounded Northerner. This one held four Odokan, three men and one woman, huddled together. They were a rare sight to see in the markets. They did not speak Republic Trade, as the Northerners and Suloi sometimes did, and citizens of the Republic did not endeavor to learn or deign to speak the language of the steppes. Since the Republic seldom engaged in skirmishes with the people of the east, it was curious to see any at the market.

Cassian tugged the cloth up higher over his nose and visually inventoried the cages he could see from his vantage point. In the other cages there were a handful of older captives, likely too old for their current work or to be replaced by new stock.

The bulk of the buyers crowded at the cages on the far side of the room from where Cassian and Peio stood. Those would be the Suloi then. Cassian aimed a glance at Peio, who did not meet his gaze but nodded. Cassian cut across the floor, past men discussing the charms versus usefulness of large-breasted women. He reached up to rub his eyes to hide the twitch of his eyebrows, and muttered a curse when he pressed too hard on his bruises.

One of the platform guards eyed and dismissed the two of them as they passed. They were, after all, just more hooded and masked buyers. Everyone wore something, though the wealthy were easily distinguished by their elaborate, artistically designed half-masks. Often painted gold, or sporting glass or jewel ornaments. As if it were a fête and not a vile perversion of society. Hoods hid hair and details of jawlines, the masks hid eyes and noses, some chose to do as he did and hide the lower half instead of the upper. Most weren't looking at each other, the order of the evening was anonymity, after all.

They passed three cells in a row containing Eanneans. Stephanus and his triumvirate cronies must be trying to quell that notorious Eannean lust for independence. A decade after their conquering they still required full garrisons of troops to hold boot to neck. These were a mix of soldiers and women. Eannean women were freer than those in the Republic, and often loudly voiced their opinions in the places it mattered. Then ended up in the Republic slave markets for their trouble, as some of these had, obviously.

The first cage he suspected to contain Suloi was obscured by onlookers. Cassian elbowed his way through them, Peio slipping behind him. Only one woman sat in the first cage, with the dusky complexion, sable, braided hair, and fine-featured face that commonly marked the roadborn, as they referred to themselves. Her face was scarred, a straight, short mark on each cheek. She sat on the straw, her legs folded in front of her. The other occupant of the cell was a man, but if he was Suloi it wasn't the only thing in his blood. His head was in her lap, as she ran fingers through his dirty blond hair. His hair and his skin, a shade lighter than Suloi bronze, indicated he was Northern or partly so.

That was all Cassian could see of him, his back was to the room, his arms clamped around himself as he shivered violently. Opium, Cassian mused. Had he addicted himself to it? Or had his captors? Opium was not a vice of the Suloi, not unless forced to it, so he was something else.

Peio breathed some petition to his god, and his hands twitched as though he would draw the mark of the Wanderer in the air, but he stopped, shoving his hands into his pockets instead. He dressed as a Republic man, pants, boots, shirts, and belt. He'd cut off his hair, the braids and twisted strands woven with colors and trophies, and no longer openly carried his bow. If no one looked closely, he passed as freedman. But you could not take the wilds out of the heart of a Suloi, even if you took them from the wilds. If they were not surrounded by those that would find the gesture suspicious, Cassian would have gripped his friend's shoulder. Suloi were not meant to walk alone, and Cassian was poor substitute for a clan.

Several cages in a row held more Suloi. Women and children, mostly. There were three men this time, which was more than usual. Suloi men had the option of dying bravely in battle. Suloi women had the sacred duty to survive, to carry on the lines. A duty that left them with few choices when their camps were razed.

As Cassian stepped away from the last cage, the arrival of the auction's organizer sent a flurry of murmurs through the room. There was very little speaking done at the auctions. Only Lucaius, who was not concerned about anonymity, spoke at full volume. He ran the auction, and took a hefty handling fee out of each sale. Lucaius was only slightly less a thug than Gallus, but with a great many more wits, and ran, by Cassian's estimation, the most successful goods-smuggling ring in the city. He was perhaps a decade older than Cassian, and wore his black hair long and tied back in a tail at the nape of his neck, and had never once, in all the years Cassian had known him, smiled. Lucaius controlled nearly the entirety of the movement of goods in the city, and therefore controlled the wealth, comfort, and secrets of many of the elite. Certainly someone could report him to the guards, but most of them were on his payroll.

Lucaius lunged onto the platform and clapped his hands together for attention.

"Welcome to the auction. We'll begin shortly. You will pay immediately upon winning a bid, and your purchases will be held only until morning." He continued on, the usual speech, but Peio tugged on Cassian's sleeve. Cassian ignored him, listening to Lucaius. He had done some work for the man, on occasion, to earn enough to pay for supplies to move slaves out of the city. It might be time for another job—

"Cassian." Peio's urgency snatched Cassian's attention. When he looked, Peio wasn't looking at him, his gaze was locked across the room, his body stiff. Cassian followed his line of sight. First he saw the biggest Meneian he had ever laid eyes on, clearing a path through the gathered buyers like a galleon plowing waves. He wore no hood, no mask. A hulk of a man with skin so black it hinted at blue as the lamplight played on it. He was dressed in the same style as Cassian's dice opponent that afternoon had been, though his clothes were in shades of red instead of tan. The sleeves of his shirt were rolled to his elbows, revealing forearms roped with muscles and gridded with raised scars. He carried no pistols, only a broad, curved scimitar at his hip, the leather belt hanging loose against the cloth beneath it, which wrapped from his hips to his chest. He was either a Meneian warlord, or descended of one, or Cassian was willing to eat his holster.

But it was not the man that Peio watched the way he might a prowling wolf. It was his companion. A woman, as Cassian had first guessed when he saw them in the cemetery. Women buyers were a rare sight at the auction, though not unheard of. But this one…Cassian tried to squint to improve his vision, to clear the blurriness from his strained eyes. He had never seen anyone like her, at the auction or otherwise.

In fact, if someone told Cassian she was the incarnation of one of the Night Sisters, he would only nod in agreement.

Because she was certainly a goddess, dressed in white stola and a turquoise shawl wrapped around her shoulders and over her head, against skin of a burnished red-brown and the shining black curls that peeked from beneath the turquoise. Gifted more generous, pronounced curves than was typical in women of the Republic, she flowed more than walked, chin high and lips set with the tiniest of tense smiles. A graceful hind in a den of wolves, marinating in the unbelievable stench of the place, surrounded by suffering, and she had the spine to manage a smile.

Gods save him from himself. He could not decide if he admired her, in every way a man could admire a woman, or despised her as he did every other person in the room. The only women of the desert he had ever seen before had been warriors employed by merchants, or slaves themselves. This one was something altogether different, and if she was here, dressed in fine, bright clothes, she could only be in the market for slaves.

She surveyed the room from top to bottom, her assessment never lingering long on any one thing. Until it landed on them. Beside him, Peio jerked as if struck, his hand grabbing for and latching onto Cassian's sleeve.

"We have to go," he said.

"We can't go." Cassian glanced around. Lucaius had ceded the stage and his handlers were headed for the cages. If they left, they'd be unable to trace the Suloi buyers.

Cassian glanced at her again, and her gaze drifted to him. He had the oddest desire to slip backward into the knot of people around him, to avoid her eyes the moment she looked at him. She had a spray of freckles like inverse stars across her nose and cheeks, and eyes large and dark beneath thick slashes of brows that were perfect counterpoint to the finer details of her face. All those acknowledgments lasted the space of a heartbeat, then his body, flight instinct honed after years avoiding trouble, seized as though he were facing down something menacing, something so much larger and more terrifying than the woman whose shape it inhabited. His thoughts fogged. And it had to be his blurred vision, but he swore, or would have, that she shone like moonlight on water.

"Are you selling that?" Lucaius snapped to the woman's companion, and the resonance of the chamber made the sound crack through the silence, waking Cassian from whatever had gripped him.

"We have to go. Now. She knows," Peio hissed, rubbing a hand against his breastbone. He shuddered, and when he turned and headed for the tunnel out, Cassian followed.

SIX

MARA LOOKED AWAY FROM the two hooded figures and to the speaker, who glowered. The man's abrupt question shocked everyone back to their own business, browsing the lives on offer. There was only a very occasional murmured exchange, otherwise everyone was silent. Once she had taken stock of the man standing beside the platform she turned back to find the man in the hood again, but he was gone. She was certain, down to her bones, she had felt a whisper of magic when she met his gaze. Irritation seized her and she snapped her gaze back to the platform, but spoke to Djar, in Meneian, as she looked at the other.

"This must be the Lucaius we've heard about. Tell him we need slaves to replace those lost on our voyage from Nasiye," Amara named the capital of Menei in her murmured orders to Djar. In the Republic, even women of high rank rarely spoke for themselves outside their home. She was not interested in proving they held no sway over her only to cause a scene. There was a time and place for pride, and this was not it. She was here to ferret out the abolitionist who had managed to evade every attempt she'd made to find him.

But if he had magic…if he was Suloi himself, that would explain why he chose to work against the Republic government and free Suloi slaves.

"You are Lucaius?" Djar said.

"I occasionally answer to that name." He folded thick arms over thick middle, eyes narrowed. Tall, broad-shouldered and wide-bellied, he had the look of a thug and the mien of a strategist. The very worst kind of scum. She preferred they had brawn or intellect, not both. It was the ones with both who invariably proved problematic. "And you?" There was menace in the question that evoked no ire from Djar.

"Is this auction not anonymous?" Djar smiled amicably.

Amara gazed around the crypt, trying to catch sight of the two men. It was nearly impossible. Almost everyone was hooded, and everyone was masked in some manner or another. They had both worn white hoods, but she saw a half-dozen others with the same.

"No mask, no hood." Lucaius gestured at Djar.

"My face is not the most recognizable part of me." Djar flicked his fingers against his jaw to indicate his skin.

"Nor hers." Lucaius indicated Amara with a jut of his chin. "You never answered my question. Are you selling her?"

"We are here to buy," Djar said. "If I may?" He gestured to indicate the cages that circled the perimeter.

"We?" Lucaius' brushy brows rose. "Has money stashed somewhere, does she?" When he reached as if to touch her, Djar's hand snared his wrist. The four brutes that stood at the corners of the platform moved in closer.

"Looking is free," Amara said, "but anything else will cost you dearly."

"Whore, are you?" Lucaius yanked his hand from Djar's grip, and Djar relaxed beside her.

"If that is the only word you can conceive of, then it will have to do."

"I can think of a few." Lucaius' eyes narrowed, assessing her more carefully.

"Do not strain yourself," Amara said, impatient. She had never cared for these small dominance battles. But they had to be played and won, a step on the way to what she wanted.

"Maybe I don't allow women that aren't for sale." Lucaius lifted a hand to signal the man nearest him. He paused when Djar turned his attention to him, long enough for Amara to counter.

"Nor their money?" Amara smiled when Lucaius' eyelids flickered, holding his stare. He made an expression that curled like a sneer but was accompanied by a laugh.

"Keep a rein on this one, aye? If she bothers anyone I'll have her on the block." Lucaius turned away, striding to the far side of the platform.

"*I saw a man in a white hood and black cloth*"—she touched her face to indicate where the cloth covered—"*with a blackened eye. Find him.*" It was not he who had rippled against her magic, making it shudder in the same way a glass of water did when Djar was tromping around near it. It had been his companion, touched with water. But he was more recognizable because of his wounds. Djar moved away from her and to the circle of cages, hunting.

Amara stepped away from the platform so Lucaius did not take her sudden solitary state as invitation, and observed the room. She drew a breath and wished, as she had upon first entering, that she had something to block out the stench. It was never just the smell of sick, filthy humans. Desperation had its own kind of malodor, something that stung her nose the same way a half-rotted corpse did. She was glad the twins, who had arrived home at the very last moment with very little explanation for their absence, were not down in the crypt with them to witness everything.

Drawing the extra length of the stola up and around her face to filter the smells, she curled her fingers into the fabric.

She could walk the perimeter of the room. She could pass the cages filled with wet, moldering straw and lives poached and not die a little at each one. She could pass them and do nothing, then forget them and continue on with her life and this assignment. She could. She must.

Amara wiped her clammy palms against her hips.

They did not need to be there long. Kiya and Bek waited topside, in the graveyard, ready to flee, attack, or thieve, depending on her success now. Her first inspection of the room suggested the slaves that drew the most interest were against the wall to her right, and so if there were Suloi, they were there. She began at the cage nearest the cemetery stairs, where she had first seen her possible quarry. That cage held only two people, a woman huddled in the corner, hunched against the stares and appraisals, hair matted and filthy about her face. Her companion was a man, curled around himself, his head in her lap. Amara turned abruptly away from them, a dull ache beginning in her chest.

The stares of the men around her helped to distract her. They appraised her as though she were for sale. She had borne such many times. But that had been a long time ago, and she had left that broken girl behind.

If either of these were Suloi, Amara could not tell by looking. There were no markings or boards on the cage to indicate any details of origin. She moved to the next. Three women, sitting with knees bent up and pressed together so they formed a circle, arms about each oth-er's waists, heads bowed to block out the onlookers. They rocked, and whispered comforts to each other, punctuated by sobs. The vile hands gripping her heart squeezed harder, the magic inside her coaxing. *It would be so easy.*

Amara twisted away from them. She sank her focus inward for a moment, listening with her magic. There was something, a trace of power, but she could not pinpoint its source, could not gauge its strength, or truly grasp it at all. Odd. Not the water she had felt in the other man. It flickered in and out of her awareness, like a flame fighting against the wind.

A flash of movement on the far side of the room distracted her. White hood, hastily ducked head, a figure fading back between others. She suppressed a triumphant smile and wove her way between the patrons and the platform in the center of the room. Djar was near the stairs, on the opposite side from her, and noticed her beeline. She waved her hand for him to remain.

There was a broken section of wall that led into a dark tunnel. When Amara did not see the two men she sought to either side of it, she stepped through. The slight change in smell was almost a relief, but not much, since this was obviously an old sewer. Amara glanced down at her shoes, scowling.

A quick walk into the tunnel revealed no one, and she pushed away her irritation as she headed back. A woman's cries echoed from the crypt as Amara returned. The woman was pleading in Republic Trade, reaching back toward her cage as a guard hefted her onto the platform. Lucaius grabbed her arm and spun her forward to face the crowd. She twisted to continue looking, crying, saying a name.

Amara recognized her as the woman who'd had a male companion in her cage. She didn't want to be separated from him. Lucaius shook her, hard, until she went to her knees, tears streaking her face. Amara bit the inside of her cheek so hard it bled. The raw copper taste grounded her. It would help no one if she revealed anything of what they were doing in a fit of empathy-induced rage. Djar caught her eye as she stepped from the tunnel and when she nodded he crossed to her side. The two men were gone or well hidden among the buyers when she looked around.

"Did anyone leave?" she murmured to Djar. He shook his head. The woman was still sobbing on the platform, crying for her cell mate as she was handed off the platform to her purchaser. She writhed and fought until the man holding her slapped her, sending her to her knees. He bundled her over to two men Amara assumed to be guards or handlers. The next were handed roughly up onto the platform, the three women who had huddled together. Amara struggled to breathe in a steady rhythm. She felt hot, and fuzzy-headed.

Lucaius called for bids. Amara pushed away the panic rising from the dark of her mind. Think of something else. What gods did the Suloi worship? The Republic pantheon? The elements, as the Odokan did? Or if they truly were descended of Old Sultanate refugees, perhaps they remembered the Wheel. Lucaius clapped his hands in quick succession and his brutes hauled the women off the platform and back to their cage as a masked man near the front nodded and counted out his payment.

The guards retrieved another woman, this one with a girl in tow, perhaps ten or twelve Turns. Amara's throat stitched closed again, memory's brutal tricks plunging a dagger into her heart. The mother held the girl to her, face pressed against her belly to save her from the stares and the sight of it all.

"We'll start at fifty for the pair," Lucaius said. Hands went up to bid, and Amara fought free of the lie her mind told her, the memory. As Lucaius repeated the winning bid, Amara called out, doubling it. She had the advantage of surprise. When Lucaius looked at her, so did the others, which prevented anyone countering.

"Two hundred," Amara repeated. Sentiment was a dangerous traitor that would reveal her if she was not careful, because those who dealt in the lives of others did not feel sentiment. In her experience men like these utterly lacked empathy and so were incapable of recognizing it in others, so she left her expression blank to hide even a hint of caring. Lucaius shrugged.

"Slave tax is thirty percent," he said. Amara did not flinch. If they thought her foolish they were far less likely to look more deeply into her identity. One of the reasons for the night market, besides it being the only place to buy Suloi, was to avoid the hefty tax the Republic put on slaves. Lucaius revealed his disdain for her by quoting it to her now.

"Very well. I'll take them now." Amara crossed between the bidders and the platform to the other side. The guards rough-handled the woman and her daughter from the platform and to the floor. The girl cried out in pain at the harshness of their grip. "Handle them more carefully. I've no use for damaged stock," Amara snapped. The handler snorted as he clapped shackles on both the woman and her daughter's wrists and attached the chain to the collars on their necks.

Amara counted the payment into her palm, trying to focus on the coins as another crying woman was dragged from her cage and onto the platform. Living in Tamar had softened her. There was suffering, as there was everywhere. But not this. This wound she had not realized still festered inside her.

The handler hung his ring of keys on a little hook on his belt made for the purpose and took Amara's money, counting it as he dropped it into a pouch at his waist. He nodded, then clipped a rope to each collar and held them out to Amara. They were rough hemp, harsh against her palms and fingers, needle-like fibers stabbing. The memories wanted to drown her, wanted to drag her back under, into the darkness. Instead she wrapped the ropes around her hands, penance for the lie she was telling, and to remind herself how far she had come, and that she would never be dragged back down. No matter what she had to do to prevent it.

"This way," she said to the woman, leading both toward the stairs. Djar came behind them, and the mother eyed him in apprehension, clutching her daughter closer and shifting nearer to Amara as they twisted through the crowd. The cage that had held the other woman and her male companion now just held the man. He was sitting up when she passed, back to the room, arms circled around his bent knees, head hanging. Amara's brow furrowed as something trembled against her magic, but a commotion behind her made her glance back. Four men had appeared out of the sewer tunnel, dressed in official-looking uniforms, with capes pinned across their shoulders. Lucaius jumped off the platform to meet them as the buyers moved hastily away, searching for escape.

"We should go," Djar rumbled, as the crowd shifted toward them. He mounted the stairs three at a time, but Amara followed more slowly, watching her new charges to make certain they did not stumble or fall.

Outside, the dank air of the cemetery was a relief from the foul, tepid air down below. She caught sight of Bek or Kiya moving in the trees that bordered the graveyard, but lifted a hand for them to stay hidden. Djar continued in the lead, toward the far northern end of the cemetery, where a rusty iron gate led to a side road in the warehouse district. The woman and her daughter shuffled behind Amara, breaths broken with sniffles and stifled sobs. Amara had seen their feet, bare, blistered, and cut. Anger tinged with sorrow beat a steady rhythm between her temples. She hoped her time in the Republic was almost over. Though she had never set foot here before, it was full of spirits and painful memories that she had spent a decade erasing.

"Do you wish Bek to hunt for the men you saw?" Djar asked as they reached the gate, hemmed-in by overgrown trees and vines and cloaked in near total darkness.

"No." Amara glanced back to see several of the patrons exiting the stairway down in the catacombs. Whoever those guards had been, they had not been the usual type she'd seen in the city. And their presence had certainly ended things earlier than they would have otherwise. "No, I don't think that will be necessary." She looked to the mother and daughter, but held her smile until she glanced at Djar again. "He'll come to us."

Seven

CASSIAN STIFLED A GROAN as Peio's boot heels dug sharply against his spine. But Peio was up and straddling the wall only a moment later. He reached for Cassian's hands and helped pull him up and they both slid down the other side, landing in a robust tangle of flowering vines sporting wicked thorns. Peio did not need to exert effort to stifle curses of anger or pain. Cassian was certain Suloi hunters were born lacking such normal, mundane instincts as to cry out when they were bleeding. Silent. Cassian, on the other hand, had to press his teeth together and slam his eyes shut as he trudged through the thorns, and they tore at his skin and clothes.

The two of them crouched together just out of the grip of the vines, surveying the house before them. A fairly typical specimen of this neighborhood. The lower class of wealthy lived here. Not possessing enough money and influence to buy in the central quarter, closer to the Assembly, but far removed from poor. Had the Meneians purchased this? That suggested a merchant of extravagant means, and also one who intended to frequent Haenna.

Cassian tugged on his earlobe as he looked to Peio. Hear anything? Peio gave a conservative shake of his head. They'd get the mother and daughter back first. Then the rest. Only the ones he had seen leave

59

with their owners. The arrival of the Assembly's guards had confused everyone, and ended things early. After this house, he and Peio could sneak back to the crypt and free as many as possible. They'd have to leave the city with them that night, because stealing directly from Lucaius was bad for one's health.

A stone-tiled path led from the locked outer gate to the interior gate. The garden between the house and outer wall held some citrus trees and herbs, their pungency released as he and Peio crept toward the interior courtyard. The path led through the house, which, like its brethren, was built on a square. Fountains abounded, in every corner and marking each doorway.

A ground-level gallery was open to an interior garden, and the surrounding building housed the various rooms. Most homes were laid out similarly, so they could make an educated guess as to where slaves might be sleeping. Peio opened the gate to the house, and went first, moving like a shadow into the gallery. After a moment a low, soft whistle like a night bird's call signaled Cassian. He crept inside and found Peio again.

Peio indicated a closed door across the garden. Situated next to the kitchen, which had an open archway, it was most likely to houseslaves and servants. Cassian waited while Peio listened. Another fountain splashed, hidden by a miniature grove of young olive trees. Something small skittered away through the lavender bushes that circled the garden, and a real night bird let loose a few quick trills. At least he thought it was a real night bird. Peio did not, apparently.

He snagged Cassian by the arm, yanking him the several paces that separated them from the gate and the front garden.

A man loomed out of the dark of the entryway, shadow upon shadow, and Cassian very nearly pissed himself.

"Gods' tits!" he cursed when he almost ran face first into the man's chest. He stepped from the shadow of the entryway and into the silver moonlight, putting a big hand each on Cassian and Peio's necks and spinning them around to march them into the middle of the garden. Cassian reached for his pistol, and Peio for a knife, and the big Meneian slammed their heads together and shoved them forward. A pop of pain momentarily blinded Cassian, then radiated down his face and neck as he and Peio dropped like boulders to their hands and knees. Cassian groaned and Peio cursed in his own language, still fumbling for a knife. The gravel of the path dug into Cassian's palms and knees as he tried to fight the ringing in his ears to make some kind of decision about what to do next. His identity was worth a fortune to Lucaius, and not only would he be strung up for thievery, so would Peio. While Cassian had accepted the likelihood of ending up at the end of rope, he couldn't accept it for his friend.

More people came to them, divested him of his pistol and knife.

"*Wheel and spokes*," someone said in Meneian, as they relieved Peio of his bow and quiver, then knife after knife, the metal clinking to the ground as they piled the weapons away from him. Cassian doubted they would find all of Peio's weapons. Depending on how intimate they wished to be in their searching.

"Welcome," a woman's voice said. "You are a great deal of trouble, aren't you?" The complexity and allure of her voice, which might have been used to sing an aria just as easily as it was used to reproach him, stole his breath and his words. Her speech was accented, though Cassian could not place its origin, he assumed it to be Meneian, though it was inflected with something else. He slumped back on his heels. The moonlight revealed the same woman he had seen at the auction.

This was a trap? She'd known they would come after her. Cassian looked to Peio, and was troubled to see him staring at the woman in awestruck admiration. Cassian tipped his head back to see her sizable companion, and when he took a look around he saw two more. His brow furrowed.

"Wait…" he said. The one crouched and digging through the pile of Peio's knives glanced up, head hidden by the wrapped turban. He paused, then rose like a spring and stepped around Peio. He yanked Cassian's hood back and tugged the cloth covering his face down. A grin split the stranger's face.

"That's the one they chased out of the gambling house!" he crowed.

"It is you," Cassian spat. "You cheated." The other stood between Cassian and the woman.

"Not us, you!" The two laughed in unison, and damn him if he could tell which had been the gambler and which the one who knew Cassian's dice were loaded.

"Investigating?" the big Meneian growled at the two of them, and their laughter cut off.

"I am glad you are already acquainted with the twins, it will make this all much easier," the woman said when silence had stretched for a beat too long. Peio shifted beside Cassian, looking from one person to the other, but settling once again on the woman. Cassian had never seen Peio make that face. It looked disturbingly like Peio had been suddenly struck dumb. "I require your assistance."

"I'm sorry?" Cassian dug his pinky into his ear and shook it, squinting at her. "You want our help?"

"Garbi," the woman called toward the stairs. Another woman descended, and when a girl came behind, Cassian realized it was the Suloi mother and her daughter, whom the Meneians had purchased. "This is Garbi, and her daughter Izar."

The two stood beside the Meneian woman, clean and in new clothes, appearing somewhat at ease. They were not wearing shackles, or ropes, only the slave collars. Cassian frowned sideways at Peio, who had dropped his gaze to the ground.

"You steal Suloi slaves and help them escape. I would like you to do that for Garbi and Izar."

"We don't steal slaves." Cassian shifted. His feet were beginning to go numb and that would cause him some difficulty when he made a run for it. "I steal valuables. Of which I'm certain you have many. Sorry to disappoint you." This had to be a trap. Was she working for Lucaius?

"I'm speaking to your friend. The one with water in his blood." She eyed Cassian briefly then focused on Peio, who shifted. So that's what he'd meant, at the auction, she'd seen and known he was Suloi. How had she known he was water clan?

"*Sanpotar*, do not speak to him." Garbi gripped the Meneian's arm. "*I do not see the Ghosts who walk the path*," she murmured in Suloi. "*I do not hear their whispers.*" She pulled her daughter behind her. "*They have no name.*"

Peio's shoulders hunched deeper with each line of the Wanderer's curse, and Garbi turned her gaze to the sky.

"Whatever you fear from him, I do not." The Meneian arced a shrewd look between Garbi and Peio.

"You will draw the Wanderer's ire," Garbi said, with concern in her eyes. Cassian looked at them again, each Meneian, then to Peio. Weren't they slavers?

"Let him come, then. You and Izar go rest, for now, yes?"

Garbi complied, leading Izar across the garden and through an archway into a small sleeping room on the ground level.

"You may stand, if you wish, unless kneeling is your preferred position?" She smiled, and even in the unhelpful light of the moon and with his still-blurry vision, Cassian could see it was an expression with enormous appeal. Were he not in this particular situation, he might be inclined to linger in staring at her.

He stood, and helped Peio to his feet. Peio gave the big Meneian behind them a cursory appraisal, then glanced between the twins, then the woman once again.

She approached them, the same flowing walk Cassian had first seen from her in the crypt. Hips weaving from side to side, sinuous, and calculated. He yanked his gaze up. She stopped in front of him. Intimately in front of him, closer than propriety dictated, at least for a Republic woman, but he knew very little of Menei and what was proper there. Most in the Republic thought Menei populated by hedonists. But the Republic thought that about everywhere save the Republic.

She tipped her head to look at him, and the turquoise cloth spilled back, pooling around her shoulders. Her dark hair was twisted around the crown of her head in braids, as was popular with wealthy women lately, save a few coils that had escaped. Without the cover, he was treated to the sight of the graceful lines of her neck and a peek of her collarbones encircled by the chaste neckline of the garment.

It was a crime that she was beautiful, a ploy by the gods to fool people into trusting her. Or perhaps it was warning, like the bright colors of a venomous serpent. But gods…if he could paint her. Or there was that piece of mahogany that had been taunting him for years, refusing to tell him what it wished to be…

Her jet eyes narrowed. "You've had an interesting day."

When he did not, could not, answer, held in confused thrall by the music in her voice, her perfect, lush mouth curved as she pointed at his face.

"Oh," Cassian said, realizing she meant his eye and split lip. "I have your people to thank for this." To his left, one twin snorted amusement. The sound broke whatever spell was on him and Cassian nipped the inside of his cheek to reclaim his sense. Her nearness made him uncomfortable, but her smell was peace, a cool, water kind of scent that seemed to wash the air like rain.

"Cassian," Peio warned, a tone in his voice Cassian had never heard before. Something was clearly wrong, or he never would have said Cassian's name in front of a stranger. He cut his gaze to his friend, who wore a guarded expression as he watched the woman. She also looked at Peio. She tilted her head.

"There is water in you," she said to Peio, and stepped away from Cassian. Cassian blinked hard, then grunted when a jolt of discomfort shot through his face and reminded him her man was part of the reason he could only see out of one eye and his head was pounding.

"What are you?" Peio asked, avoiding her gaze.

"I am not a slaver. And you are not petty thieves. So let us dispense with our adopted personas and deal in truth. I am here on behalf of another, who is seeking Suloi gifted with a particular magic. I would like your help."

"So you are a slaver." Cassian rubbed his temple, pressing against the vein that throbbed in time with the pain in his skull.

She examined Peio, ignoring Cassian. She clearly did not understand the subtleties of Suloi communication, because Peio wasn't going to tell her anything if she kept staring at him like that.

"You can tell whether I'm lying, can you not?" she said to Peio. That was their little secret. Peio's unerring sense for lies, more invaluable even than his keen accuracy with projectiles. And instead of keeping that secret, he nodded like a besotted simpleton. "So," she coaxed, "tell him."

"Truth," Peio said. She turned to Cassian in triumph, the smile back, though this one was shaped with less allure and more calculation.

"You're drunk," Cassian accused his friend. Peio wiped the back of his hand across his mouth.

"Not anymore," he sniffed, cutting his gaze away from the woman when she raised an eyebrow at him.

"So you aren't lying." Cassian shrugged. "That doesn't give me a reason to help you. In fact you've given me every reason to get rid of you as fast as I can."

"You free Suloi and send them to safety. I can offer them asylum."
She stepped toward him and he thought about stepping away, but her
companion still stood at their backs.

"Oh?" Cassian glanced sidelong at Peio, who frowned.

"I can take them where they will never fear persecution again," she
said.

Cassian dug his fingers into the back of his belt, to prevent himself curling them into fists. Not Menei. They loved magical slaves so
much they bred them. Where could she possibly take anyone where
they would not be persecuted? More importantly, why did he want
to believe her so badly? No, not want to…he did believe her. Gallus
had rung his bell more soundly than he'd realized, and now he was
out of his mind.

"The children of the Wanderer choose their own path, and would
never follow the lead of *Sanpotar*," Peio said. But it did not sound as
convincing as it should have, one of the major tenants of the Suloi
culture. No Outsiders.

"Not even if that path led them home?" she said, in a voice like
serenity made sound. Like Frixis with flute, leading people astray.
Next she'd turn them into flowers or trees. Or goats.

"Where once was home is forgotten," Peio said, "the road there
barred. We belong to each other now." Cassian heard the break in Peio's
voice when he said *we*, and so did she, her expression losing a measure
of its hauteur. She considered for a moment, and her next words were
either well-laid traps or the product of uncanny insight.

"I have come to open the road," the woman said. "The blood
remembers home, even when we cannot. You belong to the Wheel."

Cassian stepped between the woman and Peio, not caring for the
way his friend seemed so enthralled by her words, bewitching though
they were. She looked at him, something sparking in the depthless
dark of her eyes. A warmth that kindled the same in him. She glanced

over his shoulder to the big Meneian behind them, presumably to stop his interference when Cassian moved.

"I don't know what your Wheel is, but Peio doesn't belong to any-body," Cassian said. "He cannot help you."

"We will help you," Peio said, reverently, "as much as we can."

"No." Cassian whirled on Peio. "You aren't in charge, I'm in charge. Have you lost your mind? We aren't helping anyone."

"You aren't in charge! We're partners," Peio said.

"We aren't talking about this here," Cassian hissed. "We're leaving."

"My people will help you find the rest of the Suloi who were at the auction tonight, and in return, you will help me," she said.

Cassian faced her. "I don't know you, and I don't trust you." He wanted to. Why did he want to?

"I have told you who I am and what I want. I do not wish that information to leave this garden. The only way you are leaving is under my terms. Help me, or Djar will help *you* find your way into a shark-infested bay." She smiled as she held a hand out toward the big man.

Cassian sighed. "I see."

EIGHT

AMARA WATCHED FROM THE window of her room, a bedroom she had chosen on the upper level of the villa, as the smuggler and his Suloi friend exited the garden and out onto the street. Bek was with them, to take them to meet with the captain and *borrow* some of his crew for their rescue.

"I should have sent you both," she mused. "Or Djar."

"The old man is too noticeable, and I'm spent." Kiya flexed her fingers open and closed. Amara turned to level a reproachful look on her. Kiya had only a whisper of earth magic to her name, and should have known better than to waste it to win at a game of dice.

"Magic is not excess coin for spending," Amara admonished. How many times had she told Kiya the same thing? "Why were you there?"

"We had planned to bribe one of the losers for information," Kiya said from where she sat curled, catlike, into a one-armed couch in the corner of the room. "Take all their money, then give it back to them for something about the smuggler. But then that fight broke out and we had to leave." Kiya curled deeper into the chair. "I wish we'd known he was the one we wanted, then you wouldn't have had to go to that awful auction."

"You will give him his money back," Amara said, "at some point."

Kiya smiled, picking at a loose thread on the cushion. "At some point."

"Mmm," Amara said.

This was the first night she'd sent any of them into real danger on this journey, and it made a fluttering anxiousness take up residence in her chest. The only slave she had ever stolen was Djar. That night was a tangle of edges and flashes, not a whole memory, but moments of panic, fear, and sorrow. The slaves of the Republic were the first she had seen since fleeing Menei, and they were everywhere. Each a dagger's cut against scars, reopening the wounds of her past so they bled fresh and insidious into the light of everything that had come since. If she did not do something, it was likely to drive her mad. "Will you and Djar set up the basin?" she asked Kiya. The younger woman stretched, bending backwards over the arm of the bench, and grinned. "Want to look at your prince again?" she teased.

My prince. Amara felt the weight of the statement settle oddly. She did not covet Ihsan. How could she desire someone she didn't know and who did not desire her in return? It was the security of his position she wanted. The most untouchable height to which she could strive. She neither wished him ill, nor harbored warm feelings for him. Looking at him did not bring her pleasure or discomfort. It felt perverse to say that she saw him as little more than an object, which was counter to the very core belief of her. But love had never been part of her plan. Only security. Love's balance was pain, and Amara had experienced more than enough pain in her life to learn her lesson.

"The Sultana requested that I contact her as the situation developed," Amara said as Kiya rose and moved to her side at the window. Amara reached up to remove the cloth from Kiya's hair. While Bek kept his shorn very close to his head, Kiya kept hers longer, nearly the length of her hand. They were both possessed of the tightly coiled, dense but yielding hair of the southern Menei. The tight wrap of the turban had flattened the puff of her hair. Amara dug her fingers into it and Kiya sighed in pleasure. Amara kept hers even longer than Kiya's, enjoying the many options the length gave her, to correspond with her ever-changing moods.

"It needs a cut," Kiya said, skimming her own nails over her scalp. She gave Amara a peck on the cheek and left the room to search out Djar.

Amara looked out the window again. Water's gift to those born in its House was an ability to sense lies. It was always such a way with the Wheel. Fifth House mages, who commanded passion, and fire, were often gifted charlatans and liars, and so in balance, water saw truth. The Second House held dominion over mirrors, shuttered light, the truth concealed within the lie. Hidden knowledge, the truth in the deep dark. She had not learned these things until she had fled Menei and found herself in Tamar, a mage uncontrolled. But these innate abilities had proven invaluable to her in building her new life, and now.

There had been layer upon layer of deception in the Republic man and his Suloi companion, and while it was not unexpected, it troubled her. Amara did not usually engage in situations in which she was not certain of her upper hand, and much of her time was spent gaining such. That had been nearly impossible here, hunting a man they had so little information on.

She must endeavor to be careful of them both. It was obvious the Suloi had never seen a high order mage, and though she had sensed only the faintest song of water in him, there had been enough for him to recognize her power's dominion over his own.

Djar and Kiya entered the room, Kiya carrying a large copper bowl and Djar a heavy, two-handled ceramic urn.

Amara helped Kiya lift the bowl onto its stand, and Djar poured water from the jug into the basin. Amara had collected the water from a fountain in the palace, and Ihsan had infused it with his own magic. They had carried it all the way to the Republic with them. A necessary effort. Divining was a nuanced spell, one of the more complicated on the Wheel. It was weakened by distance, by how well, or how little, one knew the person they were trying to call upon. This basin of water might last another small turn, if it was not disturbed. She would very much like to be on her way back to Tamar in that time frame.

Amara stood before the bowl, her hands on the rim, waiting for the water to settle. Kiya resumed her place in the chair, and Djar took up a stance by the window. Amara breathed out, releasing the reins of her power, calling it forward. It surfaced across her skin, brilliant like quicksilver, spots and rosettes like the leopards that stalked the velds of Menei, reflective like shifting bits of mirror.

"Ihsan Sabri." Amara stroked the surface of the water, caressing it with her skin and her power. His name was spell enough to summon his magic to hers like trickle to torrent. For a Charah fed and was fed by all the mages of their House, and his magic would always be subservient to hers, even if the prince was not subservient to the merchant. She drew her hand up from the surface of the basin, and the water rose beneath it, Ihsan's likeness in miniature, a featureless copy. "Greetings, Sehzade Efendim." She bowed.

"Mistress Mutar. You have news to relay." The echo of his voice made the liquid vibrate, and its sound was hollow and strange as relayed by the water. With a large, live body of water the effect would have been less, but to contact him without draining herself, she needed water connected to him. The remaining water in the basin bloomed with ice, spreading out from the figure's feet to the edges of the bowl. A rare, and powerful manifestation of Second House magic, Ihsan was the only ice mage Amara had ever met. Some rumors had been spread that the traumatic effect of nearly burning to death had changed his magic, but there was no way to know.

"Only insignificant. We have located the smuggler and enlisted his enthusiastic support of our cause," she said, dryly. The watery likeness smiled.

"Undoubtedly. I will relay this news to the Sultana." He could have cut the contact off, if he had wished it, and that he did not suggested he had more to say, or thought she did.

"There is little else to tell, I am afraid."

"Be careful," he said, and even in the watery representation of his voice she heard weariness. "There are players here that have become more active since you left, and the Sultana fears there may be danger from quarters you do not expect."

"Your concern warms my heart, Sehzade," Amara replied. She knew he was speaking of the Grand Vizier. Amara had made the politics at court as much her business as the politics of the Merchants' Guild. She was well aware that the Grand Vizier not only opposed the Sultana, but his supporters outnumbered her in the Council. She also knew him to be a man of internal evil, for there were several former servants of his that had passed through the back door of her shop looking for aid.

"Do not let my concern mislead you, Mistress Mutar," he said. "I will await your next summons." The water collapsed on itself. Amara frowned at it as she pulled her power back into herself, under her control, the quicksilver marks fading from her skin. She had never met a cold water mage. Even those barely gifted at all were warm, sensual creatures. Ihsan had demonstrated a bizarre lack of that sensuality, more suited to someone born of air than one born of water.

Could he not be bothered at least to be friendly now that they were all but engaged? Certainly there was the condition of her task in the Republic, but Amara would not fail. He could not have been harboring some hope that he might be allowed to marry for love, and she saw no reason he shouldn't be pleased with her as a companion.

"Whatever turns his magic to ice apparently did the same to his heart," Kiya observed with a yawn. She was tired, as they all were. None of them were quite adjusted to the change of scenery and rhythm. They had not been in place long enough to accustom themselves to everything yet. Kiya and her brother had borne the brunt of the labor thus far, searching day and night to follow the leads Aysel had given them to track down the smuggler.

"You may leave this filled for now. Set it up in the common area, and cover it with a cloth," Amara directed. She didn't want to risk losing any by attempting to return it to the jug. It would lose its conductivity over time, as the water was reduced by heat and Ihsan's magic signature faded from it. The ocean would serve the job as well, but that would take a larger expenditure of power, as well as a sheltered and isolated place to stand in the water, and so she would use the basin as long as she could.

Kiya and Djar moved the basin into the other room, and Amara followed them. Bek and their new friends would be gone most of the night. The flutter in her chest threatened with teeth when she thought about trying to sleep. There would be nightmares tonight, something she had chased away in Tamar, had foolishly thought defeated.

They would need to be ready to depart the city almost immediately upon Bek's return. If they managed to retrieve all the Suloi still in the crypt, she doubted the fact would escape Lucaius' notice for long. The smuggler had reluctantly revealed he had contacts outside the city who would help transport the Suloi to a clan who would take them, or farther east, where they would not be enslaved but be forced to fend for themselves in a less-forgiving environment. He had also warned that a contingent of Vexillae had recently arrived from the capital, though he was not certain why. They would have to move in haste, and in secret.

Vexillae, Amara had learned—a little from Aysel before they left Narfour, and more once she was able to question people herself—were a vile lot. Originally a force set aside for special tasks appointed by the Consuls, they had in recent decades been assigned almost exclusively to eradicating magic in the Republic. Apparently selected at a young age and trained to the task over many Turns, they were, as far as she could discern, universally a gang of violent oppressors. Camps of Suloi were hunted, and if they were not tortured and killed, they were taken by these men who wielded Republic technology that far outstripped the peaceful Suloi's capabilities.

Djar and Kiya situated the basin and its stand near one wall, where there existed a space between the odd and, to Amara's eye, unplanned collection of furniture. They had secured the use of the home through a liberal application of money, and knew only that its owners had retired to a less populated part of the Republic to live out their days. Amara's only complaint was that to bathe required a trek up the road to the nearest public bathhouse, and she had made time only once for such an endeavor. There were aqueducts, not only visible throughout the city, but present in the back of Amara's mind, her natural sense of water that surrounded her. They supplied household water, for the water closet, and the kitchen, and the fountains that splashed throughout the house and grounds, but there was not a single basin large enough to take a bath.

Bek had located a room on the lower floor set with tile and a drain that Amara suspected was for bathing. If one was meant to stand in the room and sponge from a bucket, or be doused by servants, Amara did not consider that bathing. Connecting with water, as fully as she could, as often as she could, was one of the few things that could settle Amara's mind, still the thoughts that swirled incessantly.

Water and earth, Amara and Kiya, could be very patient waiters. Djar, however, was a man accustomed to movement and action. He filled the time preparing them for travel, packing supplies, and saddling the horses they had hired. When he had finished he perused the two shelves that held the home's paltry selection of books.

His Republic Trade was better even than Amara's, given all the time he'd spent in the Nasiye coliseum circuit, packed alongside former Republic slaves. And while it might take her quite an effort to plod through a book printed in the language, he found an intriguing specimen and sprawled on one of the lounging couches to read it. A quick glance at its pages as she passed him to and from her room revealed it to be a book on history. His one true love.

Though tinkering might be his second. He was in the process of disassembling one of the house's clocks, which lay in neatly demarcated piles on the table beside him. The Republic's machines were interesting to him, even if Amara only found them loud and obscene.

"*According to this,*" he said in Meneian, amused, "*the dispute that began the Sundering War was over horses.*"

"*Mages are treated little better than used-up nags here,*" Amara said, "*so perhaps Republic historians liken the event to a horse trade.*" Amara thought he could easily give the Sultana's new librarian a run for his money on random facts. Perhaps she would reintroduce them upon her return. It would do Djar well to have someone who could bear to listen to him debate history until lesser folk were comatose.

Kiya stood by the window, watching. Amara puttered. First to the downstairs kitchen to scrounge for nibbles left over from their dinner. A handful of crisp flatbread was all she managed, her stomach knotting in protest when she eyed the ham Taliba had made for them. The citizens of the Republic were obsessed with meat.

After her failed attempt at grazing, she returned to her room to straighten things. Deepest night descended, and the rain that came with it muffled the world. Kiya straightened from her vigil at the narrow window. "They're back," she announced.

Amara joined her. The Suloi man who had been with the smuggler had just moved through the gate, the smuggler and Bek behind him, shadows in the night. Djar laid his book on the couch and went downstairs to meet them. Amara and Kiya waited together at the window. Amara frowned, and Kiya voiced her thoughts.

"There isn't anyone with them. There were more"—Kiya looked at her for confirmation—"weren't there?"

"We may have been too late. They could have been sold," Amara said, and Kiya's eyes widened, almost as if she could see the dagger of pain that shoved through Amara's breastbone. She slid her cool, slim hand into Amara's, and Amara gripped it with a smile she hoped appeared undisturbed, instead of brave. "Have Bek bring the smuggler to me."

Amara waited by the window, focused on the gate. Only Garbi and her daughter. Only two of the people who had been in that Wheel-forsaken crypt came out of it free.

She clutched the window frame in one hand, her nails digging into the wood. And how many had she left behind in Menei, to make her own escape? To live a life full of success and ease? When Kiya returned, Amara had to force her hand to uncurl, and she turned toward the smuggler…the stranger…with a smile.

He appeared little more cheerful than when she had sent him into the night. Irritation wrote a grimace on his face, and distrust narrowed the unmarred eye. Or perhaps his mood was due more to the wet grip of his rain-soaked clothes to his body. They looked at each other for a moment, and he scuffed a hand through his dripping hair, inadvertently slinging it at Kiya.

"*Are you a mongrel?*" Kiya scoffed, skirting around him to slouch onto one of the chairs.

"*At least I'm not a thief,*" he snipped back. Kiya snorted, glancing at Amara and back to him.

Surprise zipped through Amara when she realized he spoke Meneian. Her gaze strayed over him from head to toe as he looked at Kiya. She could not recall a single person she'd met in Haenna who spoke Meneian. Why did he? Because he was a smuggler, perhaps. The more languages one knew, the easier it was to blend into situations, instead of standing out.

The swelling around his left eye was beginning to darken and show bruising that she suspected would only grow more gruesome in the days to come. His split lip was puffed and angry looking, and she thought it likely made speaking a bit painful, though he had managed the sharp syllables of Meneian well enough. If she had time she would have sent one of the twins to get mugwort for him.

"Oh?" Kiya said. "The signs posted all over the city naming you a criminal would suggest otherwise."

"This face is not on a single posting in this city." He tried to grin as he drew a circle around his face, but it pinched to a grimace immediately when his lip split open anew. Amara stepped into her room and took a cloth from the ceramic basin on her dressing table, pouring water over it from a pitcher. She squeezed out the excess and returned to the common room. When she approached to hand him the rag, his gaze drifted over her cheeks and nose. He mumbled a thank-you.

"Were so many sold tonight? Did the auction not end early? I thought you might have returned with more," Amara said.

He pressed the cloth over his lip and shook his head. "Too many guards tonight. The Assembly guards made Lucaius cautious." He dabbed at his lip again and tossed the rag on the table, too harshly. Anger.

Bek and Djar came up the stairs, Djar bearing a tray of coffee. Wheel keep him, he always knew just what she needed. Coffee would brace her. She could already smell its bitter caress in the air.

He took it to the table in the sitting room, snuggling it between his stack of clock parts—weight, counterweights, and wires.

"Those are tiny cups," the smuggler said as he settled onto a couch. He lay back against the cushions, clasping his hands over his belly and lifting his muddy, booted feet onto the hand-embroidered fabric. He laid his head back against the pillows and closed his eyes.

Amara looked at Bek and Kiya, and raised her eyebrows. Kiya gave her a bewildered look and mouthed *mongrel*, and Bek scowled in the direction of the man's boots. When he moved to physically correct the smuggler's rudeness, Amara shook her head. Bek stood behind Kiya's chair, and though she still lounged, and he was straight-backed, their expressions were the same. Disgust. Bek had a broader brow and jaw, and a bit more muscle than his sister. Kiya had finer features, and fuller mouth. With obvious differences like their sex and the length of their hair, anyone that knew them even briefly could tell them apart. They could, however, look nearly identical with the right costuming, a fact they often used to their advantage to instigate chaos of varying severity.

For their age, they were wise. But in this assessment, they were wrong. They had grown up amongst the poor of Nasiye. Amara had been poor amongst the rich. Putting his muddy boots all over fabric that could be ruined by it suggested to Amara that he was in fact highborn, instead of lower class. He wasn't lacking in manners; he was lacking in awareness. Material things and their care had little meaning to him because he'd always been surrounded by them.

How interesting. A man of privilege, slumming about in the poor districts. A noble who had ruined himself wouldn't be spending time helping others. So what had knocked him down? What did he hope to gain by what he was doing?

Amara walked to the end of the couch and hooked the man's crossed ankles with her hand as she passed, slinging his feet to the floor. He sat up, looking bewildered as he did. She took the opportunity to examine him more closely, to reassess her initial dismissal of him based on the evidence of his brawling. He had the look she associated with Republic born, who descended of the Northmen and had long ago mixed with the warmer-toned races of the south to land somewhere in the middle. There was some lingering brush of the Old Sultanate in the coloring of the Republic, just as there was in their architecture.

Republic skin could bronze in the sun, as his had, and most of them had dark hair. His was a shade removed from black, with some natural curl to it that only showed because of its current disheveled length. Where his Suloi companion had a broader, shorter face she might have associated with the Odokan from the east, he had a lean, oval face accompanied by a square jaw and straight, patrician nose that spoke of Northern influence. The smuggler's eyes, gifted the dark contrast of his nearly black brows and lashes, were an arresting shade of blue. It was a rare color in Tamar and rarer still in Menei, though she did not think it so in the Republic. Interesting. Perhaps he had the north in his family tree?

She sat on the couch across from him. He examined Bek and Kiya for a moment, gaze flicking from one to the other as if memorizing their differences. Finally he shifted to face Amara, leaning forward and supporting his forearms across his thighs. He looked away, then back, his gaze flicking to her hands and down.

Amara leaned forward to pour a cup of coffee. She had insisted on bringing the ibrik and cups, as well as her own coffee. She could not imagine the hardship of arriving in the Republic to find their coffee inferior to that available in Narfour. In fact she found they did not drink it at all. Amara dashed a bit of cream into hers, then prepared a cup for the smuggler, who watched with a suspicious look on his face.

"Do you drink coffee?" Amara lifted the tiny cup and inhaled the scent to help draw her focus away from the billowing guilt in her belly. Drinking her coffee, while others huddled somewhere in the dark. Frightened. Subjugated. She set it down. He eyed his cup, then hers.

"I'd rather not," he said.

"I'm not going to poison you." She took a sip then, to demonstrate. "I require your assistance, as I said."

"And after?"

"If I were going to kill you, I would not use poison."

"Well, that is comforting." He turned the cup one way then the other. She smiled when he looked at her. Watching her as he did it, he took the cup of coffee, lifting it toward her in salute, then downed it in one drink. Amara raised an eyebrow. He choked, coughing and staring into the tiny cup at the dregs of the coffee, his face reddening. "Gods," he said.

"It is meant to be savored." Amara pressed her lips together to prevent a laugh. Kiya snorted, and Bek rolled his eyes. "In sips." He was lucky Djar did not have the means to prepare it as he normally did, in glowing coals, until it was hot as lava.

"Savor it?" He coughed again. "Why is there sludge in it?" He tipped the cup to examine the contents.

"If it is not to your taste…"

He reached for the ibrik and poured more, looking at her askance as he lifted the pot of cream and splashed in a portion.

"Perhaps honey? Some prefer theirs sweet." She nudged the dish toward him.

"I do like a little sweetness," he said, "but it is always better in the company of something salty." His gaze flashed to hers and away. A flirt, was he?

Amara leaned against the arm of the couch, tucking one foot onto it as she studied him again. A gambler, smuggler, and brawler. Not usually her type. But there was promise of a rakishly handsome man, beneath all the bruising.

She glanced to Djar. "Is it still raining?"

He nodded after a glance out the window.

"Will the rain pass by morning?" she asked the smuggler as he took a tentative sip of his new cup. He considered the flavor for a moment, then pursed his lips as if he'd decided it was passable.

"Usually." He set the cup down. "It is a trek. You still wish to make it, just for the two? Garbi and Izar? Technically I owe you no assistance." He flicked a glance at Kiya. "Since we did not free any slaves tonight, you did not, technically, hold up your end of the bargain."

He didn't trust her to know where he met his contacts. She could see the nervousness in him, the way he tried to hide that he constantly surveyed the room, noting exits, impediments. The way he would clasp his knees as if to stand, then relax. There was not a great deal of trust to spare when it came to slaves. Whether one was trading in them, freeing them, or one of them. It was not a business that allowed the cultivation of trust. So she would not demand his. Still, she needed his help. Willing or not.

"I have heard," she said, "that you have technically been relieved of all your coin." She sipped at the coffee.

He flinched, looking to Kiya again. "Not by honest means."

"Oh? Is gambling an honest endeavor? If you had won, would it have been by honest means?"

He scratched a spot between his brows that was not bruised.

"I will see that your money is returned after you have assisted us in returning Garbi and Izar to their people and you have helped me speak with the Suloi about my offer."

"They don't speak with Outsiders." He gave her a thorough assessment, perhaps noting the finery of her clothing and judging her ability to travel in the wilderness.

"Your friend—"

"Peio cannot help you." He took another sip and set it down, looking to the rain-washed window. "I will do my best. I have some sway." He stood. "Thank you for the coffee."

He stared at the disemboweled clock with a notch of confusion in his brow. The wealthiest in Menei often had Republic technology as novelty, so she was not unfamiliar with clocks, but their ticking irritated her. Punctured the silence. Broke time into odd, arbitrary segments. She did not understand how they worked exactly. Mechanisms that lacked the elegant quiet of magic. She was glad Djar was operating on this one, so its incessant ticking did not fill the house anymore.

"I dislike the idea of traveling with someone whose name I do not know." Amara stood. "I am Amara. Djar"—she pointed—"Bek, and Kiya."

"Cassian." He ducked his head.

"Cassian," Amara repeated. She liked the sound of it. His good eye slitted, his lips parting, and he tucked one hand into the back of his belt as he looked away from her again. "There is a spare room for you and Peio. I think it best we all try to sleep a little."

"We have to leave before the light." Cassian eyed her clothes again. "It is not an easy journey," he hinted.

"Ah. I will endeavor not to burden you."

His mouth twitched. Then he left, disappearing down the stairs.

Sleep. Deep inside she cringed. Some nights she allowed Kiya to sleep with her, for the warmth and companionship. Any woman who had grown up in a harem, as Amara had, or in the orphanages of Menei, as Kiya and Bek had, was unaccustomed to sleeping alone. Amara had always slept with other women, first her mother, then her sisters and rivals, lulled to sleep by heartbeats and others' slow, rhythmic breathing. But tonight her skin felt too sensitive, her temper on edge. She could not bear the idea of being touched.

Djar waited until the sound of Cassian's steps on the stairs faded. "What do you think?"

"There are lies in him," Amara said, "but I do not know if they matter to us."

NINE

CASSIAN WOKE TO THE scent of food and followed it into the sitting room. It was still dark, though birds in the garden were doing their best to sing the sun up over the hills. A small, stocky woman with coiled hair fading from black to copper to grey at her temples was just laying out dishes of breakfast foods. She had fed him after their inauspicious arrival the night before, and the morning's offerings were a still-steaming, sliced loaf of olive-studded bread, a plate of boiled eggs, and cold salted ham. She was, apparently, part of the ship's crew. He imagined those onboard were missing her just then. Cassian greeted her and she returned it with a warm smile and an insistence that he eat.

"You're too skinny. I can make anything else you like. Beans?" she asked, patting a hand against his belly. He shook his head, suddenly and uncomfortably reminded of his family's cook, whom he'd known since childhood.

"This will do well, thank you."

She touched her heart and spent a moment lighting lamps before returning downstairs. Cassian spread butter on a slice of bread and laid a piece of ham over it as he made his way to one of the two windows that faced the entrance to the villa and the ocean beyond. All three of Amara's people were in the garden, the two men sparring with their scimitars. In the dark. Cassian stuffed half his meal of bread and ham into his mouth as he tried to watch them. A lamp burned behind him, casting too much light on the window to see clearly what was going on below. He hoped he never had to find out if he could shoot faster than Djar could swing his wicked-looking blade.

He did not know what to make of this group. They looked like Meneians. They talked like them. He'd asked around a bit at the docks, and found they'd arrived on a merchant ship that was still moored in the bay. A few contacts had even confirmed the movement of goods to and from the dock. The usual, bolts of cloth, coffee and tea, the incredible, biting spices that only seemed to grow well in Menei.

But also, cloth dyed Tamarine red. Not just the cloth, but the dye itself. It only came from Tamar. From their mages who knew how to extract the color. Not just the red, but the far-rarer purple. That explained her wealth at least, the finery she wore, the ability to buy slaves just to set a trap for him. Tamarine dye was coveted in the Republic, though they could only get it secondhand from Menei, whose relationship with Tamar was not tainted by threat of war.

Cassian stepped away from the window. His gaze was caught by a great copper basin standing against the wall. He reached up and rubbed his fingers over his stubble-rough face, then stuffed the other half of the bread in his mouth. He hadn't bathed in an age, and that looked like ample enough water to at least make him feel less slovenly.

There was a cloth over the top of it that he set aside, then proceeded to unbuckle his pistol belt and remove his shirt, laying them both over the nearest couch. He cast about for a pitcher or cloth and seeing none, resigned himself to splashing. He washed his face, rubbing away dried blood and wincing at the stubble that was covering his bruised jaw. Shaving would have to wait for another day. He scrubbed wet hands through his hair, which was becoming untenably long. He needed coin for a haircut as well, so it would have to continue in its current state. Cassian moved on to his torso and arms.

"What"—the cold, cold voice stopped him instantly, as if he'd been turned to stone or ice—"are you doing?"

Cassian turned to see that Amara had exited her room. She looked at him as if he were bathing in the blood of virgins, her lips parted in disbelief, her jet eyes wide, her hands half-raised as if she meant to grab him. He looked down at the basin, and wiped the excess of water from his face, confused.

"Bathing?" He squinted at her. His vision was still poor, despite that the swelling had gone down a bit over his left eye.

At that same moment a stampede of footsteps came from behind him on the stairs, announcing the arrival of her trio of servants. When the footsteps stopped, silence reigned, and Cassian looked at the three of them, then back to Amara, aware he had caused some gross offense, but not entirely certain what it was. She lowered her hands, and her lips pressed together. He could not help but notice she wore only a blue silk robe, belted at her slim waist and open nearly to her navel. The inner curves of her breasts were visible, and despite his respect for propriety, his gaze fixed there.

Behind him one of the three burst into laughter. Cassian ripped his gaze away from her exposed skin framed and highlighted by the blue fabric. The girl, Kiya, was nearly doubled over in mirth. Bek glared; Djar sported a menacing scowl. What had he done? Cassian glanced at the basin, and frowned.

"Was that special water?" he asked. Why would they have a basin of special water set out for anyone to use? And what was special about it? He knew nothing about Meneian religion, or what their gods might require of them. He sniffed at his hands, to see if there was a scent, but there was no smell to give it away as something other than plain water. "I would apologize if I knew what I had done. Maybe."

He reached for his shirt, eyeing the still-laughing twin as he used the fabric to dry his face.

"Your apology would not undo the damage," Amara snapped, and strode forward. The lower portion of the robe fluttered open as she moved, revealing her legs nearly to the apex of her thighs. Cassian tried to turn away, but she maneuvered in such a way that he turned right toward her as she put herself between him and the basin. She raised her gaze, slowly, up the expanse of his bared torso, and he might have thought she admired what she saw until her gaze fixed on his.

There was such a look of imminent, violent threat in her large, dark eyes that his body insisted he was about to die. The hair on his arms stood up, as if he were faced with something deadly instead of a woman he could probably pick up and toss across the room. But that look, it seemed to sink claws into his mind, into his will, into his beating heart, and turn him cold from head to toe.

Cassian took a step back, nearly tripping over the couch behind him, and instead sitting down abruptly. She turned her back on him and examined the basin, then sighed, lifting her hand to her face, fingertips against her brow and cheeks.

"*He's polluted it. I cannot use it now, throw it out and prepare to leave,*" she said, then looked at him sharply. Perhaps remembering he understood Meneian. She turned abruptly and returned to her room.

Kiya recovered herself, wiping at her eyes. She looked at Djar and said, "*He's dumber than a dead camel,*" before following her mistress into the other room.

"Go prepare Garbi and Izar to leave," Djar told Bek, who obeyed immediately.

"If she's offended I bathed in her water, is it not a simple thing to change it?" Cassian stood, pulling his shirt back on.

"It is not a simple thing," Djar replied as he walked to the basin and hefted it. Cassian was silently impressed, the basin was unusually large, and with that much water in it…. He watched the man head for the windows, and Cassian outpaced him and unlocked the one on the right, pushing it open then stepping out of the way. Djar dumped the water, glancing at Cassian sidelong as he lowered the empty basin away from the window. Cassian wouldn't say he saw gratitude in the other man's gaze, but perhaps curiosity. He turned away, returning to the couch to retrieve his belt and pistol, and tucked his shirt into his pants before buckling the belt around his hips.

"Where do you intend to take these Suloi?" Djar asked as he fit the basin back on its stand.

Cassian usually liked a man that got straight to business, but this one looked too eager to separate him from his various parts to even consider amicability. "A day and a half ride from here, depending on the weather—to a rendezvous."

He wouldn't tell them more than that now. He and Peio often didn't know until they'd reached the rendezvous. They might be there hours or days before a Watcher relayed their arrival to someone who cared.

"Just Djar, is it?" Cassian asked casually.

"Djar," he confirmed. Most of the tribes of Menei liked to distinguish themselves from each other. They were a proud people, and each could name their lineage back to time immemorial, and often did as part of their introduction. Djar had not even given a surname.

Cassian's sense that things were not quite as they seemed grew stronger with each interaction, and it made him feel itchy and eager to be done with the lot of them. If it weren't for Peio's insistence on helping them, Cassian would have run the moment an opportunity presented itself. Peio was tightlipped about what he saw in Amara that Cassian couldn't see.

Unless he was just smitten. Though Cassian doubted that. He was far more likely to be struck simple by a pretty face than Peio, who rarely looked at faces. He hadn't been able to take his gaze off her though, which was very unusual. Not just for Peio. For any Suloi. He had never known Peio to be wrong about anyone, but then, there was a first for everything.

CASSIAN AND PEIO LOADED their gear on their horses while Kiya got Garbi and Izar settled on another horse. Peio checked Cassian's effort at securing his rifle at the back of his saddle, and gave a nod of approval. Though Cassian carried a pistol everywhere, and a rifle when they were outside the city, Peio did not. The Suloi did not use modern weapons. They stuck with swords, knives, and short bows.

Amara joined them as the steel sliver of dawn touched the horizon. He'd been worried about bringing her. Her people seemed hardened enough. But she struck him as a lady accustomed to comforts, and there was nothing comfortable about a day and a half in the saddle with a night camping in the middle of it. He did not want to spend those long hours listening to her complain about inconveniences or ruined finery.

His concerns were diminished immediately upon her arrival outside the villa. She had dressed sensibly, in attire very much like that of her men, loose tan pants and shirt, belted at the waist by cloth dyed turquoise. She mounted her horse without assistance or any sign that would suggest she was anything but perfectly comfortable in the saddle. Well. Onward then. Though he wouldn't mind a flask of something to dull his nerves and irritation.

Temper lingered in her expression from whatever insult she had perceived from his use of the basin. All her civility from earlier in the night was gone. Djar and the twins mounted, and Cassian took the lead and Peio the rear. Djar took up a place within arm's reach of Cassian, which made Cassian feel less like someone they'd engaged to assist them and more like someone they did not intend to allow escape. Cassian could not help but note that it was an easy reach and swing for Djar to decapitate him, if he so chose. They had not acted overly hostile. But Cassian's days of easy trust were long behind him.

The first hour or so, making their way through Haenna and toward the eastern road, was spent in silence. Despite the darkness, the city woke around them, men moving about their homes, preparing to go to work, women beginning their domestic chores. Shutters were thrown open as they passed, children hauled buckets from wells to their homes, women rekindled cookfires and outdoor ovens. The smells of food—fresh bread, bright fruit—occasionally made their way to the little group.

The fastest route to the road north was the main road through Haenna, which crossed the canals that divided the sections of the city. But even in the lingering darkness Cassian didn't want more eyes on them than were unavoidable. So he led the Meneians through the poorer sections, on shoddier paths, where those who shouldered the worst of the backbreaking work of running a city lived. The street sweepers, the fish mongers, the transport drivers. Whores and dancers and servants. They were all crowded together in the lowest point of the city, where the smells and waste from the richer parts collected, so that a sour stench of garbage and misery permeated the place. Out of perverseness, Cassian chanced a glance back at Amara, to see how she was faring. He enjoyed making the wealthy uncomfortable. To remind them what the cost of their comfort was.

She was as at ease now as she had been while sipping her coffee on the velvet-covered couch. She caught him watching her. It was still too dark to see much nuance in her expression, but he did see the sharp quirk of her brows raised in silent question. Cassian faced forward again when they made the edge of the slums, where a secondary road crossed the High Canal, the main waterway that separated the wealthy from the poor. This road would feed them to the main road leaving Haenna to the east and to the north.

No one spoke. Not even once they had left the city. If he'd been by himself the silence would have been perfectly fine. It wasn't that he specifically wanted to speak to them, in fact he could think of not one subject he'd be interested to discuss with any of them. But he could use a distraction from the monotonous clop of hooves against the road, the glare of the sun as it rose higher in the sky, the unforgiving brightness of it in the clear sky bringing stinging tears to his eyes. The road was laid with pavers, but a fine layer of mud had washed it from the night's rain, and that kicked up around them as they rode, coating everything in wet grit.

He looked to Peio once or twice. These runs were hard on him, even though he wished to continue making them. Every time Cassian looked, Peio's gaze was fixed to the road in front of his horse, shoulders hunched, all the pride gone from him. It would come back, to some degree, when he was free of the judging silence of the other Suloi.

Just when Cassian thought he might go mad from the silence, Djar began to sing. The bass of his voice was even more pronounced in his singing, and the song had a rhythmic cadence that was at once steadying and buoying. Cassian had never heard a Meneian song, let alone a Meneian singing. In fact if pressed, he would not have thought Menei a place of songs, knowing them only as he did, as warriors and traders. His grasp of the language was not so good that he could quite make out what the song was about. But it was not long before Kiya joined in, and her brother, turning it into a complex chorus. They were soon all smiling, and laughing when one of them fell out of sync or missed a word. And after the song finished, Djar turned in his saddle to look at Amara, who had not sung, and she frowned.

Even Garbi and Izar had perked up, sitting a bit straighter. Izar, the girl, bouncing hopeful looks from one to the other.

Djar began again, on a new song, starting with a long, low note that rumbled. Amara joined him, in a sweet, clear voice that was, Cassian thought without reservation or doubt, the most beautiful he had ever heard. Djar soon faded out of the song, leaving its care to his mistress, who transformed the simple rhythm and repetitive lyrics into a masterpiece that stirred Cassian down to his soul. There were lines, none of which he understood, that made his heart ache and the absence of his family feel suddenly acute and unbearable, and others that made him feel settled and at peace like he rarely felt. When she finished he longed for her to continue, and could not help staring sidelong at her, marveling.

"What was that song?" he asked, unable to free himself from the desperate wish that she would sing again.

"A lullaby. From a mother to her lost child," she said.

"Will you sing again?" He could not stop himself from asking the question. Djar chuckled. Cassian tried to recover his dignity as she looked at him impatiently. "You can't have been enjoying the tedium of the silence any more than I was."

"No," she acknowledged. "But I do not enjoy singing." The way she turned her gaze away from all of them, and the way her people all looked suddenly bereft and sad, made Cassian wonder why.

"But you are so gifted at it," he said, incredulous.

"Gifts are simply curses wrapped in pretty cloth," she said. "I will sing one more." It was a command more than a concession. For this song she sang alone, and she sang in Republic Trade. The song was not familiar to him. It was a ballad, a story of a man born broken and outcast, who accomplished a series of deeds that brought him to the notice of his king, and was eventually made a prince, and finally King himself. She sang it with such fierce belief that he was completely taken in by it, and could almost see the story unfold before his eyes.

After that she kept to her word, and did not sing again, though her companions did, trading songs and laughs. The Suloi did not join in the singing, though Cassian knew they had many of their own. They shared their silence with Cassian and Amara while Djar and the twins found entertainment in both Meneian and Republic songs—most of those being the sort belted in taverna after several drinks fortified courage and loosened tongues. Some of the language was so coarse he thought their mistress or Garbi might show some offense. But Amara was either lost to her own thoughts or not as tender of sensibility as he had thought her. And Garbi rode in roadborn silence, a silence that only Suloi seemed capable of, a fading kind of thing that made one almost forget they were there. It was one of their habits that protected them, and made them such good observers.

TEN

AS THE AFTERNOON SUN sank behind them, Cassian began to suspect they were being followed. The road cut through rolling landscape, hills and valleys that would allow for someone who was being careful to pace them out of sight. The mountains that divided the country between east and west were far behind them, west of Haenna, and their foothills had faded and worn down to gentle slopes and wide fields in this part of the country. For about an hour he kept his suspicions to himself, wondering whether the followers were after him, or after the Meneians.

He caught only one physical glimpse of what he thought was a rider, and it was distorted by the glare of the sun at their backs. Perhaps it was another of their own group? The laundresses would have spread word of their encounter with him and the Meneians, and perhaps the darkness had not hidden the Suloi as well as he had hoped. It could be guards, or some other contingent of Lucaius'. Or perhaps some enemy or acquaintance of his new friends?

"Have you noticed our company?" Cassian asked Djar, who looked at him sidelong with a curt nod. That reaction was enough to suggest to Cassian that Djar, at least, was not expecting anyone else.

"An admirer of yours?" Djar suggested.

"I have so many, it's difficult to tell," Cassian replied. "I thought they might be comrades of yours."

"Not friendly, no," Djar said before turning to Amara, who had been following their conversation. "Amara. The Sehzade's warning—"

She lifted a hand to silence him. "You and Bek see if you can get a better look at them," she said. Djar nodded, and he and the other kicked their horses to a full run, heading back toward the city. When Peio caught Cassian's eye Cassian nodded, and Peio wheeled his horse and sped after the two Meneian men. Amara noticed when Cassian touched the holster of his pistol to reassure himself that it was there.

"That may be of very little use to you, if they are who I think they are," she said. Cassian frowned.

"Pardon?"

"Your weapon. It works by fire...does it not?"

"Have you never shot a pistol?"

A corner of her bow-shaped mouth turned up at some private amusement. "They work by fire. Even the poorest of Aval can prevent a spark," she said. He looked over his shoulder, after Bek and Djar, then at her again.

"What is an Aval?" he asked. The word wasn't a familiar one from any of the languages he knew.

Her eyebrows rose. "For one who deals in the lives of mages, you know very little about them."

"Mages? Are there Tamar mages after us?" He'd seen Suloi magic, on occasion. Plants grew better where they camped and worked, they had an uncanny way of finding their way back to any place they had been, some of the ones he'd rescued could make light, and others could listen to rooms on the other side of a house. And some, like Peio, had a sense for lies, and could find nearby water even if blindfolded. But he would never have equated them to mages.

"That is my suspicion," Amara said, coolly. As if the thought didn't make her skin crawl. If it was a Tamar mage, what business did Cassian have with them? They wouldn't be hunting Suloi, unless mages were in the habit of enslaving other mages. Perhaps they thought he or the Meneians were enslaving instead of assisting the Suloi. Perhaps the Meneians were using him in an elaborate scheme to find more Suloi and take them as slaves. If it wasn't for Peio's certainty of Amara, he wouldn't trust them further than he could throw Djar.

Could he possibly convince a Tamar mage he wasn't an enemy before he was turned to charcoal? He'd heard tales only, never met a mage or seen magic of the kind rumored to be gifted to the children of the Old Sultanate. Whatever of their powers had once been spread through the world had been concentrated under the Sultanate, and diluted since their war. The Suloi were the last dregs of it as it died out in the Republic.

"You seem unconcerned. It makes me question your sanity," he said, frankly, and she laughed. Just one short burst closer to a giggle than a full belly laugh. It had the same strange quality as her singing voice, a trick that put him at ease when he should be anything but.

"If you are afraid, then you are smarter than I initially gave you credit for." She looked at Kiya, who had moved her horse to ride near Cassian's other side. Izar and Garbi looked to the horizon, searching for the subject of their conversation. There was always a place for Suloi women in a new clan. The memory keepers. The Suloi wouldn't care if they were the last of their own clan, or not. Not like the men. Not like Peio. Suloi women were never Ghosts, but the warp and weft of the tapestry of Suloi society. And that was the reason most Suloi men chose death rather than capture. "We'll make a camp in those trees, and see if our new friends would like to join us for a meal."

"Wouldn't it be better to keep moving? We might be able to lose them once we get into the woods," he suggested.

"No," she said.

Cassian fumed in silence, because not another word was uttered for the duration of their ride. Not until Kiya decided on a spot, situated between a creek and a rise of rock in the hill. He had to give her credit for choosing the same place he might have.

Both women dismounted and Cassian followed suit, watching to make certain Garbi and Izar did not need assistance. Kiya set up a tie line so the horses could graze. Amara began unpacking their things from the mule, making tidy piles of bed rolls, cooking equipment, and food. The Suloi assisted her. Cassian watched them together as he exchanged the horse's bridles for halters and tied them to the line Kiya had prepared. He began unsaddling them, setting each set of tack together, then went to work rubbing each down with a brush. The dust from the trail could make for sores, and even this short journey could be made miserable by a horse that would not be saddled due to raw spots.

He kept an occasional eye on mother and daughter, who were likely to run. When it was just him and Peio, and one ran, he would let them go. If they chose to take their chances on their own, he wouldn't take that choice from them. They were very capable of doing so. But there was someone out there, someone he didn't think was friendly.

Amara took a bucket to the creek and crouched by the water as she settled the bucket into the shallow water to fill, unwinding the cloth from her hair as she did and letting the fabric settle about her shoulders. Her hair was free from the style she'd had it in before, a cascade of jet curls that just reached the tops of her shoulders. Kiya joined her at the water and took the bucket as they walked toward Cassian. He noticed how closely they walked together, their shoulders brushing together, like sisters. Or lovers. If they were neither, then affection was more freely given in Menei than in the Republic. He looked away when Amara caught him staring, putting more energy into brushing his horse.

Kiya took the piles of equipment that Amara had unloaded and began building a camp out of it, digging a depression and arranging the beginnings of a fire in it, laying bedrolls and retrieving everyone's things to set beside them. As she worked at starting the fire, Garbi and Izar joined her to help. Kiya chattered at them, though they gave little response. Amara left them and came to stand on the other side of Cassian's horse, looking at him over the back of it.

"Are you not concerned for your men?" he asked, uncomfortable with her nearness. Between the knowledge that someone unfriendly at best, and capable of using magic to execute their wishes at worst, and his sense that something was strange about his companions, Cassian was feeling particularly edgy. Her proximity only worsened his feeling of impending doom.

Djar he understood. He served her, he was big and strong and had a giant sword. That was all Cassian needed to know of the man. The twins were more enigmatic; he still wanted to know how they had cheated him out of his coins. But she…she was a merchant who walked with her servants as if they were friends, who sang beautiful songs, who acted like a queen but made no pretense of being such out in the woods. She did not seem the least afraid that she might be pursued by mages out to exact revenge. Cassian had never trusted people he could not categorize, and she defied all his attempts.

"Djar and Bek are lions of Menei," she said simply, as though that were an answer that made any sense at all.

"And you? Aren't you of Menei? Daughter of a warlord? Princess of a kingdom? What brought you here?"

"Princess will do." She tipped her head, an ironic tilt to one brow. "And I told you, I seek the Suloi for someone else." So was she a princess? Or wasn't she? And if she wasn't interested in talking, why did she insist on standing so close to him?

He moved from his horse to the next, which was the big bay Djar had been riding. They were hired horses, not owned, judging by the poor condition of their feet and lackluster attitudes. Amara followed him, and this time, picked up another brush and began to work on the opposite side of the horse. Cassian watched her over the back of the beast, and she smiled a little, looking away from him and to her task.

"You seem to know your way around horses," she commented, watching his work and, he realized, mimicking it. Perhaps she did not know the care of horses? That was difficult to believe, considering the obsession of the southern countries with the breeding of them. If she was noble born, as she acted, she would certainly have been taught the basics of horse husbandry.

"My mother thought them the most noble of beasts," he said. His mother had been an accomplished rider as well, and though they had never owned a great herd, he had learned their care from her. "We used to ride out to meet the Suloi clans, some even knew and welcomed us." Cassian paused, halfway through a stroke of the brush, frowning. Why was he telling her anything? He didn't talk about his family to anyone. He glanced at her again, but her attention was turned to the horse's face. For just that moment, the passing of only a few seconds, he had the distinct sense he was seeing her accurately. Quiet. Gentle, her gaze turned up to the horse's, one hand stroking down its nose, tracing the narrow end of the brush between the halter straps. His brow furrowed.

"Did your mother's slaves care for them?" Amara turned her gaze to his, and it was no longer gentle, or quiet.

"My family did not have slaves," he said, and again felt as though a stranger had spoken in his place. These small secrets he was giving her were enough to put together and unravel everything. What about her, this woman he barely knew and did not understand, compelled him to speak honestly? Lying came as easily to him as breathing. He'd been doing it all his life, and now suddenly the skill escaped him.

He stared at her in shock, and she looked back in surprise, her eyes, the same rich brown as black truffle, searching his face, her thick, perfectly groomed brows lifting. A work of art. His hands itched again, that urgency to create blooming in his mind. It would be long days before he had free time to devote to a painting or sculpture. And maybe it wasn't creativity at all that was making him antsy. Perhaps it was other, too-long-neglected desires.

Her expression changed suddenly, and he was certain she recognized his thoughts in his face. Cassian dropped his gaze and ducked, turning so he could lift the horse's front foot and prop it between his knees.

"You could not have chosen poorer beasts," he said gruffly, and brushed his hand over the hoof, trying to dislodge some of the dirt and grass from it.

"I'll do that when I'm finished here," Kiya said, from where she had just finished starting the fire.

"I'm perfectly capable," he replied, refusing to look at either woman. His thoughts and loose speech alarmed him, and it would be best if he didn't look or speak to any of them for the remainder of their trip. He'd get them to the camp, introduce them to the Watchers, and the rest would be between them and the Suloi. He wouldn't have to worry about them any longer, and he could get back to doing real work. Gods he needed a drink.

"I'll do it better," Kiya said as she rose and approached. He looked up at her, incredulous. She folded her arms over her chest and jutted out a lean hip. He set the horse's hoof down and wiped his hands on his pants.

"Please, be my guest." He was happy to hand the horse's care over to her and move on to the next, to put more distance between himself and her mistress.

They continued their work in silence. Kiya quickly outpaced him, moving through all the horses' hooves before he'd gotten to the last to brush, and that made him suspicious of her thoroughness. When she and Amara were occupied with Garbi and Izar in putting together a meal, he moved to the first horse, his own, and lifted its front left foot. He wiped his eyes with the back of his wrist, cursed under his breath when the pressure caused pain through his left, and stared.

The hoof was pristine, as if she had not only picked out the dirt and grass, but scrubbed it with soap and water as well. All of the horses were in the same condition. His uneasiness and rising certainty that something strange was going on had to be put on hold for the return of Djar and Bek.

"Not Tamaran," Djar said as he dismounted and handed his reins to Kiya. "Vexillae, perhaps?"

"Describe them to me." Cassian moved from between the horses. Djar looked to Amara for permission, which she gave with a nod of her head.

"Three of them, and they appear to be Republic men. Bristling with weapons. Pistols, like yours, larger guns. Swords. They wore leather light armor, straps and buckles with contraptions." He drew across himself with gestures as he spoke, and with each word Cassian's certainty grew. Garbi and Izar grew quieter and quieter, huddling closer together as they tended the fire.

"The Vex," he said. Why were they following? He'd made wide berth around the Vex in all his dealings, and had never crossed paths with them before. As far as he knew, he was not known to them for his efforts. But how could they be after Amara and her people? They operated from the capital, not Haenna. Someone had leaked information. The thought made him want to rage and curse. It meant his entire network would have to be purged.

He didn't want to lead them right to the rendezvous. Cassian looked the direction he had last seen them.

"The Vex?" Amara asked. "Is that what you call the Vexillae?"

"They *discourage* the use of magic in the cities." The rest he held back with some effort. Amara was looking at him in concentration and he turned away from her to meet Djar's gaze. "Did you tell anyone but me that you were seeking Suloi slaves?"

"Not in exact words," Djar said. That did not encourage Cassian.

"They are unlikely to attack us. I suspect someone has informed them you're hunting Suloi, and they are hoping to follow you to an active camp." That was the best case.

"Which is where you're taking us," Amara accused.

"Not exactly." If he didn't look at her he might be able to keep things to himself.

"Then we will continue through the night."

"What?" He snapped his gaze to hers. "To what end?"

"Nothing in our agreement gave you leave to question me. We will eat, wait for dark, and continue on to the camp." She marked the items by tapping her finger against her palm.

"They're soldiers. They are armed to the teeth and most of them poor tempered on the best of days." The last thing he wanted was to stumble upon a troop of Vexillae in the dark. And if they arrived at the rendezvous sooner, it would only mean waiting in a single place longer for the Watchers to acknowledge them, making them an easy target.

"Then all the more reason to hurry in order to avoid them." Amara turned away from him and Djar and joined Garbi and Izar to begin packing the things she had just unpacked. Cassian frowned harder.

To give himself space and time to think, he returned to the horses and saddled them while the others joined around the fire and spoke in hushed Meneian. Peio helped Cassian ready the horses again, silent and grim. Cassian affixed his bedding, along with his rifle, to the back of his saddle, thinking about their route, and how he might pervert it, to make it more difficult for the Vex to follow them.

"Tell me about these Vex," Djar demanded as he approached Cassian. Cassian pondered how much to tell him, what it might give away. Peio stopped what he was doing and wandered away, to the edge of the copse. Hearing the men described who took his life from him was too much, Cassian understood. They'd taken his too.

"They are men, usually selected before they begin school, and taken to Corsyra to be trained in swords and marksmanship. The Republic outlawed the use of magic. They believe it encourages sloth and discourages science." In reality, Stephanus knew what a threat magic was to his power and the spread of the empire he hoped to forge. He said it enraged the gods, and the priests in the temples avowed the same. Though Cassian had always wondered why the gods would have created something and given it to man only to be angry when he used it.

"I have not had occasion to deal with them, so far." He shrugged, trying to appear as if the idea of them didn't make him ill. They'd ransacked his childhood home under false pretenses. They'd tortured men and women who had served his family for decades, trying to force them to admit to powers they never had. "But laws in the capital are often not enforced in the outer cities to the degree Stephanus might wish, and many wealthy families still keep Suloi with magic for convenience, and as a means to outdo each other. Guards are easily enough bribed to let a few household slaves slip beneath notice."

"And what do they do with the Suloi besides sell them?" Djar asked.

"They exterminate them." Cassian pulled the cinch tight on his saddle and buckled it closed. He was trying to keep the emotion from his face, the memories that filled him with visions of camps, silent. His home. Cassian shook his head to banish the images and turned his back on Djar.

"Mages? The Suloi have magic, do they not?"

"Some," Cassian said. "A little. The Republic uses some of them for experiments, to make weapons that are effective against it. They pay the best prices, too." A fact he'd always thought particularly ironic.

Djar slid a gaze around their group, his onyx eyes taking in Garbi and Izar, trying so hard to appear unbroken, and his lip curled before he stalked back to Amara's side. When Peio returned he joined Cassian and the others and they ate a modest dinner of dried fruit and salted meat. When the food was finished Amara went ahead with her plan. Their barely used camp was disassembled and the horses mounted.

They rode north along the coast for several hours before Cassian made the turn that would take them into the forest. They rode right into a ferocious spring storm. Cassian thanked Luck for making up his gambling losses with the weather. She always had a plan for him, even if he could never trust it. The Vex would never be able to follow them in this deluge. The wind drove the rain nearly sideways, and the rain itself was cold and brutal. Talking was impossible in the downpour, and Cassian had to argue with Djar about direction primarily in violent hand gestures, because nothing else could be perceived in the dark and the rain.

Never ask Luck for boon or bounty, the saying went, the bitch would kill you with it.

ELEVEN

CASSIAN DESCENDED, PAINFULLY, FROM the tree he'd climbed to obtain a better view. Early dawn light was only just visible when he looked over the tree canopy. The storm had finally moved on and he needed height to get his bearings. When he jumped to the ground Djar waited for him, arms crossed, scrutinizing the surrounding woods. Cassian brushed his sap-sticky hands on his pants, sighing. He was wet, and tired, and more than a little irritable, and he was glad to be in Djar's silent company if he had to be in any. Peio would be tightlipped until they were free of the other Suloi, then probably drunk for days.

"If we head that way"—Cassian pointed—"we can break through the trees and I'll be able to get us back on course."

Djar merely nodded, and set off in the direction they'd left the other three.

"You climb the tree next time, and I'll watch," Cassian grumbled. Djar graced him with a deep chuckle.

"You are better built for such endeavors," he said.

Cassian could not deny that Djar's broad shoulders and tree-trunk-sized arms were probably better suited to tearing men into pieces than navigating the limbs of the thin pines that grew on this side of the mountains. They walked in silence that was almost companionable.

They descended the hill they'd climbed, to where the horses gathered at the base. Garbi and Izar sat nearby, Garbi working tangles out of Izar's hair. Just on the other side of them Bek kept watch. Kiya and Amara were farther, near a trickle of water that flowed between the hill Cassian and Djar had climbed and the next. Kiya braided Amara's hair, and Amara had pulled her shirt from her pants. She'd lifted the front and gathered it in her hands to wring it out, baring her lower back to Cassian as he approached the horses.

Her ribs and waist were exposed, down to the very top of her hips, and Cassian's stride stuttered with his surprise. It was not her bared skin he was struck by, but the pale tattoos that followed the path of her spine. One after the other, the entire expanse that he could see, a trail of debt marks, the last one just peeking from beneath the waistband of her pants.

That was a Meneian practice, marking those indentured for crimes with their debts. What crime would buy that much debt, a lifetime's worth? She turned, saw him staring, and yanked her shirt down, her expression tightening as she met his stare.

Before he had time to even cast her an apologetic frown for seeing something he was obviously not meant to, Suloi appeared out of the trees behind her. They had weapons drawn—attacking. Not greeting.

"Amara!" Djar lunged down the hill. Kiya threw herself between Amara and the oncoming men and was immediately tackled by one of them. These were free Suloi, dressed in little besides trousers and weapon belts. They were not, however, Suloi that Cassian knew. He didn't recognize a single face. He drew his pistol and dropped to a knee on the hill, aiming it at the nearest man.

Something struck him from behind, and Cassian fell sideways into the mud, pain smashing him into unconsciousness.

HE WOKE UP ON his belly, with his face in the mud and his hands tied behind his back. It took him long moments of slow mental sorting to remember how he might have ended up as he was. At first he was convinced Gallus had caught him and left him tied up for Sophus. But he wouldn't be outside. When he did finally piece it together into memory, he rolled to his side and looked around. The sun had fully risen now, and they were in a clearing in the trees. Cassian recognized it as the abandoned camp he'd been trying to lead them to by the skeleton of a lightning-struck pine in the center of the clearing. His head pounded, and he struggled to sit up. They'd left him on the edge of the clearing, and the others were arrayed around him, in various stages of waking. Kiya sat next to him, her eyes closed, her head bent to her chest. A pile of weapons that he assumed to be theirs when he realized his pistol was missing from its holster, sat near the dead tree.

Cassian glanced around the clearing until he found their captors on the far side. He did not see Peio or Garbi and Izar, and that concerned him. The Suloi were generally peaceful; this attack was unlike them. Though it was also unlike them to be traveling in such a small group, outside of a clan. It occurred to him that they might be the remnants of a slaughtered clan, exacting their revenge on anyone they came across, or warriors borrowed from a clan to do the same. A Hunt.

Djar, lying a few paces in front of him, woke with a start as Cassian tried to take visual measure of their captors. He got his knees under him and sat up on his heels, looking first to Cassian, then to Kiya. Bek sat just in front of his sister, and Amara was still prone, on her side, her hair broken loose from its half-finished braid and obscuring her face. Her chest rose and fell, and she did not appear to be harmed otherwise.

Kiya was whispering. She repeated something, over and over, in a language he didn't know, her eyes squeezed shut and sweat beading on her forehead. Her hands, tied behind her back like his were, twisted against the rope, her fingers reaching. Cassian saw, from the peripheral of his vision, rocks around her shifting, shaking, pebbles scooting. His mind rebelled. He closed his eyes and opened them again, and saw the same thing.

She murmured the words, again and again. A rock dislodged from the ground and skittered towards her. She grabbed it and sucked in a breath.

"Stop," Bek said to her, his brow furrowing as he looked at her, the warmth washed from her skin and sweat trickling across her brow.

"Shut up," she said back, and began whispering again, her eyes opening to glance at the Suloi who stood speaking to each other on the other side of the clearing. More foreign words hissed from between her teeth and Cassian watched in stunned silence as bits of rock flaked away, leaving a keen edge. Kiya smiled grimly, and began to work the rock against her ropes.

"You're a mage," Cassian said, stupidly. She slipped her gaze sideways at him and widened her eyes in mockery. Was she the reason there were mage hunters after them? "What are you going to do when you get loose?"

"What do you think?" she sneered. Djar made his way, on his knees, to Amara's side, and said her name.

"Don't be stupid. They'll have more in the trees besides these," Cassian said quietly. They ignored him. Kiya pulled her hands free, but left them behind her, and Bek turned his back against her side so she could cut his ropes as well.

Two Suloi came from the trees, prodding a third forward with knife points, his fingers laced behind his head.

"Peio!" Cassian called. Peio lifted his head to look at him, saw their predicament, and dropped his hands to his sides. He set his feet and began demanding and gesturing. One of Peio's captors poked the tip of his knife against Peio's side, and he barely moved, only shouting louder as blood bloomed at the point. Suloi pride. A fragile thing, and the only coin Peio had left to deal with. The argument went on for long enough that Kiya was able to finish cutting her brother loose.

"Go," Bek said softly, and they rose as one, each grabbing a weapon from the pile. Kiya darted across the clearing in one direction, Bek in the other, and they were on the Suloi at the same moment a shout went up from the far side, from the trees, warning. Arrows snapped into the ground near Kiya's feet, but she had already leapt, landing on the nearest Suloi's back like a pouncing cat, her knife against his throat, her hand in his hair to hold him. He stumbled back, silent, a grimace or a grin pulling his mouth tight as Kiya spoke into his ear.

Bek went for one of the men as he reached behind to retrieve his hand ax, and they wrestled for it.

"*Settle your friends, Outsider, or I'll put an arrow in them.*" The voice came from behind him, speaking in Suloi, in the trees, and was followed by the sound of a bow creaking as it was drawn.

"Djar, tell them to stop," Cassian warned, "or someone is going to get hurt."

Djar snapped a command, and Kiya dismounted, jumping back when the Suloi spun on her, drawing another knife. Bek's opponent drove the ax handle into Bek's chest, doubling him over. The Suloi in the trees behind Cassian called an order, and his men dropped back toward the far side.

"*Tell this one to sit,*" the archer said. Djar still knelt beside Amara, a position easy enough to stand and charge from.

"On your backside, Djar," Cassian translated, since none of them had shown evidence of speaking the roadborn language. Djar submitted, albeit slowly. The two Suloi urged Peio toward them from the far side of the clearing, and three more brought up the rear. When they stopped, they released Peio with a shove. He stumbled forward, but didn't fall. When he'd found his balance he plucked at the blood-stained, thumb-sized hole in his shirt and grumbled about it being his last good shirt.

"Peio. *What is going on?*" Cassian asked.

Peio shook his head. "*The Watchers aren't here. This is a Hunt.*" He gestured at the other Suloi men.

Cassian closed his eyes. A Hunt was when surviving Suloi hunters, men, banded together to make a suicidal attempt at revenge. It also explained why they were speaking with Peio. A Hunt was outside the bounds of clan. That Peio was a Ghost wouldn't matter to them.

"*We are not here to harm you. Did Peio explain?*" Cassian asked, not knowing which to address his question to. The one in the woods behind him answered.

"*He explained. But he is a Ghost under the employ of an Outsider. I can judge for myself what you and your friends are.*"

"What is going on?" Bek demanded. "What are they saying?"

Cassian shook his head. He was trying to think of the quickest way to explain what was happening, when Amara stirred. She made a soft, pained sound, and stiffened, tossing her head to get her muddied hair out of her face. She took stock of their situation then rolled to her knees.

"Why am I tied up?" she asked. Her gaze landed squarely on Cassian.

"For the same reason I am, I would imagine," he said dryly.

"Because you are *Sanpotar*. Outsiders. Because you ride with kidnapped Suloi," the archer in the trees said. He had to be from a Northern family. His Trade was very good, and they were the only clans that still dealt with the Republic.

Amara focused her gaze over Cassian's shoulder. "Are you Suloi?" she asked.

"You do not know Suloi when you see them, yet you mean to enslave us." The man's sneer was clear in his voice, even if Cassian couldn't see him.

There was a pause in which Amara glanced at Djar, then took the measure of each man she could see. A brow ticked up, accompanied by a short, quick sigh.

"Just because I see you does not mean I know you. And I do not wish to enslave you. If you untie me, perhaps we can speak in a civilized manner." When the awkward stillness continued, Amara made a disgusted sound in the back of her throat. "I am here as envoy of Tamar, sent by Sultana Naime Sabri, seeking mages of the Third House."

With each word from her lips Cassian went more rigid with surprise, riding a series of valleys and peaks of disbelief and confusion.

Peio went to his knees, which halted Amara's confession. "You are, I knew you were," Peio said, eyes unblinking. Amara shook her head with a look of censure.

"Right." Cassian squinted. "Of course she is." She was what? Tamaran? How could Peio know that? And why did he care?

Peio flicked Cassian a sharp look before he turned and put a hand over his eyes as he faced the trees at Cassian's back. "*Pathfinder Garai, I hold the Wanderer's eye. This Ghost means no disrespect. This is Cassian Haydar. He is a beloved friend of all roadborn, and has freed more of our people than can be numbered. I beg you forgive the trespass and let him go. Let them all go, they only wish to help.*"

If the man in the trees was a Pathfinder, or a clan head, then that explained Peio's deference and the general chaos of their situation. Wherever a Pathfinder went they were in command, whether the clan was their own or not, second only to the Pathfinder of the clan in residence. Cloth brushed and bow creaked as the man behind Cassian lowered his bow and slid his arrow back into his quiver. He shuffled out of the trees.

He limped, using a staff to walk. There was nothing otherwise remarkable about him. He was slim and tall, his skin the burnished color of dark tea, his dark hair long enough to pull back against the nape of his neck and scattered randomly with small braids. His eyes were dark as well, with the hint of the plainsmen ancestry all Suloi shared, narrow and canted. He was young and strong. Too young to be a Pathfinder. A young Pathfinder and three borrowed men from another clan for a Hunt. His clan was gone then, and he was out for revenge.

"*The Wanderer does not see the Hunt, only the hunted. You needn't hide today, Ghost,*" the Pathfinder said, his voice burdened. "Cassian," he said when Peio lowered his hands. "*I am Danel Garai, firstborn of Matia Garai, Speaker of Clan Garai.*"

"*It is my honor, Pathfinder. I would greet you properly, but…*" Cassian indicated his bound hands with a tip of his head. Danel nodded to one of the men, who drew a dagger from the straps that crisscrossed his bare chest and strode forward, slicing it through Cassian's bonds. Cassian stood, forcing himself not to stumble on legs gone numb, or give in to the painful tingling in his arms.

The Suloi were observers, and they remembered everything they observed. Showing weakness at their first meeting would put him in an inferior position, in their minds. Cassian stepped forward, clasping Danel's shoulders as he leaned in to press one cheek then the other against Danel's in a traditional greeting of respect. Then he stepped back to give him room.

"Are you quite enjoying ignoring us?" Amara asked, looking up at Cassian from where she knelt beside Djar.

"I'm not ignoring you, Princess." Cassian squatted in front of her. It was a pleasant sensation to have control of the situation; he had felt steered since meeting her. "I am enjoying my return to freedom. I did lead you to the Suloi though, so our dealings are concluded." He grinned.

"All part of your plan, was it?" she scoffed. "I'll say when our dealings are concluded."

"If you want anything else from me, you'll need to pay. On top of returning the money your girl and her brother stole."

"Untie me," she ordered. He glanced sidelong at Danel, who ducked his head in permission. A Suloi's goodwill could disappear quickly, if respect and protocol were not observed. Cassian held his hand out to the Suloi who had cut him free, and was handed the knife he'd used.

"Right away, Princess." He leaned forward to peer over her shoulder at her bound hands.

Amara turned her head to whisper against his ear, "Mock me at your peril."

The melody of her voice, lowered to an intimate whisper, even in threat, sent shivers over his skin. Cassian turned his head enough to look at her as he cut the ropes on her wrists. She held his look with irritated intensity.

"I'd never mock you…" He grinned. "Princess."

He freed Djar before standing and handing the knife back to its owner.

"These two"—he pointed to Djar then Bek as they got to their feet—"saw three Vex before we encountered that storm. It might be best for you all to leave."

"We are aware of them. But we cannot leave." Danel surveyed each Meneian in obvious curiosity. After a moment he looked up at the sky, which was now in the full brightness of morning. Clear and cloudless, as if in mockery of the storm that had come and gone in the night. "Your friend says you have freed uncountable Suloi."

"He exaggerates." Cassian's gaze strayed to Amara. She was busy dusting her clothes, though she only succeeded in spreading mud more broadly about them.

"There is a place we can stay, and talk, that will be harder for them to find," Danel said. "Follow us." He limped toward the other side of the clearing, and it was clear to Cassian that the effort caused him no small amount of pain. As he pondered how to offer help without also offering offense, Amara strode quickly to Danel's side.

"Pathfinder Garai," she said. He stopped to look at her. She bowed forward. "Forgive me, I do not know your customs. I hope"—she turned and slipped her arm into his, smiling with warmth—"that you might see fit to educate me." Danel made a sound of affirmation as he leaned into her offered weight.

Beautiful and cunning. A deadly combination. Cassian wiped his sleeve against his brow.

"Too bad." Djar stopped beside Cassian. "I was looking forward to killing you once you'd brought us to the Suloi."

"To maintain your secret identities, I suppose," Cassian said mordantly. "I would have hired someone else to kill you."

Djar laughed, and clapped a heavy, hard grip against Cassian's shoulder that nearly brought him to his knees, then trailed after Amara. Bek and Kiya followed him. Cassian looked to Peio as the other Suloi fell back into the trees. Garbi and Izar were gone. Very likely already on their way to a new clan. Sometimes the Watchers stayed to engage with Cassian and Peio, but in this instance they would have avoided the Hunt, taking only the mother and daughter.

"How do we get out of this in one piece?" Cassian asked Peio.

"Pay whatever price he asks," Peio said in monotone, his hands going reflexively to his head. His hair was short, like Cassian's. Once it had sported braids. As many as Pathfinder Garai's, the colors and ornaments proclaiming his family, triumphs, and accomplishments. Signaling that he would have one day walked in front of his clan, as his father had. Pathfinder.

Peio dropped his hands, drew the Wanderer's circle on his palm, then turned to follow the others.

TWELVE

I T TOOK HALF THE day to travel through the forest to the alternate camp, and it gave Amara time to assess their new companions and adjust herself to the change in their situation. Djar rode beside her, the twins behind, and the Suloi encircled them. Cassian rode in front, at the head of the formation but behind the leader, Danel. His friend, Peio, rode beside him.

They had been laughing and talking in Suloi the entire morning, and Amara chafed at her inability to understand the language. Its tangled, musical syllables and long vowels defied her attempts at aligning it with something she already knew. It was not a disadvantage she was accustomed to. Though at least it was not unpleasant to hear, inspiring a feeling like shaded forest roads and laughter.

The Suloi were an interesting puzzle. If these had magic, she could not sense it as she had in Peio. She could see their distant Tamaran roots, and in equal measure, the Eastern heritage they shared with Sarkum. They had sun-bronzed skin, hair in varying shades of chestnut and deeper sable. All of them wore it somewhere between chin length and the nape of their neck, pulled back in various configurations, but all with loose twists, braids, and small bits pulled back throughout. Some of the braids had colored string or ribbon woven through them.

They wore very little in the way of clothes, which, once she was over her initial shock, Amara appreciated for the aesthetic. She had never pretended she did not enjoy looking at a well-formed male, no matter the circumstance. The Suloi were all of a similar build, slim and athletic, the bodies of men accustomed to a life on the move.

What clothes they did wear consisted of pants sewn of some kind of leather, kidskin if she were to judge by the suppleness. They wore boots similar to Cassian's, that rose to their calves, and each wore a series of belts and straps in configurations that seemed dictated by personal choice—around their hips, slung over their shoulders, about their arms and thighs. These straps held knives of diverse sizes. Each man also carried a small hand ax somewhere on their person, as well as a bow and quiver. Danel's bow was the most ornate. While the others' appeared merely functional, his was carved in detail from some dark wood, with symbols on the upper and lower limbs. None carried swords or pistols.

These were not people of war, though she had no doubt they could defend themselves if the need arose.

For their part, if they cared about the differences of her and her companions, they were not so obvious about it as the citizens of the city had been. In fact she noticed they made it a point to avoid staring or eye contact of any kind, even with each other. There was no sense of hostility from them, as she had felt in the city, though they might simply be hiding it better, less empowered than the city-dwellers were.

Her gaze continued to stray to Cassian, though her view was restricted to his back. He was taller than any of the Suloi, and did not obviously share heritage with them. Amara did not want to find him attractive in any way, but she did. He was a gambler and a smuggler prone to brawls. And he was Republic born, and had at some point been of their upper class. She was certain of it. Yet she could not stop looking at him, could not stop wondering why he did what he did, free strangers. Her inappropriate curiosity irritated her so much she began to fidget with the cuffs of her shirt.

"Do you know what you wish to do yet, about the smuggler?" Djar said. Though he wasn't looking at her when he spoke, Amara suspected he had noted her fixed attention on Cassian and the fidgeting. He knew her tics too well not to notice.

"No," she sighed. "I would like to be rid of him, he only complicates things, but he speaks their language and knows their customs and I do not."

"Do you trust him?"

"I don't know." If she was able to interrogate him she might be able to pinpoint the falsehoods she sensed around him and whether they mattered to her. She had tried, the day before while they tended the horses, but had been stymied by Djar's return.

Everyone told lies. Some of them were of significance to her, most of them not. Her magic sensed their existence, but without prying, or hearing the lie spoken outright, she could not know the specifics. Still, her life, coupled with her power's inclinations, had honed her instincts to a fine point, and she had a feeling Cassian was not an evil man. A flawed one, obviously. But then, she was also flawed. Unforgivably so.

They arrived at the camp in the late afternoon, having traveled a quarter of the distance back toward Haenna. Amara was happy for the break. Before she left Menei, she had spent a great deal of time in the saddle, but it had been Turns, and she had grown accustomed to the comforts of being settled. She rode in Tamar, but not often, and not for long. Not that she would admit her discomfort to anyone, or allow them to guess. Under the pretense of examining their surroundings, she stood once she had dismounted, allowing the muscles in her back and legs to cease cramping.

The area where they dismounted was still within the trees, not a clearing like the last, and Amara had to look up to see that platforms had been built and lashed between the trunks, high above them in the branches. The warmth drained from her face, and the trees seemed to spin above her. Her blood and life were desert, flat plains, her magic water. The domain of air had never appealed to her. And even less so when her mortality as it pertained to heights had been made very clear to her when traitors to her father had used her as a threat to cow her parents.

Amara looked at the ground to try and calm herself. The memory of the ground swirling below her, her hair twisting in the breeze that blew past her as she had dangled upside down existed momentarily concurrent with her reality of standing on the platform. Bile rose in her throat and she swallowed it back, standing perfectly still until the sickening feeling passed and she felt steady on her feet.

Kiya exclaimed in glee and all but dove from her horse, finding and climbing the nearest rope ladder that hung, loosely, from one of the platforms. Bek was quick to follow. Amara turned her gaze from the height as Bek and Kiya ascended, and to her utter horror, found Cassian watching her. He sauntered toward her, she suspected to goad her about the fear she'd made obvious, and Amara turned and strode purposefully toward the ladder Kiya had climbed.

Her hands were clammy, and she could not breathe unless she forced herself to, every muscle in her body tense. Could they not have at least secured the ladders to the trees so they were not flopping and spinning about as she climbed? With every rung that took her higher, her heart beat faster, and she stared steadfastly at the tree trunk, growing slimmer and slimmer as she clung desperately to the ladder. Why build them so high, where the trees had thinned and become even less capable of supporting a platform's weight?

At the top, she lifted shaking hands to the platform and crawled onto it, staring at the boards as she inched close to the tree trunk. She could not stay up there, could not possibly sleep up there. She'd roll off in the night and smash…

She grit her teeth, squeezing her eyes shut and feeling the mortifying sting of tears. No. They could not see her fear. No one could see her afraid.

Amara clawed at the rough bark of the trunk that pierced the center of the platform and forced herself to her feet, trying to find something to put her focus on that did not suggest the distance to the ground. But there was nothing. She could see the tops of the trees farther out, even the suggestion of the edge of Haenna beyond the forest, and if she looked closer to where she stood, there was the ground. Amara tried to concentrate on the sounds of the men as they saw to the horses and unloaded supplies, tried to let their laughter ease her pounding pulse and the breaths that wouldn't even out. She studied the intricacies of the bark in front of her face, the sap that clung in frozen amber droplets, the furrows and flakes that formed the rough surface. The smell was calming at least, the bracing, resinous scent of pine.

"Amara!" Kiya called, and Amara looked out of habit. The younger woman was trotting across a rope-and-board bridge stretched between the platform Amara stood on and a much larger, multitiered one at the other end. Kiya did not mean to taunt her. Only Djar knew that Amara feared height. In her vision, the ground rushed up toward her, spinning and tilting, and Amara shut her eyes, swallowing a scream that was followed swiftly by nausea. The platform lurched beneath her, tipping one way then the other as someone below began to climb the ladder. The scream escaped her in a breathy, thin shriek and she clung harder to the tree trunk, pressing her forehead against it and closing her eyes again.

Her heart would stop. She had to get down. But she did not think she was capable of climbing back down. The thought of voluntarily dangling her legs over the edge to find the ladder rungs made her feel like vomiting.

The platform stilled, and Amara sucked in a breath, pivoting only her head to see who it was, hoping to see Djar. The only one she trusted in her fear. Of course it was not. Cassian perched on the edge of the platform, one leg tucked beneath him, one knee bent toward his chest as he observed her. Her mortification found new heights when she saw understanding in his eyes, and looked away from him.

"Please go away, or at least move away from the edge," she managed to say, though to speak felt dangerous, as if the effort it took might knock her off the platform. Her mind convinced her his weight caused the platform to tip in one direction and she could feel herself pulled toward the edge. He rose, the movement shook the platform, and Amara heard a little groan issue from her throat.

"I was going to ask if you were all right, down there, but you didn't give me a chance. Are you?" he asked, gently. And she hated him for it, for seeing any weakness in her and feeling pity. She would not be pitied, not by anyone. But especially not by a man who had probably never suffered a day in his life that was not result of his own folly. In any other circumstance she might have been able to lie or distract him. But in this moment she could only give her head the barest of shakes. "It will be better on the big platform. You can get away from the edge there." The platform where they stood was little more than a collar around the tree, so she could only assume anything of greater span would be an improvement.

"Do I have to cross that bridge?" she asked. Cassian made an affirmative noise. Amara looked up at the blue sky above and shook her head. "I think I'd like to get down." She tried to affect some kind of strength into her voice but failed. Yes. She needed to be on the ground, and she didn't care if she had to spend the night alone in the dark woods.

"I think you can cross it. I'll help you."

"Please don't touch me," Amara said desperately, even though he'd made no move to.

"I won't." He stood at her back, putting his hands to either side of hers on the tree. He did not touch her, and having him behind her eased her distress. "I would never touch a woman without her permission," he said in her ear. He had a voice suited to laughter, and she closed her eyes, concentrating on the timbre of it and the way his breath tickled her cheek.

Her tension eased another fraction. "How noble," she said.

"I think we both know I'm not noble."

Amara agreed. Freer of slaves he might be, he was also a smuggler, a gambler, and a cheater. She found enough courage in her curiosity to turn her head, then her whole body, putting her back against the tree.

"Perhaps not entirely noble then. How does someone with your particularly...*uninspiring* resume find themselves a shepherd of stolen lives?" Her breath came easier, his distraction working like magic. He gave her the barest of smiles, but it curved his cheeks and revealed a dimple. Amara let her gaze rest against his. The swelling on his left eye had receded, leaving only the dark, multihued bruising. For some women the evidence of his violent nature might have added to his appeal. That was not so for her. What she found attractive were the laugh lines radiating outward from his uninjured eye, indicating he smiled often. And that blue. She had not known she would be so easily tempted by eyes like oceans.

"I will tell you a little, if you trust me, and follow me across this bridge," he said. "Hold on to my arms."

Cassian lowered his hands from near her shoulders, to waist height. Amara gripped his forearms. He cupped her elbows and took a step back. Her body seized as she stepped away from the tree and the platform swayed.

"I started gambling when I turned thirteen," he said, and Amara fixed her gaze on his face again. It was pleasing enough scenery to keep her mind from her surroundings, and if he kept smiling enough to maintain the dimple, and talking, she thought he might just distract her all the way across the bridge. He eased backward and she followed. "My parents were often gone. I thought my life was boring and dull and I liked the way it felt to win, and to lose."

"You liked to lose?" Amara asked. She despised losing. Cassian stepped onto the bridge and released his grip on her elbows, closing his hands on the rope rails that ran the length of the bridge. She tightened her fingers against his forearms, and concentrated on the flex of the fine muscles as he adjusted his grip on the ropes and made room for her on the bridge. Was he really going to cross it backwards? Was he not afraid at all?

Nausea swelled up like a tide in her stomach.

"No, I liked feeling. Something, anything. Victory, anger." He shrugged. More evidence of his wealthy past. Someone who had fought for what they needed did not also have to find things that made them feel.

Amara's heart tumbled in her breast as they moved away from the platform and she slid her feet, shuffling more than walking, because the little gaps between the boards made her feel they would snap beneath her. If she looked down she could see the ground, far, far below. He took another step backward, coaxing her forward, and her hands seized against his arms. She let her gaze roam his face and down the smooth, bronzed column of his neck. He needed a shave, or a purposeful beard, to look less unkempt. Though the halfway point he was at now, with stubble just long enough to no longer be sharp from the razor, suited him.

"And you have never grown tired of it, since then?" Amara could not bring herself to look to see how much farther they had to go. Instead she focused on him, the fine details of his face. She had always enjoyed those distinctions in men, the little things that made them unique, like works of art in her mind. Whether they were beautiful, or masculine, or something altogether different, there were always intricacies worth looking at.

Cassian had many. She could not help but compare him to Ihsan, who was handsome bordering on beautiful, a Sabri trait. But Ihsan was cold like his magic, isolated by his past, and Amara could see that beneath his swagger and despite his secrets, Cassian was a man of warmth and laughter.

She had never been so drawn to stare at Ihsan.

"Do you know you have a way of looking at a man that makes him feel he is the only one you've ever seen?" he said, quietly. Of course she knew. The way one looked at another human defined their relationship from the moment it was formed, whether that look was anger, disdain, attraction, or fear. A water mage was infinitely capable of changing and adapting to the people around them, and that, coupled with what Amara had learned just to survive the harem, made her perfectly aware of even her minutest glance. Except for this moment, when she had merely been looking.

"You are the only man I can see right now," she said, because they were so close and he dominated her vision.

"Yes, but you were looking." He grinned, the dimple deepening, and she lifted her gaze to his eyes again. The bruised one was uncomfortable to look at, but not the worst wound she had ever remained stoic in the face of.

"I did not mean to imply I wasn't," Amara said. There was no reason to pretend she hadn't been. She'd never felt there was reason to hide attraction from someone. Nothing but discontent came from hiding it, and if both parties were amenable, telling the truth resulted in pleasure for both. "I think you know you are handsome."

He seemed amused by her candor. "I think some women find me so, but you have not seemed impressed by me thus far."

"You are rude." They had made the halfway point, where the narrow wooden bridge hung lowest. Her heart thumped at the realization and she clung tighter to his arms. "And little more than a criminal. These are not generally traits I am impressed by."

"I am more than a criminal." He glanced behind himself as he stepped from the bridge onto the platform. "Though not much more." He allowed her continued grip on him as he backed across the bigger platform, and stopped when they were closer to the others.

She released her hands from him, and realized how tightly she'd been grasping him, and that it must have been uncomfortable for him.

Amara filled her lungs with air, something she had been unable to do before crossing the bridge. The others had all ascended, and were gathered near the center of the structure. The platform here was expansive, encircling dozens of trees, as big as parts of the pier in Haenna, so that she couldn't quite see over the edge without a pointed effort. Djar stood at the perimeter of the group, watching Cassian and her with a glower and folded arms.

"Could I trouble you to let your man know he doesn't need to decapitate me?" Cassian asked.

"Perhaps," she said. He frowned. "In trade for me doing so, you and I will never speak of this"—she gestured broadly toward the bridge—"again."

"Fair enough."

Amara lifted her hand to Djar, and he turned away.

"Thank you," she said, grudgingly.

"Are you all right now?" Cassian asked.

Amara nodded. This platform did not shift, and with some distance from the edge she was settled enough to move around. Was it because he was kind that he spent his time and money freeing the persecuted? She had never met anyone that kind. Doing good just for goodness' sake.

"Are we meant to sleep up here?" she asked as they moved toward the others. One of the Suloi worked at gathering the ladders, folding them on top of the platform to prevent anyone else coming up them, which explained why the ladders were not fixed. If she hadn't been so consumed with panic she might have come up with that on her own.

"In those." Cassian pointed to a series of lean-tos, constructed of boards, away from the edge but with their backs to it. Bek and Kiya were busy setting bedding into four of them, and Amara took another calming breath. She could do that. With something at her back much of her fear would be soothed.

"Since you are in such a benevolent mood," Amara said, "perhaps you might educate me on how to broach the topic of assistance with Danel and his men." She nodded toward the Pathfinder.

Peio was sitting with two of the other men, tossing dice back and forth. Kiya joined, plopping herself between two of them and folding her legs in front of her. Danel sat in the center of the largest section of the platform, a great circle pierced through by half a dozen trees. He leaned against one, the leg Amara thought the injured one stretched out in front of him, watching everyone with a keen eye. She could tell something troubled him, from the furrow in his brow and the tense set of his jaw and shoulders.

"They want something, or we would still be tied up in that clearing." Cassian watched Danel as well. "But I do not know from which of us they want it. Let him bring up what he wants first, then you can bargain for what you wish." He paused, looking at her sidelong. "Which is?"

"I told you when we met," Amara said. "I want mages."

Kiya had told her that he had seen her use magic, but that was as far as Amara would allow his knowledge to go, for now.

Perhaps he did not believe in slavery, but that did not mean he was not loyal to his ruler, his birthplace, loyal enough to turn a powerful mage and her people, from Tamar, into Republic authorities. Djar had told her Cassian mentioned the Republic used mages as test subjects. That was not how Amara planned to spend the rest of her days. The

Sultana owed her a prince, and she first needed to complete her end of the agreement.

"These men have been through too much for me to agree to help you, at their expense, without knowing what cause you serve," Cassian said. A spark of wary admiration formed for him, that he stood up for those who were persecuted. Danel gestured to them to come closer, before Amara could answer Cassian.

When they approached, Danel spoke without rising. "You did not tell me your name."

It could hardly be considered rudeness not to stand to address her; whatever injury he had sustained had obviously nearly crippled him. Considering what she knew about the Republic's treatment of the Suloi, she could only guess he had escaped their hands at some cost to his mobility. Was this what would become of Tamar, if the Republic invaded? A country of ruined, broken people, hunted down, robbed of everything that mattered to them? Haunted by ghosts and violence?

Amara moved to kneel in front of him.

Quietly, so her voice did not carry beyond him, she said, "I am Mistress Amara Mutar, Master Merchant of Narfour." She bowed her head. His handsome, serious face was intent as he scrutinized her in flickering glances. It had not escaped her that the Suloi avoided eye contact completely. So she turned her gaze down.

"Why are you here?" he asked when she did.

"The Sultana sent me to the Republic looking for Suloi gifted in a specific type of magic. It is my hope you might be able to assist me in finding them."

"And what does your Sultana wish to do with my people?" His tone sharpened with suspicion.

"Ask their assistance with a Blight that is destroying our food crops. And in return, offer them a homeland where they will not be persecuted for their Wheel-blessed gifts."

"We do not have names for our magic, as you seem to. And the Republic has redoubled their efforts to eradicate us. Many clans have been all but erased." He shifted, failing to suppress a wince as he adjusted his leg against the boards, folding the other one inward. "I would like to help you, Amara, but I am afraid my concern is else-where." His expression became veiled. He wished to bargain.

"Perhaps there is a way I can assist you with this concern, in return for your knowledge."

"We will eat, and discuss these things," Danel said, loudly enough that it caught the attention of his men, who moved as if commanded to their packs. In short order they had laid out what was a feast compared to her dinner the night before. Hard cheese and cured sausages, and spears of some sort of dark green wild vegetable alongside dried apricots. The Suloi gathered around in a circle, and Amara's people inserted themselves into open spaces. She sat beside Danel, with his shelter at her back to keep the edge of the platform out of her mind. Cassian took a seat on Danel's other side, his friend Peio beside him. One of Danel's men produced a large wineskin and passed it to Danel.

"May the Wanderer keep us and ours to the road." Danel raised the skin and took a long drink, and passed it to Cassian, who did the same. So it traveled to each person, and finally to Amara. She only barely managed to contain her repulsion at drinking from the same skin as so many others, but did so and handed it back to Danel. The sense of each lingered in the wine, as it would have in water, and touched her mind with their essences in a cacophony she had to block out or be overwhelmed.

When Danel set the skin beside him, the others began eating. Danel offered Amara a slice of meat and cheese he'd cut with his knife, and several of the green spears. She nibbled on one as she watched the others. It was crisp and vegetal, slightly bitter.

"*Sanpotar*," Danel addressed Cassian. "Have you heard that a clan was recently murdered?"

"One in the north, yes?" Cassian didn't look at Danel when he answered. Amara watched his interactions carefully, to try and garner knowledge.

"Mine," Danel said. Cassian stiffened, his hand pausing halfway through its reach toward the communal platter of food. His gaze flicked to Peio, who gave a discreet nod.

"I might offer you my kinship, Pathfinder Garai, that the Wanderer does not turn his eyes from your road." Amara noted Cassian's phrasing, the gravity of the tone he used, the way Danel turned his head away in silent refusal.

"I am not without a clan," Danel said. "But your generosity does you credit. Instead, I would ask help in locating what is left of my people."

"How many?" Cassian's gaze strayed to Amara's, then away, and she could not have guessed what he sought by looking at her.

"One." Danel paused, staring at the platform in front of him for a moment. "My sister, Mirari."

"What do you know of her whereabouts?" Cassian had stopped eating, though everyone else continued. Amara picked at a slice of cheese as she listened.

"I know she was taken to Haenna. That is where my knowledge ends." Danel looked at Amara. "You could guide my Hunt in the city. If you assist in this, then I will consider helping you. Tell me what magic you seek."

Amara finished chewing, taking the opportunity to think. Creation magic had been lost in Tamar after the Sundering War. She had never seen a creation mage, all she knew of their power was what she had studied in books. It would be diluted, perhaps even changed in the Suloi, if Peio was anything to judge by.

"They would have an affinity for life," she said. "Perhaps plants would grow at their touch, or wounds heal more quickly. They might inspire happiness in those around them, or bring energy."

Danel nodded as she spoke.

"I have known some like that," he said, and hope flared warm. Perhaps this debacle was near to over. "But the Wanderer has seen fit to lead them on the last road."

She looked across the circle at Djar, whose mouth was set in a grim line. Gone? All of them? The entire ordeal a complete waste of her time. The Republic and its dispassion for mages had felt so distant in Narfour. And that was the cruelty of the Wheel. The threat you ignored was always the threat that spun the circle to take you at your back.

"The Wanderer does love confluence of paths." Danel shifted against the boards. "The Garai were a clan with magic like you seek. But my sister and I are the only two who remain of them. How much use to you I can be"—he gestured at his leg—"I cannot promise."

A bittersweet mix of sorrow, triumph, and caution filled her. He was only one man, and even if they found his sister she did not know how much help two would be against a Blight that was devouring two nations. And if he was not powerful enough to cure his own ailments, it suggested there was not enough power in him to cure anything outside himself. There was a small hope that it was not lack of power, but lack of training that prevented such a thing. She would have to locate his sister. And to do that, she would need help.

Amara glanced at Cassian. He lifted his hand in signal to wait, and spoke to Danel.

"Dissolve the Hunt, Pathfinder. Send these hunters back to the road. They will only be captured in the city."

Danel inclined his head in agreement. Cassian nodded to Amara.

"If I find Mirari, would you be willing to return to Tamar with us?" Amara asked of Danel. He lifted his gaze, tipping his head back to look at the sky.

"If you find her, and she agrees," he said. "There is nothing left here for us, and perhaps that is the Wanderer's way of forcing us onward." He drew a long breath and let it out slowly. "There is something else you may be interested in. We escaped with the help of my sister's friend, Benat. I do not know where he is, but she may. They were captured together."

"Is he another of the Garai?"

"No. Only some of the Wanderer's blood is in his veins." Danel lifted the wineskin and gave it a shake. "But I saw him call molten rock from the earth." He took a long drink.

Amara's gaze snapped to Djar's, and found his expression as shocked as hers must be. Even Bashir, the commander of the palace guard, could not do such a thing, and he was the most powerful earth mage Amara had ever seen.

Calling fire and earth together would only be possible by a mage who straddled the two Houses. It would only be possible by a Charah.

THIRTEEN

CASSIAN SAT WITH DANEL long into the night, after most of the others had made their way into their beds. He tried not to be, but he was aware of Amara, what she was doing, who she was talking to, at any given moment. And that awareness meant he watched, in furtive glances, when she went to bed, and knew that the girl, Kiya, lay with her.

Their whispered conversation reached him where he sat with Danel, but not its subject. They laughed together, finally slept, and he wondered again if they were lovers, or friends, or mistress and servant. He could not put the bridge crossing from his mind, her closeness, the moments when her fear had stripped her of all her hauteur. How easily she met and held his gaze, how she had looked at him.

What was she doing so far from Tamar, in the Republic, where the Old Sultanate was unwelcome at best? He could only piece together bits he had overheard, but it was not enough to form a full story and explain what motivated her. He'd seen her murmuring to Danel, and of course heard him agree to return with her to Tamar.

But why? What interest did she have in the Suloi, and why that specific magic? Danel seemed willing enough to trust her to retrieve his sister, which was no small thing. The last remaining member of his clan, sister to a Pathfinder, family. These were sacred things. It also meant Mirari was his clan's *Matrik*, or matriarch, the only one who could allow others into the clan who were not born into it. She was vital for rebuilding the Garai, and her life the only thing between Danel being Pathfinder Garai and becoming a Ghost like Peio.

If Danel trusted Amara to any extent, Cassian had to take note, just as he had Peio's opinion. The Suloi were gifted observers of people, and very little escaped their notice and instinct.

"You should return with us, to the villa," he said to Danel, to turn his thoughts. "That way I can keep you informed of what we find, without endangering this location."

Danel made a noncommittal noise, and shifted from where he sat against the tree, to lie on his back and stare up at the stars. Cassian knew the Suloi equated a constellation with their god, but not which, for they guarded it as the most sacred of secrets. He followed Danel's line of sight into the night sky. Peio had long ago passed out from too much wine. Alcohol was his vice, not Cassian's. He enjoyed it, but rarely to excess, and certainly not when he was so far off the ground death was a certainty if he stumbled the wrong direction.

There were also the mage hunters to think of. Despite that, he did not judge Peio for his choices. A Suloi hunter that lived when their clan did not was an unforgivable dishonor, the greatest cowardice, in the eyes of other Suloi. The only thing keeping Peio from walking off the nearest sea cliff to join his decimated clan was his work helping Cassian. There had been times it had been too much and Cassian had saved him from himself. But maybe that was selfish too.

"Why do you work for the Suloi?" Danel asked without looking at him. "You do not share our blood."

"My mother was the granddaughter of a Northern slave who bought her freedom near the end of her life. My parents believed that we are all the same, no matter where we come from, no matter if there is magic in our blood or not," Cassian replied. "They believed slavery should end."

"You speak of them as if they are gone."

"They are." Betrayed by people they trusted. Murdered. Their household arrested and done away with, their estate confiscated and turned over to another, one more sympathetic to the local wishes of the aristocracy. And Cassian left alone, to contemplate his arrogance, to live and relive two decades spent doing nothing but what he wanted, his misplaced resentment, the incomprehensible audacity of his sense of entitlement.

This was his penance. And it would never be enough. There would never be enough lost games of chance or rescued lives to erase his youth, to erase the pain he had caused them, to erase that two good, giving people had been snuffed out and one useless, selfish bastard allowed to remain. All that remained to him was the blood right his father had left him.

And waiting. Waiting for the man who betrayed them to die. Then he could take back what was his. Continue what his parents had begun. The real work of freedom.

Cassian heard mutterings from Amara's direction and glanced in time to see her untangling herself from the blanket she shared with Kiya. Once she was free, she stood facing the nearest ladder. He doubted she'd want his help a second time, though it was obvious she was contemplating how to get down. Danel had turned his head to look as well.

"I saw you help her," he said. Cassian nodded. "It is strange, the fears that take our spirit, isn't it?" Danel added. "How it is different for us all. That one…" Danel looked skyward again when Amara clutched her hands in her pants and stepped to the edge. "That one should fear nothing."

Cassian glanced to Danel for more information, but his expression indicated there would be none.

Amara got down on her hands and knees, moved onto the ladder. Thinking of her down in the trees and underbrush by herself turned Cassian's attention from Danel's words.

"Your men are on watch?"

"Yes," Danel said as he followed Cassian's gaze just in time to see Amara disappear over the edge of the platform.

"Forgive me, Pathfinder." Cassian got to his feet. Danel lay back down.

"Be careful, *Sanpotar*, that you do not follow the river, instead of the path. I once warned another to be careful how far they followed a stranger. That they might find themselves led down a path they did not know the way to return from, in a place they never meant to go."

"And did that come true?" Cassian asked.

"Perhaps my sister can answer that question, when you find her." Danel closed his eyes.

"My path is cast in blood. I cannot stray from it," Cassian said. Danel nodded his understanding. Vengeance. The Red Path. Once a roadborn was locked onto it they could not leave it. Danel understood.

Cassian walked to the edge of the platform. He arrived in time to see Amara dismount the ladder and step into the darkness. He crouched and made his way swiftly after her.

When he reached the ground, he stopped, hearing her movement through the underbrush to his left. Assuming she needed only to relieve herself, he waited where he was, listening. An owl hooted its superiority somewhere in the distance, and he heard other small noises, animals in the trees and the underbrush. His woodcraft was not equal to that of the Suloi—Peio was like a specter in the woods—but there were killers searching for them, and he didn't like the idea of Amara alone in the dark. She carried no weapons, and if she was a mage of any power, like Kiya, she had yet to reveal that.

What had Danel meant, that she should fear nothing? She'd shown no signs of being a warrior, though Danel might have information Cassian did not.

❦

AMARA RESERVED JUDGMENT OF Cassian's intentions until he had reached the ground. She wanted to assume he had climbed down the ladder out of concern, and not out of some perverse desire to trap her alone in the dark. When he did not move to follow her after reaching the ground, her irritation eased, and her curiosity grew.

How did a man become such a haphazard mix of vice and virtue? She'd overheard most of his conversation with Danel. He said it had been his parents' work, freeing slaves, and apparently he had taken up their banner. Yet he'd also become a man who lived on money made at the expense of others, and gambled to excess.

But his eyes. There was such warmth and kindness in them, and she could not reconcile that with someone so obviously miserable.

The Wheel had seen fit to force them together, so avoiding him was an exercise in futility. Amara stepped out from behind the tree she'd used to hide as she conducted her business. Power swirled in her belly, a tiny maelstrom of warning that sensed the intent of another, and she started to spin around, sucking in a breath to cry out, but a hand clapped over her mouth, and a blade of wicked sharpness bit against her throat.

"You're a good, quiet girl, aren't you?" a male voice whispered in her ear. Amara nodded, pushing down on her flare of power. He spoke with the hard-edged syllables of a Republic citizen, not the rounded, lilting accent of a Suloi. Revealing herself to someone she could only assume was a Vexillae would leave her with fewer advantages than she already possessed.

He removed his hand from her mouth, and wrapped his arm around her waist, holding her tightly against him. A myriad of hard, edged objects pressed against her back as he did, whatever contraptions and weapons they carried, she guessed.

"There are two ways this can go," he murmured, and the knife nicked her throat. Her magic tossed and crested in her mental grasp, reacting to her turmoil. "You can continue being a good, quiet girl while we leave. Or, you can try and fight me or warn your friends, and I'll carve you up like a roast."

"What do you want?" Amara fought against her power's whispered promises that all she had to do was let it free, and this would end. No one had power over her, whose voice was water, whose will was immutable. Amara shoved the voices away. Never again. She would rather die.

"Shut her up," another voice said, from a bit farther behind them.

"What do you want from me?" Amara tipped her head farther back against his shoulder, away from the bite of his knife as he dragged her, slowly feeling his way through the darkness, backwards. Bek and Djar had seen three of them the day before. That did not necessarily mean there weren't more.

"We were told to search for a mage that looked like a Meneian trader," the man holding her whispered against her ear. Her power swelled, breaking free under reins loosened by her sudden surge of fear. Someone had betrayed her. What did they do to mages in the Republic? They tortured them. Experimented on them. Exploited them.

Silver bloomed across her skin, freed by her horror, shining in the darkness, and her would-be captor barked in alarm, yanking away from her.

"Amara?" Cassian called.

"Help!" She lunged away from the Vex, breaking into a run, remembering a moment later they had guns. Her back ached with the imagined sense they were trained on her that very moment, that within the next breath she'd feel the strike of a bullet. "Djar!" Amara screamed. She dodged sideways into some tall, leafy underbrush just before she reached Cassian.

Cassian stumbled forward with a grunt, and dropped as if he'd been struck. Amara stopped, turning back toward him. *End this*, her magic demanded even as she silenced it in her skin.

Amara crouched in the underbrush. Enough moonlight filtered into the trees that movement and shapes could be seen against the blackness of the forest, and her heart beat so hard she could feel its pulse in her legs. She wanted to go to Cassian, she wanted to call out to him, and she wanted to shrink, and be silent and unseen. She might stop them with her magic, but at what cost? Her power was barely hers to control, its consequences too broad.

"Come out, little mage," one of the men warbled. He grabbed Cassian's still form and hauled him up and back, underneath the shelter of the platform, out of reach of arrows that might be loosed from above.

"Amara!" Djar snapped. Amara looked up. He was too canny to silhouette himself against the edge of the platform, so she couldn't see him, and she doubted he could see her. She didn't dare call back. Cassian made a noise, and she hoped that meant he was not mortally wounded.

"No. We can't see her, don't loose," someone else ordered from above.

"Is this your friend? Hmm? Shall we poke him a bit and see if he has magic too?" The voice drifted from the deeper shadow beneath the platform.

He doesn't want to, her magic said. *He wants to leave, to walk away. Tell him.* The power whispered, swirling under her skin, coaxing her. Amara shut her eyes. *Make him.* The magic trilled. But it wasn't the magic. It was her. Her thoughts. Her words. Her will.

"Last chance," came another voice. Never, never again. Amara stood.

"I'm here. Let him go," she said. Amara heard a heavy thump, as though they had dropped Cassian to the ground, and she hoped she had not just given herself up for a dead man. Somehow they knew she was a mage, yet they had not killed her outright. They wanted her captive, more than they wanted her dead, she hoped. Amara released the grip she held on her magic, allowing its silver reflection to wash over her skin, its faint glow illuminating the area around her.

"There!" Djar crowed.

"What in the gods' names?" one of the Vex cried out. Her untethered power whispered more frantically. *End it. End it. Stop them.* But Amara had a decade of practice ignoring it, and she had made herself a promise, after she had unleashed it in saving Djar so many Turns ago. Never again. The price was too high. She did not need her power to win. She never had.

A gun fired beneath the platform, the sound shocking and so loud her body jerked. Instinct made her crouch, certain they'd shot at her. But no pain came, no blood. She opened her eyes.

"Can't see a damned thing. Would you lazy sons of bitches get down here?" Cassian called, and she saw him, lying on his side, trying to load his pistol again.

Amara moved without thinking, certain they'd kill him before he got off another shot, but not her. They wanted her alive. She lunged through the bushes, which tore at her clothes, and threw herself on top of him.

"Get off me!" Cassian shoved her away, his voice panicked, trying to roll on top of her to shield her in turn. Someone grabbed her hair, jerking her back, and she shrieked in pain, rounding to claw at the man. He gripped her arms and shook her violently, so her head snapped back and haze drifted through her vision. "Damn it," Cassian said behind her, struggling to his feet. Another gun went off and he cursed again, dropping to his belly.

"We need to go." The Vex holding Amara twisted her hair in one hand and her arm in the other, dragging her backwards, beneath the platform, through the dark. Somewhere to the right his companion moved as well, a darker shape against the night. A ladder tumbled down from the far side of the platform, and another, bigger shape dropped from above. Djar. Amara purposefully stumbled, lurching forward in her captor's grip. Sharp pain webbed her scalp, but she dragged against his hold, stopping him.

"Get up." He yanked her.

"Rear!" his friend barked, but Djar's looming shadow was already on him, his scimitar slicing through the air to knock the gun from his hands. Amara's captor spun her around, locking one arm around her throat and drawing a pistol with the other.

"Gun!" Amara cried, and the man cinched his arm, cutting off blood flow and air, and she struggled uselessly, kicking at his legs and clawing at his leather-clad arm as she gasped for breath that didn't come. He lifted the gun, taking aim at Djar, and Amara reached behind her, raking at his face with her nails. He cursed, whipping his head away from her, and bashed the butt of his pistol against her temple.

Darkness and light exploded in tandem in her head. She slipped to the ground and landed on her knees. Someone cried her name. The forest floor tipped from beneath her and she fell sideways, dimly aware as her power swirled through her in silver pools of angry water. But it could do nothing without her guidance, without her will and voice, and she closed her eyes, drifting away.

Another gunshot that sounded as if it were right in her ear woke her from her stupor. Djar roared in pain, and her wits returned to her in a cold flash. Her body was not completely under her control as she propped herself on her elbows on her back, trying to see around her, to sort out the chaos. The Vex stood over her, his legs straddling her body, his arm lowering, a pistol in his grip. A pace away, Djar twisted away from them, a hand to his face. Amara fell to her back and pulled her knee to her chest, then kicked the Vex as hard as she could in the groin. He howled, doubled over, and a shot rang. He jerked, eyes wide, and collapsed on top of her. Amara shrieked, covering her face with her arms.

"Enjoy the River Nexus," Cassian snarled from somewhere behind Amara. Someone lifted the dead Vex away, and hands caught her, lifting her up. She recognized Djar's fumbling grip and towering height. She clung to him, sucking in great, heaving breaths, and he returned it.

"You're all right?" he asked.

Amara nodded against his chest. "You?" She pulled away, tipping her head back to look at him.

The left side of Djar's face was covered in blood, torn and mangled. Everything within her stilled. The sounds of the others descending, everything, drowned by slow horror. Denial surged in her, cold, and hot. Tears filled her eyes as she reached shaking hands up to his face.

"No," she whispered. He jerked away from her touch.

"I am alive," he rumbled. It was too dark to see the damage completely, to gauge whether he had lost his eye, but she knew.

She couldn't breathe. She stepped back, choking, her hands at her mouth. The tears traced hot tracks down her cheeks.

"Amara," Djar demanded.

"I did it," she wheezed, finally drawing breath as her sorrow broke free of her grip and consumed her. "It's my fault."

Djar turned away from her, and walked to where one of the bodies lay. Cassian replaced him, holstering the pistol he'd used to kill her attacker.

"Are you hurt?" he asked.

Amara found some of her control in the face of someone who could never understand how not all right she was.

"I am fine." She swiped at her cheeks. Djar needed to be treated. "I need to help Djar." She forced the quaver from her voice.

"I think you should sit down and rest," Cassian said. "I'll see to this. I'll see to Djar."

"No. I'll see to him," Amara snapped. "Bek!" She turned from Cassian. Bek strode to her from where he had been with Djar, beside one of the bodies. "Collect their things. Have Kiya help you. We'll bring them with us."

"Yes," he said, obediently. But his look lingered, questioned, and she could not bear it. She looked away.

"Djar. Go up. I want to look at your wounds."

He rose wordlessly from where he crouched beside one of the Vex, and climbed the ladder in front of her. Her emotions were too raw, her mind too busy playing and replaying all the moments she had ignored in which she could have changed the course of the outcome. The fear of the ladder mingled with those, the need to keep shuffling forward or be drowned in regret.

Danel waited at the top, leaning on his staff, his expression pinched and pained, his body tense. Amara could not imagine what he felt. There had been only three Vexillae. How many descended on a camp to slaughter its inhabitants? How much of what had gone on below had reminded him of the loss of his people?

"What power do you possess to heal?" Amara asked him, as Djar continued forward toward the sleeping shelters and sat down. Danel gave Djar a cursory examination from a distance, and grimaced, shifting his stance to turn toward her a little more.

"This was not just a bullet." Danel looked at her gravely. "They have vials of acid they throw, to cause pain. And fear. To maim. I can ease the pain, and perhaps some little of the damage. I cannot give him back his eye."

Her throat tightened as the faint hope died, and she looked down, to hide her emotion.

"I have some healing supplies in my pack, if you would bring it to me," Danel said.

Amara did so as Danel made his slow, limping way to Djar. She dragged the pack to them and laid it beside Danel. As he opened it and began pulling out bandages and ointments she knelt in front of Djar, lifting her gaze to his. He met it, held it, and they stared at each other in silence.

The muscles in his face and neck were tight, his mouth drawing a thin, harsh line. The flickering torchlight revealed the slick of perspiration on his skin. His pain was hers. She cradled his hand between her own.

Danel reached beside him and lifted a wineskin, handing it to Amara. Her hands shook as she took it. "The acid still burns him." He placed a hand on Djar's shoulder and urged him to lie on his side. "This is water. Pour all of it across his eye."

Amara pulled the stopper on the skin and began to pour it over the area. To her horror, she saw bubbles and Djar's body stiffened, a low groan issuing from his throat.

"Quickly. More." Danel grabbed her wrist and upended the skin so the water splashed against Djar's wound, washing away what remained of the acid, as well as the gore, revealing the damage in livid detail. Danel did not let go of her until the water was gone, and Djar's body relaxed. He sat up, taking a deep breath. Amara pulled a clean rag from the supplies, cupping his cheek and gently wiping the excess water away. He folded his legs in front of him and slouched forward.

Danel nodded. He reached for Djar's wound, and Amara dropped her hands to her lap. Danel set his hand over Djar's left eye, covering the damage, and closed his eyes. Amara did not try to hold on to the tears that fell down her cheeks, nor did she close her eyes or turn away. She had caused it; she would sit through his suffering with him no matter what sorrow it brought her.

Danel chanted no spell, nor drew a sigil; no light danced in his skin. In Tamar, only a Sival or Charah could command magic with a thought, by channeling their own energy. She could feel it, a whisper against her own. Barely enough to even recognize as power. Was he casting? Or had Suloi magic changed so much, shifting as the power grew dimmer within them as they moved farther and farther from Tamar?

Djar flinched, his good eye closing briefly, the lines of pain remaining in his brow when it opened again.

When Danel finally opened his eyes and pulled his hand away, some of the tension had relaxed from Djar.

"That is all I can do with magic. Mine was the weakest in our family. Drink this, it will fog your mind, but also take some of the pain away." Danel handed Djar a little glass vial. "All of it."

Djar did so, tipping the vial back and emptying it. That spoke more to his suffering than anything else. He was not a man unaccustomed to pain, nor one to take anything he did not know the origin of.

"And, this ointment will protect the skin while it heals." Danel reached into his pack, and she saw his hands shaking as he retrieved a jar and handed it to her. Even that small magic had tired him. Amara opened it, and swept her fingers through the oily surface, bringing it carefully to Djar's face.

"What happened?" she asked, whispered, because her voice had no power.

"We struggled for the gun. It went off in my face. It missed me, or grazed me. Then he threw that liquid fire at me…I do not know," Djar said, his voice hoarse, with pain or emotion, Amara couldn't tell.

"It grazed you," Danel said, the lilt in his voice easing some of the gravity of his words. Danel's magic had knitted the worst of the shredded flesh through a turn's worth of healing, so she was able to touch him without grazing open flesh, though she didn't rub it, afraid to break open the scabbing. If she were not so broken with sorrow, she might wonder at this evidence of creation magic, to know that the Third House indeed survived. But it was hard to wonder at something that had so little effect.

Djar's eyelids were fused shut on that side, from the acid itself, or the heat of the blast…perhaps the healing, Amara couldn't bear to ask. She could never forgive herself, or ask him to. She buried the shame beside the rest, in a raw, bleeding part of her soul, and covered it up with her promise to them both that she would make it better. She would make a place for them where no one could wound them, or force them to do things they did not wish to.

"*Sister of my heart,*" Djar murmured, lifting his hands to grip her wrists. Amara shook her head. She couldn't bear for him to speak to her. "*I am alive. You are alive. It is all that matters, it is always all that has mattered.*"

"*I promised you more than this.*" Amara avoided his gaze as she dabbed more ointment onto his face.

"*You have saved my life. You have saved my soul. What price is an eye?*"

"*Too high,*" Amara said. "*When I had the power to prevent it.*"

"*I would never ask that of you,*" Djar said.

"And here I thought you couldn't possibly get any uglier." Cassian sat abruptly down in front of Djar, frowning at him. Amara turned to him, her sorrow and shame igniting into fury, but Djar laughed, a big boisterous sound.

"No uglier than you, at least," Djar replied. Her anger cooled to irritation. The methods in which men coped with horror had always baffled her. When she looked at Cassian, she remembered the part he had played in it all, and that he was likely hurt as well. He'd shot that Vex. The one who had hurt Djar.

"Are you injured?" She leaned forward, trying to examine him for evidence of blood. He reached up to the back of his head, his fingers grazing a spot where his dark hair was wet in the torchlight.

"One of them smacked me with something. I'm lucky they didn't shoot me." He glanced at Djar and her. "Why were they after you?"

Danel, silent, handed her a fistful of rags and nodded to the ointment while he fashioned a bandage for Djar's eye. Amara moved behind Cassian, and carefully brushed the hair away from the wound where they'd struck him. It wasn't bad, though he'd have a lump and a headache. She cleaned away some of the blood and forest-floor detritus and put ointment on him. Danel urged Djar to lie down.

"They were after mages." Amara peeked at Djar over Cassian's head. He shook his head; he'd told no one. No one knew. No one. She had not used power once since reaching the shores of Haenna except within the villa. It was difficult for her to believe that the Grand Vizier had reach even into the Republic, but if he was desperate enough to unseat the Sultana, he might lower himself to make friends of enemies. He was even more ambitious than Amara. The difference being she suspected him perfectly willing to take lives in the pursuit of what he wanted.

Overly favored by the Fifth House with a gift for lies and charm that had gained him a majority of support from the Council, he had effectively tied the Sultana's hands. It was no secret he opposed the Circle of Chara'a. Amara would not put it past him to attempt to gain his goal by having her assassinated where no one would be able to investigate. Amara's death would end any hope the Sultana had of completing the Circle, and remove the threat the Circle posed to the Council's political power.

"Are you a mage?" Cassian asked. "I thought I saw you...glowing."

Amara opened her mouth to reply, to lie, but Djar chuckled. She glanced at his face, and saw that his good eye was glassy, and he was grinning. Danel's medicine had started working more quickly than she would have imagined.

"*Sing, oh sing, sweet water's child,*" Djar hummed, turning his face upward. "*Sing, oh sing, daughter of the wild. Sing a dream to me, tell me a lie, make it truth to me.*"

"Hush." Amara moved to his side and set a hand on his shoulder. "That is enough."

"*…sing peace and hope, that are lies to me.*"

"Shh," she said. Perhaps his euphoric distraction would prevent her having to explain herself in any detail to the other two. If Cassian worked to free Suloi, it was unlikely he was violently opposed to magic, but hers was an altogether different matter than most.

"What is he singing?" Cassian asked.

"Nothing." Amara sat back on her heels, folding her hands in her lap and making her tone dismissive.

"Ah," Cassian said, "nothing, it is." He looked at her critically as he spoke, then reached between them and pushed her hair carefully away from her temple, where the Vex had struck her. A light, brusque touch. "He cut you." He tucked a knuckle against her chin to tilt it so he could see the place the knife had grazed her skin. The soft brush of his fingers over her face, steady and kind, was gentleness in the shadow of violence. She shivered.

Cassian noticed the reaction, and his gaze settled on hers as he picked up the cloth from where she had set it. "This"—he brushed a thumb over her temple—"will be tender for some time."

"You must know much about such things," she said.

Cassian mocked a chuckle before he issued her a slight glare. He cleaned the cut on her throat and swiped some of the ointment over it. She was struck again by his kindness, his willingness to care for people he barely knew. It did not make her trust him, but it made her more comfortable with the idea of trying. She was in need of people to trust, if there were assassins after her and her friends.

"Will you help me find Danel's sister and her friend?" she asked. "I can pay you. Twice what I owe you, if it is done swiftly."

Djar hummed the tune to the song again, but his eye was closed and the melody broken as he drifted in and out of sleep.

Cassian pulled his hand away from her, setting the cloth on top of Danel's pack and scratching at the back of his head, where he'd been struck. Amara batted his hand away, and he looked at her sidelong, his bright eyes brighter with teasing. Cassian leaned backwards on his hands and stretched out his legs, watching her for a long time in silence. Did he feel empowered by making her sit through his silences? She raised an eyebrow.

"If I don't help you," Cassian said, "will you deny me the money the twins stole?"

"You would have lost it anyway," Amara said.

"It's the principle of the thing." Cassian tipped his head back. "I'll think about it."

FOURTEEN

ASSIAN RODE AT THE head of their little group. Peio brought up the rear, once again, pensive and irritable.

Behind Cassian, Amara consulted in a near whisper with Djar in an argument. She and her people had also been thoughtful and quiet since they left the camp that morning. Danel, who had sent his huntsmen back to their clans as promised, was silent and brooding, though Cassian suspected that was the man's permanent state of mood.

Cassian was ready to be back to his own routines, without strangers in the mix. No matter how pleasant they were to look at. He turned in his saddle to check on Peio, slicing his gaze across Amara as he did. She saw. A corner of her mouth ticked up, her own gaze routing over him from head to toe. Cassian faced forward again, cursing inwardly. Was he fifteen again? What was wrong with him? And did she have to be so smug about it in any case? She could have the decency to pretend she didn't notice, instead of taunting him with her blazing looks.

"I would like to go down to the water," she announced to Cassian's back. They were the first words she'd said to him since they'd left the camp in the trees. Why did everything she say make his skin prickle? The woman could have made the subject of dung heaps sound erotic.

"It would be wisest to return to the city and wait for daylight. Thieves are not uncommon at night." Cassian resisted the urge to turn and look at her, yet again, examining his hands instead. A carving. That's what he needed, something to occupy his hands. He squeezed the reins. Why had she waited so long to ask for a stop? Stopping to sightsee was foolish not just because of thieves, but because they had Djar's injury to be concerned about. Danel was obviously suffering as well, having given what pain medicine he had to Djar. But Cassian would not have called Amara foolish, from what little he had seen of her. Perhaps she had a good reason for her desire.

She pulled her horse to a halt and looked toward the water, then along the cliff. Night had begun to fall and they were finally within sight of the city. He was ready to be out of the saddle, not extending the journey. But she had said she'd pay him.

"There is a place behind us where you can get down to the shore. Although I cannot promise it will be uninhabited when we get there," Cassian said. The beach was a favorite place of illicit lovers to escape the city.

"Djar, Bek. Take Danel and Peio to the Fountain House," she ordered. "We will meet you there shortly."

"It is unwise to split up," Djar said, carefully. Her expression tensed, but she didn't respond right away. Instead she took hold of Djar's reins and urged their horses away from the others.

Cassian could only catch a few words. Basin. Ocean. Sultana. Then she said she didn't need an audience.

Djar's whisper carried better. He asked when she had ever minded an audience. Amara gave her head a little toss, frowning. She said something about the city guard.

"There is no one here that would profit from being brought to the attention of the Republic," Djar said, almost at full volume. Cassian thought it was purposeful, a kind of warning. Amara turned her horse away from Djar and approached Cassian.

"Please lead the way."

He urged his horse to a trot, reversing their direction and traveling north a bit, scanning the cliff for the segment of rock that marked the trail down to the beach. It was too narrow and steep for the horses, so they dismounted at the top. Bek and Danel remained behind to guard them and watch for others, at least in theory. In reality Cassian was glad for an excuse to keep Danel from the trail. He doubted the Pathfinder could make the trek.

"You may stay as well." Amara frowned when he started down the trail.

"It would be handy for you to have a Republic citizen at hand were you to encounter anyone on the beach, don't you believe?" Cassian asked. She was a woman accustomed to being in complete control of a situation, and he enjoyed needling her a bit too much. She flicked her hand in dismissal.

"Do as you will then, but if you observe something that causes you…difficulty, I will remind you that it was your choice."

"That sounds interesting." He brushed past her to the trail.

"It does not surprise me that you think difficult sounds interesting. It is clearly your life's motto." She came after him, but stopped when Djar made to follow her. She pressed her hand to his chest. He hadn't uttered a word of complaint through the entire day's ride, but it was obvious to everyone that he was in pain, and it was taking a toll on him. He shook his head, and Amara's expression tensed with her temper, but she turned away from him. Cassian couldn't quite decide their relationship to each other. They did not appear related, and he sometimes acted like a servant, sometimes like an equal. The way they had spoken to each other, touched each other, after his injury had suggested intimacy.

She seemed especially close to the girl too, but perhaps that was simply the way she was with people she cared about. He was certain Menei had similar ideas about unions between men and women to those of the Republic. That only unions between men and women were acceptable, and anything else was aberrant. Cassian didn't particularly care beyond curiosity. He had spent too long with the Suloi, who took a much freer view of lovers and love, to care who did what with whom. But he was curious. And he did have an…interest in what Amara might find attractive.

He led them down the trail, Amara, then Djar, then Peio and Kiya following. The cliff trail overlooked the narrow strip of sandy shore, snapping through six quick switchbacks before depositing one on the sand of the beach. Kiya and Peio discussed dice, and though Cassian couldn't quite hear them, he could tell they were getting along well. Peio did not laugh often, and he laughed twice before they were even halfway down the trail.

At one point Amara's feet slipped against the dirt, packed to a smooth, slippery surface by the hundreds who had hiked it. She fell against Cassian's back, he barely managed to stay on his feet, and they grabbed each other to stay upright. She was soft in all the right places, he was able to determine before she extracted herself from his grip.

"Shall I carry you down?" he offered only partly in jest. She feigned pondering, sweeping him with another charged look that won her back every modicum of control he had taken.

"That will not be necessary, thank you," she said over her shoulder as she continued on.

The trail ended at the beach, which was a mix of sand and polished stones, and Amara walked halfway to the water before she stopped to look up and down the cove as the rest of them joined her.

"Kiya?" Amara asked as the other woman moved to her side, while bending to remove her boots. She set them in the sand beside her. Peio took up a spot beside Cassian.

"She speaks so loudly," he said under his breath, taking a bite of dried meat. Cassian held his hand out, and Peio tore the strip in two and put some in his palm. Peio did not mean that Amara literally spoke loudly. To *speak loudly* in roadborn culture was to meet someone's eyes. And Amara was not afraid to be direct. Which Cassian liked. A great deal. It could grow exhausting, the Suloi way of communicating. Nonverbal glances and gestures, language that skirted the subject.

"I can tell her, if it bothers you." He ripped a piece of meat off with his teeth.

Peio shook his head. "*Rain flows to river, not river to rain.*" Cassian raised an eyebrow, but didn't ask for an interpretation.

Removed from the physical attraction, he couldn't decide what he thought of her. She'd fit right in amidst the various criminals he dealt with, as cunning and underhanded as any of them. He couldn't sort out whether he should respect her or be suspicious.

Djar joined them, and Cassian held the remnant of dried venison out to him. Djar took it. They stood a few paces to Amara's right, where she watched as Kiya crouched.

"What is she doing?" Cassian asked.

"She is feeling the earth for other people." Djar's voice was strained, a small sign of the pain that plagued him. Kiya splayed her hands over the surface of the sand, whispering to herself much as she had done at the camp to obtain a rock.

"How does that work?" he asked, fascinated. All the magic he had seen of the Suloi was passive, for the most part. What Danel had done to Djar the night before had been the only magic of its kind Cassian had ever seen. He'd seen the other subtle magics of the Suloi, but never healing.

"I do not know exactly. I am ungifted, a void, they call it in Tamar. But as she has explained it to me, she can sense the movement, or vibration, of people. I don't know how far. But it allows her to see what we cannot."

Cassian glanced up and down the beach, thinking. It went on for a league or so, and great tumbles of jagged stone obscured parts of it. Whatever Amara wished to keep hidden from others, he supposed Kiya's spell was a good precaution.

"I always imagined spells to be a bit more…" Cassian lifted a shoulder. "…awe-inspiring. Or at least visible."

"Did you?" Djar's voice pitched in dry amusement. Kiya rose and nodded to Amara, who unwound the cloth from her hair and folded it, setting it atop her slippers in the sand. She strode forward to where the water lapped against the shore, and stood in it, silently.

"We have stories," Peio said, in the lilt his Suloi accent gave to Republic Trade. "People burned to ash, mountains crumbling at a thought."

"Magic comes in many forms," Djar said. "And sometimes the magic you have heard stories of is only awe-inspiring for the pain it causes. Mages of the power you describe are rare." He looked at Amara as he said it, a distinct expression of regret on his face, sadness in his dark eyes. Cassian wondered what put it there, what magic had done in his life to make him equate it to sorrow.

It seemed, no matter where one came from, that magic did not only bring wonder. But pain. Cassian's mother had taught him that it was difference that made the world beautiful. And it was difference that made the world hate. The two sides of Tessis' scales, forever dipping away from balance.

"Is Amara a mage too?" Cassian asked. "Like Kiya?" He had seen her glow. He was certain of it. No Suloi had ever glowed, that Cassian could remember. Kiya had not either. Perhaps he had just imagined it. Or his vision was still untrustworthy while the swelling of his face abated. She wasn't Tamaran…was she capable of the kind of magic he'd heard stories of? If so, surely she would have saved herself from the Vexillae.

"She is a mage," Djar said. "But not like Kiya. Her House is water."

"House?" Cassian struggled to keep his gaze off Amara, standing still as stone as the waves lapped around her feet.

"Her power. The Wheel is broken into six spokes, called Houses," Djar said. "Each House is born of the one before and creates the one after. Amara's is water, which sits between air and creation."

"So she can control water?" Cassian asked. There were Suloi who had an affinity for water, like Peio. He could always find water. He seemed to see better in the dark, as well. And his sense for lies was infinitely useful. Kiya had moved earth though, which he'd never seen a Suloi do. What did Amara intend to do with the ocean?

"Not as you imagine it. Lesser water mages can," Djar said. "The same power takes slightly different forms in every mage. Their talents and personalities shape their magic."

"Lesser?" Cassian asked. How powerful was she?

"She is something different," Peio said, softly, and touched Djar with his gaze briefly before turning it to the sand again. Djar nodded. Was that what had Peio fawning over her? He sensed her magic? Magic they shared? Why hadn't he said anything to Cassian?

Cassian rubbed his fingers over his breastbone, pressing away a tangled feeling that mixed jealousy and melancholy.

It was good, good that Peio found someone he had something in common with. But…was the jealousy Cassian squashed a desire for the same? Or a fear of losing his only friend? Peio wouldn't leave with them too, would he? That was selfish. Wanting to keep Peio from something that might bring him some measure of joy. Just so Cassian wouldn't have to be alone in the world. Again.

"Yes," Djar finally said, the word hissing between his teeth as Amara turned from the water and returned to them through the sand. "She is something different." The man's voice shaped the words with reverence, and with sorrow. Cassian looked at Djar but there was none of that emotion mirrored on his face.

"Can you do it?" Djar asked Amara when she reached them. Her pants were soaked to the knee, clinging to her calves, her bare feet covered in sand.

"Of course I can do it." She tugged at the turquoise cloth that hugged her waist, unwinding it and setting it with her boots and head wrap. Djar snorted. "But there is a storm somewhere." She gestured into the darkening distance. "And the water is…" Her eyes reflected orange sunset as she looked out to sea. "…distracted."

Cassian had to concentrate on picking apart the last bit of dried meat in his hands to prevent himself staring at her. "Do you speak with water?" He took a bite. "It can be distracted? Can it be angry as well?" He had seen an angry ocean whipped by storm. But he had only described it as such, not considered the water might actually feel. Or maybe…could she speak to the gods? To Passius, and his finned daughters? To the god of waves and rain? Or maybe she was his daughter, made human. There were stories of such things. He'd never really believed them…

"Water is not sentient." Amara regarded him with suspicion. Like he was an adder that might strike at her. Because of her magic? "But…" She paused to think. "…it absorbs all that it touches, and reflects it." After she said it, without preamble, or even a glance in their direction, not a glimmer of hesitation, Amara pulled her shirt over her head and handed it to Kiya. Beneath the shirt she wore only a thin linen cloth to wrap her breasts.

Peio made a choking noise and turned his back, coughing on a piece of jerky he'd inhaled.

"What…" Cassian started and failed. He forced his gaze away from the soft dip of her belly, the deep curve of her waist, and his thoughts away from what she might feel like in his hands. "What are you doing?" he asked.

"Something I would not have to, if you had not befouled my divining basin with your blood and sweat." One corner of her mouth turned up as he chanced a look at her. "I warned you that any difficulty you incur is by your own choice. Does it offend you?"

"I cannot recall a single time in my life when a naked woman offended me. But keep going, I'll certainly inform you if this is any different." Cassian tore off another bite of jerky. He was trying to pretend he was as unaffected as Kiya and Djar. But that smile was on her mouth, the one that told little, smoldering lies about how he was the only man in the world. She held his gaze as she hooked her fingers into the pants and pushed them down to her ankles. Cassian blinked, his body completely under her control, fire blazing up his thighs and into his belly. Peio had the right idea. He should turn around. He should not look at the small swath of cloth that remained around her hips, providing only a hint of modesty.

"*Is she done yet?*" Peio asked weakly. Cassian barely heard him, staring at the pronounced curve of Amara's hips, the lush fullness of her thighs, imagining the smooth softness of her against him. Peio had peeked by this time, and his breath left him through his nostrils. He spun back around, muttering under his breath about the Wanderer turning his gaze away from the impious. The Suloi might be free with who they loved, but women's bodies were not put on display outside moments of passion, as far as Cassian knew.

"If I said that I do not regret whatever I did to your basin, would you find that offensive?" Beside him, Djar huffed a laugh, and Amara took on a more amused kind of smile.

"Ignorant, at the least," she said, snapping him from his haze of lust. She strode to the water's edge. Watching her walk threatened to send him into fits, and he finally dropped his gaze to the sand, trying to collect some rational thoughts from wherever they had scattered. The stola he'd first seen her in, and the Meneian pants and shirt since had greedily guarded the secret of her curves. Seeing them in all their unadorned glory was more torture than pleasure. He'd been trying not to let his imagination run away with him, despite his attraction.

This was akin to opening the gate on a herd of starving oxen and it would be a struggle not to picture her as she was now every time he looked at her hence. And wanting her.

"Does she do this often?" Cassian asked, then had to clear his throat. He needed something, anything to distract him from the intense longing and ache in his groin. "Strip naked in front of men she barely knows? Isn't she afraid?"

"She isn't naked," Djar pointed out helpfully. Cassian threw him an incredulous look. Djar lifted a hand to the scimitar at his hip and drew it in such a casual movement it took Cassian a second to react. Peio flinched, skipping a step sideways and drawing a knife. Djar ignored him, turning his blade one way, then the other, until it caught the light of the setting sun and was set ablaze. "Do you think a blade unsheathed is afraid? Or that it invites battle simply by being what it is?"

"Is she a blade?" Cassian asked, eyeing the weapon as Djar returned it to its sheath.

"Amara was birthed and forged in the fires of Menei pleasure houses. Her body is no less a weapon than my blade is. If someone chooses to look at it and see invitation where there is none, or take what is not freely given, that is their folly, and not hers," Djar said. "Besides. I am here, and if you forget yourself, it will be the last thing you ever do."

Cassian did not doubt that. Peio sheathed his knife, though he did not relax. Cassian shivered. At least Djar's demonstration had cooled his lust.

Amara had walked into the water by then, up to her hips. "Is she going to cast a spell?" Peio asked. "Does it require her to be naked? Kiya wasn't naked." There was a bit of pleading in his voice. Kiya snickered from where she stood on the other side of him.

"It is a difficult spell at any time," Djar said. "The more of her skin is in contact with the water, the easier things will be. She would not need these measures if you had not been so crass as to bathe in spelled water." He gave Cassian a sidelong look of disdain.

"It was spelled? Am I spelled now?"

"Don't be stupid." Kiya laughed. "It doesn't work like that."

Cassian tried not to let his relief show.

"Are there many spells that require no clothes?" Peio asked, finally turning around again.

"Only this one, as far as I know," Djar said.

"Of course, only this one," Cassian muttered.

"I did once see a fire mage burn all their clothes to ash," Kiya said in a musing tone. "But it was accidental. They were fine, though."

Cassian wondered how one might burn all their clothes without burning themselves.

Amara turned to face the beach, putting her back to the setting sun. Cassian looked at the sand. He could not watch her any longer and not feel like a complete lecher.

A flash of silver light startled him and made him look up. Something else enveloped him at the same time. A heaviness in the air. Presence that had not been there a moment before, and certainly hadn't been there when Kiya had used her magic. This felt…other. Almost sentient. Amara had called her power, and it was an altogether different thing than Kiya's, than any Suloi's. Her head was lowered, her eyes closed. Quicksilver bloomed in splashes over her body, and bled from her into undulating rivulets through the water that swept past her in slow, rhythmic waves. Something that was not quite fear swept away the remainder of his lust, leaving him cold and rooted where he stood. The Republic, and its Temples, believed that magic was stolen from the gods. They said it was man reaching too far, playing with power that did not belong to them.

No wonder Stephanus was afraid.

Amara lifted her head and opened her eyes. They had been filled with silver, and the rosettes of it on her skin swam and danced in eddies and currents, reflecting the fire of the setting sun behind her, blazing as Djar's scimitar had. She placed her hands against the surface of the water and when she spoke, hundreds of voices whispered in unison, each in a different language, saying the same words. He had never seen, nor heard anything like it, and her near nakedness was forgotten in the sheer wonder her power inspired, transforming her from woman to something higher. Could gods be offended by something they had created? Was it possible to take from them something they did not wish to give? Was this sanctioned by the god of the seas, or affront to him?

"Is that awe-inspiring enough for you?" Djar murmured, looking at him askance. Peio answered for both of them when he nodded.

"Ihsan Sabri," Amara said, her own sonorous voice lost within the chaos of the many that spoke with her, and Cassian understood, sensed, that she was calling someone's name.

Ice sheeted the surface of the water in front of her, surrounding her, freezing the surface around her hips and across her skin, and water rose up from a point in front of her, resolving itself into the shape of a man. Taller than Amara, clothed in garments of water, winking blue lights swirling through his figure. Peio whispered another entreaty to his god. Cassian thought he should be afraid. But he was numb…or awed. Or more likely, struck dumb.

When the apparition spoke, the magic whispered again, and though Cassian could not understand him, he understood some of the voices that echoed him.

"Mistress Mutar." The man's features were not quite clear, the way a reflection in water looked, washed out, shadowed. "You are looking well." He gestured at her body. "Is there a problem with the spelled water you brought with you?"

"Sehzade. It was…" Her gaze flicked over the apparition's shoulder to meet Cassian's. He had never been so unnerved as he was looking in the glowing, pupiless silver of her eyes. "It was polluted," she said. "I have news."

The silver on her skin continued to dance, shifting beneath the ice that crept higher and higher up the lower curve of her abdomen. Cassian didn't think the ice was hers. Not Amara, who was warm, both when she was angry, and when she was not. That ice belonged to the vision in front of her, and Cassian decided he did not care for the way it was inching up her, claiming her.

"Hurry then. This is a needless drain of your power," the man said.

"I can decide whether it is needless. I believe I've found the Fourth House Charah." The silver on her skin coalesced around her waist, and the ice fractured away, but immediately began climbing again.

"Are they with you?"

"No. If he lives, he is a captive of the Republic. In addition, I have located two Third House mages, one of whom is also a captive. However, the rest of their clan that might have possessed power has been wiped out."

"Find the Charah and bring him to us, if he agrees," the man said.

"Yes, Sehzade." She bowed and the apparition's gaze followed her movement, skimming over her nearly naked torso as she rose up. It was certainly the apparition of a man then, and not some magical entity without a prick, Cassian thought wryly.

"There is something else," she said. "Someone has betrayed me to the Vexillae here. We encountered three of them yesterday. I believe it to be the players you mentioned in our last discussion."

"That is unwelcome news. But I am pleased you appear to be unharmed."

"Some of my people were gravely injured. I trust the Sultana will investigate this matter and punish any she finds responsible." Amara's tone had lost some of its deference, and taken on the one Cassian was more accustomed to, hauteur. It stripped some of the wonder of the magic away, and he grinned.

"Of course, Mistress." The apparition was not amused, but instead austere. A Sultana was fairly highborn, Cassian thought. If Amara could order her about, then she must also be highborn. But the marks…she'd also been a servant. A criminal.

"I will contact you again as soon as anything changes," Amara said. The other ducked his head and drew a hand across his body. The water collapsed into itself, shattering the thin layer of ice and splashing across Amara's body as the blue glow faded from the water in front of her. Amara wavered, and took a step, then almost collapsed into the surf. Cassian tensed, and he would have run to her, but Kiya was there first, keeping her on her feet until Djar had made his way to them through the waves and swung her up into his arms.

"I'm well enough to dress," Amara protested, as Djar marched out of the water. "Put me down."

He complied, reluctantly, and kept his big hands on her shoulders while she found her balance in the sand. The sun, of which a sliver remained above the water, shed plenty of light for Cassian to see that she shivered and her lips had taken on an ashy cast that worried him.

"Was that a person? Or some kind of …spirit?" he asked, resisting the urge to pull her close to offer his warmth. It would not have been welcomed by her if she were clothed, and he suspected her ire would be the least of his punishments if he laid hands on her while she wasn't. Peio shifted from foot to foot, his gaze turned up to the top of the cliff. Danel and Bek were too far up to be seen clearly, back from the edge of the cliff and the trail. The setting sun highlighted them, but they were turned away from the beach.

Kiya helped Amara into her pants as Djar steadied her then handed her the shirt. Amara pulled it over her head, but the thin fabric clung loyally to her wet skin, and her taut, dark nipples showed quite well through it and the thin linen that wrapped her chest. Cassian fixed his gaze on her forehead.

"A man. Sehzade Sabri," she said, slurring from the cold.

"Was he trying to kill you with all that ice?" Cassian asked, more tersely than he meant to. "And is that his name, or his title?"

"He wasn't trying to hurt me. He can't help how his power manifests." She hugged her arms around her torso. "And that is his title. Prince. He is second in line for the throne of Tamar." She waved Djar away, apparently recovered enough to stand unaided. Her attention went to Peio, who made a bit of a show of looking anywhere but at her. "You can look at me, Peio."

Peio shook his head violently. "No. I've seen you naked…No," he said.

"And what do you do when you've made love to a woman, hmm? Never speak to her again?" Amara's eyes were bright and a little smile curved her full mouth.

"I…" He shook his head again and turned, striding quickly for the path up the hill. Kiya giggled, collecting the rest of Amara's clothes in her arms and running after Peio. Amara turned her gaze on Cassian, and he tried not to dwell on his new knowledge of her body. It helped that Djar was standing directly behind her as a large, threatening shadow.

But he didn't need Djar as reminder, he need only think of what she had looked like, standing in that water, clothed in the silver light of her power and summoning the likeness of a man that was an ocean away. He had no business lusting after someone like her. What else could she do with that power? Why was she here, in the Republic? Was it really just to collect a handful of marginally gifted Suloi?

"And you, Cassian?" she said his name on an exhale, exactly the way he might imagine she would say it in the throes of pleasure, and he narrowed his eyes at her. "Can you look at me?"

"Now?" Cassian asked, and once again, whether by her spell or her charm, said more than he meant to, "or after I've made love to you?"

He had thought it might sound flippant, teasing. But it sounded like the invitation his roaring desire wanted it to be.

Her lashes lowered, and she smiled to herself. As if she were only playing with him, manipulating him for her amusement. Yet…her gaze flicked to his once more, open warmth in her eyes. His body informed him, in urgent demand, that it did not care whether he was being manipulated or not, as long as he could get her alone, he'd be happy to let her manipulate him all she wanted.

She turned away, cutting the connection between them.

"You should teach your friend your confidence." Amara hooked her arm through Djar's. "Many women find arrogance arousing." She leaned only slightly on Djar as he led her back toward the cliffs.

Cassian was left to wonder at whether her words meant she found his confidence arrogant, or arousing.

FIFTEEN

AMARA REACHED THE TOP of the stairs and stopped. The twins, along with Peio and Cassian, were seated on the floor in a circle. When she'd left them, they'd been discussing the equipment that they'd taken from the Vex who attacked them in the forest. Now they were tossing dice across the floor between them. Djar was napping, or pretending to, on one of the couches. It was too small for him, and one leg was stretched out over the floor to keep him from tumbling off sideways. He still appeared drawn, even at rest.

Amara's hand tightened on the pouch of medicine she'd purchased at the apothecary. She had not realized it was opium that Danel had given Djar until she'd asked for it by Danel's label at the apothecary. She was loathe to give Djar more, but neither could she bear his pain.

"Show me again." Cassian curved a hand over his mouth as he watched Kiya with narrowed eyes. She tossed two dice toward him. Amara could not see what numbers landed, but knew Kiya had manipulated them. She had seen her lips move in a whispered spell and felt the tiny push of magic against her own. Water and earth were not in direct opposition, but they were not next to each other and in harmony on the Wheel, so she was more sensitive to its use.

"How long can you do that?" Cassian shoved Kiya's shoulder as he smiled, just hard enough to make her laugh, and Bek grinned, scooting closer.

"All day," Kiya said proudly.

"We went through five others before you came to the table," Bek said. Amara wanted to be irritated that Cassian was encouraging them in mischief, but she was too pleased to see them opening up. Of course it would be to someone who was more scoundrel than upstanding citizen. Though his faults were diminishing in her perception as his virtues came to light.

"That's much more useful than weighted dice." Cassian's voice was warm with amusement. The sound of it was growing on her. Now when he spoke a sharp little spark flared in her belly. It was that initial attraction that was always the most enjoyable. The unknown. The wondering if her interest was returned. Wondering if it would amount to anything.

"Play?" Bek said with a grin.

"You'll probably lose even if they don't cheat." Peio eyed the pile of weapons. His hands trembled as he looked away. Amara knew a warrior when she saw one, yet there was anguish swimming in circles around the Suloi. He must have lost his people. Why were his braids gone? Why had Garbi and Izar spoken of him as if he were cursed or diseased and all the others ignored him?

Since the Sundering, Tamar had enjoyed almost uninterrupted peace and prosperity, a situation that made it easy to be complacent. It made it easy to forget the toll exacted by hate and violence, the price that was paid for peace. A price not just paid by soldiers, fighters. But paid by simple people, people who wanted nothing more than to live their lives. Amara had not forgotten, exactly, but she had pushed it aside, and when the Sultana had asked her to join the Circle she had refused. She would not use her power, would never hold dominion over anyone but herself. Yet if this was the alternative…so many lives destroyed.

"Thank you for the vote of confidence, Peio"—Cassian kicked his friend with an outstretched leg—"but I'm feeling Luck today."

"You always are, and you are always wrong." Peio stood. He saw Amara when he did. His face flushed darker beneath its bronze hue and he turned abruptly to stride to the windows. She felt only a little pang of regret for teasing him. It surprised her that his embarrassment still lingered.

Cassian glanced up when his friend moved. First he watched Peio walk to the windows, then looked at Amara. There was no mystery in his eyes. No mistaking the way he looked at her. The way he had looked at her on the beach, in stolen glances as they rode. There was no question if he returned her interest. It was written in his face for anyone who cared to look. As if he had never seen anything he wanted so much. And somehow that was just as exciting as not knowing.

Her breath came short as he rose. He was not the only man to have looked at her so. But he was the only one with eyes the color of the ocean on a summer's day. They would be easy to lose herself in. He would be. A man of warmth, and playfulness. A man with eyes like water. A man who worked for something he believed in. For something outside himself. Instead of ice. Instead of someone who wanted nothing to do with her at all. Instead of someone who locked himself and his heart away from the world.

But Cassian could not offer her what she needed, only the pleasant distraction of what she wanted. As much as she enjoyed casual trysting, she could not afford any distractions, or any chance of complicating matters.

"What have you discovered about the Vex?" Amara asked, crossing to them and trying to distract herself from the heat in his gaze.

"They like knives," Kiya said, "poison, acid." Her voice grew darker. "They have Black Sleep as well."

"I'm not a poison expert." Cassian bent to pick up a leather strap sewn with small cloth loops filled with glass vials, the liquid inside them black and viscous. "Kiya says this is particularly feared in Tamar." An involuntary shudder made Amara take a step back.

"It is illegal in Tamar." But it had been used once that she knew of, against the Sultana. Against Aysel. She did not know by whom, or if they even knew. The palace had kept that secret too close.

The poison had enough water in it to resonate against her magic. Though it did not whisper, as water did, its nature still made itself known. Cold, oozing malice swept around her thoughts, stopping her breath, slowing her heart. A sound escaped her as shadowed fingers closed around her throat. Screams. There were screams in that poison. Lives given to create it. They drowned her in their suffering, in their fear, until she swirled into darkness.

Warm, strong hands closed on her arms, drawing her focus back to the world around her, to Cassian standing in front of her. Untouched by the magic in the poison. She grabbed onto handfuls of his shirt, afraid to be swept away again as he could not be. The poison would not sing to him.

"Look at me," he said, his handsome face tense with concern. Amara drew a deep breath that felt cool and untainted, and nodded. His grounding, magicless touch was exactly what she needed.

Djar stirred behind her on the couch, propping himself on an elbow.

"Amara?" he asked in a groggy voice.

"I've never been near it before," she said to Cassian, and forced a smile for Kiya and Bek, to reassure them. They'd both leapt to their feet, and Kiya's fingers found Bek's hand, clutching it.

"Can it hurt you like this, without touching you?" Cassian asked, searching her face as though he didn't trust that she was fine. Djar sat up completely.

"No. I was not expecting to sense it. I can block it." She did not wish to disconnect from him immediately, his warm resonance that helped center her. Djar and Bek had a similar effect on her, one of the reasons she, unlike many mages, was not superstitious about the presence of voids. She knew they were nothing more than another piece of the Wheel. The shore upon which her magic pushed and pulled, anchors to the corporeal. "Thank you," she said, and was rewarded with a smile, and a glimpse of his dimple.

"You're all right?" he asked. Amara nodded, dropping her gaze to his mouth. What better way to distract herself from evil than to look at something pleasant? He did not have a full mouth, as was usually her preference, but lips in the shape of a recurve, frowning now. Serious. But easy to a smile as well. That half smile faded, the heat coming back into his eyes. His grip on her arms loosened, became a careful pull, inviting her closer.

"I'll take this somewhere else." Kiya retrieved the belt with its vials of poison, giving Amara a sly look. Amara took a step away from Cassian and he let his arms fall to his sides. "Unless we can destroy it? Toss it in the ocean?" Kiya held the belt away from herself, and Bek snatched it out of her hands with a frown. He took it to the other side of the room, setting it on a table in a corner by a second window.

"No. I do not know enough about it to taint the water with it. Wait. We'll take it with us to Tamar, and give it to the Sultana's researcher." This was what he had meant when he said the Republic was experimenting on mages to make weapons against them. They were manufacturing Black Sleep. But how had they learned? Had the Black Sleep meant for the Sultana been brought from the Republic?

"Those Vex." Cassian crouched by the pile of weapons, tapping a pistol with his finger. "They weren't after Suloi, they were after you.

That…" He pointed at the poison as his brow wrinkled, his mouth drawing into a frown. "…was for you."

"Yes," Amara said. His eyes closed, then opened. She had not allowed him to watch her spell casting only to flirt and taunt, but to distract him from the revelation of the magnitude of her power, from thinking about all that could go wrong if the Vex hunting for her inadvertently discovered him and his work with the Suloi. She could not leave the Republic without the Charah. Without Danel and his sister Mirari. And she needed Cassian's help to get to the places she would need to in order to find them.

Cassian draped his arms over his thighs, surveying the weapons again before he rose.

"Every moment we spend with you is a risk to us," he said, his tone carefully neutral. "They will send more." His expression was grave as he looked past her to Peio.

"I will stay," Peio answered whatever silent question had passed between them. A pregnant pause stretched, Cassian's expression growing more troubled with each heartbeat. "And when it is time, I want to go with them."

Amara saw the anguish that flashed across Cassian's face and was quashed. Watched him force a smile and a nod. Watched him hide his feelings, the loneliness that sharpened his features briefly, so he did not burden his friend. She saw Cassian untether Peio with a grin and a shrug, and loved him just a little for it. For the selflessness.

"Then I will help, so you may be gone faster. You do smell up the place." The lie of a grin continued, and Amara glanced to Peio. The water in him saw through Cassian's lie as well, tightening the corners of the Suloi's mouth. "But I have to ask"—Cassian turned that pretend smile on her, the sharpness of his look making the lie obvious—"how those Vex knew you were here?"

"That is a very good question that I cannot answer. I can only speculate that it is because of the politics in Tamar."

"Are you here with Tamar's sanction?" Cassian frowned, staring at her as if doing so hard enough would give him the truth he sought.

"I have no way to prove it to you, if that is what you are asking." Amara glanced to Djar as he shifted, rubbing his hands across his knees as if preparing to stand. "We were sent by the Sultana to see if any Suloi retained creation magic. It died out generations ago." Some might argue that it had been wiped out when death mages were hunted nearly to extinction. The Wheel could not be unbalanced in such a way, without consequences touching across the Houses. Without weakening all magic.

"And what will you do if you find them?" Cassian asked.

"We hope to reestablish their magic in Tamar," Amara said. He didn't need to know about the crop blight, and that information, in the wrong hands, could be seen by the Republic as the perfect first blow in a war. And though there was some connection between them now, she still felt the press of untruths, shadows that veiled, a schism in him she did not trust. Those who fell from the elite usually wanted nothing more than to be back among them. And if that was what Cassian was, could she trust him not to use her secrets to reingratiate himself with his peers?

"Reestablish magic? How? It is nearly dead here…What will they be expected to do?" Cassian asked. The same questions Danel had asked. Why did he care so much about people that were not his own?

"Exist," Amara answered. "If they can perform certain magics they might be asked to, and compensated. But not forced. No mage in Tamar is forced."

Cassian pondered, looking to Peio once again. The Suloi nodded. After a moment Cassian did as well.

"I have not found anything pointing to who purchased Mirari yet," he said.

She would have to send Kiya and Bek back out. They were playing with short time, if she was being hunted.

"I did," Peio said. Cassian frowned. Peio released a breath that puffed his cheeks. "I heard…she's at the villa."

"The villa," Amara said, incredulous. "Aren't there many villas?"

"Only one that matters," Cassian said, with shadows in his voice. "Buschetto. We'll need to know for certain. And if she is there we don't have a way to get in. They'll have extra guards, and the visiting centurions."

"Centurions?" Djar asked.

"Military commanders," Peio said, with a look like he'd chewed lemon rind. He drew a circle on his palm. The gesture captured Amara's interest. That was an Old Sultanate prayer, to the Wheel. Perhaps the Suloi had kept it.

"They're returning from Aklion, in Eannea," Cassian said.

"Uprising?" Amara suggested. How free would he be with that sort of information?

"Usually. They rest over here on the way to Corsyra." Cassian scrunched his face. "And the city is always worse for it. Centurions are worse than sailors."

If he thought them honorless, perhaps she could get more information from him. Such as what their plans were for moving on Tamar, or at least what rumors he had heard. A great benefit of his status as semi-criminal was that he walked within the most fertile sections of the rumor fields. That information, about armies, was less important, at the moment, than the Suloi woman and her help in finding the Earth Charah.

"How do we find out for certain whether Mirari is in Buschetto?"

Cassian dug his hand into his pocket and retrieved his dice, giving them a shake as he considered. "How do you feel about brothels?"

"They are not unfamiliar to me," Amara said, dryly. Djar frowned, and Bek and Kiya snickered together. "What did you have in mind?"

"Suloi women are invariably kept as houseslaves and brothel girls. The Den is the biggest brothel in Haenna. If Mirari isn't there, or hasn't passed through, someone should be able to confirm who purchased her."

"The Den?" Amara had never known a brothel to be named without mention of flowers or silk or the color red, some unsophisticated reference to the parts of a woman most enjoyed behind its doors.

Cassian shifted his hand, sliding his fingers together to place one die atop the tip of his thumb and watching it as he balanced it there. "Lupanar," he said. It was not a word she knew from Republic Trade, so she suspected it was Old Corsan, a language she did not know, the mother tongue of the Republic. "A building populated by she-wolves," he added, flipping the die back into his grip and looking up at her, "can only be called a den."

SIXTEEN

AMARA STOOD WITH HEAD tipped against the glass of the window that overlooked the front garden, watching Bek and Djar, hugging her arms around herself. They'd been sparring for over a candlemark, and it was not going well. Djar's depth perception was gone, his ability to follow and anticipate Bek's movements destroyed. Now Bek moved slowly, suddenly the teacher to a man who had only days ago been a master, and when Djar missed for the dozenth time in a row, he hurled his scimitar across the garden, twisted away from Bek, and strode away. Amara closed her eyes, pain gripping hard hands around her heart and throat, squeezing tears from her eyes and a shuddering sob from her throat. He might as well be dead for what she'd taken from him.

She turned away, and saw Cassian standing in the doorway to the living area. Amara put her back to him and brushed away the tears. Cassian moved toward her as if she might explode in temper if he approached too fast.

"It will come," Cassian said when he reached her side. Neither of them looked at the other, but out the window. Bek retrieved Djar's

173

scimitar. "It is etched in his bones and flesh and sinew. His body knows how, soon his mind will realize that." Cassian tapped his temple.

A few days had done a great deal of good for Cassian's eye. The swelling was gone, though the discoloration remained, darkest on the inside of his eye and around his nose, lightening to shades of yellow and green near his temple. He still looked disheveled, several days' worth of stubble darkening his cheeks and jaw. Could he not find any time to shave and clean up?

"You speak as if you have experience with this." Amara's gaze strayed to the table set between the window where they stood and the next. The items they had stolen from the Vex were carefully arranged across its surface. The weapons were familiar, for the most part. Each man had carried knives, a short sword of the blockier, hacking style the Republic favored, a pistol. There were two rifles. Some things she did not recognize. Hollow, metal cylinders she thought might be meant to be filled with something and thrown. Pouches containing odd powders she was not brave enough to touch or smell, afraid to discover which contained the acid that had injured Djar, or more Black Sleep. They were weapons of fear, torture, subjugation.

"Not personally, but I have seen others," Cassian said. "Why do you blame yourself for his injury?"

"I could have prevented it." She did not wish to tell him more than that, but to at least purge the bare truth to someone helped with some of the pain. Some of the guilt that felt like a leaden weight around her neck.

"At a cost that Djar would have approved of?" He reached across the table to a hard leather tube and lifted it, unbuckling the cap and opening it. He peered inside.

"The cost was mine to pay."

"I doubt he sees it that way, considering he jumped the height of three men to get to you before those men hauled you off," Cassian muttered. "It is my general experience that men like Djar do not cast their lots in with people they don't find worthy." He reached to the table to retrieve a curling piece of parchment. They'd discovered it among the other things. A drawing, of her. Words proclaiming her a dangerous rogue mage, written in Republic Trade, scrolled across the bottom.

Apparently, she was in the Republic without sanction from the Sultan, which she supposed was not entirely untrue, since it was his daughter that gave the order. If what Ihsan had suggested was correct, she could only imagine this missive to be the work, by proxy, of the Grand Vizier. How else would they have known what she looked like? There was nothing about it that would serve as usable evidence, but she would take it back to the Sultana nonetheless. It, along with the small, tattered piece of paper bearing some kind of code might prove imminently useful in condemning the Grand Vizier to the darkest of prisons.

She had not taken a personal interest in the Grand Vizier before, because his machinations had not affected her personally. Anger warmed the spaces inside her. If he wanted to play games with her life and those she cared for, she'd douse his fire for good. The Sultana's hands might be tied, but hers were not.

"Are you dangerous?" Cassian asked, in a manner which she suspected he thought sounded lighthearted.

"I can be." Amara took the paper from him and set it on the table. "But only to those who make themselves my enemies."

"You are too beautiful to be dangerous." Cassian made an expression that was half smile, half grimace. He made it often, as if the words he said were forced out of him. Or he was baiting her. The deeper smile that appeared and disappeared confirmed he was teasing. She did appreciate his candor.

"There are many beautiful creatures that are also dangerous," Amara said. "You have seen a great deal of me, and that is all you inferred?" Amara looked at him sidelong, smiling a little. Cassian did not return the look, but he did flush.

"You did not appear to be hiding any weapons," he said. No, Amara thought as her smile faded. Her weapons were so hidden even she could occasionally pretend they were not there.

"It is a rare person who has never been a slave that works to free them. I find that admirable," Amara said, to turn the subject and her thoughts from more troubling topics. They had never been truly alone together. She was curious about him. It had been easy to judge him harshly, in the beginning. A smuggler, a thief, a gambler. Disheveled, evidence of brawling obvious on his face, disrespectful. Her own expectations had allowed him to fool her, almost completely. In truth, he had since demonstrated himself to be selfless, respectful, and adaptable. That he had managed to lie to her was interesting enough, that he was handsome was more so, that he still remained a mystery to her, fascinating. She did so enjoy a puzzle.

"No," Cassian said. "I'm not admirable. But the work is meaningful to me."

"It is rare to find someone who works toward what is meaningful to them, instead of only waxing poetic about what needs to change."

He shrugged the words away, shoving his hands into his pockets. Below them, Djar had returned to the garden, and took his sword from Bek. They began again.

"See?" Cassian said.

"You don't understand what he was. What he has been his entire life. This is no different than losing an arm."

"I hope our past is not all that we are," Cassian replied, quietly. "Or there isn't much hope for me." His smile was pretend. Amara missed the real one. With the dimple.

"Is your past so much worse than your present?" At least he had never been subjugated. A privilege he surely understood.

"Yes."

"That is why you work to free the Suloi," Amara said. "For your past."

He turned, leaning his shoulder against the frame of the window. She liked how expressive his eyes were. That she could read them as she did water. They always told the truth, no matter what the rest of him was saying. In this moment, he was hiding the answer to her statement behind a look of curiosity.

"You aren't like any woman I've ever met," he said. Amara tsked. There were not enough counting beads in the world to keep number of the times a man had said that to her.

"No," she said, "I am exactly the same as the women you've met."

"I've offended you," he said, bemused, pulling his hands from his pockets.

"Too many think it is compliment to elevate one at the expense of others. I find it repugnant. If you cannot compliment me for something that is mine, instead of taking away from other women, then do not bother at all."

Cassian tipped his head slightly back, as if she'd screamed at him. "You want creative compliments?"

"I do not want compliments at all, if you have nothing genuine to say," she said impatiently.

"I could try again?" he suggested. Amara exhaled through her nose. He twisted away from the window, putting his back against the wall. His mouth wasn't smiling, but his eyes were. Her irritation fizzled. "I could…" He tipped his head as if he were thinking. "…compliment your eyes? Or your lovely hands." Now his mouth began to turn up.

Amara folded her arms and raised an eyebrow.

"Are there any compliments you have not received?" He reached to her, pinching the pale green fabric of her stola near her waist. Catching her gaze with his, he gave a minute tug. Amara allowed him to urge her to his side. He released the fabric and circled her waist with his hand, pressing his fingers into the dip of her low back as he faced her, still leaning his weight against the wall.

"Very few," she said, interested in leaning against him, but standing still and straight instead.

He tipped his head closer, and she tensed, bringing her hands between them to stop him, pressing to his chest. She could not. Not with this one. No matter how attractive the man was, or how very nice he felt beneath his shirt. Or how unreasonably charming the dimple was. She did not mix sexual and emotional attraction. She did not trust the two together. All magic woke to strong emotion. And what could be stronger than making love with someone one cared for? And she could care for him. Truly care for someone that gave of himself to others who needed.

He did not move his body closer, or change anything except the tilt of his head so his mouth was closer to her ear. He followed the slope of her neck with his thumb. A simple touch that caused a visceral surge in her body. "This curve"—his thumb continued up to outline her jaw to her chin—"is perfect. I want to paint you." His thumb slid over her chin and throat to rest against the hollow between her collarbones.

Her hands slipped down, her head turning partially to his in surprise. He lifted his head away, only enough that he could meet her eyes. He lowered his hand. There was a fleck of brown in his right eye. A seed, they sometimes called it in Menei. Tamar would consider it a sign of someone balanced. Favored by the Wheel.

"Paint me?" she said, breathless. "Are you an artist as well as a smuggler, gambler, and thief?" She had met many artists in Narfour. None quite like Cassian.

"I dabble. I believe in diversifying my talents."

Amara laughed. Cassian took full advantage of the opportunity to flatten his hand against her back and pull her against him. Amara went willingly, despite the angry little voice of reason in the back of her mind. He wanted to kiss her, she could see it, the heat in his tan skin and pale eyes, the way he kept darting looks to her mouth, how his fingers were pressing, digging softly against her spine. And she wanted him to. He felt so incredibly good against her, hard where she was soft.

"You have to be able to stand still for long periods," he said, "no matter what."

"Oh?" She worked her hands up between them, to his shoulders, then slid her hands down to his elbows, pulling herself more firmly against him. There was some safety for her in his lack of magic. There was nothing there to wake hers, to antagonize or empower it. For now. "I have never been painted."

"I promise it won't hurt," he said with enough innuendo to drown her. "We can take as long as you like."

"What if I don't like it?"

"I'll keep trying until you do." He tipped his head a fraction closer, sending a surge of anticipation over her mouth. No. *No.*

"I can be very demanding." She tightened her hands on his arms to quell the desire to pet him, feel his shape beneath his shirt. A tendril of magic uncoiled in her belly. Like a cobra raising its head.

"I have no doubt, Princess." He closed his eyes briefly. When he opened them he skimmed his hand down her back. "Let me kiss you?"

Amara lifted her hand to his stubbled face, laying her thumb over his mouth. Softer than it looked, it was an easy thing to imagine his lips against her skin. Everywhere. Her breath left her harshly. "I cannot be distracted from my purpose."

"If you change your mind," Cassian said, with a broody, lusting look in his eyes, "I will be more than happy to oblige you."

"Go," she strangled out, stepping back. She curled her hands against her belly, as if it would help her put her desire, and her magic, back to sleep.

"I'll come back tonight, to go to the Den, as we planned." He dropped his hands and his gaze, shoving away from the wall and away. He jogged down the stairs, and wounded silence hung in his absence.

Amara whirled to the window again, to watch Djar and Bek. Kiya had joined them, with Peio, who had taken to the twins, it seemed. When Cassian strode down the path toward the gate, Peio broke away, running to catch up to him.

SEVENTEEN

AMARA EMERGED FROM HER room after dressing for her jaunt to the brothel. Kiya followed, giving a final tug to the stola. Cassian sat with his back to her, on the floor beside Djar, who sat on the couch. Danel was across from them on the other couch, leaning forward over a chessboard set on a small table between them. It pleased Amara to see them both engaged. Djar had never been one for extraneous conversation, but his silence since their return was different. Brooding. Danel was often lost to the haze of his pain medicine half the day.

Bek and Peio were missing. Presumably downstairs, in the interior garden practicing archery. Amara had been there when Bek, uncharacteristically shy, had asked Peio to teach him and Peio had enthusiastically agreed. He had been just as willing to teach Kiya, who could speak of little else since. For all that they were experienced, Kiya and Bek were still young. Not even three Cycles yet. Amara was very happy to see them engaging beyond her and Djar.

"Be careful." He kissed Amara's cheek. "Or they might try to keep you there."

"They could not afford to employ me." Amara smiled and Kiya returned it with her sly grin. In Menei, Amara had commanded sums equal to a princess's bride price, just to dance for those who paid. She made a thoughtful noise, looking at the girl who was as close to a little sister as Amara would ever have, and touched her face, then stroked a hand over her halo of buoyant black curls. "Tomorrow I'll cut your hair," she said.

Kiya covered it well, but she was always anxious when Amara went to the brothels in Narfour. Amara had been doing it ever since she arrived in Narfour, looking for women, and sometimes men, that she might be able to help or mentor. Amara was not certain what Kiya feared about it, she never said it out loud. But Amara always tried to give her special care following, so she would not forget she was loved and would not be abandoned.

"And the Old Lion's," Kiya said in a fake whisper. Djar didn't straighten from his hunch over the chessboard, but his good eye focused on them and he clicked his tongue in admonishment, which brought both women a smile.

Cassian turned, looking up at Amara over the couch. Meeting his piercing blue gaze again gave her a pleasant little jolt, a stroke of heat across her chest. They had not seen each other since that morning, when she'd been so very close to giving in to her desire to kiss him. If he was resentful of her denial, it did not show now. Some men could be terribly sensitive about rejection, no matter the reason. That he seemed to understand made him all the more attractive.

Cassian stood and Djar did the same.

"I'm coming," Djar said.

"No," Amara said. "You have done enough. I want you to rest, because I may have need of you once we find where she is."

He scowled, but sank back to his seat, and Kiya plopped onto the couch next to him, slipping her arms through his and laying her head against his shoulder.

"If we are not back by sunrise, you may assume that we are in need of rescue." Amara gestured to Cassian as she spoke, who followed her downstairs and out to the front garden.

"Are you certain you want to do this?" Cassian asked, jogging to catch up to her. "There can be a great deal of unpleasantness inside, the darkest shadows of the city."

"I am not a stranger to the dark, Cassian. I wonder what you think I am, that you make assumptions like that." Amara raised an eyebrow at him then looked away as she stepped onto the road in front of the villa.

"I can only guess by what I have observed. Though the more I learn about you, the more I grow intrigued."

"What have you observed?" She thought about sliding her arm through his, but any touch at all was encouragement for them both, little steps taken toward the release of all inhibition.

"I thought you must be a noble, a princess of some great warlord in Menei who is accustomed to getting everything she wants and having men throw themselves at her feet."

Amara laughed. "If that is an example of your ability to judge people then it is no wonder you fell so easily for Bek and Kiya's dice game."

"But these…" He lifted a hand behind her, stroking the backs of his knuckles down her spine, where the marks on her back were concealed by the stola. He dropped his hand to his side. Amara wanted his touch, but not that one. A sorrowful, pitying touch. She had come to grips with the marks, the trauma of each. Strikes of the hammer that forged her.

"I have been both," Amara said.

"If I ask about your past, will you tell me? Or will you keep your secrets?"

"You have seen me naked, is that not secret enough?" Amara teased. He looked at her from the corners of his eyes, mouth curving. Amara tugged her gaze away.

"I have found that the most interesting secrets women keep are not the ones hidden by their clothes."

More observant than he would have her believe. It seemed his brutish bumbling was more act than she had realized. How intriguing. Perhaps a few of her secrets as bait would urge him to reveal his own.

"I am the daughter of a Meneian warlord, an accident of magic. Both my parents had some little air in their blood, from long before the Sundering War. It was enough to tempt the Wheel." She held down the upwelling of memory, the force of the horror that accompanied the memory of her young, fragile self, and continued. "My mother and I fled after my father was murdered and his commanders attempted to sell me for the prestige, and fortune, it would bring them. We ran for nearly a decade." There was more to their escape than that. More violence. More…of her own truth. But only Djar knew all of her story.

Those six Turns had been torture for her mother, but for Amara the memories were good ones, because her mother was in them. They were family, of a sort. She had believed she was safe in her mother's care, but that was a child's understanding of the world. That nothing lay beyond their small sphere of existence.

"When I was twelve, we were caught. My mother was killed, and I was indentured." The image of her mother's death still fueled her nightmares. And when the memories came to haunt her, they stayed for days or turns, and she never slept with anyone else while they tormented her, because she could not bear the touch of another's hands, like the hands that held her back as they executed her mother. Neither did she wish for anyone to hear her screams, to know her at her weakest. She was not fragile or weak anymore.

Cassian remained silent and somber, listening but not reacting beyond capturing her arm through his. He turned her hand into his and stroked his thumb in circles across her palm. It was unexpectedly soothing, and banished some of the emotions that surfaced. Nothing could have made her suspect that he was a man to whom giving comfort came so easily. He never hesitated, when she was afraid on the bridge, when Djar's wound pained her, when the poison had overtaken her, when Peio said he would leave, and now, when shadows that he could not see plagued her.

The rest was impossible to tell without revealing things she did not wish to, so she skipped it. The palace of the King in Nasiye changed hands six times while she lived there, and she was reindentured, her debts tallied in her skin, by each new man and one woman, to sit the throne. "I fled the harem a few years after I arrived, and I took work in brothels until I could pay my way on a ship bound for Tamar. When I arrived I found a place for myself in the Weavers' Guild in Narfour, and have since made myself into a Master Merchant. And when I return to Tamar, having completed this task for the Sultana, I will be betrothed to the Sehzade." That was what she wanted, what she was working for. Once she was at the palace, she, and the others, would be out of reach of harm.

"That ice mage?" Cassian said in a voice strangled by incredulity. "The one you called out of the ocean?"

"I did not call him out of the ocean." Amara laughed. "I called his power to mine. But yes, he is the Sehzade, and you are astute, for calling him an ice mage. That is exactly what he is."

"I am not astute, I was staring at your body and dying a slow, tortured death imagining the things I'd like to do to you, and that man magicked ice all over your skin. I think it is not such a great logical leap."

"So bold with the truth." Amara stifled a smile, enjoying the bloom of heat in her belly at his words. What had he imagined doing to her? "Subtlety is not a game you enjoy?"

"I enjoy it very much." Cassian stopped, urging her to face him. Amara complied, looking up at him. "But you stripped naked before me, which was not subtle. And any subtlety I might have been capable of has been buried beneath my memory of your skin and shape." His hands curved behind her arms, not pulling, barely touching. Always so polite. She suspected he understood what it meant to her to be grabbed, held, or forced to anything. The warmth in her belly spread wider.

"I warned you." Amara struggled to keep her gaze from his mouth.

"You taunted me," he said. "And continue to. Which is an enjoyable, if also confusing game."

"How can I help myself, when it makes you look at me as you are now?" Amara sank into the building ache of desire. The last season had seen her too busy for lovers, and the lack was only highlighted now, by her internal promise not to engage with Cassian this way. But he was entirely too handsome, the messy tousle of his dark hair and the shadow of his unshaven jaw only adding to the allure of him.

"But you told me to go." His voice grew huskier, a timbre she would have liked to hear more of. "When I wanted to kiss you. And now I find out you are betrothed to a prince. So you really will be a princess, and I am afraid I cannot compete with a man who commands ice, and a throne." His expression mixed wryness with regret, suggesting there were things unsaid that would change the meaning of his words. No, he did not command magic. Or stand in line for a crown. He had no power whatsoever, that she could see. But still he made a difference, still he tried, gave what he did have to help others. She could not say the same for Ihsan.

And Cassian noticed her. Saw her. Wanted her.

Amara forced herself to step back and turn away. None of that mattered. It was not a competition. Ihsan had what she needed, and that was the end of it.

Cassian walked beside her in silence. He led them down a side street. After a few steps he paused, his face drawing tight. Several guards stood at the outlet of the street onto another, speaking with two men dressed much as Cassian was. Shirts that laced at the throat and sleeves, pants, tall boots, and pistols. The conversation seemed friendly, as though they knew each other and had just happened together. But Cassian turned abruptly onto another street, without explanation, and took them through another series of turns and side streets.

"I have not associated with criminals since I left Menei," Amara said when she grew tired of the silence. "I cannot decide if I find it exciting or tiresome."

"Does it matter that I am a criminal with a heart of gold?" Cassian asked, stopping at the intersection of a side street with the one they had turned from originally to look both ways before stepping onto it once again. They were moving closer to the city center, where the buildings became more ornate. She could see the shadowed outline of the Basilica to the west, a fat hen sitting on the nest of the city. It was a stunning building, if one could overlook the domination and subjugation it stood in celebration of.

"Would you like to play a game?" Amara asked. Traipsing through alleys and side streets had given her time to ponder him and his actions, and she thought she had come to a conclusion.

"Why do I feel the better answer would be to say no?" he said.

"A guessing game. I heard you tell Danel that you are continuing your parents' work. You implied they were gone. On the bridge you told me you gambled because you liked to feel something, anything." Amara looked up at him, but he did not look back, and he had lengthened his stride, almost as if he were trying to escape her. "There is something in your past you feel you must atone for. I might guess it has something to do with your parents."

"I knew there was a reason I avoided women with intelligence," Cassian muttered.

"Mm. Are you certain they were not avoiding you?" she asked and he tossed her an amused look over his shoulder. No, she doubted very many women could resist the charm of that dimple and those bright blue eyes. "So, am I correct?" Now her curiosity was stoked, as well as her ardor. She was not the only one with secrets.

"I cannot atone. I do what I do because I despise the Republic and enjoy causing it and its minions vexation."

"I see." She believed that, to some degree. Not as noble as she had hoped. But the idea of nobility, selflessness, those were not traits one attributed to themselves. They were labels given by others. A person always knew too much about themselves and their own motivations to call themselves noble, or selfless.

Why did he despise the Republic? His own people? She didn't ask, because he had closed his expression and tightened his mouth, walking with new tension. So she walked beside him in silence.

EIGHTEEN

"I**S THAT IT, THERE?**" Amara pointed to the end of the road, where a large building sprawled at an angle, and a single red-painted lantern hung on a post at the corner. Below it, a marble sculpture of a buxom woman draped with a cloth from shoulder to hip held a flower in cupped hands. Beside her stood a carved wolf.

Cassian nodded. The silence stretched between them again, as Cassian cast her a few looks.

"There are several girls here that I know who may be able to tell me something of use. The person we need, though, is Antonis."

"Oh?" Amara said in curiosity, and blinked at him. Cassian cleared his throat and his gaze sliced away from hers.

"Not...I don't know them that way."

"I see. And you are certain this Antonis will be here?" she asked. Cassian's eyes tightened at the corners, and he shoved his hands into his pockets. "What do we need from him?"

"He'll be here," Cassian said. "We need a way into the...his villa. Buschetto. I believe you will be more successful in that endeavor than me." He gave her a sideways look. "I cannot imagine he will not find you just as charming as I do." A flash of anger tightened his mouth, then he relaxed and smiled. "I will meet you there, if we are separated." He pointed to a shadowed alley across the street from the brothel, one stacked with a variety of detritus that would make hiding easier.

"Are you going to tell me what is between you and this Antonis?" Amara grabbed his wrist when he started forward. "You owe me a secret or two, in exchange for mine."

"I owe you?" He pulled his arm back, dragging her to him, and clutched a handful of the stola at her waist so he could step against her. He was a perfect height, his chin level with her forehead, so she would not need to do anything but tip her head back to kiss him. "Which secrets am I indebted for?" He dipped his head to her neck, his mouth close enough that his breath sent a shudder through her that stopped her thoughts for the space of several heartbeats as she hoped he would come even closer. "Your body, or your past?"

Amara lifted a hand to his face, turning it so she could look into his eyes, and oh, the heat of him. Those dark brows and bright eyes and that broody want furrowing his brow. If his expression alone could kindle such liquid heat inside her, she could only imagine what his hands could do.

"All of them." Amara sensed the change in his focus, from want to demand, his body looming closer, his expression relaxing. She was going to have to endeavor to keep a room between them at all times, or she would be unable to keep her hands off him.

A smile broke slowly across his mouth, revealing his dimple. She could be a complete fool over that dimple, there was no doubt. It made her feel like a silly, smitten girl.

"There are women in the Den who will tie a man to a post and torture him. Have you considered that as an occupation? I have a feeling you'd be very good at it." He straightened.

"What makes you think I haven't?"

Cassian appeared startled and laughed before he led her across the street and under the red glow of the lantern. Amara pulled the door open and stepped into the dim, smoky chaos of the interior.

He stayed close enough at her back that she could feel his movement. She waited just inside the door for her eyes and thoughts to adjust to the visual chaos, quelling the desire to cough. Streamers of some kind of smoke slipped through the air. They stood in the corner of a columned arcade that surrounded a central seating area that was open all the way to the ceiling of the second floor, filled with long couches and cushions for lounging. Bodies twined and writhed there, ringed and adorned with the pale smoke, turned pink by the odd red light. The smoke was cloying, and Amara suspected it might have hallucinogenic properties, if taken directly. She could hear soft murmurings and more enthusiastic uttering, most of those originating from above.

"You're all right?" Cassian stepped around her.

"I am practically home," Amara said.

"Cassian!" a woman's voice called from nearby. Amara squinted, peering around Cassian to see a young woman, with golden hair made into ringlets about her bared shoulders, come weaving through a quartet of people who had taken up position in the arcade. Hair that pale was just as rare in Tamar as blue eyes. A trait of the most northern of people, where the sun was not as generous as it was in places that bordered the sea. As she drew close, Amara saw she was not as young as she originally thought; the dim light and a liberal application of powder did much to hide the signs of her age.

"Moina." Cassian kissed her cheek. "Amara, this is Moina. She runs things." Cassian took a step back, so that Moina and Amara faced each other.

"I did not think women owned businesses or property here," Amara said, interested. Her interest was not returned, sadly. Moina made it obvious she did not care for Cassian bringing in his own female company.

"I do not own it, I run it. Are you looking for work?" The warm greeting she'd had for Cassian was a distant memory in the tone she used for Amara.

"I'm looking for a friend." Amara adjusted her posture, slightly, allowing her straight back to relax, and her hands to grip the fabric of her stola, and turned her gaze down. "We were brought to the city together, and I haven't seen her since."

"When?" Moina glanced from Amara to Cassian.

"The last auction." Amara wrung her hands, and aimed a glance about the room that she styled as shy and overwhelmed.

"I've only two new girls from then," Moina said. "If they aren't busy, you can ask them. Come with me." She held out a hand, and Amara took it, glancing triumphantly at Cassian as she stepped toward Moina. His gaze followed her movement, his lips pursed as he folded his arms over his chest.

"Cassian, behave," Moina warned.

"I always do. Is Antonis about?" He offered her the fake, charming grin. The one Amara did not like.

"The north room," Moina said. "Stay away from him, please. He's already being a menace."

Amara witnessed the change in Cassian's expression. Cold fury that burned and died, its smoldering remains lingering in his eyes as he glanced quickly about the room.

"Just…stay there," Moina said as she tugged Amara away, past the two women and two men that giggled and teased near the place the arcade turned an angle. Moina led her down the arcade, walking at a pace that allowed her to greet people, smiling and laughing as she passed them.

"How long have you run things here?" Amara was careful to keep her tone deferent and reserved. The women in power in brothels were only precariously so, and it often made them quick to put down any behavior that judged as challenging.

"A decade," Moina sighed. "Or a lifetime. However you mark your time."

"Has it been kind to you?" Amara asked as Moina turned through an open doorway set with thin, gauzy curtains. Amara couldn't tell the color of the fabric, the red lanterns shone ruby light over everything. It did make it feel like a cave. A den. Aptly named. Were the women she-wolves, as Cassian had called them? Or perhaps that was just the Republic's name for them. Naming them dangerous and wild so that the men who came could act that way without feeling like monsters.

"Gods no. But it is better than being owned by one of the big houses." They ascended the stairs and stepped onto the balcony that wrapped the lower room. The view from above was revealing, distanced as it was from the chaos. Amara paused to look, watching the activity below.

A rainbow of people, though at first glance she saw no Meneians. Northerners, the duskier skin that might belong to Suloi, or Odokan, or even someone from Tamar. A couple kissing slowly on a couch, the woman straight-backed and stiff, the man curving himself over and around her in an attempt to coax her to her back. Another couple beyond them, ensconced in a pile of cushions, a bit further along in their dance, with the woman's dress pulled down off one shoulder, a breast revealed. She had a dazed look, one Amara recognized. Drugs of some kind. Whatever made the smoke perhaps. It had the same smell as Danel's medicine. Poppy. She had seen it used in Menei, though it was less common than other drugs.

"First time in a brothel?" Moina joined Amara at the railing to the balcony.

"Yes," Amara lied. "Are these women slaves?" She had noted that, unlike the people in the auction, these did not wear collars.

"They are," Moina said. "This is one of the only places they can earn money, hope to buy freedom."

Perverse, Amara had always thought, that a profession that took so much of one's personal freedom and self away was also one of the only where they might buy back their own lives. It was the same in Menei, and Tamar, though slavery had been outlawed there long before the Sultana took her father's seat.

"Some girls like to watch." Moina eyed Amara as she looked down at the people below. Amara shook her head. At the harem, where she was first sent after she was captured as a girl, she hadn't minded watching. No one was allowed to touch her there, and she'd been a teenager in a body that was awakening. Watching had been titillating. But once she'd left, and turned in desperation to the brothels, that had ended her interest in pleasure for years. She'd been the dead-eyed girl, and the one reluctant to be put on her back, and seen her friends be the same.

Now she knew the joys and pleasures of choice, of control, and these scenes did nothing for her but bring sadness and a sense of futility. She wanted out of this land as soon as she could. A sparkling, marble and gold metropolis, built on the backs of the conquered.

"I only want to find my friend," Amara said. She hoped, for both Danel and Mirari's sake, that she had not ended up a prostitute. From just her short interactions with the Suloi, Amara could see they were a prideful people, and from Peio's reaction to her nakedness, one that appreciated the right of a woman to her body and her desires. There could be a great deal of damage done to the mind of a Suloi woman thrust into the depravity of a slave brothel.

"Come on then. How did you come to meet Cassian?" Moina asked with a bit too much interest.

"I was lost, and encountered him on the street, and when he offered to help me we began talking." It seemed plausible enough, given Cassian's propensity for offering help.

"Ah. His latest stray." Moina laughed. "Don't get your hopes up. He rises and falls, and you'll find him in some gutter days from now, devoid of money and cares. Or he'll simply disappoint you." She turned into another room, this one without door or curtain. Two women sat together on the floor. One of them was tending the second, whose lip was split and face red. Amara's curiosity about Moina's declarations about Cassian were forgotten at the sight.

"What happened?" Moina asked, with not a hint of concern in her voice.

"Antonis." The one tending the injured girl dabbed a rag against the bloody split in her friend's lip. "He's been through half the Den, and nobody can do anything but irritate him." Her gaze strayed to Amara and lit with interest.

"Are you a new girl?" she asked. She was pretty, truly young, perhaps not more than eighteen, Kiya's age. She had the look, and lilting accent, of a Suloi. Her sable hair was long, braided away from her temples and the rest left loose down her bared back, completely different than Garbi and Izar's, though she shared the same deep bronze skin. Her friend, with the injury, was Northern, like Moina, her hair flaxen, her skin almost blue pale and seemed luminescent in the red light.

"I'm looking for my friend," Amara said.

"Where is Antonis? Is anybody waiting on him?" Moina asked, sharply. "Abene, you're done for the night. No one here is going to want to look at that mouth."

"Yes, Mistress." The Northern girl's voice quavered. "Kattalin is with Antonis."

"You ask them your questions then be gone, before someone takes a liking to you and gets something for nothing," Moina said to Amara, then left. Amara watched her go, then knelt beside Abene.

"May I look?" she asked, softly, and Abene turned her face obediently toward her. It looked to her like the man had struck Abene with the back of his hand, her lip had split against her teeth. A charmer, this Antonis. No wonder Cassian so obviously disliked him. "Do you have willow bark, or mugwort creams here?" Amara took the wet cloth from the other. The two of them leaned in, and their fear and misery permeated the room as thickly as the smoke filled the downstairs.

Amara pressed gently against Abene's mouth, and Abene gave her head a little shake.

"I will bring you some tomorrow," Amara said. "Are you all right? Did he do anything else to you?" There was a dark star in her heart, burning like night, that wanted to purge all her memories, pain, and their upwelling on this man that held court over the helpless. Perhaps the Wheel would give her a chance.

Tears sprang into Abene's eyes, and she tipped forward. Amara wrapped her arms around the girl's frail shoulders and held her as she cried. The other girl moved around them on her knees and stroked Abene's back.

"What is your name?" Amara asked her.

"Sorne. And this is Abene," she said. "You said you were looking for your friend. Who is she?"

"Mirari Garai," Amara said. Abene sniffled against Amara's shoulder, and sat up. Sorne handed her the cloth, and Abene used it to wipe her face and nose.

"I know Mirari. But she isn't here." Sorne's expression pinched. "That man. Antonis. He owns her."

Amara nodded, and stroked some of Abene's hair behind her ear. The villa then. Just as Peio had said. "What does Antonis look like?"

"He's easy enough to spot," Abene said. "He's the only one dressed as a senator and acting like an emperor, when he is neither. He always takes the north room."

Amara nodded and reached out, touching Abene's hand. "What does your freedom cost?" she asked. She had spent too much already, depleting her purse considerably to find Cassian and keep herself hidden.

"Ten years or one thousand aur. They say we can make it off tips, but I've not met anyone who has done it." Sorne combed her fingers through Abene's pale hair.

"Thank you for your help. I will bring medicine for you tomorrow." Amara stood.

Abene laughed, giving Amara an incredulous look. "Why?" she asked.

"Because I can," Amara said, and left.

She returned downstairs, keeping an eye out for Moina, who she wished to avoid. She made her way around the arcade to a wide arched doorway. Even before she reached it she suspected it was the right location. There was a great deal of noise coming from within, some laughter, most of it talking. Amara glanced inside. A long low table dominated the space, with squat, cushioned couches lined against the walls. Jugs of wine and scattered goblets covered the table, along with long-forgotten plates of food.

There were a number of men and women in various states of repose, standing, sitting, lounging, trysting. In just her brief glance Amara saw breasts, chests, buttocks, and one half-aroused cock. None of those interested her, but the scene unfolding halfway between the door and the table did.

Cassian stood there, facing off with another man, who was dressed in a white cloth draped at opposing angles over his body, hemmed in embroidery, and sleeveless, cinched with an ornate belt embellished in blue and gold. A woman cowered behind Cassian, and Amara made the guess that it was Kattalin, the name Abene had mentioned to Moina.

"...so nice of you to make an appearance in public, Senator Haydar," Antonis sneered. Amara had been about to step into the room, but paused, letting the title soak into her consciousness. Now that was interesting, wasn't it? Was he being facetious?

"Back off," Cassian snapped. Some of the others in the room were watching the exchange with interest, like it was staged just for their benefit.

"Still playing like mommy and daddy, are we? Why don't we discuss this before the Assembly, hmm? I'll have the guards escort you."

Amara ducked into the room, skirting the wall, past a woman and man entwined and oblivious on one of the couches. The woman's clothes were piled on the floor. Amara snatched up the piece of cloth on top, a diaphanous piece of yellow silk, and approached Antonis from behind. Cassian saw her, and his expression contorted from anger at Antonis to horror at seeing her. Antonis saw the look as well, and started to turn. Amara twisted the cloth in her hands and slung it across his eyes, wrapping the rest around her hand to pull it taut, and pressing herself against Antonis' back.

"I was told," Amara murmured against his ear when he went still, "that you were not being treated well." She slipped around him in a circle, letting the weight of her breasts brush against his back and arm, then press against his chest. "A pity," she crooned, slipping the cloth free of his eyes when his face turned down toward hers.

He examined her, his grey gaze raking her face and hair, and finding something that pleased him, he said, "Are you here to rectify that?"

She slid her hands up his chest, and circled them around his neck, letting her head tip back to bare her throat. "Would you like me to?" she asked, and when his attention threatened to stray back to Cassian, Amara touched her fingers against the thin, hard line of his mouth, and dragged her lower lip through her teeth. His gaze fixed on the motion.

"I think I might," he said.

Amara smiled, and slipped away from him, striding to the table and stepping onto it. Antonis turned to watch her, his expression lit with intrigue. She did not need to have heard the others speak of him to see the cruel tilt of his mouth and the edginess of temper in the set of his shoulders. Cassian remained near him, though the girl had shown sense enough to escape. Amara frowned at him as she removed her sandals and tossed them toward Antonis. Cassian frowned back.

"If he isn't paying…" Amara suggested to Antonis, and indicated Cassian with a lift of her chin. She unwound the fabric from around her shoulders and waist and set it aside so only the stola remained. It was still heavy, baggy, and cumbersome, but it would have to do.

"A good point." Antonis grabbed Cassian's elbow, who jerked away from his touch. Cassian slid Amara a furious look before he stalked away. She'd deal with him later.

Amara had not danced in such a long time, but dancing belonged to the Second House, movement to water. One of the many reasons she had been so coveted in Menei. The music came from the main atrium, and was faint in this room, but enough to mark her pace by. She began, her body finding a rhythm she knew, her hips drawing slow, sensuous circles. Amara fell into the memory of Nasiye, where she had danced for kings, and warlords, and countless others. She claimed the entire table as her stage, circling its length and edge, spinning and twisting, drawing the suggested shape of a lover with the movements of her arms and hands. The song she danced to had beats that allowed for quick shakes and suggestive undulations of her hips.

Antonis made his way around the table as he watched, and sat at the head while Amara twisted on the opposite end. During one slow spin, she saw Cassian lurking in the doorway, and was both exasperated and pleased. But if he did not have enough sense to leave in the opportunity she offered, then he deserved all the punishment he got. She danced for his benefit for a moment, undulating her hips in a slow trace of the figure eight, then twice much faster, allowing the movement to flow up through her belly and torso.

In Menei she would have been wearing only bits of ephemeral silk and gauze, bells and coins to emphasize her movement. But the strength of the dance was not in what it revealed, but what it suggested.

Hints and glances, that was what people wanted. She traced her hands up her own silhouette, met Cassian's gaze briefly. She turned, making her way toward Antonis in stuttered steps, each accompanied by a change in direction of her hips.

He watched her come, with a smile, his head tipping back as she stood over him. Amara spun slowly once more, then bent backwards, circling her hands around each other as she bent, and bent, and, just before her head touched the table behind her, she lowered herself to her knees. It laid her body, arched upward, out in front of him, a move designed to make a man feel as though he were being offered something.

It was profoundly uncomfortable, and difficult to hold. But Amara did so as the others applauded, and as Antonis ran one hand up her right thigh, over her belly, then over and around her, lifting her and pulling her off the table and into his lap. Amara caught a glance at the doorway and saw Cassian had finally left, to her relief.

"Where have you been all this time?" Antonis asked, his hand sliding up her body to grip her throat. "I have never seen you before." It was not a hard grip, but it left no doubt that he was a man who enjoyed control. Too much control. There had been a time when such a grip would have sent dread through her, but Amara had left that helpless girl and those fears long behind her. He had no control over her, and never could. She was free.

She smiled at him, lifting an arm up and around so she could stroke her hand over his hair. There were small things she'd learned, as she had taught herself to enjoy pleasure with the men she chose. She did not entangle her fingers in his hair, or slip her nails up his neck. Those were intimate touches, given for mutual pleasure. To keep those separate were lessons she had taught herself as she shed her former self.

"I am new." Amara roamed his face with her gaze. He was perhaps a bit older than Cassian. His dark hair held the barest hint of grey.

"And I was only just told you were displeased. I'd like to make certain that doesn't happen again," she said. "What can I do for you?"

He smiled, a hand stroking down her back, the other finding its way under the hem of her stola and to her thigh. "My mood has already improved."

"They say you are a senator," Amara murmured, dipping her head to nuzzle the spot below the hook of his jaw. "I do not know what that means. In Menei we don't have them."

"I've heard Menei is a place of heathens," he said. In Menei, there were heathens and scholars. Poets and mathematicians. The best and the worst of humankind. Just as there were in any other place.

Antonis suddenly grabbed her hair, pulling her head back as he adjusted, then directed her attention to his right arm and chest, bared by the wrap of cloth. Amara complied, ignoring the anger of his treatment as she curved her hand over his shoulder and bit his skin, as she imagined he liked. He made a pleased sound in his throat. She slipped her hand beneath the cloth, stroking his chest, letting her mind wander. He had the soft physique of someone for whom everything was done, flaccid muscle kept shapely only by his relative youth.

"I've heard that senators have the most beautiful homes." Amara allowed her voice to reflect awe, shifting on his lap, letting her thigh brush the hard evidence of his arousal.

"Indeed. My family owns the largest villa in Haenna. We have olive orchards, and a vineyard." He reached for his glass of wine and drained it. Amara turned, picking up a nearby jug of wine, and refilled his glass. Antonis nodded in approval, then held the cup to her lips. Amara pretended to drink, then he did, and set the goblet down. The last thing she wanted was a glimpse into this man's mind by touching liquid he had. "Such a mouth you have." He lifted his hand so he could thumb her lower lip.

Amara licked a lingering wetness of wine from the corner of her mouth, meeting his gaze.

"No." His eyes narrowed. "You aren't new. You know exactly what you're doing." He reached once again for his glass and finished it. Amara filled it again, emptying the jug. She set it back on the table, plotting her escape by its use. She needed more from him though, a way to get to Mirari.

"I'd like to show you all the things I know how to do," Amara suggested, brushing her mouth against his, exhaling against the stench of stale alcohol as she did, running her hand down his chest and to his belly. She did not touch his arousal, only circled her hand between them, over his torso, his thighs. Thinking of this man would be all she needed to cool her ardor for Cassian if it threatened to distract her again. "But soon I'll have to leave. I've been sold for the latter half of the night."

Antonis shifted beneath her again, and lifted her onto the table in front of him, his other hand diving beneath the bottom half of her stola, gripping her thighs as he rose up over her.

"I don't like to share," he said, some of the temper she suspected he showed frequently revealing itself in his eyes and mouth. His hands clawed at her thighs, too hard for pleasure. Amara grew tired of him, and more determined to make certain he never laid hands again on the poor girls she had met upstairs.

"Then buy me for a night. I can dance for you, at your home. Then you can do whatever you want with me, for as long as you want." Amara ran her fingers down his cheeks, and neck, and lifted her knee in a slow caress of his inner thigh.

"How much?" he asked.

"Two thousand aur," Amara said. "For a private audience away from the Den, and everything you want." She smiled, looked into his eyes with warmth and edges, showing him her teeth.

"Or I could have you now for the price I've already paid."

"That isn't what you want." Amara ran her hands up his arms. "You want me to dance for you again. You want me to do it in front of all the men you hate, so they can see what you have and they do not." She twined her arms around his neck. It was all too easy to recognize a powerless man that despised those who had what he wanted. The men who frequented brothels were apparently the same in Menei, Tamar, and the Republic.

"You are a clever little witch, aren't you?" He dipped his head down to smell her hair, which sent a shudder of repulsion through her he mistook for pleasure. He was not convinced, and she needed to be gone before Moina found her. So she took a chance.

"If you don't, Senator Haydar already told me he would." She slipped from beneath him and stood. "And I have to serve the highest bidder."

"Cassian? Did he tell you he's a senator?" He laughed, and she saw the bright burn of loathing in his gaze. Amara nodded. He sneered, grabbing a fistful of her hair. "Well he isn't. He is nothing. Twenty-five hundred aur. You don't lay a finger on him or him on you, and in two days you come to my villa to entertain me and my guests."

Amara held out her hand. "Moina doesn't take anyone's word," she said.

Antonis smiled grimly. "No she doesn't." He sat back on the cushions at the head of the table as he reached beside him to a purse that sat on the floor. He counted out the coins he'd promised.

"And will your guards know me, and let me in when I arrive?" Amara said.

Antonis dribbled the coins into her hand, and withdrew from the same purse a piece of paper on which a wax seal was centered. He held it up to her, pinched his index and middle finger, and regarded her with a little smile.

"You're wasted here in this pathetic hovel," he said. Amara raised an eyebrow and hooked a finger through the empty jug of wine, shaking it before him to indicate she meant to refill it. "Someone else can get it." He reached for her.

"There is some just outside the door. I'll only be a moment." Amara playfully knocked his arms away with the jug, and he sighed, leaning back and letting his arms fall to his side.

"Music!" he yelled as Amara turned away. She cast him a glance as she crossed the room, then another, accompanied by a coy smile as she turned out of the doorway. When she was out of his view she let the smile drop, setting the empty jug on the serving table just outside the room as she strode past it and toward the front door. She'd need a bath to feel free of him. The money in her hand made her give a real smile.

"You're still here?" Moina said as Amara passed along the central area. She had just set a tray of food down amidst a writhing tangle of people, and wove between the trysters to Amara's side.

"I wished to speak with you," Amara said. "This is two thousand aur." She counted it, then held it out to Moina. "To purchase Abene, Sorne, and Kattalin."

"This isn't enough," Moina said.

"No? I saw girls go for half that at the auction, and they were not used up."

"I knew there was something off about you," Moina said, but took the money.

"I will come to fetch them in the morning, I expect them to be exactly as they are now, no new bruises, no damage. Yes?"

"Of course." Moina bounced the coins in her hand. "Anything else, Mistress?" She sneered a little.

"Here is five hundred more." Amara held it out. "For your assistance in a small matter."

"What is it?" Moina glared. Amara looked over her shoulder.

"Antonis has purchased me to dance at his villa in a few days. I need only for you to confirm that you are aware of the purchase, that my part will be executed, and that someone else has purchased me for the rest of this night."

"We like Antonis happy, here. That does not sound like it will make him happy," Moina said, and Amara saw tension around her mouth and eyes.

"It will make him happier than it would if you told him the truth."

Moina looked to the northern room again, and Antonis bellowed something unintelligible. Moina jerked, her eyes widening, fear flashing through them before she set her jaw and nodded to Amara.

"Thank you," Amara said.

"Where were you a decade ago, when I was fresh from the auction, hmm?" Moina asked, quietly, some of her edges softened. When her gaze met Amara's, a hard memory, a decade old, seized her from head to toe. Her own escape made into murder. Boys made fierce by paint and costume, made subservient by fear and pain.

"Buying my own freedom," Amara said.

Moina studied her. "What did it cost?"

"Blood," Amara said, "and pieces of my soul."

Moina looked abruptly away. "They'll be in good health tomorrow." She walked away.

Amara lunged for the door, needing air untainted by the smoke, and the stink of bodies, sweat, and sex. She collapsed against the outer wall of the Den, gulping air and squeezing her eyes shut. When she was calm, she opened them again. The one benefit of the red light inside was that her eyes did not need to adjust to the darkness outside.

She pushed away from the wall and crossed the street and into the alley Cassian had indicated before they went inside. There were crates stacked to one side, and a midden pile on the other, and she had to navigate between them sideways. She'd left her sandals in the brothel, and did not want to end her night by stepping in something foul with her bare feet. Though she couldn't imagine anything in the midden heap quite as stomach-turning as the man she had just entertained.

It took her a moment to see Cassian, because he did not greet her. He leaned in the shadow of the far side of the tower of crates, his arms folded over his chest, one foot flat against the wall, the other on the ground. Amara regarded him in silence, gauging the mood that hovered around him like a cloud. He looked at her with an expression she had not seen him wear before. Flat, the barest of tension in his mouth and brow, a hard look that gave away nothing of his mood. That was all right; what she couldn't sense, her power could. Entanglements. Complications that would keep her from her goals.

"We should leave," Amara said. "Your friend will be displeased that I abandoned him."

"That man is not my friend," Cassian snarled. "Though you seemed willing to be his."

Amara abhorred jealousy. Especially from someone she had made no promises to. But Cassian's jealousy was a veil for something else. His inability to deal with Antonis, perhaps. Whatever it was, she didn't care. She was unwilling to accept blame or anger or whatever emotion he was laying on her shoulders.

"When you have ascended from your baseless melancholy, you can thank me for demeaning myself to discover the whereabouts of Danel's sister, and obtaining the means to get to her." Amara paused, immersed in the sense of truths barely held in check. "I agreed to pay you to help me find the woman, not to do all the work myself while you skulk in an alley because of some imagined rival."

"Rival? Rival for what? You have no idea what is between me and Antonis." Cassian pointed violently toward the brothel.

"Tell me then. Why did he call you Senator?"

"It doesn't concern you." He lowered his hand, turning his face away.

"It made you more than useless in there, when our agreement was that you would help me to find Mirari. I did all the work myself. Therefore it does concern me." She had not meant to rise to the bait of his anger. Amara preferred to diffuse temper, rather than aid it. She didn't dare touch him now. Not with anger and restraint between them. That was a perfect recipe for poor decisions. "I'm leaving." She turned to leave him to his sulking.

Cassian grabbed her by both arms and spun her back toward him, pulling her against him. When she tried to tug away, he gripped her waist, holding her body tighter to his, and looked down at her, with that expression that made her feel the desperation of his want, and dipped his head toward hers. But the power of it was gone, because he'd grabbed her. Forced her.

"Don't. You. Dare," Amara snarled, meeting his gaze and holding it. He froze, his brows drawing down as he looked at her. "Remove your hands from me."

He lifted his hands, holding them up near his shoulders. "Forgive me, Princess. Isn't this the game we're playing? You tell me you want me, and make me want you, then tell me I can't have you right before you run laughing to the first person of rank you can find?"

"Our play was mutual," Amara said, though there were other things in his grossly warped sense of the situation that needed addressing as well. "But rest assured, there will be no more play between us. I will give Peio what money I owe you. Do not appear before me again."

The color drained from his face, and the angry tension left his body. Horror at his own realization twisted his expression, remorse overtaking his mien from head to toe, but it was too late for her to care.

She turned from him and strode away.

NINETEEN

CASSIAN SAT IN THE shade of an old, weathered olive tree, leaning his back against it. He shaved another thin piece off the hunk of olive wood he held in his hands, turning it one way then the other, examining the grain of the wood. Technically, he was trespassing, but so many hours of his life had been spent under the tree that he could never consider it a place he was not allowed to be. The tree graced the top of a hill that overlooked his former family home from a distance. The oldest olive on the estate, growing long before his parents ever took stewardship of the land.

It was not the time of year for workers to be at the olives, and so he was unlikely to be discovered. He had yet to decide if visiting it, even from the distance of the orchard, made him feel peaceful, or tormented. What he wanted was perspective, or something to help him find a way back to the way things had been, before he'd met Amara. All he could find was a deepening sense of disgust and regret. Antonis' parents had turned him into a seething, bitter wreck of a man, and now he'd allowed Antonis to dig in beneath his skin as well. At the cost of his pride and what little honor remained to him. He worked away another thin flake of the wood's outer layer. It didn't know what it wanted to be yet, but it would come to him eventually, as it always did.

He'd returned to the Fountain House after she left him, even though she'd told him not to. No lights had been lit, so he hadn't entered. Appearing at night while everyone was sleeping would not improve his chances of being allowed to apologize before someone ran him through. The look on her face when he'd grabbed her, betrayal, anger, would not stop flashing through his mind. At first he'd just berated himself for sounding like an arrogant swine. But he'd not only offended her, he'd hurt her, and he could not concentrate on anything else. It had been his mother who told him, gentle reminders as far back as he could remember, to never take away a person's choice to be touched. Especially, she had always said as she stroked his hair, if someone had previously stolen that right.

Gods what had he been thinking, grabbing her like that? Antonis had heated his temper to fury with his taunting. When Amara had appeared, he'd been out of his mind. He hadn't been thinking. He'd been afraid Antonis would reveal his secrets, or hurt her, as he did the other women, he'd felt powerless to help her, and he'd waited and waited in the alley, not knowing what to think or if she'd ever return. If she knew what he was, how he had failed, he doubted she'd ever look at him so warmly again. He'd been afraid, and angry, and he'd acted no better than Antonis.

He set his hands and the block of olive wood in his lap, closing his eyes and tipping his head against the tree.

After a few moments he picked the carving back up. He'd selected it from the bits of interesting wood he'd collected and kept in the little house he owned in the city. It was just a shack, a place to store his things and occasionally sleep or hide. The only thing of value in it was the wood and stone he kept there for projects, canvas, when he had time for them. Wood was easier, he could carry it with him, work with it when he needed something to occupy his hands. This piece had called to him when he went to the house after Amara left him, and as he worked away the outer layer it revealed sinuous, curving streaks of dark and light.

"I thought I'd find you here," Peio called from behind him, and Cassian turned to look around the tree trunk just as his friend appeared over the crest of the hill that led back down to the city. "She sent me with your money. I don't think she had well wishes to send along as well. Shall I lie and say she did?"

"No, thank you," Cassian said. He wanted to ask if she was angry, sad. If she cared at all, but he didn't think he'd like whatever answer Peio had to give him.

Peio planted himself in the grass next to Cassian, dropping the bag of money between them, his gaze going immediately to the most distant field, on the far side of the estate. A century of troops camped there. Their centurion and his comrades would be guests of Paulus Hirtius until they marched again. Cassian could only think of one reason Stephanus would have recalled the soldiers from Eannea, and that was because he wanted to move on someone else. Cassian had a reasonable idea of who that might be, though he'd only heard rumors of the border units being moved south. To protect the Spice Road, was the general consensus. Cassian trusted the general consensus about as much as he trusted a herd of cud-chewing goats.

"This is enough, I think." Peio nudged the pouch of money. "To track down the ones we can, to get them east."

Cassian picked up and opened the pouch to look at the coins, and for the first time in a long time felt sick at the sight of it. He tugged the strings closed and set it back down.

"You know she's coming here." Peio ticked his chin in the direction of the sprawling building. "When Paulus is entertaining the centurions."

Cassian curled his lip, his hand tightening on his carving knife.

"I did not know," Cassian said. He would have, if he hadn't been an ass.

"Apparently"—Peio plucked a blade of grass and chewed it thoughtfully—"she danced him into a stupor. That's what Kiya told me anyway."

Cassian refrained from commenting. She'd danced him into a stupor and she wasn't even doing it for Cassian's benefit. Of course Antonis had fallen for it.

"She also convinced him he should purchase her for a night of private use at his father's gathering. For exactly the amount of money it took her to buy three girls from the Den." Peio shook his head. "And a bit. Enough to pay Moina to play along."

Peio had never set foot in the brothel, refused because he did not trust himself not to burn the place to the ground in a fit of rage. But Cassian had complained often enough about Moina that he might as well have.

"She's really amazing." Peio's brow furrowed and he stuck his lower lip out over the grass blade as he pondered. "Cunning. And powerful. She could be a Matrik."

Cassian didn't need anyone to extol her virtues to him. He was deeply aware of them, and he prevented himself snapping at Peio by forcing calm into his voice. "She does not seem your kind of woman, Peio." Suloi women were no less confident than Amara, they were simply quieter about it.

Peio snorted. "It isn't like that. She's a mage. A real one." He frowned. "Her magic…it sings. It sings to mine. Since we met her I can feel it more than I ever have."

"Are you stronger?" Cassian asked.

Peio shook his head. "No. Just"—he squinted, flexing his hands against the ground—"more awake."

"Is that why you want to go with her?"

Peio's expression closed. "No." He let the word hang between them for a long time, and Cassian knew before he answered. "I cannot do it anymore."

Cassian nodded. It killed him. Every one they could not free bled him. There were only so many times a person could be reminded that they were not wanted by their own people before their soul was forever lost. Cassian had always known Peio couldn't do it forever.

He'd known that one day there would be nothing left of his friend. This was better, as much as it pained him. Better for Peio to leave to somewhere he might start a new life, than to remain and fade slowly away. Besides. When Cassian took back what was his, Peio would be trapped while Cassian played politics.

"I'm glad," Cassian said. Peio punched him in the arm. They grinned at each other, but the expressions didn't last long, and they both looked to the ground.

"So," Peio finally said, "what did you do? Why are you up here alone?" His voice was laced with accusation and exasperation. Cassian lowered his knife and the olive wood.

"Antonis." He sighed. "We had words, then I was an ass."

"The usual, then. You know they need you," Peio said. Cassian scoffed. She'd more than proven last night that they had no need of him at all. "If they're going in there"—Peio indicated Buschetto's sprawling estate below them with a jut of his chin—"they'll need someone who knows the way out."

Cassian picked at a flake of the wood he'd cut too deeply. He should tell her. What he was. Who he was. Rather, who he used to be, and intended to be again. As soon as Paulus Hirtius had the decency to die.

"I need to apologize to her."

Peio made a sound of agreement. "Bek told me he hasn't seen her that upset in a long while."

Cassian wasn't certain he wanted the dubious honor of upsetting her more than she had been in a while. "Are you coming?" He stood and brushed the grass from his trousers.

"When have I ever missed a chance to see you humiliated?" Peio said, cheerfully.

TWENTY

THE GATE TO THE Fountain House was unlocked, which Cassian pretended was a good sign. Peio had been working through a handful of roasted hazelnuts that he acquired on their way through the markets, and chewed one as he asked, "What are you going to say?"

Cassian strode through the garden to the front door. He stopped inside, his eyes adjusting to the dimmer light beneath the upper level, trying to see into the atrium. He could hear voices now as well, and he followed the sound around the gallery. Once he rounded the corner he saw them, Bek leaning in the doorway of the bathroom, Kiya seated on the ground in the garden, two girls he didn't know busy rubbing some sort of oil or cream through her dark hair.

Bek looked at Cassian and flashed his teeth. "Someone doesn't know when to stay away," he taunted.

The new girls watched him in curiosity, but not for long. One of them was the girl he'd tried to protect from Antonis the night before. Kiya didn't move but to turn her gaze to him and shake her head, he thought it might be a warning. He wondered if Amara had told them of his foolishness, or if they simply knew she was upset with him. He continued to Bek's side and peered around the frame of the door to the interior of the bathroom.

Djar sat in a chair in the center of the tiled floor with one side toward the door, shirtless, while Amara stood at his back, carefully drawing a straight razor against his head. She rinsed it in a basin he held on his knee after each stroke, and rubbed a palmful of oil across his scalp before drawing the blade against it again. She wore a boxy, sapphire-green, Menei-style caftan that fell to the floor, and no shoes. A decorative border of gold embroidery adorned it, cutting across her shoulders, down the sides of the fabric, and across the bottom. It had short sleeves, and a high, round neck that opened in a little V just deep enough to reveal the hollow of her throat.

"Not only do you return after I said not to"—she drew the razor once more—"but you do so when I have a blade in my hand." She rinsed it, and aimed a withering glance at him. "Your arrogance knows no bounds."

"If she cuts me because you've upset her…" Djar suggested. He didn't need to finish. Amara tapped his shoulder in reprimand.

"Want me to take him away?" Bek asked, straightening away from the wall and reaching to grab for Cassian. Peio put a hand on Bek's arm before he touched Cassian, smiling amicably.

The Suloi were peaceful, and in their culture, it was bold, rude, and threatening to meet another's eyes. Because they avoided eye contact, people mistakenly judged them as shy and weak. But they could fight. And they fought dirty, and Peio was no exception. He dressed like a Republic man, in shirt and pants, had eschewed his blade and bow straps so he would be less noticeable, cut away the braids that marked his accomplishments. But when Bek looked at him, all young temper and bravado, even he recognized the look on Peio's too kind-looking face. Smuggling was an ugly, dangerous business, and Cassian liked having a partner everyone underestimated.

"I have a story to tell you," Cassian said to Amara, as Peio urged Bek a step back. "If you're willing to listen."

"I have been told my ability to listen is one of my greatest strengths." Amara stood back and examined her handiwork on Djar. She reached for a spot that displeased her. "Why should I waste it on you?"

"I owe you secrets," he said. Bek had moved a bit back, but stood with his arms folded, and Peio offered him some whispered joke as truce. Bek burst into laughter.

"What is this story about?" Amara glanced at her young friend, holding back a smile. He liked that—the way she cared for their happiness. Not like him. Selfish. And lost.

"A boy whose life was stolen," he answered.

Her hands stilled on Djar's head, her brow furrowing. She resumed, dipping the blade in the water and continuing.

"When I'm finished," she said.

Cassian suppressed his grin at the surge of relief that filled him.

"Why do you shave your head, Djar?" Peio asked, leaning back against one of the supporting columns of the walkway.

"Because he wants to," Bek said, at the same time Kiya answered, "because he's ugly with hair." The other girls giggled.

Amara smiled in amusement, flicking a quick glance at Cassian that erased the smile, and looked again to Djar.

"I am handsomer than either of you could ever hope to be, with hair, or without," Djar crooned. "Yes, Amara?"

"You are the most magnificent lion I have ever known," she said it, and a flash of sadness passed over her face as her gaze brushed across the still-healing wound over his left eye. Then she rallied, smiling again as she stepped back to examine her work once more. She seemed pleased, and took a damp rag from another basin and wiped it, with attentive care, over his head, neck, and shoulders. Then she rubbed more oil over his scalp, so it gleamed. Cassian thought he probably

shaved his hair because it made him even more intimidating. No softness to interrupt the harsh threat of every angle.

"There. You all look as presentable as I can make you. Kiya, take
the girls to the bathhouse. Buy them new clothes as well." Amara
spoke as she took the basin from Djar's knee and dumped it.

He stood, and shook out his shirt. As he stretched his arms into
it, Cassian caught sight of all the scars that crisscrossed his body. The
ones on the front were likely blade marks. But his back showed more
measured, repetitive strokes. A whip, Cassian guessed, and along his
spine a single tattoo, faded nearly to invisibility. Cassian and Bek moved
aside to allow Djar to pass from the bathroom into the garden.

"Djar, take Bek to the apothecary and buy willow bark powder and
mugwort balm. Have them mix both fresh, where you can see them,"
Amara ordered, as she dumped the second basin of water.

"I'll be upstairs," Peio muttered, giving Cassian a sharp look as he
cut through the garden toward the stairs that led up. Cassian watched
them go to their separate tasks, glancing occasionally at Amara as
she swept up the remnants of hair she had trimmed from the three
Meneians. When it was quiet enough, most of them at least out of the
immediate area, Cassian stepped into the bathroom.

"I'll fall on my knees if that's what you want," he said. She didn't
answer or acknowledge him, continuing to sweep. "I had no right to
touch you or treat you like that. I wasn't in my mind. I was…"

"That is not an excuse. And a person is due respect of their body
and wishes, no matter who they are. Your own struggles do not give
you license to do as you please," Amara said, softly, setting the broom
against the far corner of the room.

"Amara, I know that," he said. "Antonis makes me forget who I
am. I know I should not let him…that was not me. It wasn't me last
night, and it will never be me again, please."

"I will decide after your story. Wet your hair and face," she said, a
quiet order that he obeyed.

Cassian stripped off his shirt, and hung it and his weapon belts on a hook by the door, then knelt at the pump on the north wall and rubbed water through his hair and stubble. When he rose and swiped the excess water from his hair, Amara nodded to the chair.

"You don't have to," he said. "I can pay someone," though he wanted nothing so much as her hands on him.

"I find it relaxing. Sit."

"Is that why you do it for them?" he asked.

She rubbed a towel over his head to rid him of more excess water, then refilled the two basins. Her hair was loose, not even partially tied back as it usually was, and still appeared damp, as though she'd recently bathed or washed it. The entire room smelled of whatever was in her bottles—mint, he thought, or lavender.

"I like to do it. So they know I care about them," Amara said as she returned with one basin.

"When I first met you, I thought they were servants."

"They are my family." Amara set the second basin beside the first. He'd realized that, at some point after the attack by the Vex. In the years following his family's deaths, he had come to know many people who had been exploited. Many were broken, some were not. But Amara's ceaseless capacity for compassion, the love she showed those closest to her.

He admired it, and wondered at it. Wondered if it was her nature, or some trait of the magic within her that he barely understood. She had come from nothing and had carved the world to suit her, holding on to a warm and giving soul. He'd had everything and made nothing of it, letting anger and resentment grow in the ashes of the man his parents had tried to shape him to be.

"Why does Djar keep his head shaved?" Cassian asked.

She seemed to consider for a moment before speaking. "Djar is the second-born son of a man who once commanded more tribes and territories than any other in Menei besides the king," she said. "When

Djar was born his father found him unacceptable, and sold both he and his mother into slavery for the offense." Amara lifted each bottle and set it down after shaking the contents gently. "Djar's mother died a slave, and he was made into a gladiator. His reputation was known throughout Nasiye." She looked down, a troubled expression shadowing her face for the briefest moment. "When Djar passed the age of manhood, his father sought him out. His eldest son had been killed in battle, and he wanted Djar to take his place." Amara frowned. "Djar refused and cut off his hair in front of his father, which his people traditionally wear long, to signify his detachment from them."

"How did you meet him?" Cassian could see why they were all so close. If their stories were so similar, their suffering so integral to who they were, then it only made the most perfect sense they would wish to be together, with people who understood those scars. Even those Suloi he freed preferred the company of their own people, who understood their culture and their pain. Outsiders were threat to them. If he had not already been known to some of the clans, because of his mother, he would never be able to do what he did now.

"In Nasiye. I saved his life," she said. "Then he saved mine. We fled to Tamar together."

Amara chose two bottles and poured some of their contents into one of the basins, turning it a pale blue. She lifted it and set it on his knee, and he held it in place as she stepped back. She looked at him, but did not meet his gaze, tipping her head one way then the other. "How long do you like it?"

He supposed that meant she didn't intend to cut his throat with the razor or stab him with her scissors. He held his thumb and forefinger apart in answer and she nodded, bending to retrieve the scissors before moving behind him. She stood there for so long without moving that he tipped his head back to look at her, growing nervous at her silence. An expression of misery disappeared from her face when he did, and he straightened, setting the bowl down and standing, pushing the chair away as he turned. She looked at him, and set her chin stubbornly.

"You were wrong, about everything you said. You—"

"I was wrong," he agreed. Her big brown eyes widened, brightened, and the line of her jaw softened. "Let me have another chance. And let me…" He reached, unable to bear her standing there, alone, almost in tears. Amara nodded, and he pulled her into his arms. "Forgive me," he said.

She was soft, and curved, and fit perfectly against him. He closed his eyes as the brisk, clearwater scent of her filled him. She took a shuddering breath and tucked her head against his neck.

"I should have asked you if you were all right, if he hurt you…"

"I'm all right." She took another deep breath, relaxing more deeply against him. Her fingertips touched ever so lightly against the base of his spine, but the effect was devastating. His thoughts filled with mist and his body woke violently. She trailed her fingers up his back, and streaks of sensation cascaded over every part of him. His breath abandoned him.

"How am I to keep my hands steady to shave your face"—she touched her brow to his jaw—"when you hold me like this with only half your clothes on?"

He eased his hold, though her compliment made him want to hold her tighter, and she pointed to the chair. Cassian placed it back where it had been and sat down.

Amara slid her fingers up the back of his neck, slowly, and into his hair. He closed his eyes, letting a shudder of pleasure wash over him. She did it several times, arranging his hair, or teasing him, he wasn't sure. Finally she began cutting.

The rhythm was the same, her fingers sliding into his hair, catching it, then she'd snip some away and do the same again. He had no idea how fast or slow she was going, it had been so long since he'd been touched by someone he wanted, someone who had even the smallest interest in him, that all he cared about was that she didn't stop. Each stroke brought his breath shallower and his body more languorous, until he was unconsciously tipping his head into her caress each time.

Amara laughed, and set her scissors down, shoving both hands into his hair and tipping his head back against her belly. He opened his eyes to look up at her, his body warm with want and ease, and the playful look on her face only encouraged him.

"Hold still," she admonished, but she held him as he was, sliding the fingers of one hand in slow, even strokes through his hair, the other gliding over his temple and cheek so her fingers could caress his jawline and ear. Cassian closed his eyes again, fighting the urge to reach up and pull her down to him. "Tell me why that man has such a hold on you." She strummed her fingers up his throat, then gently lifted his head away before she picked up her scissors once more.

The warm idleness snapped away at the mention of Antonis. He'd said he would tell her, but now he was reluctant, wishing for the return of the peace and warmth of just being touched. Speaking of the past only brought him misery. But he'd said he would.

He tried to focus on Amara's touch, on her nearness to dull the anger. "My mother was the daughter of a freed woman, with the North in her blood. She hated slavery. Worked against it her whole life. And because my father loved her, he took up her cause. They did what they could in the shadows, shuttling those they could free out of the Republic."

He lifted a hand to his face, rubbing carefully at his bruised eye. The healing made it itch and his irritation inflamed it. "My father and Antonis' father, Paulus, were friends. Or so my father believed. Antonis and I grew up playing together. But they betrayed us. They pretended to be aligned with my father and mother, all the while collecting damning evidence, some of it real, some of it not. Paulus called their work sedition. Convinced everyone that my parents were trying to mount an opposition to the Consuls, weren't freeing slaves, but collecting a mage army."

Cassian had to force the final words out. "My parents were arrested, and died in prison before they ever had a trial."

Amara's hands had stopped their work, and she stroked the backs of her fingers down the nape of his neck, then against his cheek, a tender touch he desperately wanted.

"Paulus was elected to the Senate." That was as much truth as he could give. Revealing everything to her would only make her hate him, and served little purpose in their shared goal. "My parents' estate was taken, their servants, men and women who had been with us all their lives, some of them rescued slaves, were imprisoned, sold, or killed outright. Tortured to admit to plans that didn't exist, powers they didn't have." He dropped his hand into his lap.

"I am sorry for your pain." Her voice was warm water, soothing, yet sorrowful, as if she truly felt his pain. "How old were you?"

"Sixteen. When the soldiers came to drag them away, to ransack our home and murder the people in it, I was at a friend's house. Artists. We'd sit around and discuss nonsense. Philosophy. Sculpture. The popular poets." His laugh was bitter. "I had run away in anger that afternoon because my father had told me it was time to begin helping them, to do something more useful than lounging about with my friends."

The shame of it overwhelmed him again. He had never said it aloud. Not even to Peio, who knew much of the story. Cassian pitched forward, pressing the heels of his hands to his brow, trying to hide from the weight of his shame and regret.

"You could not have saved them." Amara moved to his side, pressing her fingers lightly between his shoulder blades. "You would have been jailed or killed as well."

"I was the only one who deserved it. I was a selfish, spoiled child that was angry because he didn't find his life interesting enough." He propped his arms against his knees and stared at the floor. "It wasn't my art they disapproved of, just the people that came with it. How lazy they were, protected and coddled by their patrons, uninterested in helping anyone besides themselves. I thought they didn't under-stand me," he sighed, "but it was me. I didn't understand. Idiot that I was. I still feel guilty, every time I pick up a brush or a chisel."

"Is that why you decided to take up their work?" She hooked her hand over his shoulder and pulled gently, urging him back up, and he went, so she could distract him with her ministrations.

"It was out of some misguided idea that I might make up for all that I had done wrong. That I might atone. That I might be able to forget all the many, many times I had failed them. And because it pleases me to take from the people who stole from me, who turned a blind eye or acted against my parents." He smiled wryly. "So. Whatever good you mistakenly see in me, it isn't there. I'm still selfish and spoiled. Just a man now." And he was waiting. Waiting for Paulus to die, because becoming a murderer would not help him take back what he was owed.

"Hmm." Amara circled back around him. "I am rarely mistaken about what I see in people." She resumed cutting, moving to his right side as she worked. "But we rarely see ourselves as we are, and are all blinded by our traumas and our disappointments to what really looks back at us in the mirror. Do you know I have often thought that is my favorite part of belonging to the Second House? Water reflects the truth."

"Being capable of magic isn't your favorite part?" he teased. He still did not understand the language of magic. Houses. Numbers. It was so structured. So different than the Suloi magic, which was just an extension of their connection to the world around them.

"That is the magic." She flicked his ear in admonishment. Cassian smiled, looking at her sidelong to avoid turning his head and making her miss with the scissors.

"You are like them, my parents," he said. "You help people for the sake of helping people. You are remarkable."

"No." Amara shoved her fingers into the front of his hair and lifted it as she snipped bits away. "I help people because I am forever trying to save a little girl I will never be able to." She made a few more snips, and stepped back, surveying him. "Go rinse your hair." She moved out of his way.

Cassian stood and returned to the pump to rinse out the bits of cut hair. She spoke of her past with such candor, but he couldn't help but think she held more back. That there was something she didn't wish to share, or was afraid to. He couldn't very well prod her for more, when he was holding his own remaining secret close. He splashed water over his neck and shoulders as well, and when he stood, Amara was before him, holding a towel. She offered it to him, but he shook his head.

"I want the same treatment Djar received."

"You wish for me to think of you and treat you like a brother?" Amara teased him with her smile, and reached to scrub the towel over his head.

"I think you know what I want."

She hesitated, her gaze flicking to his then away, before dabbing at him with the towel, then slinging it around his neck and using it to pull him back toward the chair. He went, ignoring the desire to grab for her and pull her to him. She was reticent, as she had not been in their interactions before. He'd overstepped once. He would not do it again.

When he sat she set the basin of blue water on his leg again, and traded scissors for a razor.

"I have never cut anyone," she said when he eyed the blade. "But if you would rather do it yourself, I can fetch a mirror."

"I'd rather look at you," he said.

Amara raised an eyebrow, holding the blade out to him. He took it, and she dipped her hands into the basin to wet them. She rubbed them over his face and throat, her fingers pressing firmly in smooth, short strokes. Cassian stared up at her, at the subdued expression of concentration on her face, her slightly parted lips and quiet gaze. The splash of freckles across her nose and cheeks both served to give the impression of innocence, and highlight the unique beauty of her.

He drew his brows down. It was remarkable, that she could turn a mundane, meaningless exercise into an intimate, blazing moment he would never forget for all his days. She brought it alive, that feeling that he was living, truly awake, experiencing in exquisite detail, that feeling he wanted so badly when he lost himself to gambling, when he fought, when he stole from the people who wronged his family.

A woman like her, it would be too easy to step over the line of desire and into the realm of something much more dangerous. Something not so easy to walk away from. His breath rushed away from him as her fingers left his face and she took the razor from his hand.

She dipped the blade in the water, the only sound in the empty room, a little splash of water. One hand steadied and guided his face to angles that allowed her to see where she drew the blade, the other commanded the razor. Amara hummed as she worked, so quietly he could barely hear her, and he thought her utterly unaware that she was doing it. The only other sounds were the rough noise of the blade against his skin, the occasional swish as she rinsed it, his own stilted breath. His body was tight with tension, aware of even the barest touch of her against him, the pressure of each of her fingers, the brush of her clothes against his legs. Only when he was completely immersed in carving something, making something, did he ever feel so focused, as though time had slowed.

"How do you do that?" Cassian said, in a reverent murmur, when she had pulled the blade away and was rinsing it in the water. Her gaze met his, her lips parted in surprise, her brows drawing up. Then she smiled a little. His throat tightened. So beautiful. Whatever god was responsible for her creation could claim in her an opus. He was lost.

"What?" she asked, waiting to bring the blade back until he'd spoken.

"Make me feel everything so acutely?" His voice betrayed him, catching.

She took his chin gently in one hand to hold him still and resumed. "I don't make you feel anything. You choose whether you are alive in a moment or not." She dipped the blade again. "It is a painful lesson to learn"—she stroked it across his jaw, rinsed, did so again—"that we are responsible for what we take in of our lives."

"I think I never learned how," Cassian said, when she took the razor away and set it in the bowl.

"Everyone knows how. You are waiting. Waiting for some moment to tell you it is all right to live. Many of us do that." Amara reached for a towel and dipped it in the water, then wiped it across his face and neck.

Cassian stared at her. How did she know that? Was she doing the same? But all she did was good. How could she feel she didn't have the right to live her life?

She dropped the towel beside him on the floor. "Finished." She surveyed him critically. Her scrutiny was difficult to endure when he wanted to touch her so badly, when he already missed her touch. Amara lifted her hand, her gaze resting on his for a moment. Her brow furrowed as she reached to him and stroked the backs of her fingers over one cheek, then the other, then beneath his jaw, her gaze following the movement of her hand. The expression on her face read to him like she wasn't sure she should touch him, and he tried to take heed, but the smooth caress of her hand brushed away what remained of his inhibition. Cassian let go of the basin on his leg and reached for her, clasping the fabric at her hips and pulling her toward him, between his knees.

The bowl tipped off his thigh and clattered to the floor, splashing blue water everywhere. Amara clicked her tongue and slipped backward away from him. He let his hands fall away as she slid the bowl next to the bottles then crossed the room to the door. She swung it closed, and he heard the latch click, then she turned, leaning backwards against it. She looked at him for so long, her brows drawn down, that it became torture. Finally, she pushed away from the door and crossed back to him.

Cassian's throat was dry as he looked up at her, hoping, as she fit herself between his knees once again. She took handfuls of her caftan into her grip, drawing it slowly up her legs by small, inching increments, until it was bunched around her hips, her bare legs within easy reach of him. On the beach he'd thought her naked form the most erotic thing he'd ever seen, then he'd thought her dancing would drown him in desire, but this slow tease would definitely be the end of him. When he wanted nothing more than for her to continue inching the fabric upward and be rid of it altogether, she instead took a step so that his left knee was between hers. She slid her right leg over his as she claimed his lap, facing him. He'd been hard from the moment her fingers started into his hair, but now he ached with vicious need, so he had to deny himself the desire to touch her, or he was afraid he'd forget himself again and start clumsily pawing at her.

"Close enough?" she asked, her mouth a breath away from his. He shook his head, and she laughed softly, her gaze flicking to his. "The shave," she amended.

"You tell me," he said, his voice strained. Amara leaned into him, rubbing her cheek against his, her hands gripping his bare shoulders, the warmth of her body sinking against his. She made a soft sound of appreciation, and it washed away his self-control. He pressed his fingers against her chin, pushing her back a fraction and turning her head so he could capture her mouth with his. Her hands slid to his head as she returned his frantic kiss, urging him to slowness, quieting his desperation. He slid his hands up her thighs, taking a single moment to lightly squeeze the yielding flesh before he slid them underneath the caftan and to the pronounced dip of her waist. "I want you," he managed to groan when she released the kiss and looked at him. It was not poetry, but it was all he could come up with in the moment. The naked truth.

"I want you too," Amara whispered. "You are a sinful pleasure to look at, and despite my better judgment I cannot stop doing so."

Hearing her say it to him, despite that she had not been shy up to that point, made him consider, for just a moment, lunging out of the chair and laying her on her back on the floor. But it would be cold and hard against her, and he wanted her drunk on pleasure, not bruised and shivering. He kissed her again and this time concentrated on the feel of her mouth—its soft, supple fullness, the way she moved it against his, pressing then retreating, driving him utterly mad with the want of more.

Cassian stroked his hands up her narrow back, to her shoulders beneath the caftan, and arched her against him. The turgid weight of her breasts against his chest sent heat cascading in waves down his body. Amara swept her tongue against the part of his lips and his body became a guttering entity of heat and need. He took control of the kiss, and she let him, yielding to the harshness of his want, giving a soft feminine gasp when he sucked against her tongue and the fullness of her bottom lip. She pulled away, running that same lower lip through her own teeth as she looked at him with burning heat in her gaze. He'd never been with anyone so sure of themselves, so openly erotic. Gods what she did to him.

"They should commission statues of you. You're a goddess." He brushed her hair away from her ear and jaw, to admire the perfect beauty of those lines.

Amara smiled coyly and traced her fingers in a slow circle over his lips, sending tiny, pleasant shocks over his skin. "Perhaps I'll have one commissioned, and set it in the courtyard of the palace in Narfour." She raised an eyebrow. "Nude of course. To shock everyone as they enter." Her gaze lit with play and mischief, and he kissed her hard, because she'd mentioned the palace and Narfour. It made him think of that man, that mage, and his ice crawling up her body, and that there would be a day she would leave and he would never see her again. She'd belong irrevocably to someone else, someone he doubted deserved her at all. Cassian found the idea impossible to think of without irritation, and so he kissed her to turn his mind from it. If she was willing to give him anything before then, he would take it, grateful that the gods saw fit to allow him even scraps of what he wanted.

"It will not do you justice," he said when he released her.

Amara cocked an eyebrow. "You do not think there are artists in Narfour?"

"The Republic has the most gifted artists in the world." He skated his hands down her back, curving his thumbs over her ribs, feeling each minute rise and fall between them, the suggestion of the curve of her breasts, over the dip of her waist, then to the round swell of her buttocks. He tightened his hands on her and tucked her hips against his, wanting the pressure of her against his aching cock.

"That"—she slid her cool hands over his naked chest—"is a bold statement." Her touch lit ice and fire in its wake, wracking him with a shudder of pleasure. Her hands curved against his shoulders, squeezing as she propped her feet on the chair's spindles and slid her hips a fraction upward and back down, stroking his erection. His fingers seized against her flesh, his thumbs hooking over her hip bones, pressing her against him as he mimicked the movement from below. Her lashes lowered, her breath leaving her in a soft moan.

"Perhaps." He let out a slow exhale to find his control. "But no artist anywhere will appreciate you the way I do." He shook his head. What would it be like, to have the time, the leisure, to do justice to her? In any medium? "Others might appreciate your breasts, or your backside." He squeezed it when he mentioned it. "Your lovely legs, your beautiful face." He slid a hand around, flattened it against the curve of her belly. "Your parts. But I see all of you." He circled her navel with his thumb, thought about kissing her there. "A work of art."

Amara slid her hands from his shoulders to his neck, her thumbs drawing twin lines on the underside of his jaw as she watched him, and he thought she was considering, or looking for something in his face. Then she kissed him, softly, and this one was different than the others, and he realized she was thanking him, quietly, with tenderness. It unraveled him, what he thought he wanted, leaving him hungry and stunned.

She pulled back, her dark gaze focused on his face again, with a look that pierced him. This…it might not be a good idea. If she was tender with him…if she looked at him as she was, with admiration, his tattered heart would be in danger of wanting something he didn't deserve.

"You have a very artistic way with words." She linked her arms around his neck. "I would not have expected it."

He pulled his hands from beneath her caftan and lifted them to her head, slipping his fingers up her neck and into her hair. It was still damp, slick against his fingers. He did not tangle his hands in it as he wished to, concerned he might undo whatever she had spent the morning doing to it.

Amara's laugh was breathy. She nodded, nuzzling his cheek with her nose and mouth. "I do so adore a man who pays attention."

"Princess, I can't pay attention to anything but you when I'm near you."

"That is normally the way I like things." She smiled as she straightened, a bit sadly, he thought. Cassian followed the delicate curve of her ear with his thumb, noting that it bore five holes, though he'd only ever seen her wear one pair of earrings at a time. He'd seen Meneian traders wear a row of rings and studs in their ears and never thought anything of it. Had it hurt?

"Normally?" he teased, pinching her earlobe gently, then continuing his touch over the high arch of her cheekbone. Her brows drew down again, her gaze growing guarded.

"Cassian," she said, and his name, reshaped with the beauty of her voice and musical accent, felt like a spell to trap him for a lifetime, "you are dangerous."

"No," he said. "You are. What are we to do about it?" He nudged her curls away from her cheek again. Silver coalesced at the edge of the rich brown of her irises. It startled him so he stiffened, but then relaxed, watching it as it moved, like water, in her eyes. "What is that?" he had to whisper, from fear or awe, or both.

"Proof that I allow you to affect me more than I should," Amara said, her voice resigned, her gaze drifting away from his. "You are not in danger. Magic is fed and released by strong feeling."

"What strong feeling?" he asked, more afraid of her answer than of the magic, afraid it would give him permission to feel more than he should. Amara looked at him again, and again she paused. The silver in her eyes surged inward, streaking toward her pupils, swirling like a maelstrom. He'd never seen anything so beautiful, so elemental. Something so foreign to him.

The creak of the front gate opening cleared the mist from his mind and replaced it with irritation. Djar and Bek's voices came next, in muted conversation. All the softness, all the concession, left Amara in the blink of an eye.

"Forgive me." The magic filled her irises completely, then evaporated. "I have allowed this to go much too far." She started to stand, and he caught her shoulders.

"Wait," he pleaded. "What does that mean?"

She cupped his face in her hands as she settled back against his lap. She pressed her mouth to his, in a tender kiss that held sweetness, and longing. When she pulled away she pressed her brow to his and said,

"It means I cannot do this with you." She lowered her gaze and stood, then left before he could think of a reply.

Cassian stood, staring at the bottles and basins, then went to the door and shut it. He leaned against it and sank to the floor, folding his arms over his knees.

None of that had gone as he expected, and now he'd be even more of a wreck than he had been. Could the woman possibly be more confusing? He couldn't think, and his body still raged with want. Perhaps it was for the best.

He stretched his legs out and tipped his head back against the door. He had not realized he was in danger of falling for her, and she was leaving Haenna sooner rather than later. What was left of his heart could not bear losing anything else he truly cared for.

Cassian glared at the water pump. The cold water might shock some sense back into him, and he was in need of a wash anyway.

TWENTY-ONE

FOUR NIGHTS AND THREE days. That was how long she and
Cassian had avoided being alone together. So when he appeared
in the doorway of her room as she prepared herself for that
night's trip to the senator's estate, she was pleased and concerned.
He leaned against the frame, watching her as she applied kohl to her
eyelids. She glanced sidelong at him once as she set the pencil over the
candle flame. She blew on it, exaggerating the action for his benefit,
extinguishing the smoking ember on the tip of the pencil.

"Is it polite, in the Republic, for a man to linger in a woman's
private doorway while she dresses?" Amara rolled the pencil between
her fingers, waiting for it to cool enough to use again.

"Have I misled you into thinking I'm polite?"

"No." Amara bent toward her mirror once more, tracing the lid
of her left eye. She did not actually want him to go. She was accustomed to attention from men. Amara enjoyed being appreciated. And
Cassian had an especially nuanced way of looking at her. As though
he could see more than she intended for him to. As though when he
looked he was truly paying attention, not simply daydreaming about
putting her on her back.

Being paid attention to was novel. Even the most considerate of lovers in her past had needed a great deal of coaching. Amara had a suspicion that might not be true of Cassian. The battle inside herself, between logic and desire, rose like a tide. She'd managed to quell it somewhat by avoiding him, but with him so close, she tried to convince herself, again, that it was not such a hard thing to tryst with someone and not care for them. She'd done it before.

"That doesn't hurt?" he asked. The room behind him, where all of them spent most of their time at the Fountain House, was the quietest it had been since she'd brought the girls back from the Den. The men had gone to bathe, a group endeavor so that they could help Danel. Kiya had taken the girls down to the garden. Amara appreciated the quiet, and did not find Cassian's company a detraction from it, but a pleasant bonus.

"Not unless I stick it in my eye because someone is distracting me." She traced her lower lid then set the kohl stick down and examined her work in the mirror.

Cassian pushed away from the doorframe to stand beside her, surveying the items strewn about the little dressing table. An ivory comb, a scattering of bangles and earrings, boxes and pots of makeup. He picked one up and opened it, then replaced it, and did the same with others.

"You are hindering my preparation for tonight." Amara tried to sound lighthearted, though she felt anything but. She'd refused to allow herself to be alone with him since cutting his hair. Though in the interim had convinced herself she had the self-control to leave him alone if she was forced into proximity. That did not appear to be the truth. Her hands itched to reach out to him. She had wanted so much more time with his body, lean and muscled beneath the shapeless clothes the Republic so loved.

Amara looked at his reflection in the mirror, his profile, at the dark stubble that begged for another shave. It suited him, even better than a smoothly shaven jaw. She liked the way it made him look softer, a bit disheveled, roguish, it had just a hint of grey scattered throughout, despite that he wasn't much older than her. He frowned at a compact he opened, confused by the burgundy-hued rectangles of paper. Amara plucked it from his hand and pulled one out, closing the compact and setting it on the table. She pressed her lips against the paper, then withdrew it and pressed them together once to even out the color.

"It is an Eastern method of making lip stain." Amara turned her face up to him so he could see the color on her mouth.

"You don't need these things." He lifted his hand but stopped, and tingles zipped over her skin. He curved his finger beneath her chin, rubbing his thumb over her lips. The tingles launched from her mouth to her core. She needed to tell him to go. This was…addicting, this lack of self-control he inspired. Always she was the one holding the reins, teasing, determining the pace. But that look in his eyes…it made her feel wanted in a way no one else had.

"I like it," Amara breathed. "If you're going to ruin it, find a better way." She lifted her gaze to his. His breath hissed between his teeth, and his fingers pressed more firmly against her chin. Amara rose, and Cassian gripped the loose fabric of the front of her silk entari, which she wore only as a robe. He dipped his head toward hers, then pulled back, a pained look on his face.

"I should not have come in here," he said with apology in his voice.

"No," Amara agreed. Was a kiss so harmful? The magic waking in her veins suggested that yes, it was. But he was so very good at it.

"I have something for you."

"Do you?" she teased. "Whatever could it be?" She bumped her hips against his in suggestion.

He laughed, reaching into his pocket. Amara raised an eyebrow, and he pulled his hand out of his pocket and raised it up between them. It took a moment of concentration to see he was holding a wooden bracelet. An especially delicate, finely crafted one. One section of it undulated, like the curve of a serpent, or winding of a river.

"It's olive wood. From the tree on my parents' estate," he said. Amara took it gently from his fingers.

"You made it," she said. He gave a single, short nod. The wood was beautiful, strikingly marked with dark and light variations that rippled over the surface like water. She slipped it onto her wrist. "It fits."

"I told you I pay attention." He curled his fingers around her arm then stroked them down to trace the line of the bracelet along her wrist. Amara looked at it again, turning it slowly around.

"It is beautiful." She glanced at him in surprise. She could not remember the last time a man surprised her. "No one has ever made anything for me before."

"Good," he said, seriously. A faint blush heated his skin, as though giving it to her had embarrassed him. Warmth, affection like she rarely felt for someone with whom she had a physical connection, filled her.

"You are a gifted artist, Cassian. I could not have described a more beautiful piece."

"Then it is perfectly suited to its owner." His gaze roved over her face, his hands on her hips tightening, his fingers digging against her skin. Why did he have to be so handsome…and sad?

"Considering your talent…" She curved her hands over his waist, aching to touch the smoothly muscled playground that was his upper half. "…perhaps I should also commission you for a statue, to place in the palace like we—"

He kissed her, suddenly, too hard, though he controlled it within a heartbeat. Amara clung to his shirt, his softened kiss still shaped by desperation. She took unconscious, backward steps toward the bed. There was no logic in her when he kissed her like this. Cassian hunched, just enough to reach for her hips, as though he meant to boost her onto the bed. She had already decided she could not deny him again, but he pulled abruptly away. He gripped her head in his hands, curving his thumbs over her cheeks and looking down at her.

"I'm sorry," he said. Some of the burgundy stain had colored his lips. She swiped her thumb across his mouth, holding his gaze with hers. He started to say something else, then shook his head. He pressed a kiss to her brow and left.

Amara heaved a breath and closed her eyes, curving her hand over the bracelet.

AMARA STEPPED FROM THE carriage she'd hired and onto the sandstone pavers of the villa's sprawling entrance. A half-dozen other, more elaborate carriages were parked in a half-circle around the entrance. Their occupants were in various stages of disembarking. She thanked the driver and pressed coins into his hand to encourage him to stay. Just in case. Cassian said he knew Buschetto well, but there was no such thing as too many avenues of escape.

Despite her protests, she had been overruled in wanting to bring only the twins with her. Djar had insisted on coming, readopting his persona as a trader, with three minions, all dressed in the turbaned, desert-appropriate attire of Northern Menei. Cassian did not pass for Meneian, of course, but Menei, like the Republic, was happy to subjugate anyone, giving no preference for any attribute but magic. So they dressed him in some of Bek's clothes and hid his face with the cloth and he trailed behind like an obedient servant. They were to arrive separately from her, and either convince Antonis and his father to sell them Mirari, or steal her, while Amara did her best to distract anyone who might care.

Gauging by the number of people entering the villa, that was going to be a challenge. Cassian had planned to take the others through a delivery entrance, to bypass the guards at the front. Her smuggler was proving to be quite useful. Her hand flinched against her hip. He was not hers.

Amara moved for the narrow staircase that led to the entrance. The roof was tiled in the curved, red clay tiles she saw on so many of the buildings. Carved creatures guarded the first step of the stairs. The ornate stone balusters were adorned, every fifth one on both sides, with bronze faceplates, each making a different, exaggerated expression.

People stopped, some halfway out of carriages, some because companions whispered to them to look, some because Amara passed within touching distance. She suspected seeing a Meneian at the wealthiest estate in the city was shock enough. But her dress would have been scandalous even in Menei. She'd chosen one in the style she'd seen the noble women wearing, which gathered around the neck, often by a metal choker, as this one did. The sleeves were loose and diaphanous. Most of the dresses gathered below the bust and remained loose the rest of the way down, but this one was tighter through the bodice and Amara had cut out the sides, revealing the curve of her waist on both sides.

It briefly hugged her hips then fell loosely to her feet. She'd chosen white, for its cool contrast to her warm skin, and it had its intended effect. She wore no other adornment save Cassian's gift. The weight of the gazes and silence that followed her up the stairs was nearly tangible. But that was exactly why she wore it. If her job was to be a distraction, then she intended to excel at it.

At the top of the stairs Amara handed the small stamped slip of paper Antonis had given her to one of two pale-haired men that flanked the entrance. He barely looked at it before handing it back to her, his gaze fixed on her bared waist. She followed the sounds of laughter and voices to the atrium.

The open-air space was planted with colonnades of tall evergreens pruned into slim spikes and filled to the edges with people. In the center of the space, surrounded by gravel, sat a shallow pool for collecting rainwater. Its presence calmed her, and fed her power, filling her with water's cool, still confidence. Centered and in front of the pool, a marble statue greeted all, a woman with hands held over her heart. She was exquisitely detailed, except her face. It was a smooth oval. The High Goddess. Amara had seen the same likeness around the city, often paired with Tessis, her eldest daughter and patroness of justice.

She wove her way through the crowd. Silence spread before her and chatter in her wake, so even a blind man could have tracked her through the garden. In Menei, even in Tamar, that kind of attention had made her feel powerful. Here…she felt stifled. Pressed upon by their stares. Diminished.

She hoped Djar and the others would be quick. She did not need the extra warning of her magic's rapid shifting inside her to recognize the imminent threat here. As she walked she kept a roving gaze for women matching Mirari's description. She might be any Suloi, except her brother had said she was marked. They'd cut her face, how they apparently culled the ones they meant to kill instead of keep.

When Amara reached the far edge of the atrium she found Antonis, lounging on one of several couches arranged beneath the overhang of the roof. A handful of men sat with him, all leaning forward, exchanging hand gestures and fast speech. A debate, perhaps, or a subject of common interest. She had noticed how many in the Republic spoke with animated hand gestures as accompaniment. Very different from the more reserved, polite interactions in Tamar.

There were eight men besides Antonis, five of a similar age, in their fourth or fifth Cycle. The other three were elder, one with very little dark hair left, circling his head from ear to ear, the other two silver-haired. Four of the younger were set apart by the red cloaks tied about their shoulders, and red, tasseled cords about their waists. Soldiers. Amara knew by the bored expressions they wore, which somehow conveyed arrogance and benightedness all in one. The fifth, who sat nearest to Antonis, was dressed similarly, but did not wear the red.

"Weaponize it. Put it in with the grenades," one of elder men said, the most portly of the three, leaning abruptly backwards against his seat to punctuate his point.

"No. That will simply burn it up," one of the red-cloaked soldiers said.

"Then in pellets, so it's on the shrapnel," the first replied.

"With this new method of manufacture, the applications are endless. Bullets, weapon coatings, dumped in water sources." The soldier grinned as he leaned forward to collect a goblet from the table between the couches. "The war is over before it's even started."

Amara forced herself to continue forward, despite the shock as the word *war* put the rest of the conversation into context. Though there was no proof, she had to suppose they were speaking of Black Sleep, and its applications in a war on mages. And Tamar.

Amara stopped a few paces from the only entrance to the space between the couches, until the soldier nearest Antonis whipped his head around to look at her and fell silent, staring. His companions did the same, one after the other.

Antonis was last, looking up with boredom and annoyance at the interruption. His scowl perked to a smile, and he sat up. The water at her back, a glowing awareness in her mind, settled her when her mood otherwise darkened against the idea of interacting with him again. Perhaps she knew why their High Goddess chose to go faceless. To be so protected from the world, to be unreadable, and unknowable, might be the greatest boon of all.

Amara reminded herself this humiliation would be endured in order to find Mirari. To find the man who was a Charah. To provide all the information she'd found. To return to the Sultana and finally, finally be given what she had worked so many Turns to achieve. She would be untouchable. Those she cared for would be untouchable. Safe, at last.

But the soldiers stared at her. After speaking of poison. Of war. Would she be safe? Would anyone?

"Your timing is, again, impeccable." Antonis stood. "Our entertainment this evening, gentlemen."

Amara inclined her head in greeting and gave them all a knowing smile, though inside nervousness fluttered like minnows. Politicians and soldiers were different sorts of entities. What worked to engage one rarely worked for the other. Politicians wanted to be made to feel powerful, in control. Soldiers wanted a chance to be out of control.

The difficulty of her task had just been multiplied.

"A whore, Antonis?" one of the older men said. The only one of the three with the majority of his silvered hair remaining, oiled and carefully styled tightly to his head. He had the same cruel mouth as Antonis. The same jaw, though he sported more cushion around his. Paulus. Amara could not help but see him through the lens of Cassian's story. A man who had betrayed a family, and destroyed a great number of lives. She might rather be a whore, than a senator, if that was the distinction between them.

He looked at her too long, and not in a flattering way. Amara turned her gaze away from his. All the soldiers in red examined her with interest, one of them making a crude joke to the one beside him. Both laughed. The one nearest Antonis, who did not wear red as the other soldiers did, ignored her. He stared down at the stone tiles of the patio.

She braced herself with a smile and stepped into the middle of the couches, to stand before the man ignoring her.

"What if I am not a whore"—the water in the pool fed its allure into her voice—"but a spy?" She needed their attention on her.

The soldier's gaze snapped to hers. His companions laughed, but he glowered.

"That's better," she praised, and stroked his bearded cheek with a finger as she turned toward Antonis' father. Paulus' pale face had flushed red, his jaw tight and eyes wide. She stepped to his side. "Wherever might I hide my weapons?" She held his gaze, and smiled, and lifted her arms out to her sides. "Would someone like to search?"

Behind her, some of the soldiers chuckled. Paulus' eyes bugged impossibly larger, but he could say nothing before Antonis grabbed her about the waist and spun her toward him.

"Gladly," he said as his hands roamed over her exposed skin, tugged her against him. Amara linked her arms around his neck, taking a quick visual sweep over his shoulder to look for her friends.

"Paulus, what is this? I thought we were here to discuss Golge," the older man who had been speaking to the soldiers about warfare said. Golge. The gatekeeper city between the Golge Belt range to its east and the road into the Republic. Were they planning on deploying men into the northern reaches of Sarkum?

Amara tugged out of Antonis' hold. She'd thought they only had soldiers at the border of the mountains. The fleet in the bay...Cassian had said they'd been brought back from Aklion. What would cause them to abandon an uprising?

Dread like a boulder weighted her down, ground her thoughts to a halt. But she had to do this. If that was what they were doing, deploying more forces to Sarkum, then finding the Charah was the very best thing she could do. A man with the power to control molten earth would be invaluable against an army.

"Don't let me stop you," she said playfully. "I'm only here to pour your wine."

Antonis grabbed her arm and pulled her back to him, grinning. He smelled of the wine he'd been drinking and had the flushed cheeks and drooping lids of someone well into their cups. Useless to her, except as a distraction for the others.

"Then be about it and be gone," the lead soldier snarled, holding the edge of his goblet pinched between his fingers and waggling it at her.

"Don't you order her about, Quintus." Antonis dropped back onto his seat, sulking like a child. "I paid for her."

Paulus muttered exasperation, and the other two elders laughed.

"So serious," Amara crooned, picking up the jug of wine on the table. She poured a glass for Antonis, to keep him happy. Then she poured wine into the soldier's cup. She set the jug down and snagged his goblet from his grip. The other soldiers made low sounds of derision as Amara took a drink. She forced herself to swallow as she held it out for him.

The shock of his violence, lingering in the dregs of his last cup of wine, zipped through her, telling its truths to the water in her. All she saw was hate. For himself. For everyone else. Lust for the thrill of victory over everything. All of it to be conquered. Even people.

Men like him were dangerous. Merciless. Impossible to control. Difficult to distract from their purpose.

"Oy." One of the other soldiers thrust his cup toward her. *Why play these games? They should serve you.* Amara shook herself free of her power's whispers. She obliged the request, sloshing wine into their cups so it splashed onto them.

"Oh!" She grabbed for a rag on the table and dropped to her knees in front of them to blot at the spilled wine. It always worked. Without fail. Not a single man in the group looked at anything but her, not even Quintus, even if it was only because he was annoyed by the sight.

"I think you spilled it higher," one said as she patted at his knee. He tried to pull her up into his lap, but Quintus shoved his hands away then snagged Amara by her elbow and dragged her to him.

"Enough," he ordered. "You." He raked her with his gaze. He had pale eyes too, like Cassian's. His were not water. His were grey, like stone. "Get out of here." His fingers dug painfully into her arm, and Amara had to force herself to continue smiling, to put her hands on his knees instead of brushing his hand off her arm.

"I'll make you leave before she does," Antonis said.

"Take your toy and go, Antonis. This is men's business anyway," Quintus said. Antonis' face flushed.

"You do like giving orders"—Amara slid up, between his thighs, flexing her fingers and digging her nails against him—"don't you?" His men laughed, and Antonis snorted contempt.

But Quintus said not a word, his hand on her arm gripping like a shackle, his mouth set in a thin, hard line. Amara tipped her head and whispered in his ear, "Do you like to give orders in private, too?" His skin prickled along the back of his neck, the muscles in his thighs bunching beneath her hands, his legs flexing tighter against her hips briefly.

She cut her gaze quickly toward the entrance. Djar stood flanked by the other three, speaking with someone she couldn't see because of the press of people. Cassian was watching her in glances. Their gazes met. That was all she could see of his face, because of the cloth and the distance. There was fear in his expression. Did he know Quintus? What else would put that look there?

"You're wasting your time," Antonis said, "he doesn't even like women." That made every single man burst into laughter. Quintus peeled his hand off her arm, and Amara retreated, saw him follow her movement with his gaze, though he took a long drink from his cup to hide it. No. Quintus did not like women. He liked conquest. Power.

She called to the water, the pool in the center of the atrium, to settle her, to calm the burst of repulsion that made her want to scramble back from him. It spun a whirlpool in her mind, whispered its power to her. *Let him try.* Amara closed her eyes against the flash of her power, shoving it back. When she opened them, Quintus' stare had taken on fervor that made her skin crawl.

She turned, picking up the wine jug again, and held it out toward Paulus and his two companions. Could they see her hand shaking? Paulus made a noise of disgust and abandoned the couches.

"Senator Hirtius." Quintus rose and stepped around everyone else to move to Paulus' side. Quintus said something to Paulus, his head close to the older man's. Paulus flinched, looked at Quintus in question, then at Antonis. Then he leaned in to say something back before he turned and disappeared amongst the crowd.

"Come here, girl," the fatter of the two senators said. "Sit." He patted the couch between them. Amara glanced to Antonis, who waved her on, and Amara sat on the edge of the cushion. Quintus returned and took his same place on the couch.

"There now. Those little boys will only paw and bother at you. It takes a seasoned stallion to put a pretty filly at ease, doesn't it?" He patted her thigh just as he had patted the couch, and left it there, lightly gripping her knee. Amara swallowed bile, resisting the urge to look for the others again. Quintus was too focused on her, and he was not nearly as drunk as everyone else.

"Seasoned stallion my balls," said one of the soldiers. "She'll at least want someone that can get it up."

"You probably don't even know where to put it." Antonis laughed. The others joined him.

"Where'd you find this one, Antonis?" Quintus finally relaxed, leaning back against the couch.

"She found me. And I knew how boring it would be, sitting around watching you fawn after my father all night. You'll have to let her go, Senator Nautia. She came to dance."

Quintus looked down then met Amara's gaze across the small space between the couches. His hands flexed into fists.

"Dance?" Senator Nautia appraised Amara. "You'll stop our hearts." All of them laughed, a sinister cacophony that dragged her into her memories. It shrank her into a child's body and stripped her of strength. She looked down, trying to steady the rhythm of her breath and hold back the panic that rose. She pushed aside the memory, buried it beneath a mental reminder of why she had come. But it assaulted her. Angry men on their knees, eyes wide, mouths frozen open, hands clawed. A heart that had stopped. Her father. This memory, this nightmare. Her power reminding her. It wanted to destroy her. To drown her. She could not control who it harmed.

Aysel Attiyeh had used her magic to stop an assassin, save her lover's life and an entire camp of refugees. It was all they could talk about in Narfour.

Amara's magic had made her a murderer before she was old enough to read, a useless bystander to her mother's death before she learned to control it, and the preferred pastime of cruel, depraved men before she was a woman. She had done everything to escape it, but no matter what she did, she could not. The memories, like her power, were only dormant, never gone, leaping up at the slightest reminder, slightest weakness, to gut her.

She hitched forward, fighting back the memory, the cold, blinding panic that swept up from the darkest places inside her, squeezing her lungs, and throat, stealing the rational thoughts right out of her mind. True water could never drown her. But her power could.

Cloth brushed against her legs. Amara looked up. It belonged to the stola of a slave who exchanged the empty wine jug for a new, full one. She turned, and sank to her knees in front of Amara.

"You dropped this, Mistress," the woman murmured, and put her hand in Amara's. There was nothing in her grip, instead she squeezed Amara's hand. As she rose she let her gaze touch Amara's, briefly. It was more eye contact than any other Suloi had given her. There was understanding there. But more, there was a scar along each cheek. A face marked for death.

Mirari.

She mouthed a word, then slunk away, her fingers sliding away from Amara's. Amara tensed, thinking to grab for her, but the senator's arm tightened around her, pulling her back. Amara watched her go, deaf to the conversation between the soldiers and the senators. She searched for Djar, Bek and Kiya, or Cassian, but couldn't see any of them in the shifting crowd. What had she said? There had been warning in her face.

"They always have the worst timing, the new ones. Come…enough of your flirting. You came to dance"—Antonis clapped his hands and pointed to the space between the couches—"so dance."

TWENTY-TWO

H E COULDN'T GET TO her. She was flirting with a Vex hound, and he couldn't go near her. He'd seen the tattoo peeking from the collar of the man's shirt, the black blade's point at the base of his skull, the open eye traced at the top of it. Cassian tried to find a way closer along the gallery, in the shadows where most of the slaves and servants lurked, unnoticed. The hound stared at her; Cassian had seen him pull Paulus aside. Did he know what she was? Or suspect? It felt as though fire were a living thing under his skin, in his belly, turning his eyes hot and his thoughts into ash.

Senator Nautia said something to her. Her smile stiffened. Her gaze turned inward, glassy. The centurions and Antonis kept jabbering, oblivious to Amara becoming little more than a husk where she sat. What had the bastard said to her? Cassian stepped away from Djar, identifying a shifting path to the couches, through the attendees.

An iron grip closed on his arm. Cassian looked up, at Djar's scarred face and stern frown.

"Whatever rescue you are planning will only anger her, and prevent us doing what we came to," Djar said. "Amara will rescue herself."

"She's in danger."

247

"She has been in worse, of that you can be certain. Remain to the task she asked of you. That is the best you can do."

"One of those men is a Vex," Cassian said as quietly as he could.

Djar glanced to them again, the muscles in his face tightening. "We have to find Mirari."

"You can do that? Leave her there, in danger?" He jerked his arm from Djar's grasp.

"I give her every freedom that is hers. And she gives me mine. Every pain, every joy, every fight, every failure. Those are ours, rights we were denied too long. She knew the risks when she came, and she has not asked for help. Take her decisions from her at your peril."

Cassian's anger cooled to shame. He could never understand. No matter how steeped he was in the lives of the people he tried to save, it had never been him in a cage.

"You," Djar commanded in a low voice, "will best serve her by finding this girl Mirari so we can be gone from here." He gave Cassian's shoulder a squeeze that was more command than friendly reassurance, and crossed the garden between the High Goddess statue and the rain pool.

Cassian took one last look at Amara, as a woman dressed in the undyed stola of a slave exchanged one wine jug for another, then slipped away. He watched another moment, as Amara rose from where she sat, seemingly all right. He forced himself back to his task. He'd already failed her once in not contributing to their shared goal. He couldn't do so again.

A boy knelt on the grass near one of the columns that supported the gallery roof, picking up the shattered remains of a wine jug. Cassian approached him and crouched.

"Wanderer see you, youngest." Cassian touched his own eyes with his fingers. Paulus' guests were already drunk. They did not care that someone dressed like a Meneian was squatting to speak with slaves. The only two men who would notice Cassian or had any hope of

recognizing him were Antonis and his father. Antonis was fully engaged with Amara, and the senator had made his way into the home. The boy looked up sharply, but when he did not see another Suloi, his gaze turned down and his shoulders hunched.

A woman came to the boy's side, and Cassian noticed her feet, bare.

"Whatever it is you need, I will help you with it." The tone was not deferent, the words hard despite the deceptively cheerful lilt a Suloi heritage gave to Republic words. Cassian tipped his head back. He recognized her face for its resemblance to Danel's. As well, the telltale, blade-sized scars in the hollow of each cheek. He'd last seen her panicked and crying for her companion.

Now her jaw was set, her hazel eyes hard. The same eyes as her brother. And the mien of a Matrik, though she was not technically one yet, she was much too young. Protect the young, the walkers, the future of the clan. Protect the past, guard the stories. Mother and memory, a clan's past and future. Cassian had never met a Matrik, they were more sacred than water, more revered than the road. Protected, always. As Danel was trying to protect her now, save her.

"Mirari," Cassian said. "Danel sent me." Her lashes fluttered, the hard line of her mouth softening, her chin quivered. She was still wearing a collar. Unusual, once someone was purchased. Unusual for a Suloi woman to be troublesome enough to necessitate it.

"He's alive?" She twitched a frightened look toward the men on the couches, to Antonis, showing Amara off as if she were a prized piece of art he had just acquired. Night was darkening the sky in earnest, and they were little more than silhouettes in the weak light.

"He is."

Antonis turned suddenly, clapping his hands. The boy in front of Cassian dropped the pottery he had picked up, turning toward the sound.

"*Go*," Mirari knelt as she commanded the boy. "*I'll do this.*" The boy rose, and another Suloi, a girl only a little older than him, took his hand

and led him down the gallery. The boy raised his hand to a dark lamp Cassian had assumed was oil fed, and pale light blazed to life inside. Not oil. Magic. The girl led the boy around, holding him up at the end, as he lit light after light, all to exclamations of wonder.

Cassian's lunch swam in his stomach. After the last lamp, the boy collapsed, and all the guests turned from him to Antonis, clapping excitedly at this display. The little girl was assisted by another servant, who lifted the boy up and disappeared into a room hidden by a curtain.

Amara began dancing, accompanied by a steady, pounding drumbeat.

"*Take a message to him?*" Mirari picked up the shards of pottery. Cassian assisted, holding his hands out so she could put the pieces in them. "*Tell him they are taking Benat to Corsyra.*"

"*Danel sent us here to retrieve you. My friend is trying to negotiate your purchase,*" Cassian said. Mirari's gaze slipped upward as if she might meet his, but continued up, past and above him, her expression growing strained, afraid. Cassian sensed the presence at his back a moment before the man spoke.

"Your father must be rolling in his grave to hear you speaking that filthy language and dressed as a slave." A soft laugh. "Or perhaps he'd be proud."

Cassian spun and rose in one movement, dropping the pottery, the familiar voice cold water down his spine and leaden weight in his belly. Paulus. Cassian would always know the voice that said the final words to condemn his parents. Enemies of the state.

The drum beat harder for Amara's dance, behind Cassian, but he could see nothing but Paulus. Older, fatter, balder. Yet sinister. A hydra, smiling benevolently at Cassian. With too many faces to ever know the true one.

"Come, my dear," he said to Mirari. She resisted only a moment, then stepped to the man's side, and he put a proprietary hold on the back of her neck, his thumb laid over the back of the collar, his fingers tangled in the tumble of hair that would once have been bound in braids and twists. Her expression was still in the way Cassian had only ever seen the Suloi manage. Maelstrom beneath still surface. From his peripheral he saw her slip her hand into the pocket of her stola. "Now. Why are you dressed in that ridiculous costume?" Paulus smiled as though he thought it was funny as he gave Cassian's Meneian garb a thorough inspection, but his gaze was sharp as knives.

"Comfort," Cassian said.

"Ah. And here I thought it might be for some nefarious purpose. Thievery, perhaps." He chuckled. The collar shifted when he applied pressure. The muscles in Mirari's neck strained, her expression tight, her gaze on the stone tiles at Cassian's feet. The bruises spreading up her neck told him she had been the victim of the collar's interior barbs many times. Cassian clenched his fists at his sides.

"Of course not." Cassian did not smile. "I meant to pay." He could not stand to look the man in the eye. It lifted his memories like boats on a tide. Brought up his hatred. It stole his reason.

"A Haydar? Pay for slaves? What a very unfaithful son you are."

Cassian shrugged. "I am not my parents. Slaves have their uses."

"Yes." Paulus raised a grey brow. "And what use will you find for this one?" His fingers tangled deeper in Mirari's hair, and her eyebrows drew together.

The music's drumbeat matched the rhythm of Cassian's heart. Thump. Thump. Thump. The reedy sound of the pipes made him jumpy, or it might have been the triumphant gleam in Paulus' eyes. Was Amara still dancing? Where were Djar and the twins? He didn't dare look for any of them, give them away. He couldn't reveal them to Paulus.

"Not this one in particular. Any you could part with." Cassian smiled as much as he could force himself to. Antonis may only have been good for drinking and whoring, but his father was another story altogether. A ferret that could smell secrets and lies for leagues. Cassian cursed himself for coming. He'd endangered them all.

"I see." Paulus looked at Mirari. "Then let us strike a deal. I will trade you this pretty little thing"—he yanked her hair and her throat worked but she made no sound—"for a pittance. She has caused more problems than she's solved, in any case. She would be a perfect beast for you."

Cassian held his arms hard to his sides, kept his gaze trained on Paulus' jowled jawline, though his fingers flexed open against his legs. He did not understand the twist in a person's mind that allowed them to think it was their right to cause pain to others.

"What price?"

"You know what I want," Paulus said.

Cassian held a burst of angry laughter back, curbed the instinct to punch Paulus in the face, and smiled. "Rot in the Night Hall," he said. He would not give Paulus the only thing that remained of his father. His only chance to right all his wrongs. He would not give a seat in the Senate to Antonis Hirtius.

THEY ALL WATCHED HER. The crowd had shifted from its disbursement throughout the atrium, toward the couches, drawn by the music and her movement. Yet Quintus was uninterested, his gaze fixed on the crowd, scanning. Amara shifted her movements and her attention to him, to draw his focus back to her. His sobriety and the taste she'd had of him when she drank his wine suggested he would be easily capable of connecting her to Djar and the others.

The other soldiers reached to swat and grab for her, and Amara brushed their advances away, waiting for the last notes of the music to make a final turn and finish the dance by falling into Quintus' lap.

The crowd laughed and cheered at his brief look of surprise.

"You are not an admirer of music?" Amara said loudly enough to keep everyone looking at her, and Quintus. Sweat slicked her skin, and made her scalp itch. The spring night was muggy and smelled like a promise of rain. To touch him, to sit and have to suffer his heat raised her temper.

"A hound? Admire music?" Senator Nautia scoffed. "Do not waste your breath. They're only good for one thing."

"And what is that?" Amara asked Quintus, curving her hand around the base of his neck and giving him a suggestive smile. The back of his neck was damp, wet with his own sweat, and she suppressed a frown of distaste. His granite gaze slid from her face and down the length of her, one arm circling her waist, the other settling on her thigh. A lifetime of experience with touch had taught her the intricacies of each, the meaning behind every nuanced contact. There was no nuance in this. He was not touching her for pleasure, he was trapping her. She tried to jerk away, but his grip was just as stone hard as his gaze.

He dipped his head to her neck and took a long, loud inhale through his nose, then turned his mouth against her hair.

"I hunt," he said. "And pity for you, I do not think with my prick." He drew back, and looked her in the eyes. In the space between shuddering breaths, Amara felt a sluggish, infinitesimal brush of magic against her own.

"Let go of me," Amara demanded. She failed to prevent her desperate look into the crowd, searching for Djar. Or Cassian.

Quintus smiled and exhaled a laugh. "Looking for someone?" He spoke over her shoulder at Antonis. "It is a good thing your father is not as great an idiot as you are."

Amara bucked in Quintus' hold, looking over the soldiers and the crowd for anyone that appeared even remotely interested in her welfare. All she saw were hungry faces. Hungry for entertainment. They cared not whether it was beautiful, or violent.

"I can't let you go." He moved his arm from her waist to clamp on the back of her neck. "You want to be with your friends, don't you?" He lifted his hand from her thigh and pointed. The crowd parted, revealing the pool of water, and beyond it Djar, Kiya, and Bek. Collared and held at gunpoint by three men…three Vexillae.

Amara's gaze snapped to Quintus, and he bared his teeth. "You are the prettiest mage I've ever sniffed out. But my gods do you *stink* of magic."

"What are you?" She recoiled from him, darting her gaze over his face. Only then did she see that his skin was a subtle shade more bronze than his companions. His cropped hair would have been sable in the sun. And that shift she'd felt against her power…did he have magic? Her breath rushed out. He'd sensed her.

"I am a hound of the Vexillae," Quintus said. "I hunt magic for them."

Everything inside her went perfectly still, as if, in fact, she were a hunted beast.

"You are Suloi," she accused. The crowd murmured distaste and his face twisted with fury. Quintus jammed his hand into the back of her hair, and twisted, yanking her head back. The burst of pain made Amara instinctively cry out, but it was a strangled sound.

"No. I am too Corsan for them, and too Suloi for the Republic. My blood is tainted enough to feel your power, and that is all that matters. And you are wanted by Stephanus." He stood, shoving her out of his lap. He faced Antonis and tapped a fist against his heart. "Thank you for your assistance."

Antonis stared in mute, drunken shock, and behind them, whispers shivered through the crowd.

"This is for you," Quintus said into her ear, his hand tightening in her hair as he held a collar up in front of her.

CASSIAN TRIED TO THINK, but couldn't. Mirari's chest rose and fell with quick, shallow breaths as Paulus adjusted his grip on her.

"Revoke your claim," Paulus sneered, "or it will be you in the Night Hall." His sneer turned into a grim smile. "And your friends as well." He indicated Buschetto's entrance with a tilt of his head. Three Vex stood there in a loose triangle, each with a Meneian in their grasp. Collared. Djar, Bek, Kiya. Cassian's chest felt suddenly empty, silent, then filled with stone. He thought about the knife tucked into the cloth at his waist. Where Bek had shown him to hide it. There would be nothing more satisfying than to plunge it into Paulus' heart. But that would only land him in prison or on the gallows. Neither would it help anyone else. "Revoke your claim, and you may all walk out of here."

Cassian scowled, the decision ripping him apart, turning him mute.

"Take a jug of wine as a bonus," Paulus mocked.

Mirari spun into Paulus, her hand flashing out of her pocket, and hammered downward with a fist clutched around a shard of pottery, cutting a jagged line across his throat and over his collarbone. He staggered back with a garbled shriek. Cassian grabbed Mirari by the arm, yanking her after him as he moved away from Paulus.

But the senator continued to cry out, grabbing at his neck and pointing at them in accusation. "Murder! They've murdered me!" The wound was not deep, but it bled like it was, staining his fine white toga a graphic red.

No sneaking out now. And Cassian wasn't leaving without the others. Guests' conversations stuttered out, and gazes turned to them. A woman screamed. The crowd broke apart like scattering gazelle, trying to get away. No one even moved in Paulus' direction. Mirari still clutched her pottery shard, bloodied, just as her stola was, holding it in front of her as if it were a sword.

Cassian whirled to look for Amara. Antonis had just leapt to his feet, shoving past Amara and the Vex that held her, Senator Nautia getting up to follow as Antonis ran toward Paulus. The four centurions moved after them. Amara's gaze met Cassian's as the Vex snapped the collar closed on her throat. Cassian lunged forward when her face contorted in horror, his stomach dropping completely, but Mirari caught his arm and yanked him to a stop.

"*Take me to my brother.*" Mirari tugged him toward a hallway. "*You cannot help them. But we can still run.*"

Cassian cursed the unfamiliar Meneian clothes and lack of his pistol and rifle. He needed Peio, but they'd sent him up to the hill and the olive tree to keep an eye out for anything suspicious.

Antonis, accompanied by Senator Nautia and two of the centurions, got Paulus to his feet, and led him back toward the couches. The guests moved inward, toward the rainwater pool, to watch the drama of the Vex and their Meneian captives unfold. The wealthy loved nothing more than to watch something lurid. Like sorrow. Like pain. Like death.

Antonis pointed to Cassian. "Take that man into custody. And kill that girl. In fact—kill them all."

The Vex holding Amara lifted a hand to stay the men that moved to obey Antonis. "Not the mages, I'm afraid. Stephanus wants them."

Mirari grabbed the back of Cassian's shirt, turning to face the guards that stalked toward them, but Cassian could only look at Amara. Gods how he'd failed her.

AMARA IMAGINED THE SOUND of the metal closure snapping into place echoed through the entire atrium. Her breath stopped halfway through an inhale. She reached up, touching the tips of her fingers against the cold metal. Her thoughts were slow, confused, nothing of what she was seeing coming together into a picture she could put words or action to. Every small movement—her swallow, her inhale—pushed barbs on the inside of the collar against her skin, so she had to hold herself stiff and still to prevent their touch. The Vex's grip in her hair allowed him control of her head, and he tipped it forward again so she could see her friends. Her family.

More men shoved and bullied Cassian and Mirari toward the others. Bek lay on his belly on the ground, a Vex standing with a boot in his back. A second man had his hand over Kiya's mouth and a pistol at her temple. A third held Djar by the collar around his neck, a dagger poised between the ribs that guarded his heart. Little streaks of blood along his neck glistened in the lamps the boy had lit. Djar seethed, looking to her for an answer, but she had nothing to give. Cassian stood with his hands raised, his jaw set in anger, a rifle pointed at his back. They shoved Mirari to her knees at his feet.

"What do you want?" Amara's voice was too dull. A stranger's voice. One she thought she had forgotten, one that belonged to her, and didn't, a servant's voice. Broken, tired. Not afraid, defeated.

"Nothing that we don't already have," Quintus said. "You'll come with us. You and the Suloi. That's it." He pushed the back of the collar against her neck. The barbs pricked her, sharp points of startling pain on tender skin, freezing her body and setting free her fears. And the fears of all who had worn the collar before.

The strength went out of her legs, and Amara dropped to her knees. There was blood on those barbs. The blood of everyone who had worn it. And their pain became her pain, their fear hers, their suffering infused her. Her magic writhed as the foreign memories and feelings assailed her like a rain of arrows, until she screamed.

Cassian lunged forward, and the man behind him jabbed the muzzle of the rifle against his back, jerking him back by a handful of his shirt. Amara tried to breathe and couldn't, tried to surface from the torrent of suffering that rushed over her. She collapsed forward to her hands, unable to hold herself up against the mental assault. Her heartbeat slowed, and she managed to suck in a single, deep breath. She sank her weight back over her heels and pressed her face to the ground between her arms. Her heart beat a sluggish cadence in her chest, until it was all she could hear. The memories were all she could see. Tears and sorrow. Fear and despair. But they were gone. She could not help them.

"Senator Hirtius," Quintus announced, "we thank you for your information, and your service to the Consul will be noted." He reached down, his hand closing on Amara's arm. She didn't resist. It was too familiar, too easy to fall back into the mind of the girl. All they had needed was a collar to erase everything she had become and replace it with everything she had been. They had collared her in Menei, when they dragged her away after her mother's death. Prisoner. Captive. Criminal. She had not escaped after all. No one who wore this collar had escaped. And all those Turns of fooling herself...

"Take the women, the mages. Kill the others." Quintus yanked her to her feet.

The man standing over Bek drew his pistol and aimed it downward. "No!" Amara cried. Bek wore a mask of hard, forced calm, and when her gaze met his, a spark of hope lit his eyes. He wanted her to save him. Thought she could. But then he looked away. He closed his eyes, and the Vex cocked the gun he held.

No. She could save him. She *could.* Amara forced the cage around her magic open, crying out with the effort to force loose her mental grip of control.

Water rushed into her mind, cold and clear.

The lamps the boy had lit nearest Amara, on both sides of the atrium, winked out. Then the next. And the next. Until all had been extinguished. Dark and cold to counter light and heat. Water to fire.

Startled cries filled the air, and Quintus tightened his grip, shouting a command to his men to stay.

Her power raced across her skin, silver in dark night, reflecting a moon that had not yet risen, quicksilver streaks of truth and twisted reality. Someone clapped, confused, as if it were all part of some show for their entertainment. It was accompanied on the tail end by shouts of alarm, mutterings, and a sudden shift of movement toward the exit. The water in the pool rose in answer to her silent call. Moisture swept up from its surface, mist pouring from it into the courtyard, and billowing upwards, obscuring everyone and everything. There were a few short, sharp screams of fear.

"Stop her!" Paulus shouted with panic-sharpened voice.

Quintus drew his pistol, jamming it against Amara's temple. "Whatever you're doing, stop it."

"Be still." Amara closed her eyes, her thoughts becoming the mist, her will becoming the water's, ephemeral figures coalescing and rising from the blanket of vapor, filling the crowd with spectral, whispering shapes. They crooned and sang, reminded everyone that there was nothing to be concerned with. To be calm. To be silent.

Be still. Be quiet. Be still. Be quiet.

The magic sang because she did, in voices old and new, languages she knew and did not, commanded, seeped into the cracks of each will, through weaknesses every person had but did not know, until each man and woman in the courtyard stood as if in a daze, quiet. The pistol sagged in Quintus' grip, and his hand loosened its hold on her. The whispers continued, chittering, coaxing.

Amara turned, putting her hand over the barrel of Quintus' pistol and pushing it away from her. It hung in his limp grip. His magic stirred under the press of hers. Answering her magic's call.

"Give me the collar key," Amara said around a throat closing in disgust and a heart thudding too hard. *Kill him,* the magic whispered. *He would have killed you. Tortured you.* A figure rose out of the brume that shifted at their feet, leaning to whisper in his ear, ephemeral fingers twisted into hate-filled claws, teeth sharp as daggers, words sweet and alluring. Amara had never known if the mist manifested as what she wanted, or what her magic told her she did. She had learned enough at the University to control it, and asked nothing else.

He reached into his pocket and withdrew a key. Amara took it from him and fumbled it into place in the collar. It clicked, and opened. She pulled it apart. The metal fell away, landing on the grass at her feet with a thump. Quintus stood, hand still raised, staring at her, uncomprehending as the figure swirled away from him. Grey eyes hauntingly vacant. Bile rose in her throat as she pried the pistol from his slack fingers.

Amara did not look at anyone as she walked around the pool, fog parting before her, whispering her wishes as she sang them into the minds of the people around her. She could not look. When she looked at someone under her magic's control, she could feel their thoughts, the threads of self that remained to them. Always it was terror. Terror she had known most of her life, terror she could not bear to inflict on another, no matter who they were. Strip them of their will and overlay it with hers. That was her power. The Wheel's *gift*.

When she stood before the others, she lifted her hand, directing the haze around the other three Vexillae, locking them more power-fully under her magical control. It loosened her mental grip on the rest of them, and the crowd began to shift, a few mutters of fear. Magic took stamina, and stamina took practice. Practice she did not have. She could not hold them much longer.

"Put your weapons down," Amara commanded, and combed through the mist, through her magic, to release Bek and Kiya's minds, Cassian's, and Mirari's, finally Djar's. The Vex submitted, and the moment she was free Kiya whirled, slamming her knee into her captor's face as he bent to put his pistol on the ground. His head snapped back and he fell to his knees, staring mutely at Amara. Waiting mindlessly to be commanded even as blood streamed from a broken nose. The blank look, the obedience, made her ill. Her hands shook. Anger and disgust rose up, at herself, at what she was, and her hold on her power wavered, weakened, and she could feel the will of each person slipping from her grasp. Breaking away. Cassian shoved the man behind him, pushing him to the ground and taking his rifle.

Bek launched to his feet, retrieving his knife from the man who had stood over him, flipping it into his hand and raising it to kill.

"Stop!" Amara said. Djar grabbed the knife and yanked it from Bek's hands. "You will not murder them while they are defenseless."

Djar tucked the knife into the fabric at his waist, and Bek stared at her in surprise.

"That is exactly what they would do to us!"

"You are better than them. I will never allow you to forget it," Amara said. Bek glared at the Vex, lethargic under the grip of her power. His lip curled, and he took a step closer.

"Obey me, Bek," Amara said. There was no power in it, but Bek flinched, and inside, she fractured, watching someone she loved look at her, even for an instant, with fear. He had not known before. Had resented she never used her magic. He knew now. She was glad her power was already failing. Before it hurt someone. Before she lost her grip and revealed herself to be not a savior, but a monster.

The wounds she'd covered so long ago reopened, bleeding shame into her thoughts.

Amara collapsed to the grass, her power streaming out of her control in fluttering ribbons, the mist sinking into the ground, the illusory figures dissolving. A man shouted and a woman began to cry behind her. One of the Vex groaned as her hold on his mind seeped away, and Amara could only sit in the grass and claw at her arms, at her throat, where the repulsive power was strongest. Pain stung as she dug her nails against her skin, tears filled her eyes. It was slow poison, would turn them all against her. That silver in her voice, the desire in her magic. Lies.

Hands closed on her arms and hoisted her to her feet, and Amara let them. What did it matter? She didn't deserve to be free, she'd known it, all this time. Unconsciousness nipped at her, her magic spent. Her magic had done its foul work and now would make her even more useless by forcing her into sleep. She knew she couldn't fall asleep, not now. But a mage depleted had little choice.

"Come on, Princess. Stay with me," Cassian said. And in the moment before the black of mage sleep took her, Amara wondered why he only sounded annoyed, and not afraid.

Twenty-Three

AMARA WAS DEAD WEIGHT, her head lolling, clutching at her own arms but fading in and out of consciousness, and as Cassian fought to get her to her feet, the Vexillae recovered. One of them grabbed a discarded pistol lying on the ground beside them. He aimed it at Cassian, and before Djar could draw the knife he'd taken from Bek, an arrow appeared in the Vex's throat.

Cassian swiveled a look around the villa. Peio knelt on the roof above the gallery, and when Cassian looked he stood and ran closer.

"Run!" Cassian dragged Amara to her feet, catching her around the waist, and Bek joined him, snaking an arm around her other side. Another Vex grabbed for Kiya as she turned, another arrow struck him down.

"This way," Cassian shouted, so they could hear him over the panicked stampede of the villa guests.

Cassian took up a limping jog toward the darkened archway that led down into the cellar beneath the home. The secret tunnels his parents had used for the slaves they needed to hide or move in and out without notice. Djar took Amara from Bek and Cassian, hoisting her like a limp bag of grain to his shoulder. They followed Cassian through the cellar, dark but for a nearly burnt-out torch that cast pale light around the barrels of wine. Mirari ran forward to open a door on the far end of the cellar, as shouts came from behind them.

"Bek, help me with this." Cassian indicated one of the long, three-tiered shelves where the wine barrels rested. They could slow their pursuit, at the very least. Kiya and Djar followed Mirari through the doorway. The four centurions and Vex hound came down the stairs from the atrium in a jumble. They were briefly disoriented by the dim light and the rows of casks. Cassian grabbed the edge of a shelf, which held a dozen casks at least, and Bek caught on immediately. Together they shoved and pulled, and finally rounded to the back of the shelf when the soldiers broke into a run toward them.

They glanced at each other, Bek nodded, and they lunged in unison against the shelf. It rocked forward, teetering, then slowly tipped, dumping wine barrels onto the stone tiles. They exploded in waves of crimson liquid and shards of wood. The rack fell on one of the soldiers, whose cry cut off abruptly. Cassian tugged Bek toward the doorway where the other had gone. It led to a stone ramp, which they charged up, and deposited them on the eastern side of the villa just as Peio climbed his way down the uneven stones of the wall from the roof and dropped beside them.

"The carriages," Djar said. They ran for the courtyard and into the melee of guests trying to escape. They were fighting for the closest parked carriages, some quite violently. A man lay in the gravel, bleeding from a knife wound. Cassian had never seen a better illustration of the *culture* of the elite. Refined until they were threatened, then they were no better than the lowest street criminal.

"There!" Bek pointed to the carriage Amara had arrived in. The driver was just turning it around to make a run for it. Kiya burst into a sprint, moving like a racehound, then vaulted the back of the carriage and had her knife to the driver's throat just as he drew his whip back to crack it at his pair of horses. Bek threw the carriage door open and Djar levered Amara in through the narrow opening. Mirari jumped in first, and cradled Amara's head and shoulders in her lap as Djar and Bek tried to climb in without stepping on her. Cassian clung in the doorway, his feet on the step, and Peio waved them on.

"*I'll catch up*," he called. He ran back toward the villa.

"Peio!" When Cassian tried to jump off, Djar caught the back of his shirt to stop him. The driver called the horses forward at Kiya's urging, and the carriage lurched as they jumped to a trot. From his vantage outside the windowless carriage, Cassian could see Peio harrying the centurions and guards as they tried to secure a wagon or carriage to follow. He killed no one else, that Cassian could see, and narrowly missed several shots aimed in his direction.

They turned abruptly down a side street, nearly tipping the carriage. Cassian clung to the doorframe and leaned forward to try and see if his friend was able to escape, but the high walls of a stone bridge blocked his view.

Once they were deeper into the mishmash of streets in the poor district, Cassian was able to draw a deep breath and think beyond escaping. He twisted and hunched to look behind him, but could only see Amara's legs and everyone else's feet. The working she'd done in the ocean had nearly knocked her off her feet. He wondered what magic did to her, that its use could send her into unconsciousness. Was it life-threatening? Or some combination of the magic and the trauma of being collared? Thinking of her face when the hound had put that collar on her filled him with violent fury enough to make him think, briefly, about jumping from the carriage to hunt him down.

Djar banged on the carriage, or Cassian assumed it was Djar, from the way the cheaply constructed box shuddered, and Kiya urged the driver to stop with a tilt of her knife. Cassian jumped down.

"This is too noticeable," Djar said as he wedged his way out of the door and shouldered Amara's still form again. Cassian wanted even just a moment to make certain she was at least breathing, but Djar pointed. "We run from here."

"This way." Cassian broke into a jog.

THEY RETURNED TO THE Fountain House because they had nowhere else to go. Djar carried Amara up the stairs, with Bek and Kiya quick behind him. Cassian, torn, lingered in the archway leading to the front garden and the gate. He wanted to be with Amara, and he feared for Peio, who had not caught up yet.

"Basha!" Mirari gasped, streaking past Cassian toward Danel, who rose from the bench he had been occupying in the interior garden. She crashed into him, which alarmed Cassian, but Danel weathered it, locking his arms around her and ducking his head against hers. Cassian slapped at his pockets and pouches, digging around until he found the single collar key he possessed. It wasn't exactly a skeleton key, but it plus a pick could usually get the job done. He approached the siblings and held it up, and Mirari yielded as he tried it in the lock.

"What happened?" Danel asked.

"Did you know?" Mirari murmured, tipping her head to look at her brother. Cassian admonished her with a grunt as he tried a different pick inside the lock. She ducked her head again. "That she is a mage? Of old blood? I have never seen anything like it. All of them...all of them were her captives. Can you imagine it?" Mirari spoke quickly and softly, trying to hold still for Cassian's work. "Like Damla."

"Is she all right?" Danel asked Cassian.

"I don't know," he said, then exclaimed in triumph as the collar unlocked. Cassian flinched at the bruised and torn ring circling Mirari's throat, but it was not the worst he'd seen. Most festered, if the collar was left on. Perhaps, if she possessed Danel's same skills, her magic had mended or prevented the worst of the damage.

"Will you watch for Peio?" Cassian asked. He needed to see Amara, or he was going to go crazy.

Danel's expression shuttered. "I cannot see the Ghosts outside a Hunt, *Sanpotar*. You know that."

"He saved us," Cassian snapped. "He saved your sister." Danel looked away from him. "Bah." Cassian waved a hand at him in angry dismissal.

"I will watch," Mirari said. Danel said her name in low warning, but she ignored him.

"Thank you." Cassian hurried to the stairs

No lamps were lit, only a single candle burning in the common area upstairs. Smart. Light drew attention. The three women Amara had purchased from the Den sat together in a huddle against the wall near the top of the stairs. Cassian could make out nothing of their expressions, though they all looked up when he arrived. Djar stood watch at Amara's door.

Cassian crossed to him and stood at his side. Amara's door was open. The moon shone brightly through her window, across the bed where Kiya lay spooned around her. Bek sat hunched in the single chair in the room, his knees pulled to his chest. He looked young and lost. Cassian crossed to him and crouched next to his chair, reaching up to squeeze his shoulder. Bek took a long time to finally look at him, eyes large and troubled in the silver light.

"You did well," Cassian said.

"If I hadn't gotten caught—"

"I got caught too." Cassian patted his shoulder firmly as he rose. It was easy to be put together for someone else. But not for himself. If they hadn't been there, Cassian might have fallen apart, useless and afraid for her. How could he possibly keep her safe from the Vexillae now? He'd thought the handful who'd caught them in the wilderness were aberrant, but Stephanus knew she was in Haenna. Had informed important people about her. He was hunting her. Did he know what kind of power she held? How could he possibly know she was in Haenna?

Amara thrashed, and a low, strangled cry issued from her throat. Kiya bolted up, kneeling at her hip, and held her hands.

"*You are safe, Sister. We all are,*" she said in Meneian.

Cassian walked to the side of the bed opposite Kiya and sat down. Amara's body had relaxed, but her brow was furrowed.

"Why is she like this?" He wanted to touch her, pretending to himself that it was to comfort her. But she had all the comfort she needed in the others. They were her family. He was nothing so special. So he dared not, with all of them so on edge. He did not know how obvious their attraction was, if he was allowed to give or claim comfort based on their few small interactions. It felt like more than it should have.

"It is mage sleep," Djar answered from the doorway. "When a mage expends their magical reserves and taps their body's energy to cast, it can kill them. Their body shuts down as defense, I have been told. To do what she did is difficult enough with one person. I have never seen her control more than two at a time, and I had to carry her then."

There had been nearly a hundred there, between guests, guards, and servants. Every one of them held in thrall by her singing and the whispering mist. Gods' blessings and curses, was that the kind of power in Tamar? No wonder Stephanus feared them. But…

Cassian looked down at her, at her face, sculpted by silver and shadow into an artist's rendering of beauty made person, and knew he could never fear her. What purpose in giving the power of subjugation to a woman who could not bear to wield it?

He curled his fingers into the linen sheet, trying to curb his need to touch her. But he could not suppress it, and reached for her, glancing sidelong to Kiya, who only nodded. Cassian smoothed his fingers over the furrow in Amara's brow. He rested his palm against her forehead. This was his fault, wasn't it? All he'd had to do was tell Paulus yes. Gods take him if he'd been the reason for lasting harm to her.

"Does she need a physician?"

"She will wake on her own, when her power is replenished by resting, but there is no telling how long it will take. And we cannot stay here much longer," Djar said. No, they could not.

"Then"—Cassian touched her hair—"you should leave. We can take her to your ship. You have Danel, and Mirari. Is that not what you came for?" He did not want to part from her. From any of them really. It had been so long since he had felt a part of anything but his own endless vendetta. But their worlds did not mix well. And he'd made a promise to his parents, or their graves anyway, so many years ago. He'd take up their torch. Once Paulus was gone, Cassian could take back his father's seat on the Senate. He could make a real difference. As they had. He could right the wrongs of his youth, repay them for the time he wasted chasing a silly passion.

"It was. But we cannot leave without the other. The Charah Danel spoke of."

Cassian still did not know what they meant when they said Charah. Neither did he particularly care. He would selfishly hoard any more time he could be with them, but at the same time worry twisted within him. Mirari moved next to Djar.

"Your friend has returned. He says it will not be long before the centurions reorganize and find out where we have gone." She glanced from one to the other of them, then asked, "You called Benat a Charah?"

"Danel told us your friend called magma from the earth. Is that true?" Djar asked.

Mirari took a war pause before she asked, "Why?"

"If he did, then he needs more training than anyone here can possibly provide him. A Charah uncontrolled is a great danger to everyone around them."

"No," Mirari said. "He is kind. He just wants…" She frowned. "What is a Charah?"

"They are the strongest of mages"—he nodded to indicate Amara—"as she is. The strongest. One for each spoke of the Wheel."

That explained Stephanus' hunt for her. Cassian stood, hot with urgency. "We have to leave. We have to split up. Too many people have seen you coming and going from this house. Stephanus must be frothing at the mouth to make an example of her." Which was likely what he intended for Benat as well. "Mirari, where is Benat?"

"In the city. Assembly guards bought him at the auction."

"Wait…" Cassian frowned. "Was Benat the man with you in the cage at the Night Auction? The opium slave?" Poppy addicts were impossible to manage, indolent one moment, mad the next, and their cravings could kill them. And he apparently possessed powerful, uncontrolled magic. He would be no help in his own rescue, and if he was still at the Assembly, even Peio couldn't break into that place.

"They're going to move him," Mirari said, "to Corsyra."

Djar cursed.

"Someone amongst my contacts will have heard when." Cassian stroked Amara's hair. "Some of you can go to the ship. Danel and Mirari can take some into the woods."

"We should not move Amara more than we have to," Djar said.

"I have a place she can stay until she is recovered. It's safer than here, at least for a short while."

"Where?" Djar asked.

Cassian grimaced. Amara wasn't going to like it.

TWENTY-FOUR

AMARA OPENED HER EYES. She did not recognize her surroundings, or remember how she had gotten there. The phantoms of nightmares threatened at the back of her mind. When she tried to capture them, they broke apart like cobwebs in a breeze, drifting away. But she didn't need the nightmares, she had the memories. The still-tender skin of her throat burned where she had clawed it, where the collar had torn it.

Her head ached. Tears spilled down her face. She sat up, hugging her arms as gooseflesh broke over her skin. She hadn't been simply asleep. Mage sleep was different. Only twice before had she experienced it, and its distinctive after-effects were unmistakable.

Her body felt foreign to her. Her abraded skin and broken nails were surely someone else's. The tears fell more thickly, blurring her vision. Despair flooded her. She staggered to her feet, frantic, as if she could outrun it. Could she? She thought she'd left that part of her in Nasiye. The monster. The killer. Subjugator. Her stomach heaved. Amara swallowed it back and swiped her wrist across her eyes so she could see.

She needed to wash. Wash it away, the feel of the collar. The sound of her voice, of her magic's voice. The song. The voices of those who had borne her power before. Traitors, liars. Thieves of lives. Monsters of songs. *Sing, oh sing, sweet water's child. Mirror a lie that is truth to me.* Not a lullaby, a warning. She was a nightmare. *Sing, oh sing, your will to me.*

The room spun as a sob tore from her throat. She tasted blood, and realized she'd bitten the inside of her cheek. Wash it away. She could endure this, if she could just wash it away. The room was a nightmare of tables and piled detritus. Beside the bed there was a rickety wooden chair with a half-broken seat, a window covered with a stained length of cloth, and as she moved, rotted floorboards creaked beneath her feet, sending little puffs of dirt up between them with each step. Against the wall opposite her bed she saw a basin, one edge broken away, a two-handled jug on the floor beside it. She rushed across the room, all of five steps, and poured water from the jug into the basin. Flecks of glaze floated in the water, as well as dust and a single spider. She scooped it out, and splashed the water up her arms, washing away dried blood, revealing the long, scabbed-over scratches she'd inflicted on herself.

Amara collapsed to her knees, knocking the basin off the table. It shattered on the floor, splashing water across her dress. She held the empty water jug in her lap as the darkness swelled up to take her again, dragging her down. Like drowning in the ocean. She could not tell if the brine in her mouth was from her tears, or if the room was the dream and the drowning the reality. Her question was answered when a rat appeared from a hole in the wall, lifting its whiskered nose to scent the air, fixing her with a beady stare. She did not scream, unable to bear the sound of her own voice. Instead she scrambled backwards through the broken pottery. A piece sliced her palm and her leg.

A door she had not noticed in her run for the water swung open and a male figure moved through the doorway, blotted into obscurity by the blazing sun behind him. But she knew Cassian's shape and posture too well not to recognize him, even if she could not see his face.

"No!" she croaked when he crossed toward her, slamming the door closed behind him. She could not bear to look at him. To see how he would look at her. "No," she said again, when he took the jug from her hands and brushed the pottery off her lap.

"Djar told me I should not take any of your choices from you, Princess, but I'm not going to let you sit on this floor and bleed." He sounded apologetic, but he wouldn't even look her in the eye. He slung an arm underneath her knees and one around her shoulders and lifted her up to carry her back to the bed. She fought, an inhuman shriek issuing from her throat, and he had to sling her onto the bed or drop her on the floor.

"Go away." She turned her back to him, and squeezed her hands between her knees so she would not have to feel them shaking.

"I'm going to go get something to treat your cuts."

The door swung shut behind him, and she turned to look. Dust swirled away from the door and through broken shafts of light between the makeshift curtains. Her hysteria ebbed, but her thoughts would not order themselves. There was more, more than the sucking sorrow that wouldn't release its grip. People who needed her. But how could they? Who could possibly need her? Everything about her was a lie. She was an imposter. Fooling everyone into believing she was worth something, worth her own freedom. That she deserved freedom, despite what she could do to anyone else on nothing more than a whim. They would be better without her. Safer.

Her eyes burned, her throat ached, and the very air around her crushed down on her, so she felt the only thing she could do was curl into a ball and let the world go on without her. They would all be better for her absence. Better without threat of her.

Cassian returned, and she hated him for it. And needed him. Needed someone to see her drowning, and know what to do. To fix what could not be fixed.

"Don't touch me," she whispered savagely. He sat on the bed beside her, and held out handfuls of torn cloth.

"Bandage your hand," he said. He tipped the bits of cloth into her lap. She stared at them, shame burning like mage fire in her heart as he stared at her. Judged her. Saw the true depth of her darkness.

"Leave me under your own power, or do so under mine," she said. Her magic coiled and snapped awake in response to her shame. The water puddled on the floor from the broken basin sent up streamers of mist.

"Are you going to make me?" Cassian asked, calmly, eyeing the rising vapor. Her heart seized, and she knew, knew she had to drive him away, to protect him. She couldn't be trusted. Not now that she'd let it go. Not now that it existed in this new world she'd made for herself.

"I can," she said. "I will. I can make you do anything I want you to."

"I'm not afraid of you, you know." He lay backwards on the bed beside her, his legs on the floor, his arms folded over his belly. "I haven't known you that long, but I know you've probably never even stepped on an ant on purpose."

"No?" She plucked at the bandages in her lap, wanting to curl up beside him and let him believe in her, hold her until the pain eased. But she couldn't. She could not let him continue to care for her. "I murdered my father."

"Did you?" His voice was so infuriatingly calm. "Why?"

The memory was fuzzy, but the emotions were as perfectly preserved as lemons in salt. The feeling, of not understanding completely, but knowing...knowing she had done something wrong. Something she couldn't fix. Those men. One had dangled her over the balcony, by an ankle, over swirling sand on hard stone. Shook her like a dust rag so her mother would stop threatening him.

"His men wanted to take me from my mother. Sell me. He argued with them." She lifted her hands to her throat, to the raw scratches that burned at her touch. "I was six." Her voice broke, her words became sobs, and she purged it to him as she cried, as unable to stop it as she would a roaring flood. "They hurt me. And they were hurting her, shaking her because she was crying, because she was afraid, using her to threaten my father."

She was there. Again. A little girl, crying. Screaming. "Stop," Amara cried. "Please." She closed her eyes around the tears. "Please stop." She begged. She rocked. As she had in the moment, chanting the word. *Stop. Stop. Stop.* Until the water in the fountain had turned to mist and engulfed them all. Until they obeyed her. Until their hearts stopped and they fell to their knees, then slumped, lifeless, on the tiles. And her father…she'd had no control. The fear in her mother's face as she had bundled Amara up in her arms. Where there had been no comfort.

It was Cassian sitting up that broke her from the nightmare.

"Gods and hells, Amara," he croaked, "please don't make me sit here and listen to you cry and tell me I can't hold you."

"You cannot help me," she sobbed. Her father had loved her. And she'd killed him.

"I know," he said. "I know I can't. I also know the lies that trauma tells a mind, to give itself a warm home to live in, to warp the truth into a cage." He touched her wrist. "I don't have the key to your cage, Princess. But you can open it from the inside. You could let me sit in there with you."

"I don't know how." She couldn't stop the tears. They bled kohl down her cheeks, so that grey mingled in fat drops on her dress, alongside blood. She wanted his comfort, but she didn't deserve it.

Just as she hadn't deserved her mother, who had sacrificed herself for her daughter's crimes.

"You have to forgive yourself. You were a child, and you did not hurt a single person last night. Not a single person, and we all know they deserved it."

"They are not the only ones I have murdered," she purged. "Boys." She tipped her head back. "Turned to jailers. And I took any chance they had of ever becoming anything else, to free one man." They were supposed to execute Djar. She'd turned them on each other.

"And Djar? How many people has he killed? Yet he does not let it blacken his soul as you do."

"You sound like him. He doesn't understand either." No. Djar believed in her. Loved her. They loved her. Because he and the twins had blinded themselves to the truth of her. Just as Cassian had. Djar fought men who fought back. Took their lives. Not their will. Not their self. Amara swiped at her cheeks and wiped the dampness against her dress. "You should be afraid of me." She could not abide his gentle words and the tortured look on his face. She was not strong enough to stand away from him when she felt so broken. She could take from him. He wanted to give her comfort. She should take it. "Now that you know how repugnant my magic is."

"You saved our lives and did no harm in the process." Cassian slid his hand to hers and gripped it.

Amara squeezed her eyes shut. "No harm? I make slaves of people. In Menei I was a prisoner, a servant. I have no desire to turn others into mine. Yet I can. I can make you leave right now, if I want to." If she did...if she made him do something against his will, she knew she would not survive it. It would break her.

Cassian laughed softly, looking at her sidelong. "Would you like to know a secret?" he asked. She turned her head to meet his eyes. He reached across himself to gently cup the back of her neck as he leaned close enough to whisper to her. "You don't need magic to make me do what you want me to."

A sob escaped her, and she leaned into him, burying her face against his neck, tucking her arms between them and crying quietly. Cassian wrapped his arms around her.

"I don't want this power. I have never wanted it," she cried. "I am a monster in pretty packaging."

"You are not a monster," Cassian said, "but I agree that your packaging is very pretty." He shifted, lying down on his side and bringing her with him. Amara relaxed into his control. Into his hold. He smoothed his hand down her back, molding her front to his in the process. "I wish I had words for you. I wish…" He didn't finish, only let his breath out slowly, and nuzzled his nose and mouth against her brow and hair.

She closed her eyes. Took a breath that shuddered, as his touch and his presence steadied her. An aura silent of magic in the presence of one that was too loud, quieted her to something she could bear. A shore upon which she crawled from the dark deep of her magic and fell against to breathe, and taste the air again.

She came out of her mind, and into her body. Her eyes ached, dry and swollen. The cuts stung. Her throat hurt from her wailing, and the collar.

"I was afraid for you," Cassian said. Not afraid of her, but for her. Someone who had never known powerful magic. Thrust into the grip of water's strongest servant.

"Idiot," Amara whispered. Cassian laughed, and kissed her brow, then cupped her jaw in his hands. His gaze roamed her face, settling against her own in silent question. He tipped his head closer, then pulled back, uncertain. Amara pushed closer and Cassian tipped her head so he could kiss her, and she let him, because it brought a shimmer of joy with it. Her body felt leaden and dead, incapable of the heat she would need to tryst with him. But she wished for it back, for the distraction. To feel connected to pleasure again, to something far removed from the shadows that clung inside her now.

"Bek would probably like to see you," Cassian murmured. "They all worried, but he has shouldered a great deal of blame."

Tears burned again, the memory of his face. His fear. Flinching from her.

"You need to see the people you helped." Cassian shifted, lifting up to his elbow. "The people who love you."

"Where are we?" Amara pressed her hand to his shoulder, to urge him back down. She was not ready yet. There was nothing in her to give to them, to comfort them. She was empty of anything but despair.

"My home," he said.

Amara let her gaze rove up the wall behind him, to the ceiling, made of more rotted boards. She rolled to her back to look around. The tables, she realized, were covered in carvings in various states of work. Something tall stood in the corner, draped with a cloth. A canvas, she guessed by its shape. Crumpled paper was scattered across the floor. The rat was back, snuffling at a discarded apple core.

Amara swallowed a sound of dismay. "It's disgusting."

Cassian laughed again. "I know. But we had to get out of the Fountain House and thought it best we split up. The others are on your ship. Peio and Danel took Mirari and the Den girls into the woods." He watched her as she took another look around the room. "I would rather not have had you see it, but now that you are here I like it. You should stay."

She turned her head, their gazes clashing. The tone had been teasing, dry. The look in his eyes was not. No. Some part of him meant every word.

Amara swallowed the tightness in her throat. Blinked against her burning eyes. She was so accustomed to rescuing others, to adopting them to her, like droplets to an ocean. But Cassian would not come.

Not to her. Too much anchored him here. And she could not abandon everything for him.

"I must look frightful." She cut her gaze away from his.

"Not once since I met you have you ever looked frightful," Cassian said. "You are so beautiful…" He stroked his knuckle against her temple. "Someone who puts others so far above herself that she is crushed by it. I feel unworthy to even walk beside you. I have never put a single soul before myself."

"Is that what you see in yourself?" She pressed her hand over his heart. "That is not what I see."

He traced the curve of her ear with his thumb, then stroked her bare arm. The warmth of his hand was welcome, making her shiver.

"Someone wise once told me we do not see ourselves as we are," he said, "that we are blinded to what really looks back at us in the mirror."

Amara scowled at him, and he waggled his eyebrows. A smile fought her and won.

"I also told you that water reflects the truth. And there are many freed Suloi who might claim you put them before you."

"Bah." He leaned down to touch his nose to the corner of her mouth and placed a soft kiss there. "Enough. Do you want more rest?"

"I don't know." If she closed her eyes, Amara had no doubt the nightmares would come for her again. Perhaps he saw that fear in her face, because he settled on his back beside her and patted his chest. She lifted up to look down at him.

"Why don't you put your head here"—he grinned as he closed his eyes—"and I'll stay to make certain the rats don't get you."

"That is very comforting." Amara glanced toward the center of the room. The apple core was gone. She shuddered, scooting closer to Cassian and hooking a leg over his. He made a low sound of approval, and she laid her head in the crook of his shoulder. He felt good, warm, and solid. And open to her. Eager to give and receive affection. And it took that for her to understand that she had missed that, in her more casual interactions. Not that she regretted them, but that she had not realized how much she had wanted such honesty. Or at least, had not wanted it from those others.

"Would you like to know what it is like growing up in Haenna?" His voice was gravelly, tired. Amara hugged an arm over his chest and nodded. "It may come as a shock," Cassian drawled, sleepily, "but it is very boring here."

His voice was the rhythmic shift of sand beneath water, timed to the slowing cadence of her heart. Its timbre coaxed her into a sleep clean of pain and memory, and his steady, magicless presence at her side held her there, sea cradled by steady, silent shore.

TWENTY-FIVE

THE LOW HUM OF voices woke her. The room was dark, cut with the flickering light of candles. She rolled away from the wall to look. There were a dozen candles scattered around, dancing and flickering. It transformed the space from filthy bachelor quarters to artist's nook. The unreliable light somehow highlighting the art instead of the mess. The warm glow inexplicably cheery and comforting. For a moment she thought she was alone. Then she saw that Kiya sat on the edge of a long table on the far side of the room, leaning forward, and Bek sat in a chair near her swinging feet. Cassian was there as well, standing in front of them both, near the item she suspected to be a canvas.

His shirt was off, tossed onto a nearby table. To protect it from the paint, she thought. Intrigued, she sat up as quietly as she could, hoping to watch him unnoticed. She had never watched anyone paint anything. She considered herself an artist when it came to clothing, stitches, embellishments, and shaping. She had watched blacksmiths and jewel smiths. Weavers. A sculptor once. And she had seen many finished paintings. Never one in progress.

Cassian scratched the back of his head with the wooden end of the brush he held. He blocked the painting from view, unfortunately, but her view of him was pleasing enough to make up for it. The candle-light was particularly loving to him, casting shadows to outline the muscles of his back and arms, darkening his hair, warming his skin. Amara rubbed her hands against the bed to quell the desire to touch him. She looked down at them when she felt out-of-place friction. He'd managed to wrap her cut hand while she slept. Not the one on her leg though. Too decent to go diving beneath her dress without her permission. Not quite the mannerless rascal he liked to play.

"How do you pick the colors?" Kiya asked, leaning forward farther to peer at the board that held a mishmash of paint.

"Practice," Cassian said.

"And getting to know your subject very well?" Her teeth flashed, and her dangling feet kicked faster, and Cassian glanced at her, allowing Amara a quick view of a raised eyebrow. Bek snorted, stretching his legs out and folding his arms over his chest.

"I only paint things I enjoy looking at, yes." Cassian focused on the painting again. Curiosity nibbled at Amara's insides, but she was too charmed by the scene to interrupt it. In the back of her thoughts there were other matters. Pressing things to be thinking of. But these moments were important too, peace and calm stolen around the whirlwind of life. These were the moments that all the others paid for. The balance of a life lived with purpose, were the moments without it.

"You could sell these, instead of gambling," Kiya suggested.

"Not without a patron, and trust me, twin one, no one is going to be my patron," he answered. Amara heard something else in his voice. Remorse, or sorrow. Because his parents had disapproved.

"Besides, how would all the other gamblers make money if Cassian wasn't there to lose to them?" Bek said. Cassian didn't turn, but kicked his foot backward, nearly upending Bek's chair. Bek snickered, and Kiya grinned, and Amara's heart was squeezed and too full all in one.

Kiya and Bek jumped into a good-natured argument about which of them should be twin one, and which twin two.

Cassian ignored them, continuing with his work. His hair was a mess, he'd clearly been shoving his hands through it. He slid his right hand into his pocket, dabbing at the canvas with the left, which held the brush. He tapped the brush against the paint-strewn board, then swept it in short strokes, tilting his head and leaning to one side as he did. Then he did the same in the other direction. Kiya and Bek mirrored the movement. It was unexpected, how deeply the sight pierced her. How comfortable it was to watch him, and them together. How quickly her mind took the image and extrapolated it to the pleasure of always waking to such a sight. To how much she would love to be a part of this side of him. See it from start to finish. See *him*, from start to finish. To have known him as a boy, and see him when the grey had overtaken the black of his hair and age had refined him.

Restless to escape the gravity of her feelings, Amara slid off the bed. The frame creaked, as did the floor. All three looked to her. Kiya slipped off the table and Bek sprang from his chair. As Kiya bounded her way through the mess, Cassian set his brush down and tugged a cloth back over the painting, raising a small wooden bar to keep the fabric from touching the wet paint. Kiya slung her arms around Amara's waist and squeezed until Amara gasped for breath.

"How are you feeling?"

"Well." Amara cupped Kiya's face in her hands, assessing her. "And you?"

"I'm fine." Kiya's dark gaze bored into Amara's, reluctance in the firm set of her mouth. "Thanks to you."

Amara had to think of the scene she had just witnessed to push away the panic that rose with the oblique mention of her magic. Kiya stepped back when Amara offered her a stiff smile. Bek hovered farther away, his angry expression his best effort to cover the guilt that made his eyes tighten at the corners.

"Bek," Amara said. He took a step closer, looking at Cassian without moving his head. He shrugged and smiled. Always he tried too hard to be Djar, stoic and silent without the other's age and maturity. Without his mechanisms for dealing with the torrent within. Amara could not bring it into the open with Cassian present. That would be an unforgivable revelation of weakness for a boy of only three Cycles.

"Kiya thought you'd want to bathe before anything else," Bek said.

"Yes." Amara wanted to be rid of the dress and all the marks and the oily, lingering feel of the people who had touched her. Wash it all away. But the other matters she had pushed out of her thoughts came back. "Are we safe here?"

"Unlikely for much longer. It would be best"—Cassian turned his back as he spoke, snagging his shirt from the table and pulling it over his arms—"for you to finish your business and be gone as soon as possible." The words were matter of fact, the tone even. But Amara was certain if she could see his face it would tell her a different story. Her magic swirled at the touch of lies.

Kiya looked at her sidelong, with eyebrows raised. Bek stared at the floor. Cassian busied himself with arranging the items strewn about the table. Blocks of wood, small implements for shaping them into something else. One of the posters with his face, or at least a poor representation of it, a knife.

"That bath?" Amara said to Kiya. "And you may tell me what I have missed."

Kiya grabbed a bundle of clothing and laced her fingers with Amara's to lead her outside of the hut. Hut seemed a generous description, but it was the best Amara could do for the thatch-roofed square that might have better served as storage than a place to live. Certainly if she compared it to her own living space above her shop. Or the palace.

The palace. A prince. A place where no one would ever be able to put a collar on her. A place where she would never fear so much for her friends that she let her power out of the depths where it belonged. A man who did not inspire feelings in her that would make it impossible to keep her magic in check, buried. A man who did not know her darkness, had not seen it. Ihsan was what she wanted, and needed. Surely, Cassian only felt like something she wanted because of the trauma that had plagued her since arriving in Haenna. The feeling would fade, she need only weather it until she was away from him.

To distract herself from the tightening of her throat, Amara squeezed Kiya's hand.

"We can't go to the main bathhouse, but you can pay to take a bath in a wine barrel," Kiya said apologetically. That would not be the worst place she had bathed. Her mother had often snuck them into livestock pens to bath in the water troughs. There had also been the waste-laden, scum-crusted water in the streets of Nasiye.

Kiya led her expertly through the maze of alleys and huts that matched Cassian's, skirting midden heaps and foul-smelling puddles and piles. Two half-starved mongrels followed them for a few turns but lost interest quickly, disappearing into another alley. In Narfour, strays were considered denizens of the city. Many people left scraps and bits out for particular neighborhood favorites, and many of the bricks in the road were hollowed out to hold water for birds and other passing animals. Here the poor creatures were lucky not to be kicked or otherwise abused in passing.

"How long did I sleep?"

"A day and a half," Kiya said as she led them through an archway connecting two squat buildings and into a little courtyard. A hard-packed dirt path led to a wall, and to either side, fabric hung as partitions between barrels. At the wall on the far end, a woman sat next to a steaming cauldron, and a gaggle of young girls sat around her in a circle. Three of them were sewing, two were tossing rocks into a circle sketched in the dirt, and the last fed wood to the fire beneath the cauldron.

Kiya paid and the girls went to work filling a barrel with buckets of hot water from the cauldron and cold water from a pump near the archway. Amara glanced up at the night sky. Blazing bright and strong, directly above them, she traced the shape of the Wheel. Six stars in a circle around the seventh, hard to see initially, until someone pointed it out. Her mother had looked to it every night, had told her the story of how the spinning of the Wheel had created the sky, and then the world. Sun for moon, water for fire, dark for light. Chaos and order. From that balance came magic, and from magic came life.

And what was her balance? It had seemed so clear. For all the pain that had begun her life, she was owed peace. And yet, here she was, tangled in the pain again.

"Here," Kiya said. They stepped between the hanging fabric and Kiya pulled another one closed, so they were surrounded on all sides by linen washed thin and spare. Amara undressed and stepped into the barrel. A standing bath wasn't her preference, but anything to wash away the feelings that clung to her skin was better than nothing.

"*The guards are hunting us, and there are posters of you around now,*" Kiya said softly in Meneian. She scrubbed a cloth over Amara's back. Over the indelible marks that made erasing what she had been impossible. "*Cassian confirmed that the Charah is still held at the Assembly.*" She dipped the rag in the water, soaped it, and handed it to Amara. The soap smelled like fat and lye, a flat, slightly offensive smell. Her soaps in Narfour smelled of lemon, lavender, and olives. "*But they are going to move him. In two days, to the capital.*"

Amara scrubbed at her fingers with the cloth, running her thumb across her broken nails. How could they steal a single man from the heart of the city government? They would have to wait until he was being moved.

"*Does Djar have a plan?*"

"*He wanted to wait for you.*" Kiya shook out the clothes she'd brought as Amara climbed out of the barrel. A very undignified kind

of thing to have to do while wet and naked. Kiya handed Amara a
threadbare towel.

"*Then I want you to tell him that we will all meet, tomorrow morning.
First light.*"

Amara dried and dressed. This last thing. Then they would return
to Tamar, she would have what she had worked for, and all of this
unpleasantness could be forgotten. Locked away with the rest of it in
her mind.

All of it.

BEK MET THEM OUTSIDE the hut and took Kiya to return to the ship.
Amara thought of joining them—a sleep rocked by the ocean would
be restorative. But she wanted Cassian's company more than she
wanted the ocean. A thought she did not allow herself to ruminate on
for even a moment. There were dangers in a feeling like that.

Inside, Cassian had cleared off the smallest round table and pulled
two chairs up to it. A half-loaf of bread sat on its surface, next to a
dish of olive oil, a scattering of olives, a hunk of cured meat, and a
broken-off bit of hard cheese about the size of an apple. The candles
that had been burning when she woke still flickered, though most
were almost burned down. Someone had cleaned the floor. If she had
her guess it had been Bek, far more fastidious than his sister. When he
was troubled, he cleaned. A fact that had been most beneficial to the
state of Amara's shop.

Cassian sat in one of the chairs, slouched into it with one arm
draped over the back, legs stretched out and crossed, his other hand
occupied with two dice. He watched her as she entered and crossed
to him.

"May I join you?" Amara asked. Cassian gave the empty chair a
push with his boot, then straightened.

"I thought you might be hungry."

"Thank you. And where did this bounty come from?" Amara sat. Cassian drew a hunting knife from his belt and hacked off a few bite-sized pieces of cheese, then cut slices of the meat, something marbled with a great deal of fat.

"A friend." Cassian cut his gaze to hers and away.

"Did you send my twins to steal this?" Amara took a piece of the cheese. It was hard and crumbling, salty and sharp, speckled with bits of something crystallized. Absolutely delicious. She'd never tasted one like it. She took another bite-sized morsel, watching Cassian from beneath her lashes as he pulled off a piece of bread and dragged it through the olive oil.

"I suggested there was food to be had in the market when vendors were distracted." He shrugged. When she exhaled through her nose, he grinned at her and winked. "They're the best at blending in, Princess. And you needed food. Unless you want whatever roots and fungus Mirari and Sorne can scavenge in the woods."

Amara wrinkled her nose. He stared at her a moment, then looked down at his hands.

"Looking at you has become my new favorite pastime," he said, quietly. He scrubbed his hands against his thighs and sat up with a forced smile, turning his gaze to the ceiling.

"You have an exceptional talent for it," Amara replied, taking another bite of cheese. He dropped his head, gaze fixing on her again. A streak of brownish paint marked his jaw, and the candlelight made his blue eyes a shade of indigo. Amara swallowed her bite and looked down. There was heat in her face. She looked at him fiercely. Cassian blinked in surprise.

"What?" He offered her a chunk of bread. Amara took it from him but didn't eat it. She picked at the crumbs.

"You do not know magic," she finally managed to say, in as neutral a voice as she could. He tugged at his ear, squinting at her before he folded his arms on the table and leaned forward. "You think it is whimsy."

"There is nothing whimsical about you. And if you mean I do not know how to do magic, then yes. If you mean I don't know anything of it, I think you're mistaken. I've known Suloi all my life. And now you."

"I mean Tamar magic. Wind that speaks across leagues, water that conveys an image, earth that shatters at a command, fire that is malleable…" Her brow notched. "…shadow that destroys."

"No, I do not know that magic," he agreed, studying her now.

"Why doesn't it frighten you?"

He leaned back again, eyes narrowed, arms folded over his chest. "In the Republic," he finally said, "gods play with us at their whim. There is no warning. No rules. One day your house may burn down. You do not know why. Perhaps you did not light enough incense for Veyna, that she would look favorably upon your home. Or you have angered the High Goddess by saying her name outside of prayer or not marrying soon enough." He sighed. "You never know. But you"—Cassian gave her a playful smile—"you are human. There is something very comforting about dealing with a human. Even if they have magic I don't understand. Humans can be cheated, you see. And gods cannot."

"Do you believe in gods?" Amara kept her voice neutral. She did not wish to insult him.

"I believe in Luck," he said, "though I am not entirely certain she believes in me."

"Luck is a goddess?"

"She is. But that is not her name. The stories go that she hates her father, who named her, so any who call her by it raise her ire. So we all simply call her Luck."

Amara dabbed the hunk of bread she held into the puddle of olive oil and ate it. "That seems needlessly complicated."

"She is one of the less complicated of the pantheon." He cocked his head. "Do you worship anything?"

"I am a child of the Wheel. I am beholden to its balance. To its turning."

"It is sentient, this Wheel?"

She picked apart a slice of the meat and ate it. Unctuous and flavored with mustard seed. She didn't like it, but was too hungry to care. The little seeds insisted on lodging in her teeth, which distracted her from the question.

"It is the collective conscious of all, magic, life and death, a cycle. It cannot be confined by ideas like sentience." The subject brought her too close to the question that remained unanswered. Why her? Why did she have to be born with a power that brought her nothing but misery? If the Wheel spun for balance, in her it had failed. She needed away from the subject, away from the threatening twist in her belly.

"Are you painting something risqué, that you must hide it?" She pointed. "I wish to see it."

He tensed, then recovered with a shake of his head. Amara rose, thinking she might play with him and forget the gravity of her feelings and fears in the process. His eyes scrunched as she took a step toward him, and toward the painting beyond.

"Just a little peek?" She edged closer. Cassian set his boots against the floor and pushed his chair farther from the table, to give himself room to grab for her if she tried to pass him. Amara pursed her lips together to hold a smile, and he slowly shook his head. "Oh come," Amara sighed, putting her hands on her hips.

"There's a viewing fee." Cassian had readopted his lazy sprawl, hooking his arm over the chair again, and it brought to mind their time in the Fountain House together, after she'd cut his hair.

"Oh?" If he asked for a kiss she wasn't going to tell him no. She wanted to forget. To be as far away from what was inside her as she could be.

"Tell me something. Anything. What do you do in Tamar? Do you spend all day stripped of your clothes, relaying messages to people?"

The sparkle in his flame-darkened eyes was charming and carnal. Her more difficult thoughts were forgotten in a surge of lust.

"I am a merchant. I deal in the finest clothes in Narfour. I make them," she said. "So it would be very poor advertising to go about nude."

He laughed. "Would you make clothes for me?"

"No." She smiled. "A common criminal cannot afford the pieces I make. Nor an artist who does not know the value of his work."

"Cruel," he said. He stretched a leg out, hooking his boot against her ankle, and pulled. Amara stepped closer at his urging, the curl of desire that warmed her glowing stronger. "And here I'd give you anything you asked for."

"What do you have to give?" she teased. She stood close enough that her left knee pressed against his right when he bent it to give her room. A man's lap had never been quite so inviting.

He gestured at himself with a sweep of his hand.

"Hmm, no thank you," she said.

He made an exaggerated expression of offense, hooking his leg behind hers and forcing her closer, then squeezed his thighs together against her knees. "Then what do you want?"

"The painting."

"No," Cassian said, "you didn't tell me enough about you."

"There is nothing else to know," she sniffed.

"Oh yes there is." Cassian caught her wrists, and rose up, his body brushing hers as he did. "Tell me everything, and I will still never know enough about you."

She tipped her head as he pulled her to him. That expression was on his face, desire cut with sadness. As though he didn't think he was allowed to want her.

She could not bear it. Could not think of what she wanted from him, what that would do to her. That there was no line between her physical and emotional needs when she looked at him. That line was the key to the chains that held her magic. She shouldn't cross it.

Amara made a quick movement for the painting in a bid to distract them both. Cassian sighed in exasperation and tugged her back. Amara pulled away, running the opposite way around the table, and he slung the chair in her path. When she tried to avoid it he caught an arm around her waist and turned her toward him again.

"You can see it when it's finished."

The tentative surge of elation at their play dissipated, and her gaze flashed to his. He closed his eyes as if it pained him. She would not be here when he finished. He knew. They would rescue the Fourth House Charah and leave. Cassian glanced at the painting, and Amara took a step toward it, then darted forward out of his grasp.

"No, no," Cassian chided as he caught her by the wrist and tried to spin her back toward him. She slipped free and ran to the other side of the table.

He chased her and she dodged him, leading him in a loop around the little table, pushing the chairs in his way, giggling. She caught a handful of the olives as she made another circuit and threw one at him.

"Are you trying to bring the rats back?" He ducked her second missile.

"This will keep them occupied and away from me." She threw the last fruit at him and it bounced off his chest. He came for her and she grabbed for something else, but missed. Cassian caught her around the waist and she squealed, trying to squirm free as she giggled and he laughed breathlessly. He levered her around, so her chest crashed against his, then bent enough to lift her off the floor.

She huffed in surprise, catching fistfuls of his shirt in her hands. They stared at each other.

"I don't want you to go," he said in a voice like rough-hewn cedar. Amara frowned, but when she opened her mouth to speak he captured it, and her breath, in his.

It was not a soft kiss, not a coaxing one. It was pure desperation. And lethal. A tender kiss would have allowed her time to think, time to step away. Not this kiss, hot and hard and fast. Amara went soft in his hold, her body wresting control from her mind. When she responded to him, Cassian's hushed sound of pleasure turned her to molten glass, ichorous and searing hot. Her magic shuddered in her mental grip, clawed fingers curling around the lid she kept on it.

"You don't belong to an ice prince," he whispered when they pulled apart.

"I belong to myself." Amara cupped his face in her hands.

"I know"—the dimple appeared—"and I like you that way."

Curse him. Curse him all the way around the Wheel and into the void. For knowing exactly what to say to make her heart march off with her good sense.

"This between us is dangerous in ways you cannot understand."

"I care about you. I want you. What is there to understand?" The loneliness showed again, the same she had seen when Peio announced he wished to return to Tamar with her. Cassian walked with her to the bed, and she could not bring herself to stop him. He set her on the edge and crouched in front of her, looking up into her face. His hands cupped her knees. She circled her thumb between his brows, then fanned her fingers over one black eyebrow.

"You do not know what happens to mages"—she steadied herself with a deep breath— "mages in the throes of pleasure. They cannot control their magic."

"And I will become a thoughtless husk if you cannot control your magic?" he asked, carefully, a smile tugging at the corner of his mouth. Amara dropped her hand into her lap. "I'd likely be one anyway, at whatever moment you lose control." His smile was warm, and suggestive. "Am I mistaken in thinking I am not your first? What have you done in the past to control it?"

"It…" Heat painted across her breastbone and she looked at the wall with a frustrated sigh. "…it isn't the physical pleasure." She could not look into his eyes. "It is the combination of it and…" She laced her fingers together. "…emotion. Magic and emotion feed each other. I cannot control my emotion and my magic all at once while also letting go with my body. So I do not tryst with people who inspire particularly strong emotions."

"Strong emotion." His fingers pressed tighter against her legs.

"Yes," she breathed. Her magic swelled out of the darkness, mist and shimmering silver.

"What emotion?" he asked. She closed her eyes as she felt the cold bloom of power inside her, and shook her head. "For me?"

Amara opened her eyes and looked at him.

TWENTY-SIX

ARGENT THREADED HER IRISES. Moonlight through jet. It shimmered just beneath her skin like the flickering of minnows in shallows, little more than a flash that was gone by the time he turned his attention to it. Beautiful and visceral, he wanted to capture it for all time painted or drawn, and something in him suggested he might be better served to run. More than just a woman, it reminded him. Closer to god than mortal. In every way capable of destroying him. Maybe she already had.

Kiya had warned him, not because he had asked. But because she understood what he wanted. Too many women he knew had that knack. That hound's sense for infatuation. It was Kiya who had removed all the water from the home. Kiya who had lit the candles. Fire, she had said, to balance water. Fire, to cut through Amara's spell. Cassian hadn't understood why he might need that. But after Amara's explanation, he thought he might be starting to.

Inside, his mind and body warred. Rejoice at this evidence that she cared about him. Rage that it was pointless. Show her he cared too. Save himself from the inevitable aftermath of going too far with someone he could never have. It was a mess in his head, his desire, his worry for her.

Those demons that chased her were not small. She was twisted around herself, blind to her own truth and wounded by it. He was not a hero, the kind of man who could stand between the ones he cared about and every danger and pain that came along. He wasn't made that way. But for her, he wished he could be. He wished he could take her pain, the way she tortured herself, and excise it from her, so she could see what he saw. Peace, and justice. Like Luck in the harbor, with hands outstretched to offer welcome to those who needed it. Patroness of the lost, the damaged, the mistreated. The only real goddess he had ever known.

"Let me care about you, Amara. I already do. You cannot make me stop."

"I cannot stay here. Everything I have ever worked for is in Tamar. And this place…" she hissed the last word, and closed her eyes. But it did not hide her magic as it flared more powerfully, shining silver between black lashes. It woke bright in her skin, those rosettes of mirrored glass, in which he could see a shadowed reflection of himself.

Cassian lifted his hands from her knees and hovered his fingers over her wrist, where silver pooled like mercury, shivering and shimmering. Her eyes opened. Cassian traced the wavering edge of moonlight, and it curved and reformed around his touch. He breathed a laugh and stroked his hand up her arm from wrist to bare shoulder, watching the silver break apart and reform in the wake of his touch.

"Extraordinary," he said. "You are extraordinary."

"I know." Her mouth curved in a smile, black lashes lowering over silvered eyes, and he was gone. Gone for a woman who knew herself and didn't, peace and pain reflected in itself, something like him but evolved to near perfection.

"Please," he whispered. He needed her. Yes, it would break him when she left. It would crush him to think of her in a faraway, near-imaginary place, married to a prince. Even if that was what she deserved. But he could worship her now, and hope a piece of it stayed with her. Mattered to her.

"I will already miss you when I go," she answered back, threading her fingers into his hair, pulling him so he knelt and fit himself between her knees. His body remembered her touches, fingers slipping through his hair, nails clawed into his shoulders as he kissed her after she shaved his jaw. "You wish to open a wound that will not heal, so you will always be in my mind."

"Absolutely," Cassian said. "Let me live in your memory and your magic, because I think when you go, there will be little left of me here."

"Men," Amara purred, "are so very fragile." She nodded silent consent, her posture softening toward him. He etched the generous curve of her hips into his memory with his hands.

"Be fragile with me, I promise to take care of you." He could do that. He could not be a hero and save her from her hurts, but he could give every inch of her body and her heart the attention it deserved, for this one time.

"You do have the most capable hands." She took his in hers, entwining their fingers. Her skin was cool, and when her magic flared in silver light the water scent of her permeated the air, washing him clean. "I have wondered if you are more smuggler or artist when it comes to a woman's body?"

"There is nothing for you but art, Amara." He'd never hated his little hut more, the creaky, slapped-together bed frame and lumpy bed. This was a woman who should only ever sleep on sprawling beds with silk and finest linen, the kind of thing draped with gauze and velvet, like he'd heard some people describe the courts in Nasiye. Things he could never give her. Not now.

"I do so love your words." Amara stood, so he knelt at her feet. The stola she had changed into was plain, white, the kind that was held up at the shoulders, little more than artfully draped cloth. She unfastened one shoulder, holding the fabric up with a hand against her chest as she slipped the other arm free. Amara knew how to make undressing into an art form, into a weapon. A knife point held to his neck would have had the same effect, a speeding pulse, breath held, all his awareness focused on a single moment, a single movement. She'd kill him or free him with a flick of her wrist.

Amara smiled as if she could see his thoughts, and lifted her hand. The stola dropped, pooling at her feet and over his legs. Cassian rose up on his knees, fingers digging, and pressed his brow to her belly. He stroked a kiss below her navel, and her fingers dug into his hair, curling to hold him to her. There was nothing under her stola, just the water of her scent laced with the soap she had used when she'd bathed. Just her skin, warm and earthen and spotted with swirling mirrors, her curves, unadorned with anything but magic. She had teased him on the beach, and he'd been intrigued, but now she was his, for the moment, and he was enraptured. Paralyzed by the insistent heat that filled him and the beauty before him.

"Up," she urged, her hands moving down as he complied. She skimmed his arms with her touch, then up his stomach and chest, to the buttons of his shirt. Her fingers were adept, making quick work of something he would have bungled in his current state of mind. He could hardly string thoughts together enough to decide what to do with her. She shoved her hands under the shoulders of the shirt and pushed it off his arms while he was still thinking. When he blinked in confusion she laughed as she leaned into him. The heat and weight of her breasts, the distinct pressure of her nipples, and the smooth, soft press of her belly to his naked skin woke him from his arousal-induced stupor.

"Leave me a wit to do something with," he murmured as he wrapped his arms around her.

"I am not particularly interested in your wits at the moment," she said into the curve of his neck. He wanted to laugh, but it was all he could do to remain standing as her breath, followed by a warm, lingering kiss against his throat, sent a cold shudder through him. Her fingers worked between them, unbuckling his pistol belt, which he took from her before she dropped it on the floor. Cassian placed it carefully down and when he straightened she unhooked the top button of his pants. All he could feel were her fingers, curved over the waistband, pressing against his low belly, how achingly close to his cock they were, how her touch felt like the only thing he had ever needed. She had said something else to him.

"What?"

"Your boots." She blinked the silver out of her eyes. It did not go completely, just receded then crept back, water washing the shore of her dark eyes. Cassian watched it as he maneuvered out of his boots and kicked them away. It pulsed with her breath, glowing stronger on the inhale and the edges of the silver softening as she exhaled. There was no medium in the world that could capture it. Moonlight, mirrors, water. Mysteries and truths, reflected and refracted, dancing on her skin, in her eyes, with her very breath. Visible, tangible proof that he was wanted. That she cared for him. Sadness lapped at the edges of his desire and he shook his head to banish it.

"Beautiful." He pulled her back to him, hugging her as he turned and fell onto the bed, with her on top of him. Amara gasped and laughed, lifting her head to look down at him.

Her hands coasted over his chest and ribs as she sat up over his hips and his mind spiraled into his groin, his hands to her hips, gods her hips, urging her down as he arched up. She rose on her knees instead, denying him any relief. "These are in my way." She tugged at his pants.

Cassian fumbled at the buttons as she pressed her hands to his chest and lowered her mouth to his. He shoved his pants over his hips but that was as far as he could get before he lost the battle with his need to touch her and kiss her. Her mouth on his was slow and sultry, and she shied back each time he tried to kiss her harder or deeper, and he made a low sound of protest. He wrapped an arm around her waist and twisted her beneath him. She was all curves and softness around him and he lost himself to it for a moment, propping his weight against his elbow and knee so he could slide a collection of curls between his fingers.

She stared up at him in silver silence, and he drew his finger along her ear, and jaw, painted his thumb over her parted lips, down her chin and throat. Her body curved up when he rubbed his hand down her arm and brought her fingers to his mouth. He kissed each fingertip, circled his thumb against her palm in a slow massage. Her lashes fluttered lower over her eyes, and the magic in her skin swirled in time with his touch, which delighted him. Her fingers curled over his when he stopped and she brushed her hand up his arm, leaving pebbled flesh as she went. She trailed her nails over his chest, sending sharp pulses of sensation from his nipples to his hips.

Her other hand traced his spine, washing his body with shivers, and when her fingers tightened on his buttocks his hips heeded the pressure, driving his aching cock between the warm press of her thighs. The dampness of her arousal made her skin slick, and her breath whispered when he pulled back, rubbing himself against the place he wanted to be. She shifted with a plaintive mewl, her legs spreading in invitation, and Cassian's hips settled against hers. That was where he wished to stay, his thoughts gone, his body under her command, but his pants were locking his legs together. He stood and shoved them the rest of the way off, and Amara watched him, raking him with a glowing gaze and a smile of approval.

She sat up before he could return to her. Then she stood, her body meeting his, heavy breasts, supple belly, heat, and chill. Her arms twined his neck and he explored the hourglass shape of her again, reveled the feel of her silken skin. Amara shifted against him, pressing a knee between his own, tucking her hand into the space between their hips to grip his erection. Cassian exhaled, resisting the urge to close his eyes and drown in the sensation.

"In a hurry, Princess?" He took her wrists and grasped them behind her back in one hand, which arched her against him in the best way possible. Her hair, damp at the nape from her bath, spilled over her shoulders, ink on loam.

"We have been dancing for some time." She shifted, circling her leg around the outside of his, sliding her calf up his. "And I am ready to play."

He marveled for a moment at her balance, but he'd seen her dance, this was a woman in control of herself, of every movement she made. He kissed her shoulder then placed a necklace of the same along her collarbones. She turned her head against his, cinching her leg against the backs of his knees. Cassian released her wrists, thrusting the fingers of one hand into her hair and taking a handful of her backside in the other as he kissed her neck. Amara melted into his hold with a throaty warble, her freed hands gripping his shoulders.

He pet her, kissing her neck, her jaw, nipped her earlobe, and her hips moved in languid torture against his, drawing little, erotic circles that nudged his cock and drowned all his coherent thoughts.

"Have mercy," he sighed, framing her breasts with his hands, tracing their silken undersides with thumbs too rough with callus to touch her skin. She shivered, her gaze flashing to his, lips parting as her breath shuddered. The look on her face, made otherworldly by the silver in her eyes, was also tender, and trusting. And the man in him superseded the animal for a moment. Some had touched this woman, his goddess, with something other than worship. Had touched her without caring. Without knowing, or wanting to, all that she was. Yet here she stood, burdened but unbroken, trusting him with more than her body. Trusting him with her pain, with her care. He was not worthy of that, but he would try his best to be, even if it was just for this night.

"What is it?" She laid her head against his shoulder. Her hair whispered against his chest, her leg slipped away from his, and he wrapped his arms around her slim shoulders. When her hands found his waist, her thumbs circling over his hip bones, he lost his grip on his thoughts. Who knew that skin was so sensitive? She outlined his navel with a fingertip and drew it down, and Cassian closed his eyes, unable to feel anything but how badly he wanted that touch to continue along his length, the grip of her hand again. The grip of her body.

"You expect me to think…" He faltered when she fulfilled his wish, stroking then holding, as if it were a lead and not his most sensitive body part. "…when you're touching me?"

Her laugh was breathy, and she stroked again, urging him backwards with her, to the bed. He paid no attention to their tangle of limbs and bodies as they maneuvered, only knew the feeling of her hand, each expert brush, graze, and nudge of her fingers. She lay facing him, draping a leg over his, pinning him with it and her explorations. Cassian closed his eyes again, sinking into sensation, and she kissed his brow, his temple, his ear, dragging his earlobe through her teeth, then stroking his neck with soft lips and his arousal with teasing fingers. It was just as tender as the look she had given him, and how had she known he wanted that more than anything in the world?

"Amara." He kissed her, urging her hand away before she sent him crashing. *Stay.* He thought in desperation. He knew she couldn't. That he wasn't what she wanted, or needed. Not for more than this. Maybe she felt the need in the kiss, because she responded with passion, less control, nipping at him. He urged her to her back and sat up, kneeling between her legs. He clasped her hips and pulled her to him, and she obliged by wrapping her legs around his waist. He spent long moments memorizing the graceful shape of them with his hands, massaging up and down her inner thighs. Amara's head pressed back into the bed and her hips, tilted up and resting on his legs, lifted.

Cassian drew one hand after the other between her breasts, over her ribs, her stomach, brushed them over her mound but only to tease. He pressed the heel of his hand against her, too high to hit the little nub where her pleasure centered. Her eyes slitted open, glaring at him in reprimand, pushing up with her hips, tightening her legs around him. He pressed his hand up, along the same trail he had drawn down, and palmed her breast, the dark point of her nipple centered in his palm. She moved into the touch, her legs dropping away as he rose up over her, undulating and moaning as he circled and plucked at her nipple. With his free hand he drew lines down her thigh with a whisper-soft touch, followed the sinewy valley at the joining of thigh and pelvis.

Her moans became a soft cry when he dipped his head to play his tongue across one breast then the other, his fingers making their way incrementally lower, toward her shifting hips. Everything there was damp, plush, and warm, and he wanted hours to touch and discover, so he could learn what made her make those sounds, those little, approving purrs that broke her voice into smoky pieces. When her hips began to move in the suggestion of the rhythm he would want when he was inside her, he firmed his touches to measured strokes. She reached above her, for something to grab, and found nothing, arching as she gripped fistfuls of sheet and pulled it down. Magic flared bright on her skin, the rosettes blooming larger, and Cassian thought he heard whispers.

He shook his head to banish them. She'd aroused him so much he was losing his mind. He ducked down between her thighs. Her hands followed, grabbing at his hair, cupping his head, as he kissed her below, breathed in the musk and water of her body. He was not entirely aware of what he did, only that he followed her, where her hands pushed, where her body rose to meet him, tasting arousal and bright magic with each kiss and lick. His body ached from head to toe, his thoughts fuzzy and limping. There was nothing to care about except every inch of her and him, of touching her in as many places as he could, making them somehow one entity.

When her throaty cries suggested he was close to sending her into her own release, he stopped, dragging his cheek up her inner thigh then kissing the inside of her bent knee. Amara went limp against the bed, eyes closed, breathing in soft pants.

When he rose over her on all fours, looking down at her, she opened her eyes.

A silver maelstrom spun in them. A hypnotizing window into something he could never understand, into a universe that would consume him if he let it. And he wanted to. She could have him. She already did.

She grabbed for him when he lowered his hips to hers, her hands skating into his hair again, her legs wrapping around his. Cassian pressed against her opening, and thought he might tease her, and himself for a bit, but Amara had other plans. With a shift and rise of her hips she seated him inside her, tightening her legs to drive him fully inside.

His surprise was eclipsed by the shock of hot ecstasy that just about ended their tryst right then. He exhaled hard, clawing at the bed, trying not to hear her long, low moan of pleasure. Quakes of near climax shuddered through him. Gods…

"Give me a moment," he managed.

She relaxed, combing her fingers through his hair, weaving a pattern on his back with her nails. Cassian closed his eyes, moving into her touch, allowing his body to ratchet down, to prepare itself for what he suspected was going to be a battle of endurance. He refused to disappoint this woman during what might be his only chance to do this with her.

"You made me too eager," she murmured when he ducked his head to hers to brush the tip of her pert nose with his lips. Her freckles were black stars in silver sky when her magic moved beneath them, and he watched, dazzled. Was his lack of magic boring to her? Did all mages glow as she did? Was that what she was accustomed to? Did she feel more because of the magic? There was so much more to know, and he was greedy for the knowledge. Cassian dropped to his elbows, touching her hair, her neck, dropping kisses on her throat. Her body was hot and tight around him, a steady thrumming of pulse beating between them, his heart, or hers, perhaps her magic. He didn't know and didn't care, but he did live for it, in that moment. She shifted, giving her hips a little buck to tell him he was trying her patience.

"I like you eager." He tilted his hips to push deeper, watching her lashes quiver and her lips part around a gasp. "As I have been since I met you. A bit of turnabout. Hmm?" He withdrew, just a fraction, and returned, and pleasure then impatience took her expression. Amara wrapped her arms around his back, and pushed, urging him to roll. He submitted, and when she was on top of him, she sat up.

Pressing her hands to his chest and tucking her legs beneath her, she lifted, a sinuous movement that left him breathless just to watch, never mind the sensations of it. And she continued to move, a carnal kind of dance. Her body and movements liquid and graceful, her hands on him, and on herself, her magic pooling and cascading on her skin, the glow of it brightening until he could see nothing else. Spinning, churning, and calling, a million voices in one entwined with hers, her hands on his shoulders, whispers and songs that drugged and possessed him.

Her back arched, her hips driving down against his, she clung to his shoulders as she cried out and her magic swirled open to envelop her, sweeping him out to an empty sea in his own mind, waves of climax crashing over him and blinding him to anything but the silver, misty glow of her.

The candles went out, and the darkness devoured him, mind, body, and soul. Severing them. Leaving him alone. The shock of it left him breathless and senseless.

Then he recognized this…emptiness. When she had taken the minds of everyone at his family's estate, this is where she had sent him. Though he had been more aware of the world around him at that moment. Could see. Now, he was separate from that. From his body, from their pleasure, from time. So not the same place, just somewhere similar. He should have been shocked, frightened, or at least had the good sense to wonder what had happened. But he didn't.

The world stretched before him, darkness and silver, a mirror.

All around him voices sang. Haunting songs, quiet songs, songs with the same resonant beauty of the ones she had sung on their ride into the wilderness. Countless voices together. Singing hope, a rise from darkness. Singing the end of struggle. A world without war. A world with truth and gentleness in it, and justice.

Peace.

Amara's song.

Slivers of silver mist parted the darkness, gossamer rivulets rising from a mirror-like surface below, glowing, like moonlight, shaped like people. In their midst a figure stood, glowing like the water of an inlet bay on a summer's day. Turquoise and beautiful, with a familiar halo of heavy curls. It did not wear Amara's face, only her shape, only her essence. In each amorphous figure around her burned a bright, blue-green light that pulsed in answer to the peaceful, thrumming song that emanated from her. Ribbons of energy strung between them, swirling around Amara, but not connecting.

Cassian tried to reach for her, tried to speak, but no matter how hard he tried, how hard he *wanted*, he could not move, or speak. His struggle to free himself of whatever held him earned him the attention of the vaporous figures. They turned to look at him from eyeless faces and flowed toward him, billowing back into the fog that made them, rolling like a storm in the dark. They coalesced, flowing and smoothing until something else stood before him. Himself.

They looked at each other.

You do not belong here. The words, presumably from his reflection, were spoken in the whispers that filled the oblivion that surrounded him. Voices mingling and separating, murmuring, and shouting, waves upon the sand. Its lips didn't move.

Where is here? He could not speak. Was this thing…her magic? Or her?

This is the font, where the Wheel spins.

His reflection turned, pointing into the oblivion that stretched away. Beyond the water figure of Amara there was something else. A shadow upon that backdrop of endless nothing, dark flames and writhing smoke. And another, a storm contained, lightning and tempest, flashing and bright. Between them all, the shadow, the storm, and Amara, spun a sphere. Its pale light barely registered in the sucking blackness, cool like winter sun. A filament of something like light or power connected everything but Amara together.

His reflection pointed at Cassian, touching a finger to his chest. *You are void.*

The mist dissolved again and plunged through him. Cassian felt as though he had fallen into an icy lake, or that it had fallen through him. Tendrils of burning cold twisted through his thoughts and heart, and the mist emerged behind him as a new figure. His father, grey-haired and dressed in the blue hemmed and belted toga of a senator. *And Unbalanced.*

Cassian needed to gasp for breath, the ice lingering in his body, but he didn't exist here. He had no lungs, or hands, or a body at all. *You cannot exist in the past and in the present.*
Scion.

The figure pushed harder against his chest. The touch sent him crashing back through silver mirror and dark ocean, the fading edge of his physical pleasure, and into a mind drowning in shame.

Cassian gasped awake in his body, and Amara was cupping his face, staring into his eyes, tears in hers.

TWENTY-SEVEN

H IS EYES CLEARED, THE glowing silver ring around them winked out in the dark, and Amara breathed again.

"Cassian…" She stroked his hair away from his brow. What would he say? She'd known she shouldn't have made love with him. She'd known it and done it anyway, and her vile magic had sought out a victim as soon as it was free of her grip. Until the instance she felt it break free she'd been lost to him, lost to them. Lost in unrestrained joy. Then in a nightmare. She hadn't even felt his mind, just that he was gone.

He hugged her so tightly she could hardly draw breath, burying his face in the slope of her neck. Her hands shook as she tried not to cry again, tried not to despair about what she'd done. Stolen from him, again.

"That is as close to the gods as I have ever been," he said. "I wish you could see what you look like, in that place. Beautiful. You sang, there."

"Where?" She drew back. Her eyes had adjusted enough to the darkness when she lifted her head that she could make out the outlines of his face, and that he was looking at her. Normally she found the dark comforting. Its embrace like the deeps of the sea. But in this moment, she would give anything to see his face more clearly. To see the expression that went along with the reverent words.

"I don't know. Your magic…it spoke to me. It called it the font but all I saw was darkness. And you."

"The void?" Had she killed him? She pressed her hands between them, to his heart. It beat a steady, strong rhythm beneath her touch, and he laughed. The warm sound was incongruous with the fluttering panic in her breast.

"I'm here. You didn't harm me. Will that happen every time?"

"I don't know. It's never happened," she said. "I'm so sorry, I shouldn't—"

He silenced her with a kiss.

"You should," he said. "We should." His mouth smiled against hers. "Many times. For practice, hmm? Either I will grow accustomed to it or you will control it and in either case it will be a very pleasant hobby." His hands took a leisurely tour of her back, legs, and arms.

She pulled away from him, got off the bed. He let her go. The bed creaked behind her as he sat up. Amara fumbled in the dark toward the table beneath the window, where candles had been burning before her released power had snuffed them. There was more light there, and she found matches and struck them, unable to bear the darkness and the way it pressed all around her. Taunting her. When there was darkness the rest of the world was gone. It was just her and whoever she was with, and she could be whatever she wished. But with Cassian… he knew too much. She was stripped to more than just her skin. He'd seen her power, been a victim of it, seen it break her. He knew her weakness. And still wanted her.

"Would you like to know what it feels like?" he murmured. Everything inside her seized, and her fingers tightened on the edge of the table. "You power? Has anyone ever told you?"

"Everyone I have taken with my power is an enemy, or is dead because of it." She couldn't look at him. She couldn't bear to see fear or disgust. Or something worse. Pity.

"I am neither of those things. So let's consider me, for the moment, an authority." The bed creaked again as he shifted.

"I do not wish to speak of this," Amara said, sharply, without turning to him.

"Just now...there are no monsters. Only you, your magic. Light and songs. The most beautiful light. Like sun on warm water. Songs that right wrongs, soothe pain."

"And when I controlled your mind?"

"In the middle of it, all I wanted was to do what you told me to do. And after...there were no lingering effects. I will not pretend I liked it," Cassian said calmly. "But I much preferred it to a bullet in the back. I am not afraid of you. And I never will be, no matter how hard you try to convince me."

Amara closed her eyes. "You're mad," she said.

He laughed. "A bit. For you. I'm less worried about your magic than whatever it is you do that makes me senseless and illogical. Come back here."

She obeyed, and he pulled her into his lap, then tumbled her onto the bed. When he rose over her, Amara frowned. "You aren't afraid that what you feel isn't part of my magic? That I make you feel what you do?"

"Were you not the one who told me that you don't make me feel anything? That I choose what I take in of my life?" He grinned in triumph. Amara rolled her eyes. Impossible man. He drew swirls and circles along her collarbones. "This...prince you are to marry," Cassian said, more reluctantly. She flinched, turning her gaze back to his. "Does he know? About your power?"

"I do not believe so. Not what you saw at the villa." A lifetime of lying to someone. Hiding all that she was. No matter. She'd already been doing it for a decade. And she'd never intended to be close to Ihsan.

"I thought the Sultan in Tamar had a harem. Are you to be one of many wives?" His brow furrowed, his mouth curving in disapproval.

"The Sultana," Amara corrected, "is betrothed to one man. And the Sultan in Tamar has not kept a harem since the very early days of the Old Sultanate."

"Oh?"

"Harems are notoriously competitive, cut-throat places. Can you not imagine the ramifications of one full of magically gifted women?" Amara raised an eyebrow.

Cassian hissed through his teeth and nodded. He swept his gaze over her, then lifted his fingers to her neck, to the scratches from the collar. The ease winked out of his expression.

"This feels like my fault," he said in a reluctant whisper.

"You did not put a collar on me," Amara said.

He squinted, and scratched at his jaw. When he looked away from her for a long moment, her chest constricted, and her throat went dry. A steady pulse beat in her belly, a warning. Lies coming undone.

Cassian let his breath out in a quick push. "Paulus found me. He wanted to know what I was doing there. He…offered to trade me Mirari for my blood right to my father's seat."

"I don't understand," Amara answered, searching his face. Guilt tightened his features, and cold dread knotted in her belly.

"I was underage, when my father was killed. I couldn't take his seat on the Senate. So Paulus was elected in his place. I retained my right to the seat. When he dies, I can take back my father's place. Our home. Everything. And I will. I'll undo all the pain I caused. And Antonis Hirtius can rot in the Night Hall."

Amara sat up.

"You're a senator?" she said, carefully.

"Not yet." Cassian sat up too, reaching for her, but that cold twist inside her was rising up, filling her limbs, warming to something hot, and angry.

"That villa…Buschetto. That was your family's?" Lies. Lies she had sensed but ignored. Fool, fool girl. "Were you…" She could hardly get the words out, could hardly meet his eyes to try and discern the truth in them. When she understood…when she realized… she turned to foam, adrift on a cold sea. Fragile and empty. "This was all just to get back at them? Did you put me and my people in danger to fulfill some revenge?"

"What?" Cassian drew back. "No…Amara. No."

"He would have given you Mirari for this thing…this right to your father's seat? The seat that got your family killed? And you want it back? Power. That is what you want." She jolted up. Her heart sped. Her eyes burned. "You said no for spite and did *this*." She held her scratched arms and broken nails out to him, then clapped her hands over her heart. "You risked our lives and freedom and made me turn into a monster!"

The tears were back. And they made her furious. This weakness. This crack she had allowed for him. The cold grip of deep, dark water made her mind and body slow.

When she tried to scramble off the bed, he caught her arms, forcing her to face him.

"You are not a monster," he said. "If there is a monster here it is me. Please. I didn't realize—"

"Liar," she choked. "You made your choice. You chose yourself. Your pride. You put me and the people I love in danger. I was a fool not to believe you when you said you never acted for anyone but yourself."

"Yes I did. I did. I am selfish, and broken, and worthless," he snapped. "I have always been. But you"—he released her arms and cupped her shoulders—"you are peace. You are mercy. And justice. Why can't you see that?"

She wanted and despised that touch, the tenderness in it. The adoration. The lies. "You know nothing about my power."

"I do not understand why your gods gave it to you, why it is in the world at all. I don't. But I do know this"—he wrapped his arms around her and dragged her against him—"who better to wield it than someone who understands the cost? Who has been subjugated, broken, and built anew? Who has seen the worst the world has to offer and stood up on the other side of it, whole and still...*still* merciful? Who else in the world could possibly hold such a power without becoming a tyrant? No one. No one but you. Pain for power."

"You do not speak to me about my pain." Tears pooled and spilled from her eyes as she pulled away from the warmth of him. "I don't ever want to speak to you again."

She lunged from the bed, away from him, and his lies, and grabbed up her clothes. And that...that was the price of care. The price her power exacted, sucking all the joy, all the potential for connection from her hands. The price no one else would ever understand.

"Please don't go." He stood as Amara pulled her stola on and clipped it in place. "It isn't safe out there, in the dark. Let me take you to the ship, or wait until they come in the morning."

Amara strode to the door and flung it open. She looked at him, holding back a tide of mourning as moonlight poured in and painted him in silver and shadow.

"I told you," she said, "I am not a stranger to the dark. And tonight, it has a great deal to fear from me." She slammed the door behind her.

AMARA CLIMBED ONTO THE ship's ladder as the two sailors held the rowboat steady. As soon as she stood on deck and saw Djar, she crossed to him. His habit of early rising was a benefit, for once. He took in her appearance, her tangled hair, her mussed, smudged clothing, and her face, and said not a word. He held out his hands when she approached, took the clothes that she unslung from her body, and stood between her and the crew as she climbed onto the ship's railing then dove into the ocean.

She sliced through the surface and into the dark, cold embrace of the water. It had been too long since she had been swimming, truly swimming, not just immersed in a tub filled with piped water. The cold and the impact momentarily stunned her, but she was a practiced swimmer, and allowed herself to float to the surface without fighting the water's push. She shoved her hair out of her face. It had suffered far too many abuses in the past small turn and the salt in the water was only the latest of these. Once she was back in Narfour, with her oils and lotions, she would be able to put herself back together.

She looked up. Djar peered over the side of the ship, looming high and broad above her. When he saw her he lifted a hand then turned his back.

Amara began a slow, even stroke, intending to swim around to the other side of the ship, then climb the ladder once more. The water sang to her. Its song the same steady, unknowable rhythm of a mother's womb, each life within its depths a flicker inside her power. They knew her, did not distinguish her from the element of their home. A water mage was never in danger from the creatures that lived within it, a unique aspect of the Second House.

The sea's cold, liquid caress as she moved was cleansing but not as settling as she had hoped. Cassian was a problem water could not solve. He was a problem she could not solve. Her trek through the city had given her plenty of time to examine her feelings. Plenty of time to build him into an evil villain then deconstruct him back into something bearable. Her inability to cope with her magic was not his responsibility. He could not have known of that particular consequence.

Yet…he had gambled lives. Though that was hard to believe as well. Had he known what Paulus had intended, when he told him no? Now that she was not drowning in the pain of her surprise, she struggled to believe that of a man who had given up power and privilege to live in the slums and free slaves. Yet, this was best. This anger, this hurt. A knife to cut the ties between them.

Amara rolled to her back and floated, letting the water cradle her, rock her, its dark depths spinning away beneath, the sky lightening above. The sea reflected the sky, though not perfectly. Clouds became shadows in the water, incorporeal light became edge-less blades. The Second House knew that mirrors could only show things as they appeared, not as what they were. Reflections were lies that looked like truth.

She closed her eyes, caring little for the stares of the sailors above. They could look as they wished. It gave them nothing she cared about. A body was no different than a robe, something draped and fitted across the soul. It might hint at what was beneath, or reveal it completely, or not at all. But that fact did not alter the truth of what was inside. And what people saw and believed based on her skin and her body was only a perception. The truth of her, of anyone, was buried deep, to be shown and given only as she saw fit. Something that could not be touched or viewed unless she allowed it. She had allowed Cassian as she had allowed no one else. Giving him both her secrets and truths.

Was he worthy? And was she? He had seen into the depths of her, been trapped by them. And still how he had looked at her, both clothed and naked. When he could see inside and out. He'd looked with warmth and worship. She wanted to go back in her memories, to hold that look against all the others she had received from admirers, but her thoughts seemed only able to produce that one. Because it was the only one born of the truth of her. The others, even her favorites, were fading in comparison. The furrow between his brows. The blue of his eyes, like the water that soothed her now. Kind, and patched together. Not so different than her. Than any of them. Imperfect.

"I told Danel we'd meet him this morning," Djar called. "We'd best make our way to shore." His voice sounded too distant, and Amara opened her eyes and looked around, realizing she had drifted quite a distance from the ship. She ducked beneath the surface once more, swam until she needed air, and surfaced again. And when she climbed the ladder, she left her thoughts and her wounds behind her, in the dark water.

AMARA HAD BEEN IN the camp for nearly two sunmarks by the time Mirari and Sorne returned from their trek into the deeper woods to gather foodstuffs. They crouched down near the fire and Katalin and Abene joined them and set to work sorting the spoils. Amara saw ramps, the young coils of ferns, roots, and a few fungus. Her stomach churned in anticipation.

She walked to them, and Mirari stood, brushing her hands off on her stola. The blood that stained it had turned rusty brown after an attempt to wash it. Mirari had belted it with torn bits of cloth so it was less cumbersome to move in.

"I have not had a chance to thank you, for what you did for me at the villa," Amara murmured. Mirari smiled, though her gaze fixed on Amara's throat.

"I"—Mirari lowered her chin—"know what it feels like to be crushed by memories. I wanted to warn you, about the Vex. I failed."

"No. You acted, which is the best that any of us can do." Amara huffed, closed her eyes, and turned away before Mirari could say anything else. Was acting the best she could do? Look what had happened when she acted.

The day was cold and damp. Amara hugged herself as she stood in front of the fire. It didn't matter that it was spring, and that the sun was shining. They were deep in the shade of the forest. While it was true that a mage had affinity for the weather and temperatures that belonged to their spoke on the Wheel, she had grown up in the hot, humid climes of Menei. Despite her time in Tamar, she had never quite come to terms with even its mild cold weather. Haenna and its environs shared many similarities with Tamar. If not its magic.

The camp where Danel and Mirari had set themselves and the Den girls up was northeast of the city. The three girls from the Den had managed to settle themselves to some extent. Sorne worked in an easy, practiced rhythm with Mirari, who fell into a leadership role in a quiet way that suggested she did not realize she was. The Northern girl, Abene, seemed undisturbed by the forest, but Katalin leapt at every sound, cringed at every sighting of bugs, eyed the simple food with trepidation. Cityborn, Amara suspected.

Amara was tired of waiting. Danel and Mirari had made a trek into the forest while Amara was in mage sleep, to speak with Watchers. Watchers, if she understood correctly, were both forward scout and messenger service for the Suloi clans. The Watchers had promised to relay that Danel required assistance in taking revenge on the Republic. He hoped some hunters would answer his call for help. He and Mirari were masters at answering questions without answering, and Amara had simply given up asking exactly what they were waiting for. How they might know that other Suloi had chosen to assist them in rescuing the Charah.

The answer came in the form of four shadows materializing out of the woods when the sun was just past its highest point in the sky. One of them she recognized immediately, though he came separately from the other three. Peio. She wondered if he knew. If he had spoken with Cassian. He had not been with the group in the woods when she, Djar, and the twins had come to find them.

Amara could not help a twinge, looking past him for the inevitable moment Cassian appeared behind him. She had not seen them apart outside those private moments she had spent with Cassian. She hoped to see Cassian, and hoped not to. If she was smart, she would leave the frayed, severed bond between them alone. She would not repair it and make her leave-taking more painful.

But Cassian did not appear. Peio ducked his head to her, his gaze fixed on the ground as he walked past and went to greet Danel.

"This Ghost would offer—"

"No," said Danel at the same moment Mirari said, "You are welcome in this camp, son of the Urbina." Danel snapped her a fierce look. Mirari tipped her chin up and turned her face to present her cheek, and nothing else was said. Amara marveled at their discourse. Wordless and complex. Peio sat down across the fire from Amara, next to Bek, who had been tasked by Djar with sharpening every blade available to them. Peio began unloading his considerable arsenal, which made Bek's grin spread wider and wider as each knife was laid on the ground beside him.

The three other Suloi hunters, who waited on the edge of the camp until Peio had vacated Danel's immediate vicinity, greeted the Pathfinder with bowed heads and a touch of each cheek to his. Mirari rose from her work with the other women and waited, hands folded in front of her, as each of the hunters presented themselves to her, touched fingers to head, then heart, then dropped to one knee and traced a circle in the dirt at her feet.

Amara was intrigued by the circle. The Suloi did not acknowledge the Wheel, from what she had gathered. Yet the circle was the Wheel's symbol. Had they kept that, over the generations? Even when they kept so little else, and now followed their Wanderer god?

"You have called and we have answered, Pathfinder Garai. May we hunt for you, avenge for you, and bring honor to our names in so doing," one of the three said, the shortest and bulkiest of them. Was this all the help they could expect?

"Do you have a plan for this rescue, Pathfinder?" Amara asked. This drew the attention of the three newest Suloi to her, and though they did not stare overtly, as citizens of the Republic had, their downturned faces did not hide their furtive glances. It might have been her Meneian heritage that drew their notice, since she doubted Meneians dealt with the Suloi in their native places. Or perhaps it was her Tamaran magic, which was still too near the surface to hide completely from anyone gifted even the smallest amount. Perhaps it was simply her sex, and that she spoke more forcefully than she had ever heard Mirari or Sorne do.

"Djar and I have discussed. There are three places to cross the River Mytra, and no way to know which they will choose. But, it seems likely they will choose the nearest, as that cuts the trip to Corsyra by nearly a day, though the second bridge north is the largest."

And what did she care about what bridge they crossed? "I see," she said. Though she did not. Danel was apparently aware of this, because his usually somber expression brightened a fraction with humor.

"There are too few of us to take on an entire transport. The bridge will allow us to cut them in half."

"Peio," Djar called. He stood at the edge of the camp, near where the trees thinned, keeping watch. Peio looked up from his sharpening. "Do you think you can take Bek and get back into the villa?"

Peio and Bek eyed each other, then Djar. "Of course." Peio shrugged. As if Djar had asked him to fetch cloth from the market.

"I want those firebombs we left behind," Djar said. Peio scratched the back of his neck and looked at the sky, then nodded. That seemed to satisfy everyone but Amara. She looked from face to face. The only one who seemed even remotely interested in speaking to her was Peio, but she knew he wanted to speak about Cassian, and she did not. She left the fire, heard Peio sigh as she passed by him and Bek, and wound her way through the tangle of underbrush to the edge of camp and Djar.

"Explain."

He adjusted his sword belt over his hips, then flashed his teeth at her in something more like a snarl than a grin. "I'm going to use their weapons against them. And if we're lucky, we won't all be killed in the process."

TWENTY-EIGHT

AMARA STOOD IN THE cool shadows of the pine trees where they had made their new camp. It was her turn to watch the road. It was a distant ribbon of golden-hued stone, cutting through scrub and grass just beginning to green up from spring rain. There had been no one on it yet that morning, but it was still early. The night spent sleeping on the wet ground had put her in a foul mood, and so she had volunteered to keep watch for the return of the twins. Kiya and Bek had volunteered to observe the Basilica for the departure of whatever caravan would be moving the Charah.

They'd left the forest near Haenna shortly after the arrival of the Suloi hunters who had answered Danel's call for help. Danel had stayed behind, though no one had said outright he would only slow everyone and be a liability in battle. Beyond that, Mirari had all but commanded him to stay, citing his role as Pathfinder to their two-person clan. Sorne, Abene, and Katalin had stayed with him. Amara, Mirari, Djar, Peio, and the three Suloi, who had yet to introduce themselves, had ridden north for half the morning to stake out the bridge Danel had chosen as their point of ambush.

Amara had neither wanted to go with the ambush nor stay with those whose roles did not serve well in battle. It should not have been that way. Never had she vacillated so when it came to choosing her role. But she was not made for battle. For violence. It was not her way, nor part of her abilities. Even Kiya could at least wield a blade with some skill. Amara had used them as props for dancing, on occasion, but that would certainly not protect her in a real battle. Perhaps in another incarnation the Charah of the Second House would have been a very useful asset to have in such an instance. But she was not.

The thought rankled. She had never been useless. Had never had no role to play.

You are peace. Justice.

Cassian's words, his earnest declaration, warmed her and wounded her. He had been drifting in and out of her bitter thoughts for all of their long ride, and now this morning. Every time she looked at Peio he looked away, as if he had been staring in the way that people had of working up their courage to speak to someone. She did not want him to speak to her about Cassian. She did not want to hear about Cassian's intentions or innocence. In the end, his reasons did not matter. She was returning to Narfour. She was going to marry Ihsan, and she was going to put all of this behind her.

Amara lifted the spyglass she held and fit it against her eye, scanning the farther distances for sign of Bek and Kiya. She didn't want to think too terribly hard about their plans to rob a guarded caravan of its most valuable captive. They were sadly overmatched for such a task. And that was yet another reason a fierce desire for Cassian's company would occasionally surface and dominate her thoughts. He would be another fighter, at the very least.

"Behind you," a female voice said softly, so she would not startle Amara. The rolling lilt of the accent identified the speaker before she appeared. Mirari came to Amara's side as silent as a doe picking its careful way through the trees. She had that same sense about her. Something wild, and graceful. Innocent, and wary. Wise beyond the youth that showed in glass-smooth skin and unwrinkled brow. She did not speak much, but obviously preferred Amara's company if she could not have Danel's. She all but ignored the other three Suloi, and they gave her wide berth, almost as wide as the distance they kept between them and Peio. Though their avoidance of Mirari felt respectful; that which they gave Peio was charged, threatened. Mirari did not ignore Peio the way the others did. Did not call him a Ghost and pretend he didn't exist. And for his part, he treated her with a mix of awe and respect. Akin to the way he treated Amara.

"It is not time to switch," Amara said.

"No. But I was awake and no one else was." She curved her arm beneath her tumble of sable hair and swept it up and off her shoulders. She had small objects woven into it, colored string wrapped around small braids, a feather here, a coin or bit of metal there. Like a magpie. Amara could only imagine that they held some significance to her, but Mirari was a person who could only be known on her own terms. That much Amara could sense. Questions would get her nowhere. Mirari would volunteer the information, or she would not.

"They should be leaving soon. I expect we'll see the twins before evening, telling us such." That was the plan. Bek and Kiya would ride out as soon as the caravan was packed and showed signs of moving, to give them advanced warning of its passage. Amara tried not to worry about the two of them, alone in a city hunting for them. They were wily. Orphans raised in the streets of Nasiye, stealing to eat and dodging guards who would have cut their hands off in punishment. They knew how to handle themselves. Djar believed them capable, and so must she.

"He isn't a monster," Mirari said, quietly. It seemed to match the mood of the forest, cool and murmured. But it jarred Amara. At first she thought the other meant Cassian, but realized, when she took in the distant, regretful look in Mirari's eyes, that she was speaking about the man, Benat. The Charah.

"Who ever said he was?"

"I did." Mirari's expression smoothed to hide the sorrow she could not banish from her eyes. "I said it."

"Because of his magic?"

Mirari glanced at Amara, though her gaze was focused on Amara's throat, and not her eyes, something Amara had noticed all the Suloi did. She'd thought perhaps Mirari would look her in the eyes, since they were both women. Because she had done it at the villa, to save her from her own mind.

"Because I thought he was." Mirari turned her head away again, focusing toward the road. She wrapped her arms around herself. "I thought he had betrayed me."

"But he had not." There was more to the story. The weaving of it was in Mirari's words. Her tone, the way she stared vacantly. Amara knew that look, that demeanor. She was ashamed.

"No. Not him. I thought he had, for a moment. Until they tried to kill him. And now he is alone, and they are probably torturing him." Her voice cracked, and she swallowed, blinking at her tears. "They gave him so much of the poppy. So much. I thought it would kill him. But it was much worse. It stole his soul."

"We are here to free him," Amara said, with the soothing tone of still water. Mirari huffed, and turned her tear-filled gaze on Amara once more.

"I do not know if you can," she said. "Even if you break him out of the cage they've built for him, the one up here"—she tapped her temple—"is stronger."

"I see," Amara said. *You could let me sit in there with you.* Cassian. Understanding as he should not have been able to. A criminal with an artist's heart, an artist's eye for details. Her details.

Amara closed her eyes, forced herself to focus. She knew too little about the Circle and Chara'a. She did not know what this man, Benat, was capable of, and how much use she would be against him. If he was mentally unstable, and capable of what Danel had seen, then he was a dangerous man indeed. Even if he wasn't a monster, as Mirari said.

"All we can do is move forward. He cannot stay a prisoner of the Republic. His place is in Tamar."

"You will let him decide for himself," Mirari said. "Or he will be your slave as much as he is now theirs."

"I will let him decide if he is able. If I deem him capable of making rational decisions and controlling himself. Is what your brother said true? Did he summon molten rock?"

"He was trying to protect us. We were fleeing the Vex quad that came for my clan. They chased us, harried us, until we could run and hide no more. And Benat was…" Her brow furrowed. "…he was wounded. He was exhausted. And different. Different than the man I met. The man I…" She trailed off, her eyes closing and her breath hitching. And Amara understood. Love seemed to be more antagonist for the two of them than dream come true.

"We cannot decide his fate here and now, the two of us. We can only wait. Is it not the most excruciating of practices?"

Mirari smiled, her eyes opened, and she lowered her lashes. "Yes."

"But it is my understanding that your people are talented hunters, travelers. You must be more accustomed to waiting than I am."

"I am not a hunter. Before the Vex came, I had never wielded anything more dangerous than a carving knife." Her smile disappeared. "There is blood on my hands now. There is no greater abhorrence to my people than murder."

"Even if it is self-defense?"

"He was only a man looking for firewood," Mirari said. "But he saw me. He would have told them where we were hiding." Her hands shook and she grabbed at the hem of her shirt. "Women are supposed to be gentle."

"And does gentleness require that you lie down and die?" Amara asked.

"We keep the camps. We keep the stories. We keep the souls"—she circled her hand over her chest—"of our people within us."

"You believe you cannot do that now?"

"The roadborn believe women are the cairns that mark the road home. The rock against which to put one's back to face the world. The strength of the shield arm, the haft of the spear, the arms of the bow against which the bowstring strains. But not violence."

"No matter where I go," Amara said, gently, "or what culture demands of them, I see that women are the strength of nations." She reached between them and gripped Mirari's hand. "Their watchful, infinitely flexible strength of compassion. The flame that burns inside them which allows them to be whatever they need to be, in the moment that requires it. One action you have taken does not define all that you are. You, who can see a man where others see a monster."

When Mirari lifted her gaze to Amara's, revealing her eyes to be the soft, yellowed green of spring grass, Amara felt as though a dagger had been plunged into her heart. Her own words drifting and forming the way the mist of her magic did, into the shape of her own truth. Tears stung at her eyes.

"Only those who hurt can so easily see the hurt in another," Mirari coaxed. "Is it not pain that gives compassion? Trauma that leaves wisdom where it treads?" She paused, looking over Amara with a gaze that saw far too much. "And where is the monster that you see?" Mirari stepped forward to wrap her arms around Amara. Amara clung to her. "Why is it so easy to forgive in others what we cannot forgive in ourselves?"

Amara could not reply, or risk letting lose a lifetime of unraveling shame.

"I will forgive whatever haunts you, Sister, if you forgive me," Mirari said.

Could she? Could she forgive herself, and her magic, as she would have forgiven anyone else?

TWENTY-NINE

ASSIAN ROLLED OUT OF his bed, stumbling over the table in the center of the room as he staggered for the door. A steady pounding was issuing from it, and he was too groggy, his head thumping in time with the knocking, to pause to think about who might be on the other side. He did think of it the moment he threw the door wide, letting in the late-morning sun and blinding him temporarily.

"Balls," he snapped, throwing an arm over his eyes until they adjusted. Someone grabbed his arms, yanking them down, and Cassian blinked rapidly. It was Bek, with a panicked look on his face that immediately sped Cassian's heart. "What?"

"They took her," Bek said, the three words tumbled together. The young man's eyes were red-rimmed, and he seemed just as likely to bolt as he was to stay and explain. His panic stabbed through Cassian. *Her.*

"Amara?"

"No!" Bek said. "Kiya. We were supposed to watch. But they saw her. I told her not to go any closer but she never listens to me. You have to come with me." He tugged.

"Wait." Cassian took a deep breath that settled his panic from absolute to something he could manage. "Just let me think. Where are the others?"

"Outside the city. We came back so we could ride ahead when the caravan left and tell them. We watched them pack all morning. Kiya wanted a better count of men to tell Djar. I don't know how they saw her, but they did. They've got her chained up with a bunch of others."

Cassian shoved his fingers into his hair, gripping it then reaching to pull Bek inside and shut the door. Even if Bek rode to tell the others now, it might be too late to help Kiya. But what good was he going to be? Him and Bek against a score of guards.

"We need help," Cassian finally said. But what help? Peio was his help. All his other associates were criminals, and they weren't in the business of helping people just for the sake of doing it.

"Maybe the ship's crew?" Bek suggested weakly. Cassian shook his head. They were merchant men. Or pirates. He'd gotten a look at the captain when they split up after Amara's display of magic. That was not a crew capable of battling ground soldiers.

"Do you remember anything about the men you were watching? Colors? Faces?" Some of the senators could be bribed. If one of them was in charge of this particular exchange, then there might be some hope of purchasing Kiya back. The money to do so was a problem to be dealt with next. Bek scrunched his face, squeezed his eyes shut. "Think about anyone that appeared to be in charge."

"I saw soldiers. I think. They didn't dress like the ones at the villa. The ones in red. These had"—he gestured at his chest—"breastplates on." He frowned. "I saw that other man"—his eyes popped open—"the same one at the villa the night Amara used her magic. The old one who was talking to you."

Cassian's thumping heart slowed, and his body numbed. His pulse beat in his cheeks, and hands, and for the length of an indrawn breath he was adrift.

Paulus. Again. He would never escape that damn family. They ruined everything of his. Took it all. His parents. His home. His money. Everything he'd ever cared for, everything that had ever mattered. Now he had Kiya. Cassian could offer Paulus all the money in the world for Kiya and he would just laugh. He would never be bribed by a Haydar. Not for money.

There was only one thing Paulus wanted from Cassian. The one thing he swore he'd never give them. He'd never had the power to dig them out of the Senate. Not with words and righteousness. But he could let them die out. Antonis couldn't take his father's place as long as Cassian never gave up his blood right to that seat. It was the one thing he could give his parents. The only revenge he had.

But what would they think of this? Of their son, wallowing in his anger? Failing. He could succeed this time. He could redeem himself in some small way. For the damage he had caused. With his lies, and selfishness. Amara might not ever forgive him, but at least he could make sure she had the people who loved her around her. He could give her back Kiya.

"I can fix this," Cassian said. "But you can't come with me. You wait for Kiya, and as soon as I've freed her, you'll take her to the others."

"What are you going to do all alone?" Bek said, incredulous.

"I'm going to make a trade."

CASSIAN STOOD IN THE outlet of the side street into the Basilica promenade, where the caravan stood poised to begin travel. The grand arch that straddled the wide street from Haenna proper spanned the sprawling courtyard. Soldiers on rearing horses crowned its top.

The Basilica itself had taken a generation to build, its stone blocks larger than the men who had toiled to build it. Smaller arches than the entrance to the courtyard graced, in triplicate, the façade. Those were painted with frescoes framed by ornate stonework. Statues marked every corner and flat surface along the building's riotous roofline. Gold glinted from its domes and cupolas.

It was a wonder, a stunning building that stood as testament to all the Republic could accomplish. And it was nothing compared to the coliseum, comitias, and basilicas in Corsyra. Yet its tainted heart was revealed in the scene playing out in its courtyard.

Cassian counted fifteen soldiers, one supply wagon, the Vex hound and his companions, and a four-wheeled platform with a metal cage bolted to it. The platform was hitched to four heavy-boned horses, who stood placidly as their handlers prepared to leave.

He didn't see Kiya until he looked into the line of captives tied to the back of the supply wagon. One after the other, strung together by the rings on their collars. She was on the end, her hands bound in front of her with rope, her angry face turned toward the ground. Cassian watched as one of the guards paced the length of the line. He wore the breastplate and the dull colors of the Assembly guard, boots and short sword. They dressed more for ceremony than practicality when traveling within the heart of the Republic, or he'd be in full armor. Small mercies. Cassian kissed his fingers and aimed them at the sky in the hopes that Luck would see the gesture.

There were eight prisoners, three Suloi, four Northerners, and Kiya. The guard poked at the Northern men with his unsheathed blade, and one of them lunged out, knocking into the guard with his shoulder. Two of the guard's friends joined him, subduing the man by beating him to the ground. That pulled on the others, who tried to back out of the fray but couldn't avoid it because of the ropes connecting them.

"That is enough, you pack of dogs!" That was Paulus. Cassian had to scan the entire caravan to find him. When he saw him, flanked by the two ranking soldiers, Cassian took one last look behind and around, to make certain Bek had done what he'd asked, instead of following him. He was supposed to remain outside of town, on the road to Corsyra, where Cassian would send Kiya when he had negotiated her release.

With a single deep breath and another whispered prayer to Luck, Cassian stepped onto the Basilica promenade. His father had served here most of his adult life. One of the youngest senators because his own father had been taken early by consumption. Cassian would have been the youngest ever, if Paulus hadn't had so much sway and convinced them Cassian was *too* young. The truth was, he had been too young. He didn't know anything of the suffering of the bottom rungs of Republic society. Not yet. Not until he had spent years among them. He had wanted what was *his*, not for any good he could do, but because of his anger.

"Paulus!" he called as he crossed the stones. The guards who stood in each major archway had taken note of him as soon as he had walked into the space. He needed Paulus to acknowledge him before he was arrested for trespassing. The man looked up when Cassian spoke, and surprise, then that terrible, congenial smile took his face, and he stepped away from the soldiers to stride to Cassian. Gods how he hated that smile. He could see it in his dreams. The smile he'd seen given to his parents countless times throughout his younger years. A smile that meant nothing. A wolf's smile.

"My goodness. You are bold, to show your face to me after you ran away with my gift for the Emperor." Paulus continued to smile, though his gaze smoldered.

"*Consul* Stephanus," Cassian emphasized the correct title, "has enough slaves." He had not realized that Paulus supported Stephanus' bid to build an Empire, and make himself Emperor. It should not have surprised him. Paulus would have supported Stephanus wanting to anoint himself a god, as long as it secured him a position with money and power.

"Not that kind. Now, what brings you out of the slums?"

"I have a deal for you." Cassian hoped he did not look as desperate as he felt. His stomach was roiling, the palms of his hands were clammy, and to his own ears his voice sounded unsteady. "You let me walk out of here with that girl"—he pointed at Kiya—"and I will withdraw my claim on my father's seat."

Paulus' eyes widened, then his expression relaxed into a more calculating smile. "In front of the Assembly?" He pointed at the Basilica. Where Haenna's Assembly met to give Paulus their complaints and taxes and support to take to Corsyra and the Senate. Where Cassian would have to testify, in good mental health, that he willingly gave up his right to his father's seat as Haenna's Senator.

"Of course." Cassian mocked a little forward bow. Paulus' smile tightened, and he turned to signal to a priest acolyte, standing in the shade of one of the century of pillars that surrounded the Basilica with several of his brethren. Taking the appeals of the Assembly to the gods, no doubt.

The young man trotted across the stones to join them. The Vex hound did the same, though Cassian thought the man stalked more than trotted. He took a place on Paulus' other side.

"Cassian, you did not have the honor of meeting Quintus, the emperor's personal hound."

He'd put his hands on Amara. Had hurt her and frightened her. Gods knew what he would have done to her if they hadn't escaped. Cassian took a step toward him, and the grey-eyed beast smiled, his hand heading for the hilt of his sword.

"You're magic touched." His nostrils flared and his lip curled. "Took her for a ride, did you?"

Cassian swung, unable to think beyond the red veil of rage that singed him, and Quintus snorted laughter, weaving out of the way and shoving Cassian sideways. Cassian rounded, and Paulus stepped between them.

"Not now," Paulus snapped to the Vexillae. Quintus relaxed, but his stony gaze remained focused on Cassian. "Pathetic," Paulus said to Cassian. "I heard you had become a slum rat. Brawling and gambling. How proud your parents would be. It is well you've decided to do this. There is no more honorable thing you could do for the people of Haenna than disappear."

Cassian exhaled hard, blinking away the fury and the sting of Paulus' assessment. He gave a sharp nod.

"These two will bear witness," Paulus said. "One for the laws"—he nodded to the hound—"and one for the gods." He tilted his head toward the acolyte. He stared at Cassian as if the look alone would wring the words from him.

"The girl first," Cassian said. Giving anything to Paulus before getting paid for it was a mistake Cassian had seen too many people make. He couldn't do anything lethal to Cassian, not before he had testified to the Assembly that he gave up his blood right. And Cassian would have a better escape plan then. For now, he just had to make certain Kiya got out.

Paulus waved his hand impatiently, and the hound raised a fist then pointed to Kiya. The guards unfastened her from the others and led her over, where Paulus unlocked her collar.

Kiya glanced from Cassian to Paulus before asking, in Meneian, "*What are you doing here?*"

"*I'll explain later. Go to the outskirts. Bek is waiting for you.*" Paulus would try something. Cassian was not fool enough to believe there wasn't a scheme behind that man's easy smile. There always was. The faster he acted now, the better.

Paulus breathed a heavy sigh. "Are you quite finished? You're wasting my time and that heathen language sounds like dogs barking."

Kiya scowled at him, rubbing her wrists.

"In exchange for the release of this woman, I offer an exchange of what is mine." Cassian withdrew the paper with his father's stamp, and his own signature, from where he'd tucked it into the back of his belt. "With gods and man as witness, and by the authority of my blood, I forego my right to my father's seat. I cede that right to Antonis Hirtius, and those that come from his blood."

Cassian handed the paper to Paulus. The words themselves came easily, but as he said them he felt dizzy, sick. Beside him, Kiya's brow furrowed slowly deeper, her mouth parting in surprise, then turning down in protest. But when she started to speak, he clasped her wrist.

Paulus smiled along, nodding at each stop. As he took the paper, Paulus glanced to Quintus, who reached for his sword. Every muscle in Cassian's body seized in surprise, and he slung Kiya roughly behind him, making her stumble and fall to her hands and knees. He put himself between her and the men.

"Run!"

"No—"

"Now!" Cassian jabbed at Quintus' face. The man was built like a brick wall, and his jaw felt made of rock. He barely moved at the impact of Cassian's fist. He swung his arms together as if he meant to crush Cassian in them. Cassian ducked down and grabbed for his pistol, but the hound knocked it from his hand with the flat of his blade. The gun went off, drawing the attention of every guard and soldier in the square. Quintus bared his teeth in a feral grin. Cassian snapped his hand toward his knife, but a guard near the arch leveled a rifle at him. Kiya scrambled to her feet, darting for the side street Cassian had entered on.

"Kill her," Paulus said on a sigh.

The rifle glinted in the sun as the guard shifted, aimed, and fired. The bullet passed close enough to Cassian that he heard the air sizzle around it. He whirled with a cry. Kiya stumbled, rolled, then she was up again and gone, between buildings. Quintus clapped heavy hands on Cassian's shoulders, yanking him off balance, and before he could regain it, he was in manacles.

A soup of panic and relief churned in his belly, making it feel as if he might vomit. "You can't do anything to me," Cassian snarled at Paulus when the hound spun him around to face the man. "I still have to stand before the Assembly to make this formal."

"You bargained for her release. Not her life. And not yours. The Assembly will take these witnesses' word as enough. They are beyond reproach. You, on the other hand, are a gambler..." His expression sharpened, his smile turning to a smirk. "...and a thief." Quintus gave Cassian a good shake for emphasis. "You've escaped justice for too long. I should have known what you were up to, all these years. Fruit never falls outside its mother's shadow, does it?"

"Spending too much time worrying about yourself to notice those around you has always been your greatest weakness," Cassian said.

"And your father's self-righteousness is yours, I see." Paulus struck him, backhanded, with the heavy ring of his office. Cassian felt something crack, pain spidering across his face and eye socket and searing a path through his nostrils. "Gods I've wanted to do that for years." Paulus laughed. "Take him to the Assembly prison. He can hang with the rest of the thieves tonight."

THIRTY

"**I** WANT TO GO BACK for them," Amara said to Djar, glancing from the descending sun to the road leading south.

"I need you here. You are the only one who can control the Charah if he is violent." Djar didn't look at her as he spoke, instead surveying the bridge as Peio and the other three Suloi hunters examined it for weak points. "Besides, what will you do if you find them? If they are captured?" They had expected to get more details of the caravan's composition when the twins arrived. But they never had.

"I cannot answer that until I know why they didn't come." She should not have allowed them to stay behind, in a city hunting for them.

Their absence had distracted Amara, her worry for them completely eclipsing her focus on freeing the Charah. She could hardly think in a straight line, let alone conceive of a plan to ambush a caravan of soldiers and an unpredictable mage. Kiya and Bek were brave and capable, but they were still, in her mind, children. The closest thing to younger siblings she had ever had.

"The Sehzade commanded you to bring back the Charah. And even if he had not, or if you do not care, you know as well as I do that the life of this man…this Charah, is vital to Tamar. If he stays in the hands of the Republic, if they turn him or break him, or use his blood to make poison, he will turn the tide of war even more in their favor than it already is." Djar's voice was flat, emotionless, to match his expression. For a single instant, she hated him. But she also knew him. Knew his heart. The twins were his family too, and their absence pained him. He was not callous, she knew that. But he did understand battle. And war. He spoke to the greater good, to seeing beyond the moment.

Amara looked out of the trees and to the bridge. The river, fast and swollen with spring melt, wound through a narrow, deep channel, and a single wood and stone bridge spanned the distance between the steep banks. This was the river that filled the cisterns responsible for Haenna's aqueducts, and irrigated its fields, though this far from the city it was a wild thing.

She had not been able to go near the bridge; its blinding height above the river channel made her ill to even look at from a distance. Djar hoped his plan to trap half the caravan on the far side would isolate the Charah and his guards from the rest. If it succeeded, they had a chance. If it did not…

"There," Mirari announced.

The caravan appeared, just a dark shape in the distance, haloed in dust. The Suloi returned swiftly from the bridge, to get out of the open and into the trees, and everyone lay on their bellies in the underbrush. None of the day's heat had reached the ground beneath the trees, and its wet cold seeped through Amara's clothes. She watched the oncoming group of soldiers and wagons through the screen of tangled branches.

Perhaps they had captured Kiya and Bek. That was, despite its awfulness, the preferable case. If they had, she had some hope of rescuing them. At least she would know where they were. After a few more moments, the sounds of the horses and wagons reached their hiding place. Wheels rattling on stones. Men's voices laughing and talking. The clop of hooves.

They moved slowly. Fifteen soldiers, a wagon of supplies, enough pistols and rifles to end everything in very short order. And one iron cage big enough to fit a single man. There was no doubt who sat huddled in that cage, and besides the two men positioned in the driver's seat, four guards rode in a loose circle around it. One of them, Amara recognized. Quintus. The other guards around the cage must also be Vex then. It was wrong of her to hope they were killed in the impending ambush. Especially wrong because she did not wish to do it herself.

There was no sign of Bek or Kiya, and Amara's panic climbed higher, into the back of her skull, the frantic feeling that had clawed in her belly and chest now occupying her completely. But she had to hold still, to bear down on her need to run to their horses and return to the city that moment.

The road was about two hundred paces from the trees. If they were noticed before the bulk of the soldiers crossed the bridge, they would lose their fight. Amara tried to concentrate on that, on Mirari clasping her hand from where she lay prone beside her, her breath quick and shallow, her gaze fixed on the cage and its occupant.

Benat was slumped within the bars, his head lolling, curled in on himself like a child. He looked much the same as he had when she had seen him at the auction, when she had felt that stirring of magic and not known what it was, or where it originated from, fool that she was. If she didn't bury her own magic so deeply, this entire debacle may have been avoided. She might have been aware enough to recognize him for what he was. They would not need to be out here when Bek and Kiya needed them.

That was the task Djar assigned her. Control the Charah. Reserve her magic and her strength in case he woke. In case he was made unpredictable by the opium that imprisoned him. And when they took the collar off him…there was no telling what he would do without pain and drugs keeping him cowed.

She needed to care about this, about him. Because her power was unpredictable, hard to control because she did not have practice. In trying to control him she might harm someone else. She needed to concentrate on that. But she only saw Bek and Kiya in his place. Somewhere she couldn't save them. Her panic turned black and cold. The still, heavy depths of deepest ocean, the place her anger lived, stirred.

"Wait." Djar's low command made her realize her gaze had strayed south, toward Haenna. She snapped her attention back to the caravan. She'd thought his warning was for her, for the magic that swirled in the darkest part of her heart, beginning to whisper. But the command had been for the three Suloi hunters, who were moving forward on their bellies, bows clutched in front of them, faces stripped of emotion. They had agreed to help retrieve Benat for the chance it offered at revenge. They stilled, slinging impatient looks in Djar's direction, until Mirari said something in Suloi with a distinctly chiding tone.

The group of soldiers that immediately preceded the wagon stepped onto the bridge, a sturdy thing built of stone pillars that disappeared into the depths of the channel and wooden supports.

Each Suloi had one of the firebombs stolen from the Vex who had tried to capture her in the woods, what seemed like a lifetime ago. They required fire on a fuse, then, as she understood it, they would explode within a few seconds. Cassian had tried to explain it to her, long days ago, but her attention had been focused elsewhere. On him, on his voice, and smile. On the way he felt comfortable, that same feeling of right as the moment she placed a finished garment on its new owner and noted the perfect fit of it. He had fit so easily into their family.

That sorrow mingled with the black anger in her belly, winding around her magic, whispered louder. She had to focus on something else. Not him. Not the twins. The task at hand.

A line of prisoners plodded behind Benat's cage, tied to the back of the wagon. Seven of them. Four of the pale, barbarian Northerners in their furs and leathers, three Suloi, looking ragged and stoic. Only two men among the lot of them. They had walked leagues today. She could see the blood that stained the stones behind them. She knew that pain, the unbearable ache of bruised feet, the sharp slice of cut soles. The dull agony of hopelessness. Kiya and Bek were not among them. They were still in the city then, and they would not have failed to come unless they'd been captured or prevented from riding by some other means. Amara's breath shortened, her gaze skimming back toward the road, toward Haenna.

Mirari's hand tightened incrementally on Amara's with each soldier that went over the bridge. It was narrow, with room enough for the carts, only one at a time. The driver had to take the supply wagon over at a plodding gate, to prevent it turning and becoming wedged against the stone wall of the bridge.

Long, breathless moments oozed by. Sweat beaded between Amara's breasts, itching and tickling. Djar shifted his weight in little increments to prepare to run. Peio took stock of his knives. He held one so large she might have called it a short sword, and another that was more knife-sized, and several more strapped to his person as backups. An entire leather belt crossed his torso, over his shirt, filled with small knives not even the length of Amara's hand. She'd seen such before. They were meant for throwing.

As the supply wagon rumbled over the bridge and its front wheels bounced onto the stones of the road beyond, each Suloi with a firebomb withdrew it, palming matches as well. Matches were the Republic's answer to Lightbringers. Something to create fire from nothing. The sweat on Amara's skin turned cold, and her breath stilled in her lungs as she focused again on the wagon.

Get the Charah out. That was her and Mirari's combined task. Free him and control him.

"Wanderer keep us," Mirari whispered, "and stretch the road straight and clear before us."

Each Suloi traced a circle in the dirt in reaction to her quiet prayer. Amara traced her own, with a thought to the Wheel and the water. Such prayers were not common in Tamar. The Wheel was served by working toward balance. It did not dole out favors for rituals or desperate pleading. Still, it might turn for them in this. To free its fourth-born child.

But perhaps her prayer went unheard, or the Wheel turned for spite, because disaster struck in the next instant. Quintus stopped, his gaze swinging unerringly toward where they waited in the trees.

"Hound," Peio snarled.

Quintus shouted an order, to get the Charah over the bridge. The caravan fractured apart and reformed with the wagon in the front. Quintus slashed through the rope that held the line of prisoners to the wagon, and the driver snapped the reins on the team of horses.

"Stop them," Djar barked. He leapt to his feet and ran for the bridge. Quintus spurred his horse, racing past Djar to the wagon. It careened onto the bridge in an awkward turn, tipped nearly to one side, and the guards had to shove it free when it lodged. The Suloi ran after Djar, but it was a long sprint on foot. The guards got the wagon unwedged, and it rumbled across the stone span. One Suloi lit his grenade and threw it. It clattered onto the bridge and tumbled to the middle, behind the wagon.

"No!" Mirari screamed, but her voice was lost in the explosion that rained fire and rock and tore an enormous chunk out of the middle of the bridge. A black-shelled inferno burst across the stones. A man's scream was cut off. The explosion left Amara's ears ringing, and Mirari clung to her where they lay on the ground.

Amara tried to search the smoke and raining debris for evidence that the wagon, and the Charah, had escaped the blast. She got to her hands and knees, then to her feet. She leveraged Mirari to hers and they staggered out of the trees.

"Can you see him?" Mirari asked, gripping Amara's sleeve and standing on tiptoe. The bridge was a mess of black, acrid smoke, broken, crumbling stone and pillars collapsing into the chasm. Through the screen of it she could just make out Djar, side by side with Peio, fighting the soldiers trying to make their way across.

A gust of damp wind cleared the remains of the bridge. The wagon's back wheels hung off the broken edge of the bridge's far side, prevented from plummeting into the river below by the heavy horses scrambling and pulling as three soldiers tugged on their harnesses.

"No," Mirari breathed. Then she ran, fast as a deer, toward the bridge.

"Stop!" Amara called, running after Mirari. She'd have to dodge through the fight and milling soldiers on this side to even get to Benat, then cross the narrow remaining strip of bridge to reach the wagon.

On the other side, Quintus was trying to bring order to the panicked horses and disoriented men. His shouted commands about the wagon could barely be heard over the rush of the river. Amara could not see Benat, trapped in the cage and dangling over the river, because of the broken remains of the bridge's parapet. If he fell into the river in that cage…

As she ran, she looked for any of hers that could assist, but they were all engaged. Djar and Peio fought off those soldiers trapped on this side, and the other three Suloi were attempting to hold back more who were trying to cross the bit of rock and mortar that remained. It was so narrow it had to be taken in single file. Mirari was going to be killed. Even if she managed to cross the ledge, they'd shoot her if she went near the wagon, if her extra weight didn't send it plummeting into the water first.

As Amara arrived at Mirari's side, just on the edge of the cluster of fighting, the soldiers on the far side of the river fired a volley of shots. Amara dropped to her belly and Djar and the others dove for cover behind rubble from the bridge. Mirari sprinted for the southern parapet, where a span no more than two bricks wide still connected to the far side. Gripping the parapet, Mirari used the pause while the far side reloaded to shimmy to the other side. She reached the other side and vaulted onto the angled, dangling wagon.

"Shoot her!" Quintus barked.

Mirari tried to reach through the bars to Benat, who was still listless, curled against the back of the cage, the only thing between him and plummet of several times his height into the water below.

"Wake up!" Mirari screeched, grabbing the bars in her hands and trying to shake the cage, to startle Benat awake. "Please, Benat, we need your help!"

Amara got to her hands and knees just as a soldier on the far side finished loading his pistol, leveled it, and shot at Mirari. Amara couldn't hear her gasp, but saw her arch back in pain, then tumble sideways off the cage. She managed to hook her arm through the bars, but hung, clinging to the cage, over the water. Amara stood and ran, only a few paces to the bridge. She could not tell her breath from her heartbeat, both were fast and hard, and the world contracted and dilated around her, devoid of anything that made sense. Sounds reached her, but she didn't know what they were. Smells, smoke and river and copper blood.

Mirari screamed for help. Benat didn't move.

She had to help. She should be able to help. But her power was as likely to doom them all as save them.

Amara gripped the rough stone of the parapet and took a step onto the crumbling remains of the bridge. Her breath rasped in her ears, and the world spun a lazy circle around her, transforming the rushing river below into a sucking whirlpool. She slid her right foot sideways, pressing her belly against the parapet, and forced herself to shift her weight. Then again.

"Please, Benat, help," Mirari begged, trying to climb the cage, but not strong enough to pull her dangling weight up. Amara could not turn to look at her. She had to keep her belly pressed to the stone and her back to the gaping hole where the bridge had been, her chin tipped down so she could stare at the top of the parapet in her grip or she would freeze. Another sliding step. She wasn't breathing. She took a quick sip of air. She was cold all over, and she had to fight every muscle in her body seizing as she forced another step. Her heel dipped into the space where a brick was missing. She lurched forward, bending over the parapet and holding tightly, shaking.

"Don't shoot that one!" Quintus yelled, and Amara looked in time to see him shove the rifle another soldier leveled at her into the air. Its shot shocked her. Quintus met her gaze and charged toward her as three other soldiers advanced on the wagon, and Mirari.

Three large steps remained between Amara and the far side. She could make it if she ran. She had to let go of the parapet.

Let go.

Let go.

Her hands clawed tighter. She had done this with Cassian. That bridge had been higher. A quick breath, which she held, and launched herself toward the other side.

Amara landed on her hands and knees, feet dangling off the crumbling edge, and crawled, tears in her eyes, to the wagon. With fire surging through her blood, fear and energy, she managed to force herself to climb onto the slanting wagon. It teetered like a child's balance board on the edge of the broken bridge, wheels and cage over open air.

Quintus grabbed for her arm, missing because Amara let go of her grip on the front wheel and slid along the tilted wagon floor to the cage, her feet tangling between the bars.

The wagon jerked, sliding farther over the bridge. Mirari made another attempt to climb up the bars, but blood soaked her sleeve and back, and her left arm seemed useless. Amara stood, leaning against the top of the cage, gripping the bars in one hand and reaching for Mirari with the other, over the side of the cage. Water ripped past them, far, far below.

Quintus leapt off the wagon as it jolted, then began to slide, tipping over the edge of the bridge. "Cut the horses loose!" he bellowed. Mirari grasped Amara's hand, and another jolt sent the entire wagon plunging toward the river.

Amara's heart seized painfully, then slammed, and she sucked in a breath. She tried to scream, but they hit the water, and it filled her lungs and froze her to the bone. The rushing current tried to snatch her off the cage, and pull Mirari away, but Amara held fast to both, though it felt as if she'd be torn in half.

Benat's power rumbled awake. Breaking over his skin as gold cut with fire that blazed through the murk of the muddy water. Magic like rattling earth and inferno from the heart of the world. The riverbed shuddered. Stones from the bridge rained down into the water around them. For a bracing, hope-filled moment, Amara thought he was helping.

Color flashed and rolled over Benat's skin. Moving with magma's indiscriminate power. Rage. That was all Amara felt, its hot, acidic tang against her tongue and poisoning the water of her own magic. This was not a mage in control. The numbness that permeated her froze to ice as he moved within the cage, horror creeping like slow vines up her arms and legs.

His hands twitched forward, grasping the bars. His eyes opened, and he looked straight at Amara. They were not in opposition, earth and water. But there was a great deal of the Fifth House in his magic, and it did not like hers. Nor drowning, apparently. Power rolled white hot, then red, then black, through his eyes.

Amara tried to rein in her magic, but it frothed and twirled because of the threat of his and her desperation for air. Benat heaved against the bars, and the iron groaned, bending open. One bar snapped, tearing a deep gash across Benat's forearm. He ignored it, pulling and forcing until he could emerge from the cage. He caught Mirari around the waist and pulled her away from Amara, yanking Amara off the cage with the same movement. The current grabbed her and flung her away from them.

She slammed into a rock, a boulder or debris from the bridge, and clung to it despite the explosion of pain through her ribs. Amara clawed free of the water and sucked in a deep gulp of air. The river had slung her a significant distance from the bridge, to where the high walls of the ravine had lessened, and their slope was less severe. If she could get to the bank, she could get out.

"Amara!"

She wiped her eyes against her soaked shirt, trying to free them of grit and the sting of the water so she could see. Bek lay on his belly on the steep, sloped bank, Kiya's arm gripped in his hands as she waded toward Amara, reaching. Amara grabbed her outstretched hand and kicked against the current as Kiya pulled her toward the shore. Amara crawled onto the muddy bank, gasping and coughing. Kiya sat beside her, and when Amara looked at her, Kiya cupped Amara's face in her hands, her eyes full of sadness that felt deadlier to Amara than anything else around them. Something was wrong.

Amara clung to Kiya's arms, drained of strength down to her bones. That look. Her mother had worn that look when she told Amara that her father was dead. That Amara had killed him.

"They took him," Kiya purged, tears overflowing her eyes and streaking through dust and blood on her face. Amara concentrated on her, trying to understand. But she was too cold, and there were too many things to try and concentrate on. Kiya's side was covered in blood. It streaked her hands, her face. Her skin was ashen.

"What happened to you?"

"Cassian told me to run. They shot me…it's only a graze. But he didn't get away."

Was he…was he dead? Amara looked around, trying to find something that made sense, whether it was Kiya's words or the battle. Her heart fell into a funny, slow rhythm, and her head filled with buzzing. Her magic stirred, churning to languid life. She'd lost the Charah. She'd lost Mirari.

"Did you hear me? They have Cassian."

"They'll hang him," Bek said, "I heard them." Amara could hear the anguish that she did not see on his face.

Kiya grabbed Amara's hands and tried to tug her to her feet. But Amara was rooted to the ground. There was nothing she could do. Amara's hands spasmed open and closed as she stared up at Kiya's dirt-stained face. At the wild sorrow in her eyes, the defeat that tightened her expression with pain. Nothing. All the power in the Second House was hers to command and she could do nothing.

Metal clashed around them, swords. Shouts. Firing guns patterned the battle with drumbeats. Her thoughts filled with murderous, rolling magma. The Charah crawled out of the river, dragging Mirari onto the bank only a few paces downriver. He looked at her, with that black, boiling lava in his eyes.

"Run," Amara told Kiya and Bek. "Run now."

Benat clambered to his feet and stumbled toward Amara, and she knew, to the deepest, quietest corner of her soul, that if he laid hands on her, he was going to kill her. He was stone and fire, the heart of a volcano made man, torn asunder and in agony. She could feel the silent screams of his fear and pain as vibrations within her power. His very soul was at war.

You are peace.

But what could she do?

Her magic unfurled, rising, racing over her skin and into her sight, coloring the world in silver truth. Everything disappeared, its color bleeding away to blackness. Amara stood alone. In the depths of the darkness, in the place where everything began, and ended.

Mist swam and spun in eddies as though pushed and shaped by a current. It rose into figures and melted away. Its voices were deep ocean songs. And as she listened, across the darkness, turquoise sparkled like sun above her on warm surface water. Voices. Bleeding together into a river of power and peace. That was water, she knew. The Second House. Empathy and emotion. Sensuality and gentleness, stronger even than stone. Stone could be worn away by the constant caress of water's ceaseless wash. But water could not be broken. It shaped the world, its valleys and cliffs, but could not be shaped or contained, flowing and reforming around all its obstacles.

The mist coalesced and rose in front of her, until she was staring at a incorporeal apparition of herself as a girl. Amara knew that mist. The stuff of her nightmares. But it had never been this, a picture of herself. Always it was monsters. Claws and teeth and whispered lies. Now it was her. Stripped of her fears, and her traumas. A smiling, laughing girl who was sweet, and innocent. One that Amara looked on now and did not miss. Her innocence was a part of her, but not who she was now. It was not her strength.

Shimmering fissures of turquoise opened across the image's skin. Cracks and wounds. Knitting together and healing into brilliant marks. But Amara understood. Those scars were strong. Stronger. Liker mended cloth made more beautiful for its patchwork intricacies.

The little girl turned to mist, then Amara's mother. Brown skin and dark eyes. A soft smile.

"Habibi," she whispered in all the voices of magic, "strength is forged in pain. *You* were forged in pain, so that you could love. Be mercy, peace of the Wheel. Be kindness in the dark of horror. Show them."

The vision disappeared in a wash of heat and fire. Amara blinked, woke to the sound of screaming and hot tears on her face. Mirari, Kiya. Benat had stopped four steps from her, where Bek had intercepted him. He held Bek by his throat, his skin turned to stone, cracked and bleeding the heat of fire. An arrow bounced off his back.

Amara ran to him, wedged herself between him and Bek. She pressed a hand to his chest and held his outstretched arm with the other. Where her hands touched, steam rose, hissing against his heat and anger.

"What are you?" he rumbled, the anger of fire and slow roll of earth shaping a voice like ancient stone.

"Peace," Amara hummed, "I am peace. Be still, Benat."

She reached within herself, within her power, and touched the shimmering water in her mind's eye, a ribbon of wild river that sliced through the land behind Benat. She let it take her over, mist rising from the surface, billowing up and filling the ravine until it spilled onto the banks, and figures stepped free of it, a faceless, sexless copy of herself for each person around her. Together, they sang.

Amara sang. She sang the lullaby her mother taught her. About safety in a mother's arms, about the quiet of night. The silence of the silver moon. The mist rose until it blinded, her song echoing inside it. Beneath her hands Benat's body cooled and relaxed, until he released his grip on Bek and collapsed. Mirari crawled forward, cradling his head in her hands as he slumped to the ground.

Amara closed her eyes, spreading her awareness into the mist. To each and every soldier who still stood. They dropped their weapons at her command, guided and compelled by the mist that poured from the river. She pushed harder, farther, stretching her soul and power along the miles of waterway, following it to Haenna. To the aqueducts that laced the city like arteries. The mist gave her eyes a wavering image of the city, like a reflection in clear water.

Sleep. She sang. Her mist swept up from the river, the aqueducts, the canals, the brackish water that filled the catacombs, and laid a blanket of tranquility across Haenna. She searched, forcing the mist wider, into every alley, every building, every window, until she felt him. That steady, silent shore, a mind she knew because it had been within her own. A body that was hers as much as it was his.

He stood next to two others, on a platform built of wood. Amara could only see pale images, but she could see the confusion as her spell filled the main courtyard of the Basilica. She'd stretched herself to the limit by then. Her heart beat in a body that felt as fragile as glass, her skin stretched paper thin over her magic and her soul. Harnessing the wild, rushing power of the river into a quiet mist was not a feat she had ever tried, and in the back of her thoughts she was aware that it was killing her.

In that same distant awareness, she could hear someone calling her name, hands on her. Come back. But she couldn't. Couldn't leave him there. Her mist crept closer, touching each person who stood gathered in the vast open space to watch. Her weakening grip on the spell wavered and slipped when she understood what she was seeing.

Gallows. Not so different from the scene she had witnessed when her mother was killed before her eyes. Had sacrificed herself for Amara. And all these people, here to watch it. To marvel at and be entertained by murder.

Anger rose, coloring her vision in violent shades. They did not deserve peace. They did not deserve the sleep she had given to everyone else. They deserved the death they had wished on others. On strangers. The whispers of her spell changed, its intent warping the singing figures into clawed harbingers. *Die.*

Mercy. Spoke of the Second House. Be mercy where there is none. That was her own voice, in her own thoughts. Her tortured heart, fluttering and pounding as she drained her own life to try and save Cassian's. When she focused on him once more, she saw the man he hated. Paulus. He was screaming orders, slamming his fist against the platform as he pointed at her mist then Cassian. Cassian, despite the noose the hangman was slipping over his head, was smiling. He was smiling at her, though he couldn't see her. Just her spell.

Amara commanded the mist forward. Intent on the man who would pull the lever to drop the hatch below Cassian and the others. *Not this time.* But her heart faltered. Her lungs seized, and for a moment whose span she couldn't name, she was gone. Drifting. Green light like spring circled her mind, and she was drawn back in her body, staring up at a circle of concerned faces. Mirari's firm hands cupped her face.

"Enough," Djar snarled at her when her eyes opened.

"Forgive me," Amara whispered, the movement cracking her lips, stripped of moisture, so that she tasted blood. She closed her eyes and dropped back into the spell. The mist had already faded, sinking into the ground. Amara spread her awareness into it, her mind possessing the mist and all whom it touched, calling to the water throughout the city to give it power. On the edges of her mind, she saw the glow of green. Mirari, trying to keep her heart beating.

But she was too late. As Amara's vision woke in the mist, the hangman reached the lever to drop the platforms beneath all three men. He pulled it. Amara screamed, twin visions of her mother and Cassian dropping. She pushed everything left of herself into the spell, and the mist surged forward and up, over the platform, and Amara's vengeance rose out of it to face the hangman, wrapping its clawed hands around his throat.

Cut them down. The hangman repeated the words, eyes glassy, and swung around to obey, moving so slowly Amara couldn't breathe for watching him. It took lifetimes, in her perception, for him to unsheathe his sword and slice through the first rope. A stranger.

Then three steps to the next. That man kicked and struggled and the hangman missed his first attempt. After two more clumsy swings, the second man dropped. Cassian's rope didn't twitch or buck, as the second man's had, and the stillness birthed sorrow.

When the hangman finally sawed through Cassian's rope Amara forced more of herself into the mist. It took the last trickle of herself and her power, and shaped it into an ephemeral body so she could walk across the platform and peer below it. She could feel nothing but emotion in this body made of water, but in the far-off distance, she knew she was crying, could feel her drained body dying all around her consciousness.

Cassian lay on his back on the stones below, wheezing, but smiling.

In a weak, croaking voice, he said, "I hope this means you forgive me, Princess."

THIRTY-ONE

HE MOMENT HE SPOKE to the Amara-shaped mist it disappeared as if dissipated by wind. Cassian rolled to his side with a groan, wincing against the bruised, hard pain in his neck and throat. Gods and hells, that was much closer to death than he had ever intended to be. In truth, he wanted to lie exactly where he was. Maybe shed a tear or two to try and rid his body of the quivering energy that made his hands unsteady and his vision blurry. But whatever she had done would not last long. He'd seen how the others at Buschetto had recovered once she turned her attention away. He rolled to his belly then his knees, working his hands against each other to try and loosen the ropes around his wrists.

He had to duck low to get out from under the gallows platform. Night had not yet dropped its full cloak of darkness. Some light lingered from the setting sun. Enough for him to observe the courtyard waking from Amara's sleep spell. Cassian divested the first sleeping guard he encountered of his knife. It took a few sweat-inducing moments to work the knife around in his hands to an angle he could use it to cut at the ropes. Each of those moments made him clumsier, as people rose from where they had fallen asleep on the stone.

The rope frayed and finally weakened enough he could loosen it and twist his hands free. He tucked the knife into his belt and circled the platform, until he saw Paulus, sitting groggily on the stones near the stairs that led to the gallows platform. Cassian crouched in front of him, gave his cheek a friendly pat, and pulled the rolled-up signature paper out of the place he'd tucked it.

"I've changed my mind, Paulus. You can rot in the River Nexus on your way to the Night Hall. And Antonis is welcome to join you." Cassian ruffled the older man's carefully styled hair and got up. He strode out through the confused and milling crowd, and into the streets.

The city was transformed, eerie and silent. All around him people still lay on the ground, some had dropped whatever they were carrying. Some had fallen asleep mid-task, though he saw no one who had been injured by doing so. The mist was sliding back, into the canals, into the grates for the sewer, sinking away, revealing the city like a magician's cloth slowly lowered.

She'd put the entire blasted city to sleep. Cassian grinned.

"Love you too," he murmured. Maybe she didn't want to love him, and truly he couldn't blame her, but he had some small understanding of what she had chosen to do. For him. Hopefully it had not cost her what it had at Buschetto.

Cassian ducked into the safety of a tight, cluttered alley, and leaned against the wall of one of the buildings. He touched his fingers to his bruised and aching throat. His head pounded, and his hands still shook.

Too close. Much too close to looking the lord of death in the eyes. Amara gave him a second chance. He was going to thank her, and make certain she'd forgiven him for his selfish choices. He couldn't leave Haenna. Couldn't leave the network he'd built over these long years, couldn't give up helping those he could. And he didn't think he could convince her to stay. But damn it to the Night Hall, he was going to try.

HE WAS WAITING IN the woods with Danel and the girls from the Den when Amara returned. Djar cradled her like a child on his horse. Cassian's elation, his plans to spill his heart to her, evaporated in the same manner her mist had. He took her from Djar and to a spot that Danel indicated, a shabby pile of blankets cushioned by leaves. Cassian gripped her smaller hand in his as he knelt beside her. It was cold and limp.

"What is wrong? What happened? Is this because of me? Mage sleep?" Cassian touched his knuckles to her cheek and withdrew them at the coldness of her skin.

"It is not mage sleep, and it was not only you," Djar growled. "We cannot linger here."

As he spoke, three Suloi hunters Cassian had never met assisted Mirari in unloading a man from the horse he was tied to like a sack of barley. They laid him on the opposite side of the fire from Amara. Sweat broke across her skin. She jerked her head to the side, and her hand curled against Cassian's. He looked first to the stranger, then to Djar. Was that the mage they had gone to save?

"What else? Tell me what's happening to her."

"His magic," Djar said. "She is trying to hold him and it is killing her."

"Hold him? Hold him from what?"

"His magic is tearing him apart." Peio squatted beside the man and examined his face. Cassian couldn't see him well because of the darkness and the wavering fire. But he looked Suloi, a bit. Mixed blood though. He was too tall and broad to be only Suloi. His lips peeled back from his teeth and the tendons in his neck strained as his body twitched.

"How can we make her stop?" Cassian squeezed Amara's fingers, then laced his own through them. Hers were so slim and graceful. But cold. Would they let him hold her? He couldn't bear this.

"We silence his magic or she'll kill herself holding him." Djar gave Benat a look that suggested he was perfectly willing to silence his magic with a scimitar through the chest. Mirari dropped to her knees beside Benat, hovering over him.

"How do we do that?" Cassian prodded.

"The same way the Republic did." Peio adjusted the strap of his quiver against his chest. "Poppy."

"No!" Mirari snapped.

"Miri," Danel said, his voice tired. "What would Benat do if he woke to find he had unwittingly killed someone who had helped him? If it were his choice, you know what he would decide."

Mirari did not respond, only turned her gaze down, to Benat's face. "Where will we get it?" she asked. "The entire city will be looking for us now. Looking for the mage that attacked Haenna."

Attacked seemed a violent word for what Amara had done. Again, without harming a soul. Except her own. Cassian wanted to lie beside her, to try and chase the chill from her skin and the strained lines from her brow and mouth.

"There was some with the supplies we took from the Vex. It may still be at the Fountain House." Peio adjusted his quiver strap against his chest. Cassian finally noticed the small wounds on his friend's arms and back. They'd fought a battle to get Benat, and Cassian had been no help at all. Causing more problems by staying away than he would have by joining them. She might have been angry at him, but at least he wouldn't have been so far away she was forced to overextend her magic. Along with holding Benat together. Whatever that meant.

"We cannot wait to find out. We have very little time to get far enough away from Haenna to outrun any Republic ships they send after us," Djar said. "We have to leave now."

He'd wanted hours to explain things to her. To tell her if she left she would take parts of him with her. He wanted a chance to beg her to stay. But she couldn't. She was in danger here, and he had no power to protect her. Whatever the other mage meant to her, to Tamar, that was important. She was risking her life for it, and the only thing he could do was help her in her chosen task. And if she took all the beauty out of his world when she left, then that was the price exacted for the moments he'd had with her.

Cassian stroked her hair away from her face and kissed her temple. "Forgive me for the improper goodbye," he murmured in her ear. "Thank you, for bringing me peace. For letting me love you, for a little while." He stood, and looked down at her for a long moment that was not long enough. How could he let her go, now, and not ever know if she made it safely to Tamar? "Are you certain the opium will work?" he said to the others.

"It has worked for the Republic until now," Mirari replied bitterly. "He only woke because he nearly drowned."

"I will make certain it works, or the Sultana's Circle will be short one Charah," Djar said. Cassian met his gaze, and they exchanged nods.

"Take her to the ship," Cassian said. "I'll get into the villa and bring any poppy I find to the docks."

Kiya and Bek came at him at once. Kiya wrapped her wiry arms around his neck in a fierce hug, and Bek slapped him hard on the back.

"Come with us," Kiya said, her gaze pleading.

Cassian smiled regretfully. "She has no need of me where you're going."

"But...we do," Kiya said. Her brother draped an arm over her shoulders, and though he wore an expression of irritation and censure as he tried to turn Kiya away, Cassian thought he knew enough about young men to see the hurt that festered beneath.

"Oh? Not enough destitute gamblers in Tamar?" He smiled when she stuck her tongue out. "I have work here, twin two. I cannot." That was half the truth. He couldn't live in the same city where Amara was living out a life that didn't include him. And he didn't have a right to be near enough to mar whatever happiness this future she had planned would bring her.

"Tell her I said goodbye." Cassian turned, swallowing back an upwelling of emotion. That was something to be examined later. With a strong drink to accompany it. Peio rose from where he sat beside Mirari and Benat, and came silently to Cassian's side. "My friend..." Cassian's voice betrayed him a little. Peio ignored it, gripping his shoulder and bowing in Mirari's direction.

"My path parts from yours," he said to her. "Thank you for daring to see a Ghost."

"May our paths twist together again someday." Mirari laced his fingers together then apart before lifting one hand in farewell.

"Peio—" Cassian began, but Peio's fingers dug into his shoulder.

"I am honored to have shared my road with yours, for a time," Peio said to Kiya, Djar, and Bek. Kiya kissed his cheek, and both men gripped his offered hand. "Sun fall to light the path before you, and rain fall behind, to guard your passing."

Peio dropped to a knee next to Amara's prone form and drew a knife, which he used to prick his thumb. He swiped the drop of blood across the back of her hand.

"My water to yours, Sister River. I am beholden to you. A droplet to the sea, and if you ever have need of me, you need only call my name. I was once Peio Urbina, first son of the Speaker of Clan Urbina. Call, and this Ghost will come."

Everyone was silent at Peio's pledge; even the three hunters had been listening, if not looking at him. Peio stood and walked into the dark. Cassian ran after him.

"I thought you were going with them," he said, when he caught up.

"You are the only clan I have left, Cassian Haydar. And even the roadborn who carry the Wanderer's tears know that the blood of brotherhood has always been stronger than water."

THIRTY-TWO

AMARA SAT ON A wooden bench along the railing of her bedroom's balcony, breathing in the damp, brined air of Narfour. In her absence the weather had warmed somewhat, and the pots of vines and flowers she kept near the railing were beginning to climb again, to spill their bounty over the railings. Her bedroom overlooked the water and she stared north, into the haze of the horizon that glimmered over a dawn-lit sea. This was the first time she had ever looked out over the water and the city and not found joy and peace in the experience.

Her body was weak, thinned by several degrees after a mage sleep devoid of anything but what water Havva and her friends could get her to drink. It had been the longest mage sleep Havva had ever heard of. The entire journey from Haenna to Narfour plus a small turn.

"This is utter foolishness. Just because you've woken does not mean you are well," Havva said as she strode through Amara's bedroom to stand in the frame of the balcony doors. "And that basket of adders is no place for you to be when you are so depleted."

"I did not do all of this, endure all of this, to falter now." The travel on the ship had been a race against her slow death. In her unconsciousness she had battled the madness that bubbled up through the fractures in Benat's mind and his furious power. They'd had to ration the poppy Peio and Cassian brought them from the Fountain House. So to keep Benat asleep, to prevent him sinking their ship, Amara had given of her power until she nearly ceased to exist.

Even now, after so much time unconscious, her magic was nothing more than a hum of a memory inside her. Only when they'd been separated, when Benat had been taken to the palace infirmary and knocked into oblivion with enough poppy to put down an elephant, had she slipped into real mage sleep. At least, that was how Kiya had described what happened. Her magic was returning, but no quicker than her strength.

"It isn't going to impress anybody if you pass out in front of them. Take a few more days. Eat. Get sunshine. Let all those people down-stairs take care of you, you stubborn mule."

"You must be looking in a mirror if that is what you see," Amara said under her breath. "I do not wish to impress him. If he is not impressed with what I have accomplished simply for the privilege of this marriage then the man is unsalvageable. Let him think whatever he wishes. I do not care." She looked out to the sea again, and thought of Ihsan's face, instead of the one she wished to. The one that was always in the back of her thoughts.

"You are more yourself than I thought." Havva gave one of her hearty laughs. "It is early yet. Have something to eat. I'll bring it to you." She disappeared back inside and when she returned, she set a cup of tea and a plate of flatbread and labneh on the little table beside Amara's bench. She settled beside Amara with a sigh. "Tell me about the Republic. How many hearts did you break, hmm?"

Oh, how she'd held it away. Held every thought of him, every memory of his touch and dimpled smile and bright eyes. Every time he tried to sneak his way into her mind she pushed him brutally away. It would fade. She told herself. It would die.

But the only thing dying was her. A slow bleed.

Havva's words sliced her open, because the only heart that had been broken was her own. Tears filled and overflowed her eyes, tracing fat trails down her sunken cheeks. Her breath squeaked as she tried to inhale, and Havva's tawny brows rose.

"Oh my girl." She pulled Amara into a hug. They were friends, bonded by their similar pasts, despite Havva being old enough to be Amara's mother, she rarely acted as such. But the motherliness came now, and Amara allowed it for the vain hope it might ease her pain.

"I couldn't even say goodbye," Amara whispered. Her first reaction when she had woken in Narfour had been fury. She'd nearly died trying to save him and he didn't even say goodbye. She'd needed to know he was all right, and all she had was the story relayed to her by the others. Her last sight of him had been him lying at the bottom of a gallows platform, smiling up at her. Still her pulse raced when she remembered it. The sight of him falling. Amara choked. Havva pet her back and made a shushing sound.

There were so many unfinished threads between them. So many things to say, and feel. The distance had done nothing but make the tear of his absence in the fabric of her new self that much more obvious. The fury had faded to the dull ache that accompanied resignation.

He'd stayed without her. And she didn't know what that meant. Was he honoring what he thought she wanted? Was that what he wanted? To live in that horrible place, broken and alone? Didn't he know what he'd done to her? Torn her open and placed himself in her heart? That he was woven amongst them all now. Kiya missed him. Bek did. There was no telling if Djar missed him, sometimes he was a closed book even to her. But, she knew Djar had not despised him, and that was as glowing a recommendation as he gave.

"I know it hurts," Havva said. "I know." She had once had a separation just as abrupt, though more devastating. The man had abandoned her, with a child on the way. Amara took a deep breath, and nodded to herself. Yes. It was not as bad as that. She would survive. She had survived much worse. But even as she thought the words, the dull ache in her chest continued, unabated.

So she would not linger here, ill and weak. She would go to the palace, and look the Sultana in the eye, and take what was owed her for the price she had paid. She would find out what the Sultana intended to do about Benat. He was a danger to himself at the very least, but more frightening, to the entire city. It had never occurred to her what a rogue earth mage was capable of. Commander Ayan had impeccable control of his power, had been known for it while studying at the University. A single angry episode from Benat and Narfour, centuries of architecture and history, would fall into the sea.

She and Havva sat in silence as Amara forced herself to eat some of the food. Her long unconsciousness, the mage sleep, her mental and magical battle with Benat, had stripped her of everything. And in the silence when no one was there to speak with her and distract her, she was faced with the agonizing realization that all she wanted was Cassian. She wanted him to lie beside her, pat his chest as he had their only night together, to invite her to lay her head, and her burdens, upon him. She had not realized she had, how much lighter she had been for his willingness to let her be exactly as she was, to hold up her pain and her past alongside her. She had not realized until she had woken without him, and the full weight of it was upon her again.

"I cannot sit here," Amara said.

"You are very weak," Havva said.

Amara rose, her hands tight on the railing to give her quivering legs time to adjust to the change in position. A brief feeling of weightlessness drifted through her head, and she thought she might faint.

"Worse than my son, that's what you are. He'd report for duty on broken legs." Havva rose with a sigh, wrapping a thick, powerful arm around Amara's waist and helping her inside.

"I'm not going for duty," Amara stated as Havva set her on her bed.

"Oh, I know what you're going for. I've never liked that plan, and you know it. I like it even less now. Wounds need to bleed before you cover them up. Or they fester." Havva frowned at her. "But you know all about that."

AMARA CHOSE HER FAVORITE entari, one she'd sewn herself of Eastern silk in brilliant, green-tinted turquoise. She'd found the cloth at a Meneian merchant's booth during the winter market three Turns before. When the light moved across it, the fabric looked just like the brilliant bays of the Sun Sea. It had been too beautiful to ruin with embroidery, and Amara felt most herself, and most aligned with her House, when she wore it. The more common brocade and velvet used to sew entari gave them stiffer shapes that did not move with the body beneath. This was the most risqué Amara would dare be in Narfour, wearing fabric that suggested her curves and moved like rippling water all around her. And before all that had transpired in Haenna, she would never have worn it at the palace. But she felt vulnerable, for her depleted magic, and her wounded heart. Beauty could be as much a shield as iron could, or a weapon more adaptable and precise than any dagger. She would need that this day.

Djar came with her, as did Danel and Mirari. They were apprehensive in the city. While Amara found comfort in the familiar architecture, arched doorways, latticed windows, breezy layouts to take advantage of the cooling sea winds and the press of familiar humanity, Mirari shied at every noise and flinched when people drew too close or looked too long. Danel was more stoic, but his tension showed in how tightly he gripped the staff he used for walking. They had not done themselves any favors by insisting on wearing their same threadbare, travel-worn clothing and foreign hairstyles. Mirari called Tamar clothing confusing, but Amara suspected she was just trying to cling to the one thing that was familiar. She had not enjoyed the many layers and buttons of caftans and entari when she arrived in Narfour, either. Now, Amara found them comforting, a ritual of the life she had built herself, one brick at a time.

Neither Danel nor Mirari had been allowed into the palace until Amara could vouch for them, despite Benat being in the infirmary. Some paranoia from the assassination attempt lingered in the palace, it seemed.

The separation from Benat had been difficult for Mirari, whose eyes showed shadows in the hollows. In contrast, Amara had been very careful to hide her fear of making the trek to the palace, of being in proximity to Benat again. But she did not sense him once they had passed through the Morning Gate. She did not know if that was because he was so deeply unconscious or because her magic was an empty well, being refilled a drip at a time.

The day was nicer than the one that had found Amara at the palace accepting the assignment to travel to Haenna. The courtyard was dry, and busy. Full of curious onlookers who stared at their passing. Despite her silent glare, Djar twined Amara's arm with his to help her walk. Mirari walked on her other side and though she wasn't as overt in her concern for Amara, she was obviously ready to move in if Amara so much as stumbled. Which she did. Twice.

The palace, despite the bright, sunny spring day, felt cold and forbidding when they stepped inside. Or perhaps that was how Amara felt inside. This visit did not carry with it the same potential the most recent visit had. But she knew, sometimes achieving something she'd worked hard for felt anticlimactic. Triumph would settle soon enough. It was always jarring, travel and return. The times she had traveled with her ships to Menei had left her tired and out of sorts for long days.

She told herself that all the way to the library, where the guard who met them at the entrance escorted them. He entered to announce them, leaving the door open enough that voices from inside drifted out. The Sultana's, and a man's, in what sounded like a good-natured, if heated, argument.

The guard returned from the interior with Samira. Samira bowed to them, pushing the library doors open all the way. When she saw Djar, her subdued, controlled expression fell to pieces. Her hands tightened around the cloth of her entari. Her gaze bounced from Djar to Amara and back, and her eyes glazed with tears. Amara had never seen so much emotion from her before. But she understood. The wound to his eye and subsequent scar were shocking.

The glaze vanished from Samira's eyes, replaced with fierce heat, sparks drifting through the honey brown of her irises and flickering across her skin. Mirari whispered something, perhaps a prayer to her god, and stepped back, dragging Danel with her. Yes, the fury of a fire mage was something to fear indeed.

"Are you lonely today, Samira?" Djar asked. Her lips parted, and the fire faded, and she gave a single, mute shake of her head.

"Not today, Djar." Her voice warbled on the last. Djar grinned at her. Samira smiled back, regaining her composure. She took quick, practiced measure of Mirari and Danel, then turned away to lead them all inside.

Amara had never been inside the palace library. She glanced up at Djar's face and found it suffused with lusty greed, his gaze flitting from shelf to shelf, up and over the books and tables, open tomes, and shelves of rolled parchment. If she was in the palace, at Ihsan's side, then Djar could use the library whenever he wished. She could speak with Aysel about finding Kiya and Bek a place in the guard, or perhaps even apprentice them to Aysel for her more…covert skills. They would like that, and it would give them a better outlet for their inquisitive natures. Yes. This was what she wanted. For all of them. Their comfort and happiness were what her sacrifices, her pain, paid for.

She squared her shoulders and untangled her arm from Djar's when she was close enough to the Sultana she thought she might walk forward on her own. The Sultana stood on one side of a tall table, Mathei Attiyeh on the other, three books laid out and open in a line between them. They both turned as she broke away and walked toward them. Amara bowed slowly and carefully. When she faltered as she straightened, Mathei, who was closest, laid gentle fingers against her elbow.

"Sit," he said, firmly, as he pointed toward a bench against the wall. Amara grit her teeth. "Or fall on your face in front of the Sultana, whichever pleases you most, Mistress." He pulled his hand back, and behind her, Djar cleared his throat to hide a chuckle. Perhaps on a different day, Amara might have found his candor refreshing. Today it rankled.

"He means," the Sultana said, "that we have all been informed of your lingering weakness, Mistress Mutar. Please do not feel as if you have to hide it. No one will think less of you for needing rest." The Sultana held a hand toward the same bench. Amara wished she had enough strength to manage a walk that indicated her displeasure, but instead she sank gratefully onto the offered seat. Her hands shook as she folded them in her lap. Humiliating.

"I would like to introduce Danel Garai," she announced, to take the focus off herself, "Pathfinder and Speaker of the Garai Clan. And his sister, Mirari Garai. They are friends of the Charah, Benat."

"Is he all right?" Mirari blurted. "Please, no one will tell me anything."

Mathei stepped between the Sultana and the Suloi, and gave the two of them a sweeping assessment that oozed disdain. "It is proper to bow to the future Queen Sultana of Tamar before you speak to her, and perhaps you should consider subtlety when you make demands."

Amara flicked her gaze to Djar, who tensed to step forward, but Danel spoke. "My sister is as much royalty as this woman, and men do not speak to her at all unless spoken to first."

Mirari grabbed her brother's wrist, throwing him a look of reproach. Mathei's face and neck turned red, and he and Danel met gazes for a moment that would have spit sparks of temper if they were fire mages. Mathei's eye twitched, and he drew a breath that had every indication it was to fuel an outburst.

If Cassian were there, he would know what to do. Amara resisted the urge to close her eyes against the thought of him.

"Let us attempt some civility, if we might," the Sultana said in her quiet, cool voice. "We share blood, if not culture. I would be honored to learn of yours and teach you ours, Master Garai."

Mathei relaxed marginally, moving around the table to stand beside the Sultana and put the piece of furniture between him and Danel. "To answer your question, Mistress Garai, your friend is physically sound. That is all I can say for him. I was hoping you might tell me more, and have been anxious to meet you."

"Forgive my brother," Mirari said, her accented Republic Trade heavier for her nervousness, "we are not accustomed to walls."

"Do you know why Benat is so unstable?" The Sultana's gaze drifted swiftly over Mathei in a command for silence. Mirari wrung her hands then spread them, her gaze fixed on the books on the table.

"He was not, before. He was kind, and..." Her cheeks darkened and she lowered her face. Danel shifted, putting a hand on her shoulder.

"We have not known him long. We met him just before our clan was taken. We did not know he had magic until he used it in an effort to save us from being captured."

"We don't know anything about magic. Not magic like yours." Mirari glanced toward Amara, and down again. "But Benat...I think he was confused. Burdened. And when the magic came, he could not..." Her breath heaved, and she gripped her hands together. "...he could not bear another thing."

Amara suspected that was just the bare bones of a twisted story. If they were going to help Benat, they would need to know more. When she looked at the Sultana's face, she saw a flicker of the same awareness in her eyes. The Sultana met her gaze, a question, and Amara shook her head. She did not know anything more than that. "I can only speak to what I experienced when he showed his power to me," she said.

"And you are certain he is a Charah?" The question was only formality, and Amara answered it with a quick nod. "What is the nature of his magic?"

"Earth. But not like Commander Ayan's." Amara shifted on her seat. "There is fire in him."

"Yes." Mathei nodded. "This is what I was telling you." He tapped his knuckles against the center of the three books they'd been looking at. "It wasn't just Vural Tekin who was unhinged. The Fourth House Charah is conflicted, historically. Torn between the steadiness of earth, home, and duty. And fire, passion, anger, and lies. They are the most different of harmonious Houses, and it was that which drove Vural mad."

"Who is Vural?" Mirari asked, her voice desperate. Amara understood some of this history. It was required reading at the University, even if one was taking private instruction. Vural had died at the end of the Sundering War, had exhausted his magic and himself, pouring it into the creation of the Engeli.

"Was," Mathei said. "Vural Tekin was the last Fifth House Charah, who lived two hundred Turns ago. He was a madman who murdered twelve of his brethren to build a wall for another madman." Mat's eyes slitted as he surveyed the brother and sister, then he looked down at the table, shoving a few papers around. "He died in the effort as well."

Amara suppressed a grimace. That was another way to phrase it.

Mirari sucked in a sharp, gasping breath that was half sob, and Danel put his arm around her shoulders, glaring murder at Mathei. "Benat is not a murderer. He is afraid," Danel said.

"So was Vural," Mathei countered. "Fear and anger are two edges of the same blade. Use one side and you reveal the other."

"And both are the twisted mirror of kindness," Djar said in his quiet, resonant voice. "Vural lost his brother and his love to the Sundering War, to destruction mages. The world no longer reflected his hope for it, and it broke him."

Amara loved that tone he used, gentle, but with unquestionable authority. He did not use it often. Only when something mattered. She smiled at him, and he returned it.

Mathei drummed his fingers against the table, eyeing Djar from head to toe. "A fellow student of history, I see. And what books have you read on the subject—"

"A discussion for later," the Sultana interjected. "I am certain our guests would like to visit their friend. Samira, will you escort them?" She turned to Amara. "Would you like to go as well?"

Amara tensed, pressing her lips together to stifle the vehement 'no' that bloomed on them.

"I will go," Djar said. "So you may continue speaking." Amara gave him a grateful look, and he followed Samira and the Suloi from the library.

"What can you tell me about their magic?" the Sultana asked after the doors had closed again.

"It is diluted," Amara answered. "Passive, for the most part. Danel was able to heal Djar's injury to some extent." Amara touched her fingers to her eye. "But obviously not completely, and you may have noticed he also suffers from injuries he has been unable to heal. His sister kept me alive when I overextended myself in Haenna. But I do not know what use they will be against the Blight."

The Sultana traced the edge of a book on the table, quiet for a moment.

"I know that an apology is not enough, that I am in some measure to blame for the loss of Djar's eye. I do not know what to say or do in balance for the wrongs done to you and yours during this errand."

"It is not necessary. I have fulfilled my side of our bargain, and as I know that you are a woman of your word, I expect that you will fulfill yours."

"The Sehzade is not in the palace today, I am afraid," the Sultana said, apologetically. "He is consumed with new Blight samples Rahal Charah has sent from Sarkum."

Of course he was. Amara released her irritation in a breath, and smiled.

The Sultana inclined her head. "When you are ready to face the Council, I will announce your betrothal. It is still contingent upon you joining the Circle. They will only accept a noble, and that is the only method by which I can make you one."

"I understand." The price for standing on the summit of the mountain she'd been climbing for so long. For her freedom, and a better life for the ones she loved. Amara would stow Cassian in the depths of her heart, where his memory could not wound her. "I am prepared to sit for the Council as soon as you deem fit. But if you have no further need of me today, I might prefer to wait for my friends in the garden."

"Of course. Mathei, will you escort Mutar Charah?"

"Happily." He offered his arm so she could pull herself to her feet. Amara smiled at him.

"I owe you coffee, don't I?" she asked.

"It is not important," he said. "Only when you are well. I would enjoy a chance to discuss the Republic with you." He pushed the library doors open and continued speaking as they walked. "What you saw, what the people are like. Their technology? I have heard of guns, of course, but have never seen one."

"We brought many items back with us. Including several guns, and explosives."

Interest lit his face, but it was shadowed. The tools of war that Tamar did not have were of course interesting. But they heralded misery. More pain.

They walked in troubled silence through the halls toward one of the interior gardens near the infirmary. Before they reached it, a voice, sharp and angry, stopped them.

"No, I said."

She and Mathei glanced at each other, and he also appeared intrigued by the interesting mix of panic and rage in the words. He lifted a finger to his lips and pointed to the intersection of the hall, where a left would take them to the garden and a right would reveal the speaker.

"I have told you the price for your defiance." That voice she knew. The Grand Vizier. Her fingers clawed against Mathei's arm as her buried anger over Djar's eye billowed upward. The Sultana had been generous with her offer to shoulder the blame for Djar's injury, but no. Amara knew exactly who she would exact her revenge upon, and her prey had just presented itself. She let a long, deep breath settle her more into herself, searching the fathoms within for that pool of magic that had always been a vast, dark ocean. It responded sluggishly to her search, there, but dormant.

A quick, hard crack split the moment of silence in the hall, something else Amara recognized, the sound of someone being struck. Mathei's dark brows notched, his mouth turning down. They strode forward together, rounding the corner of the hallway wall.

The Grand Vizier stood facing them, halfway obscured by an alcove, his son before him with his back to Amara and Mathei. One of his hands was in his father's grip, raised between them, and Cemil's face was turned away; his right hand gripped his father's so that the two of them were locked together like stags with entangled antlers. Amara could not tell who had struck whom, but the moment she and

Mathei made the turn, she felt fire. Heat like rage, a wall of it that warped the air and stung her nostrils.

"Is everything all right?" Amara asked.

The Grand Vizier looked up abruptly, a smile flashing into existence. He released his son's hand and drop his other arm, to try and disguise the fact that they were quarreling. Cemil's shoulders hunched and eased and he turned, releasing his grip on his father. When he rounded, his eyes were narrowed and on fire, but he corrected that with a blink and a sneer.

Amara had very few interactions with Cemil Kadir. She only knew him by his reputation as a man who enjoyed excess in everything. There was almost never silence at his home, or his father's, she supposed. Socialites of any level seeking to rub elbows with their betters, or simply find entertainment, knew there would be a party wherever Cemil was, with ample alcohol. He was, besides Ihsan, one of the most eligible bachelors in Narfour. Now that it was clear his father was not going to succeed in making him Sultan by marrying him to the Sultana, women threw themselves at his nonexistent mercy daily. Many of them made special orders at her shop before doing so, wasting perfectly good cloth and intentions on someone who did not deserve them, or so she heard.

Though she could understand the initial attraction. He had fire's hand in his creation, those usually sharp edges softened by the warm beauty of his mother's Fourth House roots. Squared jaw and brooding brows, with eyes that should have been hazel but were made hammered gold by the fire in them, the only other person besides Bashir Ayan she had ever seen with golden-hued eyes. His hair was the darkest shade of brown before black, kept on the edge between groomed and enticingly disheveled.

But anger was not attractive, and Cemil stunk of it, to Amara's water-enhanced senses. It poured of him like fetor off midden heap. His face, made more rugged by the day or two of stubble along his jaw and cheeks, bore the answer to her question of who had struck whom. When her gaze lingered on the red streak along his cheek and the cut across his cheekbone Cemil's sneer wavered. He reached up to wipe his wrist against the mark, and dropped his gaze. Interesting that his attractiveness was not his father's. In fact he looked nothing like the man save for the color of his hair and his fire.

Amara cut her gaze to the elder Kadir. How he smiled, all charm and serpents. They had crossed proverbial swords as it pertained to the Merchants' Guild and Amara's rise within. And while she would only have called him a rival before Haenna, he was her enemy now. She thought it only fair he know that.

"I should expect a man of your esteem to control himself more appropriately, Grand Vizier," Amara said. Mathei made a subtle shift beside her, turning into a more defensive stance.

"A family quarrel, Mistress Mutar. And what a surprise, and pleasure it is to see you. I had heard such disturbing rumors about your health. Is it true…your magic is completely depleted?"

"Temporarily," Amara said.

"Of course. You appear as fit and lovely as ever."

Mathei's arm tightened against hers, and he moved as though he might step between the two of them. She appreciated his gallantry, but she did not require protection from Behram Kadir. If anyone needed protecting, it was him.

He had tried his fire mage charm on her countless times before, and it was no less emetic now. But Amara had a lifetime of practice with men who believed themselves desirable. She smiled to hide her disgust and simmering fury.

He closed the distance between them. "Your timing is perfection. I have a gift for you, a token of thanks on behalf of the Council that I had just asked Cemil to deliver to your man. The big one." He smiled wanly.

"Djar," Amara said.

"Ah yes." The Grand Vizier took her hand in his, brought it to his lips as his gaze skated her body, riding the silk she regretted wearing for only one loathing-filled instant. His lips were warm and dry against her skin, discordant like cat's tongue. Before she could snatch her hand away, he had deftly clasped a golden chain studded with garnets and rubies around her wrist. He straightened, and Amara tugged her fingers from his grasp, closing her other hand over the bauble.

Cemil's golden gaze rested on her wrist, then lifted to hers and cut away. He appeared suddenly pale, stiff in place as if being held there by invisible hands, his lips pressing so hard together they were bloodless. Amara's brow furrowed, and the words of concern that she might have spoken were cut off by the Grand Vizier.

"For your service to the Sultana, a small token of our thanks."

"So obviously attempting to curry favor with a mage of the Circle, Grand Vizier?" How Mathei managed to make his accusation sound so friendly, Amara could only admire.

"Mistress Mutar"—the corners of the Grand Vizier's mouth ticked up in amused chagrin—"Mutar Charah and I have a long history as comrades in the Merchants' Guild, Master Attiyeh. It is not uncommon to offer such…niceties, as gifts. She had, by all accounts, a harrowing time in the Republic. This bauble is the least we could do for her service."

The gold and red gems were gaudy and out of place next to the beautiful, subtle wood of Cassian's bracelet. She forced a smile and a tip of her head. Behram Kadir was a master of control, and he knew she could not refuse this gift. Gifts made the Wheel spin; generosity was never refused in Tamar. No matter what the real motives behind its delivery were. And because he knew she could not refuse it, he controlled her. This gift was nothing but a show of power. To show that she was not more powerful than he, who could subjugate with *generosity*.

"I will give my thanks when I am announced to the Council, as betrothed of the Sehzade and Second of the Circle," Amara said. His smile burned, but he bowed his head, touching his hand to his belt as he did so. "Forgive me, Grand Vizier, but I was just on my way to visit the Fourth House Charah, you'll excuse me of course."

"Of course." They met gazes for a moment, and in the depths of his pupils she saw the fire burning. The triumph. No matter. He thought he'd won. He thought she would not move against him, because no one else in the palace seemed willing to. They only sat back and waited, hoping for the Wheel to find justice for them.

Amara turned, and Mathei hurried to keep up, pulling slightly on her arm to slow her. "You've riled him." Mathei glanced over his shoulder.

"That is the least I plan to do." Damn the Wheel and its justice. She would exact her own. A listless whisper from her magic was all the warning she got before pain arced through her arm and she crumpled to the carpet.

He was awake. That awful, angry fire…she said his name, Benat, before that pain stole her consciousness.

THIRTY-THREE

"Y OU ARE IN NO shape to face the Council," Havva said as she pushed the clothes in Amara's wardrobe back and forth, examining them.

"It's downstairs, on the dressform." Amara eyed Havva sideways from where she sat at her dressing table. It had taken every bit of her weak, lagging energy to sew the new caftan and entari for the girl, Kumru, who had been cut up at the Lily by her patron. But she was due to take her test for admission at the University, and so Amara had stayed up late into the night to finish.

Havva went downstairs and returned, bearing a set of caftan and entari in golden green. She laid it on the bed, then set her fists against her hips. She eyed Amara in the mirror, her mouth set in a line of disapproval.

Amara had to prop her elbows on her makeup table to trace her lids with the kohl. Otherwise her hands shook too much. And every time her gaze strayed from her work, it settled on the wooden bangle on her wrist. The memory of the moment when Cassian gave it to her was so detailed that her body reacted as if he were standing in the doorway, watching her—warm, and hungry. But her heart ached—cold, and empty.

Below it hung the bracelet Kadir had put on her. She hadn't removed it, for fear one of Kadir's many lackeys would see her without it and report the slight to him or anyone else in the Council. Once her betrothal was official, she planned to fling it into the ocean. Or sell it for coins she could use toward helping someone Kadir had hurt or shamed. A more balanced reaction to the audacious flaunting of his power. Touching it turned her stomach. Looking at it made her head hurt. Red had always been her least favorite color.

"I am fine to face that herd of old goats. I only overexerted myself, is all," Amara said dismissively, though her true feelings on the subject were more complicated. She'd been told, when she woke from her sudden attack while at the palace, that Benat had not moved so much as an eyelash the entire time Amara was there. Whatever had hurt her and knocked her unconscious had not manifested at all for those watching the unconscious Charah. Was he seeking her even in his poppy-induced sleep? Mirari had said he was kind, but…Amara shuddered. She had not imagined the pain, or the fire. She knew that. But she did not entirely trust that anyone else would believe her over the evidence they could see with their eyes.

They would have to wake him eventually. The only delay was that the palace's head physician, Ceylik, believed he needed more time for the physical abuse he suffered while under the "care" of the Republic to heal. Havva agreed, that if he did not wake in physical pain, they would all be better for it. Then, they would wean him slowly from the poppy, switching instead to a concoction Havva knew for holding someone in sleep. For now, Amara had vowed to stay as far away from him as possible.

Kiya strode into the room and threw herself on the bed with a groan. "You've deliveries downstairs," she said. "Heavy deliveries." She sat up then moved to Amara's back, picking at her curls, arranging them, pinching some between her fingers to survey her handiwork of the night before. Amara had bathed, and Kiya had made an effort to repair the neglect Amara had heaped upon her hair and skin during their troubles in Haenna.

"I'll deal with them when I return. Do you wish to come to the palace with me today and meet Attiyeh Charah?" Amara asked. Kiya pursed her lips and shook her head. "As soon as the betrothal is official I plan to ask to apprentice you to her for the guard," Amara said. "I thought that was what you wanted."

"I'll meet her soon. Not today. Today is your day"—Kiya grinned—"Princess."

The word was as sharp as a needle, straight through her ribs to prick her heart. Her smile faltered, and Kiya's own smile faded in turn, her gaze falling to the floor. She gave Amara's hair one last half-hearted fluff then left.

"I'll make certain Djar and the carriage are ready. Mirari said she and Danel will go to visit Benat," Kiya called from halfway down the stairs.

Amara set the kohl pencil down, and wrapped her hand around Cassian's bracelet, breathing away the tears that bit at her eyes. No more tears. She had learned long ago that the only thing to be done when one felt they could not go on, was to take another step. And another. Into the blindness. Into the pain.

❦

AMARA WAS NOT ACCUSTOMED to having to sit quietly while her temper simmered like water about to boil over. Her outrage, when shaped and applied carefully, had only ever aided her. Here, as evidenced by the Sultana's smooth, unruffled expression, anger was a deadly fault. Amara took her cue from the other woman, who had spent her entire life in this particular arena.

"The Council agreed that a marriage to a noblewoman would hold the Sehzade in the line of succession," the Sultana said. Ihsan sat to her left, on the bench she used to occupy in the Sultan's court. Amara sat near his left side, though not close enough to touch.

The Sultana sat in her father's seat on the dais, covered and surrounded by a shelter carved of wood in repeating circles cut with the spokes of the Wheel, and shimmering gold. She appeared serene and beautiful despite the downward spiral of the situation, a vision of calm in a frosty blue and silver entari.

"But Mistress Mutar is a merchant. A successful and wealthy one, I will grant you"—the Grand Vizier inclined his head with a smile as if granting a boon—"but that does not make her a noble."

"She is Charah of the Second House," the Sultana pointed out without moving. She did not even appear to breathe. Amara could not understand how the woman could sit there so composed while the Grand Vizier played games with her. Amara had believed the politics of the Merchants' Guild to be underhanded and distasteful, but this was unbearable.

"Am I misinformed? I had thought she refused a place on the Circle." The Grand Vizier looked at Amara. Where he looked, so did the entire Council. Beside her, Ihsan shifted, his back straightened, his fingers tightening briefly against his knees. Warning her, perhaps. But that was unnecessary.

"The Sultana has agreed to my marriage to the Sehzade on the condition that I stand as Second of the Circle." She held his gaze until his smile faltered.

"Then it is settled," the Sultana said.

A whispered tide of irritation rose and fell in murmurs through the room. Amara caught glimpses as men looked to each other. Upset that their chances of marrying their daughters off had been stolen by someone generally considered unworthy. She maintained her smile, though her teeth clenched. This triumph did not burn as brightly as others.

"I am afraid"—the Grand Vizier's gaze cut from the Sultana to Amara—"not."

Ihsan's breath hissed out, and Amara denied her instinct to look at him, to understand what he did. Instead she held the Grand Vizier's gaze as he spoke.

"The Council cannot accept another Sabri marrying a mage of the Circle. You claim the Circle will be unbiased, but how can it be, if both heirs to the Sabri line have claim on its members?" A ripple of quiet agreement. Yavuz Pasha, whose entire family bought their clothes from her, would not meet her gaze. The two Viziers who sat directly behind to the Grand Vizier frowned at her. To Amara, it felt as if the floor and bench beneath her vanished, leaving her weightless, rudderless. Wordless.

Silence rippled. Ihsan lifted his hand, as if he might reach for hers, but she was certain, even if he did touch her, she would not feel it. And the Grand Vizier knew. How he frowned. As though it troubled him. As though taking this thing she had worked for since coming to Tamar—had now bled for, had broken her heart for—caused him anything but pleasure. She could see that truth in his eyes, burning like the fire that was often there. Could feel the heat of his triumph against her depleted magic.

The reason for the bracelet became viciously apparent. The Grand Vizier had always had every intention of preventing her marriage to Ihsan, and the bauble was his consolation prize to her. An attempt, perhaps, to ensure she would make no move against him in the Guild.

How long had he planned this? How long had he known? Amara's breath flowed in, and out. Each breath calcifying around her wounded heart, protecting it from the sharp edges of her broken plans.

"Please consider a place on the Circle, Mistress Mutar," the Sultana said in measured tones. "It will assure your noble rank, for which you have more than proven yourself."

Amara gripped the edge of the bench she sat on, staring unseeing at the windows behind the Viziers that sat across from her. Oh yes. The Sultana's promise was broken, but still she would expect Amara to be the noble one. To sacrifice herself for the Sultana's grand schemes. She could join the Circle. Amara had refused previously because the Circle was no less a set of shackles than actual chains. To stand in the Circle would make her a noble, but not one nearly equal in rank to what she would have been after a marriage to Ihsan. Not a woman able to dictate her own destiny.

"I will consider your offer, Sultana." The words echoed hollow in the room, sounding to Amara as if they had come from someone else. She stared unseeing as they watched her. Ihsan cleared his throat.

"Do you have a better solution, Grand Vizier?" Ihsan's words were sharp as icicles, his cold power wafting across Amara. She did not care, and did not hear. Sitting through the remainder of their negotiation felt as she imagined holding back the tide might feel. Impossible. But she managed.

"I am certain the Council and Sultana can come to an agreeable solution," the Grand Vizier said with a deep bow.

The Sultana dismissed them. Amara managed to keep her seat, and her composure, while the Sultana and her entourage left and the Viziers filed out after her. Ihsan stood and offered his hand.

Amara stared at it, then looked up at him.

"Trust her, she will find a way to make things right. To make this happen," he said. The most he had ever said to her. As dispassionately as the ice that so obviously ruled his emotions. How had she ever thought she could bear him? Bear Turn after Turn of that coldness? It would have been difficult enough before Cassian, but now...her heart, her light and dark. They were his.

Amara ignored Ihsan's offered hand and stood.

"You may tell your cousin not to waste her time. Consider my proposal withdrawn."

✿

THE GARDEN OUTSIDE THE Council Hall was a welcome, cool respite from the press of body heat inside the chamber. Yet she could not enjoy it. In fact she was not certain she could enjoy anything, ever again. Turns of her life, her effort, her sweat and blood and humiliations, *wasted.* There had never been any hope for her to climb out of her past. She could see that now. No. Those at the top would always ensure that those at the bottom stayed there. In fact they probably found it amusing to watch those below them circle and leap and fall, like fish trying to escape a bucket.

"Do you know"—a hand closed over her wrist—"that he only gives these to people he hates?" Cemil hissed in her ear. Amara spun, trying to yank her hand from his grip but he levered it up, holding it between them. He was pale, sweating, dark circles beneath his eyes, where fire snapped and whipped.

"Get your hand off me or I'll put you in the infirmary where I put the Earth Charah." Amara yanked again, and Cemil pulled her a step closer, his lip curling. She was not afraid of him. Water did not need to fear fire, and her power outranked his. She was, however, filled to the brim with loathing.

"These were my mother's. These baubles he hands out as favors. His little joke. His revenge on her."

She had left him. Cemil's mother had disappeared when Cemil was a boy. Walked out on the Grand Vizier and his legendary cruelty. Everyone in Narfour knew that. Amara would have applauded the woman, except for her appalling lack of maternal responsibility.

"And *you* don't deserve to wear this." Cemil's mouth kicked up on one side, and the fire in his eyes burned white. Heat curled around her, and her magic rose in response, only barely enough there to shield her. The bracelet melted from her wrist.

Amara yanked away, and Cemil let her go, smiling.

"If you were not such a disgusting little pig I might thank you."

"Perhaps you should." Then Cemil walked away. When he reached the gallery he stumbled on the step up, leaned on a pillar for a moment, and then continued.

Drunk. Amara bent to retrieve the melted mess of bracelet. The stones might be repurposed, at least, to help someone in need. To balance Behram Kadir's vileness. She rubbed her hand over her wrist, though she was undamaged from Cemil's outburst.

Cassian's bracelet was not so lucky. Char darkened one side. Her breath shuddered, despair coloring her vision grey and watery.

This palace was toxic, doing its best to be the death of everything she held dear.

❧❧

AMARA, WHO USUALLY PREFERRED the company of others, was grateful to be alone when she arrived home that night. She closed and locked both the front and back door to the shop. Her youngest apprentice was a Lightbringer who had dutifully left a mage orb, as well as lit oil lamps for when the mage orb faded. Amara tossed her lightweight ferace over the back of the settee near the back door, then draped herself on the couch.

She closed her eyes, but opened them immediately. She gripped her wrist, Cemil's attack still hovering on the edge of her emotions. Her fingers curled over the wooden bracelet, and the anger swirled away. She sat up, and slipped the piece off to examine it. The charring from his fire appeared to be minimal. Perhaps one of the jewelry-makers could polish it away. She wondered, if the Wheel had spun differently, what Cassian might have chosen to do in Narfour.

Gambling was not legal in the city, and the City Watch kept a close eye on it. Where there was gambling, there were other unsavory activities. People preying on others. She wanted to imagine he would be happy, with her. In a city that did not need him to wade into its sewers and secrets to rescue the brutalized and neglected. Her fingers tightened. But didn't it? Narfour was not a perfect city. The events of the day stood as testament to that. There was oppression here too. She'd played by their rules, done everything she thought she was supposed to. And they had laughed in her face. They didn't see anything in her but her past. The girl she had been. A murderer. A captive. A prostitute. Unworthy. The Sultana might want her magic, but she had never wanted the person who wielded it.

She rose. A bath would help wash away the lingering feeling of Cemil's manhandling. And perhaps help silence the hopeless ache that was both bottomless and quiet. It was not unfamiliar. There had been a similar hole in her when her mother was killed. They never filled, those holes. Cassian had fit like a piece she had not realized was missing, until it was gone.

The stack of deliveries nearly blocked the stairs. She shouldered aside a rolled carpet, one of the handwoven kind from the interior valley. Each maker had their own pattern, their own secret designs they wove into each. Amara loved them desperately, imagining the hands that made them, the stories they told. Whenever the Weavers' Guild sent traders to the valley, Amara requested one. The carpet, rolled and bound with burlap and rope, slumped against the haphazard stack of crates, sliding to the floor at the base of the stairs. The stack wobbled, and when she lunged to prevent it toppling, she banged her knee into one of the items.

"This Wheel-damned day," she sighed, sinking to the lowermost stair. She slid the item she'd kicked across the stone floor and propped it against her knees. Wrapped in burlap and tied with twine, it was an odd package. Most she received were obviously for the shop. Crates and bolts of cloth. Ribbons and seed pearls or beads for embellishment. It wasn't large, perhaps as wide across as her elbow to her fingertips and tall enough to make it rectangular instead of square. Curious, she plucked the knots from the string that held it. She peeled back the top half of the burlap.

"Oh." Breath and sorrow shaped into a sound like a word. It was a painting. Unfinished, the linen canvas showed around the edges, framing the oval image in the center in irregular patches of beige. She knew exactly what it was the moment she saw her own brown skin and curls. His hands had touched this. There was love in it, she could see it from the exquisite details. She wanted to hug it to her, but feared damaging it.

It was not until she had blinked away the tears in her eyes that the image resolved itself completely to her. Cassian had painted her standing, hands held open and away from her hips, in a dress he'd fashioned to look like water, wave and river, flowing away from her and into the background. Her face and hair, her body were the most finished aspects, everything else was only partially imagined silhouettes and shapes just suggested with strokes of white or grey. She touched her fingers to her mouth, then to the painted figure's. She gingerly lifted the canvas to turn it toward the light so she could examine the details in the light of the mage orb and lamp.

Something fell out, making a soft sound on the stone floor. Amara set the painting aside, leaning it carefully against the stairs. She picked up the bit of paper that had fallen and unfolded it.

I'm sorry I couldn't finish it. I wanted to. I thought I could convince you to give me the time it would take. Years, months, days, hours, minutes, to stare at it, to know it so well it became a part of me. But I cannot finish it without you, I cannot bear to. I hope it makes you think of me, sometimes.
It isn't quite the naked statue you had commissioned, but you don't need any help causing an uproar.
You tell that ice mage to take good care of my princess.
-C.

Her inhale broke in thirds around her tears as she rubbed her thumbs over the surface of the paper. Over ink that had splattered where he wrote his initial. How had she tricked herself into believing she could still marry Ihsan? There was a gaping hole where her heart had been and no prince could fill it.

That place she had wanted for so long, beside a prince, untouchable, and completely removed from where she came from. She did not want it. She did not belong there. She was already a princess, to a man who stood up to oppressors, who sacrificed everything to do so, just as she had. She could make a difference for others, exactly as she was… exactly where she was. She could do something to make certain that Tamar did not get swallowed by the Republic.

THIRTY-FOUR

CASSIAN HAD LOST COUNT of how many times he had looked at the piece of paper with his father's signature on it. His blood right. The damn thing had nearly cost him his life, and Amara's. How had he never noticed before, how much his signature resembled his father's? The same careful script with thin, long loops. He had it back, thanks to Amara. And what was he going to do with it? With anything?

He hadn't followed her, and he regretted it every day he woke up. He'd spent his last coins to send her the half-finished painting on a trade ship bound for Menei. He bribed the ship captain with the coins, a bit of his father's finery, and promises of a rich merchant who might be talked out of some Tamarine dye. He didn't know if Amara would oblige that part, but he trusted she could handle one greedy merchant captain.

There was nothing here for him but his imagined purpose. But the Assembly had found him out, dismantled his networks of informers and no one would work with him. He had no money, no ability to help anyone. Could he free slaves? Yes. But he had no way to get them out of the city now, no one who trusted they wouldn't be revealed if they worked with him.

"Do you want any of this?" Peio asked, stripping a bit of flank off the rabbit he'd been roasting over their small fire for the last half hour. Peio liked his meat just a moment removed from life, and Cassian would prefer his one step removed from charcoal. But he was too hungry to complain, and so he nodded.

They'd been hiding in the woods since the night he'd watched Amara's ship disappear against the horizon. Visiting the city between changing camps every night, starving between the game Peio could hunt. Neither of them was particularly skilled at foraging for spring bounty. That was a task left to the women in the Suloi clans, and Cassian had grown up believing vegetables and meat magically appeared on his table every night.

Peio made quick work of breaking the rabbit into two portions and handed Cassian his half. They sat across the fire from each other, silent as they ate. Crickets chirped all around them, and small things scurried through the underbrush. The fire was small and kept little more than coals. Cassian did not know if they were being actively hunted, but the only people that camped in the woods were Suloi and criminals, and so anyone that encountered their fire would assume them of interest to the Assembly.

Cassian had been trying to construct an apology for Peio ever since they'd watched Amara's ship go, but words failed him. Peio had shared Cassian's same purpose, though his reasons were perhaps more noble. Less about vengeance and more about loyalty. And now neither of them could help anyone, and Peio was stuck here. He could have gone with Amara, to a new life where he might have been more than a Ghost. Cassian could see him fading, back to the near-husk he'd been when Cassian first found him in that cage in the catacombs.

He picked at the rabbit, pulling stringy meat from the bones, and set the paper in the dirt beside him. He wondered what Amara would think of Peio's half-cooked rabbit. He suspected she would eat it without complaint. He wondered what elaborate and delicious food she might be eating in the palace.

Gods he missed her. Cassian closed his eyes. He could still picture her perfectly, as if she were right in front of him. Soft, silken skin as warm as earth, eyes so dark he could barely distinguish the pupil, the high arch of her cheekbones, the point of her chin, the pretty way her cheeks rounded if she smiled when she didn't want to. That spray of freckles, little dark kisses he'd never had a chance to count. Her pile of curls. Her curves. His hands flinched closed, his gut clamping at the memory of her body tangled with his.

She was a world away and still she could stop his thoughts, his breath. She'd done it the first time he saw her, and she did it every time he thought of her.

"Do you know why the Wanderer traveled?" Peio studied the remains of his dinner, instead of looking at Cassian. Peio had never told him any roadborn stories. The Suloi kept their secrets. Outsiders were kept Outsiders, even when they were friends of a clan.

"Tell me." Cassian wrapped his arms around his knees and tossed the bones into the fire.

"I will tell you the way the Urbina tell it, but I know each clan tells a different tale, and who is to say which is right?" He stretched out on his back, to look at the stars that could be seen through the trees above them. "He wasn't roadborn. There were no roadborn when the Wanderer lived. There was only the Great Meet when clans came together to trade for the winter, and sometimes, they made treaties to camp and share hunting grounds for the next year. Those treaties were often bound by marriages between the children of the clan leaders." Peio slipped into Suloi, his voice taking on a cadence almost akin to a chant. "That was how the man, Can, met Damla. He had no magic. And she was one of the most powerful of the clans from the north steppes, where water ruled. River Sister, they called her."

Cassian blinked, lifting his head to glance at Peio, but his friend only continued to stare skyward.

"At that time, the magic of the Old Sultanate spread as far as the Odokan plains, into the northern reaches of Menei, and even touched the outer edges of the northern tribes. Magic was everywhere. It was in the plants, and the earth. The water and the sky. The storytellers say that before the Sundering War, when you spoke into the silence all that came before answered you from the void. The realm of the spirit, where magic and soul are one and the same."

The story itself seemed to weave a spell, even the woods around them had fallen quiet under the rhythmic influence of Peio's voice. Cassian wondered if that place, that vast plain of nothing, when he had somehow been inside Amara's magic and her mind, was that realm.

"They say that magic does not die, that it lives in the void only between mortal lives. That it carries the memories of each body it inhabits. In the Suloi, it lives in all of us, a spark for each, to tie us together, so we are forever bound to each other, and can find each other in the void beyond. It is why, to live on beyond your clan…" Peio's voice grew strained, but he shook it off. "The Suloi believe that if magic meets one it has known before, it will remember. It is a special thing, when magic is reunited. A rare thing. They believed that is what happened to Can and Damla. Because they loved each other from the moment they met."

Cassian ground his teeth. He hated tragic love stories, and he had a suspicion that's what this was going to be. He lay down, mimicking Peio's position, only he pulled a blanket over himself to protect from the cold spring night. It was that chill, he was certain, that caused the prickling of the skin on his arms and up the back of his neck.

"They were separated on their wedding night," Peio continued.

"I knew it," Cassian groused.

"The armies of the Sultan came." Peio slung Cassian a chastising frown. "They razed the Great Meet, searching for shadow wielders. The mages he hated. Many, many were murdered. In the chaos, Can lost Damla. He gathered together all he could of the survivors, and fled into the night. He hid them from the armies, and took a group of his clansmen into the army camp at night to steal back those they had taken prisoner. Then they fled, north. Because that is where he was certain Damla would have gone, home. Though he did not know where her home was."

"Did he find her?" Cassian knew he was going to regret asking.

"No," Peio said. A long, terrible silence followed. Cassian wallowed in it, black melancholy filling his thoughts and a deep, painful ache starting in his breast. Like if he did not get up and move he would die.

"He wandered from river to river, looking for her. For his river. And her magic sang to him in his dreams, and he followed it, all over the world, they say. And his clan grew with the stragglers he found from the Sundering War. And finally, he followed her into the void, where she waited for him. And after he died"—Peio pointed to the sky—"the stars appeared in the sky, to light the way for all who came after."

Cassian pressed a hand over his eyes. "If you ever feel the need to tell me a Suloi story again, just keep it to yourself."

"The Urbina believed we are descended of Damla. That she fled that night, that she carried and bore Can's child. That she searched for him too, and that one day, they will both return, and be reunited, and that is when the roadborn will remember the road to the home that was forgotten. It was always Damla who opened the road, and Can who led us down it."

Cassian peered at Peio, and the light from the coals between them cast his friend's face in odd shadow. "I have an unpleasant feeling you're trying to make a point."

"No point." Peio sat up and tossed another handful of sticks on the coals. "We say to pine for one we miss is to follow the river. And I only wondered if you were going to follow the river until you waste away?"

"What alternative do you see? We can't exactly charter a ship." They didn't have the money, if they even made it to the docks without getting arrested. Or being turned in by whatever ship captain they petitioned. And what would he do in Tamar anyway, if they even let him step foot off the boat? Peer at Amara through the palace windows? He supposed being impaled on a Tamar spear for trespassing might be a less painful death than starvation, or heartache.

"She said she came to open the road," Peio said. "That the Suloi are wanted back in Tamar."

"I'm sorry to put lie to your histories, my friend, but there is no road to Tamar that does not lead through Republic garrisons, unforgiving mountains, and end in death. You may be welcome, if we make it that far, but I do not think they will be pleased to see a Republic man on their doorstep."

No, they were talking of war in Haenna. No matter that Amara's sleep had harmed no one, the Assembly had only seen that she'd thwarted one of their own. That news was passed to Stephanus' and his already well-fermented paranoia bubbled over. He'd sent several centuries on boats to stage in the Eannean Islands while his new fleet was finished in Haenna.

"Don't you think someone should warn Tamar?" Peio scratched at the beard that was beginning to cover his face.

"Want to take a stroll over half the earth, do you?" Cassian said.

"I thought we could take a ship. I've saved some money." He paused, looked hard at the sky. "I cannot stay here," Peio said, quietly. "If I cannot help others, if I cannot prove that I lived on for a reason, if I cannot atone for my sin…"

The sin of living. Cassian had argued with Peio, when they first became friends, but he did not have the power to undo an entire cultural truth just to save his friend's life. And what right did he have to tell Peio his beliefs were wrong? Cassian didn't have any better answers. Just kinder ones. And he owed him. Peio had given up his chance to go with the others back to Tamar to stay with Cassian. They were brothers, of a kind. Cassian had nothing left in the world more important than that, and if he were being truthful about the ache in his heart, Amara. What else was there?

Cassian lifted the paper. He stared at his father's handwriting, and his own, so similar and yet different. What did he think joining the Senate would accomplish? His parents had been prominent citizens, well loved. And still they had failed to make a difference beyond the individual lives they saved. His heroes, both of them. They sacrificed everything for others. Just like Amara. And what was he?

"Ever since you broke me out of that cage, it has been about that piece of paper," Peio said. Cassian lowered it enough to look over its edge at him.

"It's all I have left of them. All I have left of who I am, and who I am supposed to be."

"What do you think that paper will allow you to do that you have not already done?"

Cassian frowned at him. "As a senator I will have actual power. Power to help."

"Have you ever counted, Brother?" Peio's voice lowered, and he poked the fire with a stick. "Do you know how many your parents saved?"

"Dozens, I think. From their accounts that I saw."

Peio leaned onto one hip so he could dig in a pouch on the opposite one. He withdrew a rolled bit of parchment and held it around the heat so Cassian could take it.

"What is this?" He unrolled it. There was nothing on it but little hashes.

"I wanted to save one person for every member of my clan who was slaughtered or taken," Peio said. "One for every sin." Cassian began to count the hashes. "Three hundred." Peio cut his counting short. "There were three hundred in my clan. We reached that number a year ago, and I was not around to count the ones you saved before I met you."

Cassian rolled the paper again and handed it back.

"Our paths"—Peio smiled bitterly—"are the trails our feet tread while we are looking at the road we want to take. You could not have saved all these if you had been a senator."

He was right. What was the Senate anymore? It once had represented the people. It once had been about choice, elected positions.

Now, Stephanus had changed it. To keep those families in power that were loyal to him and his plans.

Cassian was a thief. A criminal. And that's exactly what he wanted to be. The kind of man people dismissed as a useless drunk. The kind who could live in that shadow between wealthy and poor, navigate both in a way he would never be able to as a senator. That was the only place he could occupy, if he hoped continuing to free the Suloi.

Cassian's uncertainty settled away. This was what he was good for. The small victories. The few lives he could save. What he was meant for. Not harboring some imagined destiny in the Senate, where no one would hear his voice or listen to his ideas.

"Maybe next time don't wait so long to make me see sense, hmm?" Cassian said. A true Pathfinder, in Suloi legend, was not just someone who could guide along the physical road. But one who could see the cultural way forward for his people as well. Cassian thought it the greatest of tragedies that Peio would never lead a clan. A task for which he would have been perfectly suited.

Cassian dipped the corner of the paper with his blood right on it into the coals. He watched it burn until the signatures were gone, then dropped it onto the fire.

"I didn't make you see sense," Peio said as they watched the paper burn. "If it weren't for her, you'd never have started thinking about the other paths there might be. Other places you might go."

"What places?" Cassian frowned.

Peio grinned. "She opened the road. Now someone has to lead the roadborn home."

THIRTY-FIVE

"**I** AM MISTRESS MUTAR, AND I am Kumru's sponsor for testing," Amara announced to the mage that received them at the University entrance. The man, though barely so judging by the wispy stubble he tried to pass of as beard, eyed Kumru. Kumru shrank, trying to slink behind Amara, turning her face down and away. Amara gave her chin a tap with her fingers then folded the girl's hand between her own. She dropped an imperious frown on the adolescent, and he squared his shoulders and nodded before he turned to find a proctor.

"What did I tell you?" Amara prodded, gently, pulling Kumru beside her again. The scars on the girl's face were still livid, red-brown against her honeyed skin.

"Battle scars, not wounds," Kumru mumbled.

"Again."

"Battle scars." Her voice quavered, but her gaze showed more determination and her back straightened. Amara urged her shoulders back and stroked her fingers against Kumru's throat and under her chin to tilt it up. Then she brushed at the fabric of the entari, embroidered with flowers and lattice, and straightened its collar.

"If you let them pity you, you will never be more than you are. You will allow that monster to defeat you, do you understand me?"

"Yes, Mistress."

"What else?"

"That this test is only an opportunity. But not my only opportunity," Kumru recited, her gaze flicking up and down and around the interior of the room. A golden and grey marble foyer was the introduction to the University. It was nestled between two of the House schools, a squatting fly between the grand, circular domed wings. Six of them around a central atrium that was a maze of stairs and secret alcoves. The University mimicked the Wheel, with its six schools and central hub. Of course two of those schools were cordoned off. Gathering dust and being forgotten.

"May I help you?" a woman of willowy stature and beaked nose asked. She squinted at Kumru over that nose, and smiled warmly at Amara.

"Ah. I see. Another one, then?"

"Proctor." Amara smiled, releasing Kumru's hand and stepping forward to kiss each of the older woman's cheeks. "I had hoped I might see you today. This is Kumru, she is Fourth House." Proctor Ozdemir, whose age was indeterminate though she was at least as old as Havva, was Amara's choice for receiving the underprivileged mages she sometimes brought to the school. Not because she was lenient on them, but precisely because she wasn't. Demanding in a way that assured them they had earned their place. A first battle won in the war they would fight for the rest of their lives.

"Kumru. The test takes all day. You are prepared for that? No food or drink is allowed once you enter the testing hall."

"Yes, Mistress." Kumru offered a quick, awkward bow.

"I'll arrange a ride for you, and see you as soon as I'm able so you may tell me all about it." Amara urged Kumru gently forward. The proctor offered Amara a little wink as she guided Kumru through the foyer doors and into the atrium. Amara smiled, and turned to leave.

Outside, Havva waited on the steps with Djar, Kiya, and Kumru's mother. Bek had stayed behind to man the shop.

"All is well?" Havva asked. Amara nodded.

"She will do well," Amara assured Kumru's mother as she gave a worried look behind them. The woman nodded. "Can I offer you a ride somewhere in the city? You are welcome to wait at my shop."

"No. I think I'll walk. I'm too nervous to sit still." She offered a tremulous smile. Amara nodded, and Djar and Kiya waved farewell to her.

Amara questioned Havva with a look.

"I went to the city prisons yesterday, as you asked."

Amara walked down the steps, signaling Havva to continue with a look.

"Our knife-wielding friend is still safely ensconced. Though I doubt he will be after trial. None of those lower-city tribunal members care about a girl from the Lily." Havva's gaze cut sideways and she stopped, examining her nails before staring obliquely into the Grand Market beyond. "I have been told that Captain Akkas can be bribed to do almost anything. As long as you can convince him it is humiliating to the palace."

Amara exchanged a look with Djar. Captain Akkas. She remembered vague rumors that he had been dismissed by the Sultana, after some sort of minor infraction. But she had not given them too much credit. While she was not of an especially friendly disposition toward the Sultana at the moment, the woman wasn't a fool. She suspected there was more than a minor infraction involved.

"How interesting," Amara said. It was always useful to know who could be bribed.

"Djar has been telling me about your encounter with the Grand Vizier's son," Havva said.

"Odd. I told him not to speak of it." Amara narrowed her eyes at him.

"I should slit his throat for putting hands on you," Djar said. "What he did is a crime. You should report it."

Kiya harrumphed agreement.

"Don't be absurd," Amara said. "The Grand Vizier would never allow his son to be punished for such a thing. If the Sultana cannot even stand up to him to keep her promises, what do you think she would do to deal with such a small thing? No."

"Djar also tells me you've refused the Circle," Havva said, her voice neutral, though her gaze shifted between Amara and Djar.

"Oh, no. I'll join their Circle," Amara said, crisply. "I forgot, for a time, where I came from. And who I belong to. I forgot that I am not the only person who has crawled from the bottom to the top and been shoved aside."

Havva smiled, slowly.

"The Circle is supposed to be impartial, yet they only have a prince and a noblewoman on it." Amara looked toward the palace, looming over the city on its cliff. "Someone has to ensure the decisions of the Circle are not skewed in favor of the wealthy and powerful."

"That's my girl." Havva chuckled.

Amara smiled grimly, twisting Cassian's bracelet around her wrist. Yes. Just like water, which bound all things together and mixed them up. Top to bottom, inside and out, side to side. A mighty equalizer.

THE HALL OF CHARA'A was the largest single room Amara had seen in the palace, rivaling the soaring expansiveness of the University atrium. But the size of it was not what struck her first. It was its song. All magic sang to her, the wispy notes of air, the hard beats of earth, fire's sinuous undulations. This room was a harmonious chorus, with notes she had never heard before, a bright, clear thread that evoked joy. A shadow pitch, smoky and whispered. The song stopped her the moment she entered, and she lifted her chin to stare at the ceiling, at the runes etched up each wall in mosaic tile. Large windows let in the cool, damp spring breeze and the sounds of birds and the city beyond.

The stone seats, padded with sewn cushions, rose away from the floor like stairs. The colors of the cushions were made in the colors of the Houses, and created a discordant rainbow around the room. The Viziers filled the seats, the Fifth House weighted most heavily with bodies. A number of earth mages occupied the benches in the section for the Fourth House. Havva separated from her to cross the floor, greeting people as she shuffled between them to find a seat.

"Should I?" Kiya whispered. The sound would have carried, if the room was not already overpowered with the chatter of its occupants. Amara nodded. Djar took Bek to stand near the doors when Kiya broke off to follow Havva. Alone, sitting in the section meant for the extinct Third House, sat Mirari and Danel. They were pressed shoulder to shoulder, Mirari's head lowered, Danel's gaze fixed unseeing on the opposite side of the Hall. A pang of guilt stung her. She had not done well enough by them. Too concerned with herself. After this, she would remedy that. She would make certain they were not neglected nor exploited.

"Please come forward, Mutar Charah." When the Sultana spoke, the room quieted. For the most part. Those in the Fifth House seats continued chatting. Spurred on by the Grand Vizier, who held court in the center of them. Of course he would talk through her joining. The insufferable bastard.

Amara shrugged out of her ferace, revealing the same water-soft, pale-teal entari and matching caftan she had worn the day they'd refused her betrothal. She laid the ferace over a bench in the Second House section, nodding a greeting to those water mages she knew who were seated there. A wedge of turquoise stone set into the marble floor, meant to represent the Second House spoke, pointed to their seats, and she followed it to the center of the room.

Her favorite clothes were put to much better use today as she strode across the vast floor toward the Sultana. The movement made the fabric swish and swing, curling around her legs and shifting away, water hugging and caressing her body. What could not be silenced with respect was silenced with sex, as most male eyes in the room focused on her strut across the floor. Amara schooled her smile as she stood before the Sultana. Victories were almost more delicious when they were achieved without the other party's knowledge. And none of them realized they'd handed her their reins.

There was a small, amused smile turning the corners of the Sultana's mouth. Amara looked up into the seats, directly at the Grand Vizier, whose unrestrained expression of annoyance pleased her.

"If you are ready to begin?" The Sultana pulled a cloth away from a wooden scepter which clutched a faintly glowing, milky stone in carved fingers. She handed the cloth to Samira.

"I am." Amara watched the stone, its faint, pulsing light. Almost like a mage orb. But something swirled beneath the surface. Shadow, then flashes, like lightning. So faint, and yet she was certain she could hear a song of magic coming from it. A tinkling, like bells or chimes.

They walked together to the seam between the turquoise in the floor and the marble of the center, and the Sultana set the scepter into a hole in the stone.

"Amara Mutar, Third of the Merchants' Guild, of both Menei and Tamar, Charah of the Second House. You must choose the manner in which you will serve the Circle." The Sultana placed her hands against the stone and released her hold on her magic. Amara had never seen the Sultana's magic, and for a moment was dazzled by the pure white light that poured from her.

"You must link your magic to the Circle to be bound to it," the Sultana said in a soft, low voice meant only for Amara. Amara pressed her lips together and closed her eyes, resting her fingertips against the cold stone. Not bound. She would serve. As she had always been meant to. The Sultana nudged Amara's fingers with her own, and that bright, pure light burned into Amara, dragging her away from the room and depositing her in darkness. In void.

Amara almost screamed, afraid she would meet Benat in the emptiness, see his fire and his rage. This was the place she had been trapped, holding him. Commanding him to sleep. But he was not there. When her fear subsided she realized there was sound. Dripping water. Drop after slow drop, plinking and echoing into infinity. She knew what she would face here. What she had already faced. What Cassian had faced and come away from with nothing but love.

I am not afraid of you anymore, she thought into the nothingness.

Countless figures rose, unfurling from the emptiness to stand before her. The closest stepped forward, and raised its ephemeral hands, stretching them toward Amara. It was not a monster. There were no teeth, no claws. Water was emotion, reflected what was inside a person, not what was outside. Her power had mirrored her fear back to her, made monsters of her memories.

What do you see now, mirror?

The figure changed, faded and reappeared. Amara stood before her own reflection. A woman who knew who, and what she was. Water to quench fire. Love as salve to hate, soft and yet unbreakable. Water. It existed in the place between air and earth, second creation of the Wheel. Calm flexibility. Nothing could stand against it, nothing could harm it. Resilient. It turned violence to peace, silencing the ripples of those things which disturbed it. The softest of substances, yet, nothing could stand up to it over time, not even stone.

Equalizer.

The figure turned to look behind it to its brethren, into the infinite, and each misty figure began to glow, softly from the inside. That pale meeting of blue and green, like ocean in warm sun. These were not manifestations of her power. These were other water mages. Those monsters in the dark, that had reached for her in her nightmares, were other Second House mages, reaching out through their magic. To lift her up. How blind had she been?

You were wounded, spoke of the Second. *And what are you now?*

Amara opened her eyes, the day-bright Hall of Chara'a and brilliant assault of the Sultana's magic piercing painfully.

"Justice," Amara said. "I will serve by justice." The magic sang its song amidst her words, voices of the past, and present. Languages she spoke, and some she did not. All the Second spoke with her, claimed their place on the Wheel. Her power, dormant and recovering for so long, rose like a tide within her, and overflowed, spilling as silver mist onto the floor around her and the Sultana. Her quicksilver moon met the Sultana's winter sun, the two pale powers different, yet complementary. The mist filled the room, rolling across the floor, and around the perimeter figures rose with glowing hearts of turquoise. Their power bled together, and that same turquoise light traced the lines of the Second House spoke set into the floor, following it to the center of the room to outline the circle there. Songs like bells echoed, lullabies that soothed.

"Justice of the Circle. You are bound to its service, from this day, until your last."

Amara's magic raced back to her, the mist rolling up and swirling around her like a cloak, then dissipating. All along her limbs, and deep within her magic, she could feel the warmth of hundreds of others. Droplets to make an ocean.

A needle pierced Amara's core, dipping and pulling, and stretched taut between her and the Sultana for a moment. Naime's eyes flared wider and the warmth disappeared from her skin. The glow of her pulsed, fading for the blink of an eye then returning. She seemed Unbalanced, but quickly regained herself, her hands tightening against the white stone, which warmed against Amara's hands.

Amara stared at Naime, watching the change, the tremor of her lashes, the set of her mouth. A lie. A weighty, draining lie, like a garment draped over her. Amara lowered her gaze to the stone, glowing more brightly than it had before Amara's proclamation. Pure white light turned opalescent by the variations in the stone. Magic trapped.

"What is the price of a Circle of Chara'a?" Amara asked in quiet accusation. Naime waited a breath before she met Amara's gaze.

"A price I am willing to pay." The Sultana looked over her shoulder and Samira came forward to take the stone and scepter.

"Mutar Charah." The Sultana bowed to her. Still occupied with the lie she sensed shrouding Naime, Amara did not notice at first as everyone in the room stood. She did notice when they bowed. Her heart thumped. Her throat filled, tightened. This was what it felt like, to stand at the pinnacle of the mountain she had clawed her way up. Breathless.

She scanned the entirety of the room. The only one whose bow left something to be desired was the Grand Vizier, who leaned on his staff and only ducked his head when she looked at him. No matter. She did not need him to bow to know she had emerged victorious in this particular battle.

Amara smiled at him. And oh how he burned.

THIRTY-SIX

AMARA KISSED THE OTHER water mage's cheek. The girl smiled.

"Is that all you need, Mistress? Otherwise I'll be back at first light to finish the seams on that entari for Yavuz Pasha's wife."

"No, that is all. Thank you, Zeynep," Amara said.

The girl nodded and gathered up her apprentice's smock, waving as she trotted down the stairs.

Amara's home was not as lavish as some. Other houses on even this same street had large common rooms, with separate bathrooms and bedrooms with doors that closed. But hers was simply one large room, so that she could have the light from all the windows in the space. Her bed was tucked up against the west wall, right beside the doors to her balcony. The bathtub, which had been one of her first purchases after taking over the shop, was tucked at an angle into the corner, where a drain directed the water into a pipe and out into the street gutters.

She had yet to install a pump. Why do that when so many water mages were happy to oblige moving the water up for her through the system devised for magic users? Pumps were for voids. Djar complained often of her refusal to use the modern amenities engineered in Menei, since there was not enough magic there to rely on it for their infrastructure. They had, of course, stolen those designs from the Republic.

But in truth Amara liked the intimacy of listening to another water mage sing the water into compliance. She'd always lamented the fact that her Charah powers did not include the more mundane ability of lesser mages to control water's path.

Amara poured a jug of day-old milk into the water, then a few splashes of her favorite scented oils and a scattering of rose petals. A good soak would settle the uneasiness that coiled beneath her skin. Tomorrow, she would at least wade in the ocean. It was still chilly weather for swimming, but the connection would do more to restore her power than anything else.

She shed her clothes, and blew out all but one of the candles. The brazier was burning below, but it felt unbalanced to be in a room with such a large amount of water and no fire. Light footsteps sounded fast up the stairs, then Zeynep appeared on the landing, panting.

"There's a man at the back door," she huffed. Amara glanced to the balcony doors, which were cracked so she could listen to the pouring rain. He must be desperate to brave the spring downpour.

"Did he say what he wants?" Amara crossed to the large mirror on the wall and pulled the silk entari she used as a robe from its hook. She tied the robe closed. It was the last thing she wanted today. To deal with anyone. To give anything else. She was battered, and bruised, her spirit wounded, though recovering. There was very little left in her to give to anyone. But that was the choice she had made. To be a rising tide that lifted everything with it.

"I can't understand him." Zeynep frowned. "It doesn't sound like anything I've ever heard."

"Is he lost?" Perhaps a sailor up from the docks? It had happened on occasion, when a ship came in from a long haul and all the crew ruined themselves on cheap alcohol. Meneian sailors were notorious for their love of Tamar arak.

"He keeps saying your name, as though he's angry."

An angry customer perhaps. Amara took a step toward the stairs but the man shouted from the base of them, and he might as well have cast a spell to freeze her in place.

"*I know you're up there, Princess. Come down, or I'm coming up.*"

Zeynep startled and squeaked in alarm at the shouted words, spinning to grab for a vase perched on a table near the landing. Amara's blood surged, the hair on her arms standing on end, and her magic swirled awake in her belly. But the strength siphoned out of her, and when she said his name, it was little more than a whisper. He catapulted up the stairs a breath later, and poor Zeynep stumbled out of the way with a cry. He paused at the top of the stairs, searching the room for her. When he saw her he strode forward, but stopped after only three steps.

Amara stared at him, unwilling to believe he wasn't a torturous vision concocted by her exhaustion and raw emotion. If he wasn't real, and she believed, even for a moment, she would be shredded. Even her misty, twisted dreams of him left her in tears when she woke.

But Zeynep saw him. Amara dared to breathe. One inhale. When Zeynep bolted for the stairs behind Cassian, Amara was able to summon a handful of wits to stop her. "It's all right. He's a friend."

"Oh," Zeynep said, quietly. She set the vase back in place and leveled one last incredulous look at him before heading down.

The only sound was the water dripping off Cassian's clothes onto the tiles. He was completely soaked, his shirt clinging to his body, his hair plastered in wet waves against his head and temples. A single, deep shudder wracked him, but he did not look away from her.

"You came." It was all she could say. Everything else would take her to her knees. She would empty herself of all the pain of his absence, of waking without him and a world away. Of realizing the world she'd labored for in blood and sweat and sacrifice was not the one she wanted.

He lifted his hands and let them fall again. "Of course I did. Did you think I could be anything"—his brows drew together as if the words hurt him—"anything after you? You erased everything I was. Everything I thought I wanted. And all that was left was you. I thought I could let you go. But I can't."

"Cassian," she tried to make the words come.

"Please tell me I'm not too late." He took a single step toward her, his wet boot squelching. He grimaced then laughed. "Have I ever once not looked like a pathetic fool in front of you? I am Luck's favorite personal jester, I think." He shook the water from his hands and sluiced the water from his hair.

"You do not look like a pathetic fool. You never have, to me," she said.

"Did you…" He frowned, looking around the room again, and past her, to the bath, then her robe. His brows rose. "Are you…a princess now?"

"If you are asking if I am married, the answer is no. I withdrew my proposal." She did not know what to do. To run to him or make him come to her. She was hopeful and afraid. Afraid to reach again for a joy that had been taken from her.

"Oh," Cassian said. "I…" He heaved a sigh, his shoulders lifting and falling with the action. "I burned my blood right."

"Oh," Amara said. There was a pressure building in her chest, her throat, her eyes. He was blurring in her vision, and she couldn't seem to keep her breaths even.

"Don't make me do this again," he said, softly. She blinked away the tears.

"What?"

"Watch you cry," he said.

Amara laughed and smiled and reached for him, and the space between them disappeared. He wrapped her in a wet, icy embrace, pressing kisses across her forehead and cheeks then tipping her face to his and branding her mouth with a kiss that felt more real and wanted than anything she had ever had.

"Gods I missed you," he said when they parted. "My house was fine, before you stepped foot in it. My life was. I was."

"You weren't," Amara murmured. Cassian laughed, rubbing his thumbs along her jaw and narrowing his eyes at her.

"All right, I wasn't that fine." His gaze lowered when she shivered, looking between them, at her robe, now soaked by his clothes.

"I missed you too," she said. He lifted his gaze to hers again, its focus shifting to her mouth and down and back in quick succession.

"I have so much to say to you." He rested his brow against hers and closed his eyes. He shivered, then wrapped his arms around her and pulled her close. The hair on his jaw and cheeks, at that halfway point between stubble and beard that just made him appear a bit wild, scratched at her face.

"Did you come all this way for another shave?" She inhaled the fresh, cold scent of the rain, the salt of his skin beneath it, that warm, flat, magicless scent that felt familiar and peaceful to her. How had she managed in his absence? This simple embrace rooted her in place, tie-lines pulling her out of the darkest depths and into the sun-bright shallows of her power.

"I'll take it," he said. "I'll take anything you'll give me." His arms tightened when she shifted to pull back.

"Then take a bath." She tipped her head back to smile at him. He sighed, tipping his head to look past her, and raised an eyebrow.

"That's too pretty for me, Princess. But I'll be happy to watch you take one. I'll even scrub the places you can't reach." He grinned play-fully, but the look he gave her was both lusty and unsure.

She rose on her tiptoes and whispered in his ear, "We will both fit." Then she tugged him with her as she backed toward the tub. He resisted only long enough to get out of his boots, then followed. When she stopped at the edge of the tub, the smile on his face relaxed.

"Amara." He pressed his nose and mouth against her temple. "I cannot do this if I cannot keep you." He looked down at her, desire and sadness somehow entwining in his expression. "Just me, and you, and no one else. Anything else and I…" He closed his eyes. "Forgive me."

"I will not forgive you for being honest," she teased. "Promise to always be so. Promise to always let me see you as you are, real, and vulnerable, and I will be the same for you, as I am with no one else."

"I couldn't tell you how I felt. I was afraid to tether you. To tell you and have it proven I wasn't what you wanted. I was just…afraid."

"Not a tether. You anchor me," she said. "A shore upon which I can rest," she corrected, searching his face, and herself.

His eyes closed, and he took a breath and released it slowly. One side of his mouth lifted in an amused smile when he opened his eyes. "I was so afraid you'd be married. Gone from me forever, because of my foolish delusions."

"It is not foolish to want to do good." She brushed the wet hair off his brow. "And you are not the only one who stubbornly refused to turn from the furrow they had made." This was the Wheel's mercy, Cassian standing before her. This was its turn from pain to joy. She'd been so tenaciously holding on to the idea that she would turn it the way she thought it should spin that she had not been able to see what it was trying to give to her. Thankfully, the Wheel was not easily deterred.

"Can I do any good here?" His gaze shifted down as he slipped his index fingers beneath the collar of her blue entari, easing it away from her neck and off her shoulder. He dipped his head and kissed her shoulder, then along her collarbone. Amara let her head fall back, and he held her by the shoulders as he pressed kisses across her throat. She dropped her hands to his belt, tucking her fingers into it and tugging his hips against hers.

He lifted his head to look at her face, his expression distant, lost to desire, as he stroked a hand over her bared shoulder and down her arm, pushing the entari down and open to bare one breast. Amara watched him, the minute changes in his face and eyes, the tension in his jaw she thought reflected his control over himself.

"Oh," she said, her body already warm and eager for his hands, "yes." She circled her arms around his waist, leaning against him. He traced his thumb over the rise of her bared breast where it pressed against him. Her breath whispered out, her nipples tightening at the soft touch against skin made even more sensitive by the chill.

"I've made you cold." He turned them so he could dip his fingers into the water to test its temperature. "How do you heat this?" he said in fascination, releasing her to turn fully toward the tub and look around for the answer to his question. Amara put her hands on her hips, frowning. Then she grabbed fistfuls of his shirt and tugged him backwards against her.

"If my bathtub is more interesting to you than I am, perhaps I have mistaken your reason for coming," Amara said against his ear. He spun, grinning, teasing with the laughter in his blue eyes. His answer was his mouth to hers, a soft exhalation of her name. She met his kiss, liquid heat pooling in her core as his hands stroked down her back and pulled her hips against his. She might have been rewarded with the feel of his arousal against her, but for his belts and weapons and pouches that prevented the amount of contact she wanted. Amara made a disappointed sound, trying to tug his shirt free of his belts, and failed. She wanted to touch him, and bit his lip in rebuke for the trouble of it. Cassian's breathy laugh was half groan. He released his grip on her to reach between them and yank his shirt up.

"Better." She tunneled one hand beneath to stroke her fingers across what she could reach of the flat, muscled plane of his stomach.

He hooked two fingers in the tie at her waist and pulled it loose. Her entari fell open and he brushed it off her shoulders. "Much better. There are no clothes in the world beautiful enough for you," he said. She smiled, pleased, sinking mentally into the easiness between them, as if they had never been parted. She examined the buckles of his belts, trying to determine her way through them. Cassian started on his shirt, yanking it up and over his head, and Amara chose his pistol belt, unslinging it and setting it carefully aside. Cassian kicked it farther away from the tub and wiggled his eyebrows at her when she gave him a questioning look.

"Water's no good for the powder," he said. "In case you planned on splashing. Which I do."

Amara pulled his knife belt loose and tossed it with the other. Then the last, and he unbuttoned the pants as she dropped the belt on the floor. She urged him backwards as he pushed the pants down and stepped out of them. She gave the hard, hot length of his erection a firm stroke of greeting.

"We could skip the bath," he croaked, tugging her to him, kneading her backside with his fingers as he rubbed himself against her belly. "I can still warm you up."

His skin was icy beneath her hands, so she shook her head and pointed to the water. He huffed a sigh as he climbed in. He looked uncertain as he sank in, gripping the sides a bit too hard. But the uncertainty cleared as Amara joined him, sinking to her knees over his outstretched legs. He lowered his hands into the water and ran them up her thighs, his skin warming with the heat of the water.

"Come here." He tipped his head back against the tub edge, pulling her on top of him. His eyes closed and his arms circled her back. She tucked her head into the slope of his neck, stretching her legs out along his, surrendering to the warmth of the water and the closeness of him, allowing herself to believe. Believe that it was real. That it was hers. This thing between them, his body and heart, and smile. That it would not be taken from her, that she was safe, here. She had thought she needed the safety of a position far away from where she began to feel what she felt in Cassian's hold. But she had been so very wrong.

The candle snapped and flickered, and each little shift made a shushing sound in the water, but they lay together in silence otherwise. Her magic hummed inside her, a song of rightness. There were so many questions to ask, so many problems to solve, but for this moment, they didn't matter, drifting away on the silence.

Cassian's hands stroked one after the other down her back in slow rhythm. From shoulder to flank, out of the water, and under it, smoothing and claiming. The movement of his hands replaced the silence, dip and sweep, the sound of little waves on the rocky shore of a pond. His fingers danced over the bumps of her spine, circled in the small of her back. He bent one leg up, tipping his knee against the side of the tub and allowing her to settle deeper into the water.

He traced the crease where her thigh and buttock met, soft, reverent touches. His fingers curved over her inner thighs, stroking her legs apart around him.

Despite the warmth of the water, her skin prickled when he dragged slow fingers up her waist. He adjusted her against him so he could curve his thumbs under both her breasts. He played his fingers across them, a broader sensation than the pinpointed surge that came when he caught her nipples in between his first two fingers and pinched, gently. She gasped, pressing her feet against the opposite end of the tub to push herself higher against him.

He sucked in a breath as she moved against his torso and erection, lifting his head up to look at her. She could see the glow of her magic reflected in the water on his skin and around them. His gaze darted about, taking her in, and she could not read the serious expression on his face.

"I'd forgotten, a little"—he stroked her damp hair away from her face—"what it looked like. I didn't think it was possible to forget."

"What does it look like?" she asked.

"Moonlight. That particular kind you see on the quietest nights, over the water. The light that defies the dark." He smiled, embarrassed. "Moonglade, my mother called it. That streak of silver on dark water that races toward you on the shore. And you want to follow it, wherever it leads. Or I do, at least. I did, in fact. I followed it here."

She had missed his words. The artistry of him. Amara kissed him, petting his chest, and belly, drawing back and up enough to put space between them so she could trace the muscles of his body, little dips and swells. Cassian nipped and sucked at her lips and tongue, and caught the backs of her thighs, tugging her hips to his, tucking her knees against his hips and sending a wave of water over the tub edge.

"Told you," he breathed against her mouth. "Splashing." He brushed his hands up her back, to her shoulders, lifting his hips beneath hers in a wordless request. His erection slid against her, a slick, shivery rush of pleasure. When she murmured her approval to him he did it again, pinning her hands to his chest with his own, and lifting her a bit out of the water. Amara sat up, and took a cloth from the table beside the tub, wetting it and rubbing it with soap. When she worked the cloth over his chest and shoulders, Cassian sighed in pleasure.

He sat up with her urging, allowing her to wrap her arms around him and continue her attention on his broad back. He adjusted her legs to circle his hips, placing kisses along the slope of her neck and shoulders as she worked. His hands held her hips, rocking them against his, teasing her to distraction. The water moved with her, sloshing against the sides, and spilling.

"There isn't going to be any water left," he said against her neck, inciting a wave of shivers over her skin. "If you're done there, I have another part you're welcome to wash." He nipped her earlobe. "Vigorously."

Amara giggled, and Cassian took the cloth from her and reapplied soap, giving the cloth a quick sniff. "Even your soap smells better than anything in Haenna," he said as he massaged the cloth against the back of her neck.

The scent of lemon and lavender filled her nose, and his strong, gentle touch turned her muscles to liquid. She leaned into him with a soft groan, and he chuckled, lifting her hair away from her skin with one hand, working strong, slippery fingers up and down her back. He rinsed the soap away before he released her hair.

Cassian slid down into the water again, holding her to him with one arm while he tossed the cloth away with the other. He coaxed her body to lie along his with his hands and shifts of his legs. And when he seemed satisfied, he slid one hand over the back of her thigh and to her sex, rubbing gentle fingers over her most sensitive skin. He shifted beneath her, freeing his erection from between them with his other hand.

He slicked the head of his cock where his fingers had been, staring into her eyes with his own so dark she could hardly tell they were blue. He looked almost sleepy with the drain of his want, and that alone was enough to send a desperate surge of need through her. He stroked his thumb along her bottom lip, and she nipped it, then sucked it into her mouth, watching his face as she rubbed her tongue along it.

His eyes closed as he groaned, sinking into the tub until his head was nearly underwater. Amara had to brace her hands to either side of him to keep herself above the water. He cracked one eye to glare at her when she released his thumb, only his face visible above the milky water.

"You want to drown me in this tub, do you?" he grumbled.

"I thought we were making love," she purred.

"Not yet." He pushed up so suddenly that more water spilled over the side, and caught her hips between his hands. He thrust himself against her, and she pressed her thighs together around him to provide some friction. His breath hissed from between his teeth. "Do you know how often I've thought of my one night with you?" He pushed and withdrew again, torturing her, gliding across the ache between her legs in little thrusts, teasing her deprived and desperate body toward a climax it was raging for. Amara shifted, just an increment, a tilt of her hips, and on his next push he was inside her.

"No." She watched the tension of pleasure wash over his face and tighten his jaw. The sight of it was almost more pleasurable than the full, smooth press of him inside her. "Tell me."

"Uhm." He blinked, hard, his hands clutching at her hips, moving her once. He dropped his head back against the tub with a harsh exhale. "That was unfair."

Amara took hold of the tub edge to either side of his head and used it to slide them apart and together again. Cassian grabbed for the sides, arching underneath her. The water swirled around them. It had lost its heat some time ago, and now its touch chilled her, so her skin prickled with cold and with pleasure as she moved. Small, slow shifts. Just enjoying their closeness, the threatening bloom of her power, the arcs of sensation over her and through her.

Cassian sat up, threading an arm around her waist. "I have never done this in water before, and you are very slippery. Promise if your power takes me over again you won't let me drown."

Before she could say a word in response, he switched their positions, pressing her back against the tub, guiding her legs around his hips.

"I was never able to tell you what I saw," he whispered, dragging a hand down her body, then around and under her backside to hold her as he thrust again. "To tell you that you can take me there anytime. I did not see monsters in that darkness. I liked it there. I felt you there."

"I know," Amara breathed, wrapping her arms around him to hold on as he moved. It was not the easiest lovemaking she had ever done. They were almost too slippery, sliding apart and losing their grip. But his laughter made up for it, and his teasing, and the deep, emotional joy of coming together with him in a way she never could with anyone else.

"That's it," he said, after a few failed attempts at keeping a pace that would finish things. He stood up, water pouring off him, and flicked a rose petal off his chest. He caught her wrist and hauled her up as he stepped out, then slung her up into his arms and tossed her on her bed. She cried out in protest.

"You'll get the blankets all wet—"

"Could not care less at the moment," he announced as he climbed on top of her, dripping water everywhere. Amara frowned at him, but forgave him the moment he was inside her again. Hot pulses surged through her hips and thighs, and every sensation seemed to burn more intensely for the absence of the water's cool caress. And because of the absence of the water and its steadying effect, Amara's power, though not recovered, stirred more strongly, breaking loose.

Mist rose from the bathtub, from the water on the floor, and rushed them. For one desperate, breathless moment she thought she might scream. But Cassian bent down and whispered in her ear, "I will go wherever you send me, as long as you go with me." His warm, rough voice and soft touch anchored her back in her body, reminded her that it was she in control, not her power. The mist stopped, swirling across the floor, climbing the bed posts, but did not touch them.

Cassian propped himself higher on his elbows, to look at it, then down at her. "You're all right?"

"Not if you don't hurry up," Amara said as she wrapped her legs around his hips. He grinned, ducking to touch his nose to hers and offer a brief kiss. He rolled them to their sides, slinging her leg over his hip.

"I'm so sorry," he murmured, rubbing the scruff of his beard softly against her neck as his hips moved with hers, "that I kept you waiting." His words were breathless, his hands on her body moving fast and holding hard. She saw silver flashes of her raging power on her skin and reflected on his, and closed her eyes against the sight of the mist that cocooned them. But she could not hold it back forever. When her body succumbed to the rhythm of their dance, shivering her apart and washing in waves of heat and cold, all she could do was hold on to him as the mist fell across them. He pulled her hips hard to his, his body tensing as he nuzzled his face into her neck and groaned. But she couldn't see, everything muffled by the grey, whispering mist.

She clung to him, waiting for that inevitable tug when her magic yanked his mind away from him. Instead she felt him relax in increments. Then he rolled onto his back, bringing her on top of him. The mist began to sink away as she took her power back in hand.

After long moments in silence, Cassian gave a pleased sigh.

"I liked that much better," he said. "I like getting to see you sweaty and well pleasured, with your hair all messed up. And not angry and walking away from me. Not that I didn't deserve it."

"I am not sweaty," Amara sniffed. She touched her hair and sighed.

"No?" Cassian said. "Well I did not work you hard enough then. Let's see if we can remedy that." He rolled on top of her.

THIRTY-SEVEN

N HIS ENTIRE LIFE, Cassian had never seen a more intimidating pack of women than those who strode through the double doors of the library where Amara had left him and Peio. And that was a considerable concession, considering the kinds of matrons his mother had kept company with, and the Suloi women he knew.

Mirari was among them, and three who were strangers. The one beside Amara was a princess at least, if her attire had not given her away, the very regal way she was looking at him like he was a pile of dung marring the pristine scape of the sprawling library would have. A woman flanked her on the other side, short. Her hair contained in twin braids. She wore swords on her back and storms in her eyes. Behind her a woman dressed in muted red shades, with the same kind of quiet repression he'd seen in every Suloi he'd ever met.

Mirari stepped to Cassian's side and he ducked his head so she could press her nose against his cheek.

"*Welcome back to the shared path, Cassian,*" she murmured in Suloi. "*Wanderer has kept his eye on your road.*"

"*You are well, Sister?*" he replied. Mirari smiled weakly and repeated her greeting to Peio, who looked like a starved man handed a roast to be greeted by someone who shared his blood. Amara had promised to find him a better place to stay than the rough and unwelcoming inn Peio had spent the previous night in.

"Efendim, I'd like to introduce Cassian Haydar. He was instrumental in our success in Haenna," Amara said to the woman in the diadem. "Cassian, this is Princess Sultana Naime Sabri ilr Narfour, heir to the Tamar Sultanate."

Naime nodded to him and took a seat on one of the benches tucked between bookshelves. "Coffee please," she said in Trade, perhaps for his benefit, and her pretty friend in the red hurried away to obey. A servant then? But she had a very different mien than most servants he'd known in Haenna. The ones his parents employed had been like that. Servants by employment, not by mandate.

"I am grateful for your assistance, Master Haydar. Though I would prefer it if I knew your motives. Tell me why you came here," she prompted as soon as the one in red had left the library and closed the doors. Well, he could admire someone who got straight to the point.

Cassian was caught up in his curiosity about the furniture, tables set low to the floor and cushions for sitting, bookstands that formed the shapes of Xs that were lined along the benches in between shelves. Frescoes decorated the walls above the benches, though there were few of those. He wasn't close enough to make out their subjects, but they were wrought in riotous colors that called to him. Perhaps he would have time to examine them more closely, later.

There was one table of a normal height, but no chairs, and an array of dishes sat on it. Ceramic bowls and colored glass plates, ornate metal dishes with lids that looked like pointy hats. He pulled the top off one and peered inside. Small pink candies. He took one and popped it in his mouth. When the flavor hit him, he glanced at Amara in confusion. She raised an eyebrow. Rose? It tasted like perfume. He didn't think spitting it out was a good idea. The crunch as he slowly bit down on it was loud in the otherwise silent library.

"The Republic has not been a friend to me. My"—he crunched again, and Mirari, between him and the balcony, flinched— "friend"—he indicated Peio with a tilt of his head—"believes the Suloi may be interested in assisting Tamar in stopping the spread of Stephanus' new Empire."

He crunched, then quickly finished the candy and glanced around for something to drink. Amara indicated a pitcher of water, which he went for. After he'd poured a glass he turned and saw he'd left a trail of dirt across the intricate design of the carpet. He offered Amara a sheepish grimace and she pressed her lips together to avoid a smile. The Sultana examined the trail of dirt as if it perplexed her. He was going to have to polish up his manners, and his boots, if he was going to spend any more time in this palace. It would be an adjustment, speaking to royalty, instead of criminals.

The Sultana's servant returned, bearing an ornate tray of silver and porcelain. Upon it was a larger set of the same kind of coffee vessel and cups Amara had used to serve him his first cup what seemed like a lifetime ago. She took a moment to pour and distribute the beverage, and when Cassian almost declined, Amara's eyes narrowed, and he accepted. The woman in red tucked the tray under her arm and as she turned to leave, noticed Cassian and the trail of dirt he'd left on the carpet. Her face scrunched, then smoothed, but the look she cast him as she left was…very judgmental, if he did say so. Did the boots and shoes in this place magically resist mud?

"And your name?" The Sultana looked at Peio when the doors closed once more.

"This Ghost has no name." Peio kept his gaze directed at the Sultana's feet. She frowned.

"His name is Peio." Cassian glared sidelong at him. Could he not start over here?

"How might the Suloi assist us? We were not certain the Suloi even existed until Mutar Charah arrived in Haenna." Gods. Mutar Charah was such a formal title for her. A step down from princess, maybe? He had trouble keeping the formality of everything in line with his very happy, informal memories of the night before.

"I cannot speak to their magic," Cassian replied. "But I can tell you they are likely the best forward scouts an army might ask for. And they are much more familiar with the tactics of the Republic than you are, I would imagine."

"And what would they want in return for this…service?" She was cold, this one. Pretty and cold, like a marble statue of the High Goddess.

"A home," Mirari answered for him. "Where they are not hunted. Where they may be as they are. The home they once had."

"If a Matrik and a Pathfinder can vouch for the road, and the destination, I believe we can convince those left to return with us," Cassian suggested without looking at Mirari.

"I am not a Matrik," Mirari said. "And I will not leave Benat here, alone." She looked at each person with suspicion.

"He will be safe and treated well," Amara said. There was song in her voice, that whispery touch of magic he had not understood the first time he'd heard her sing. The one that could calm, as it did now, settling his feelings and making him feel steady.

Mirari turned her back on them and paced to the doors that overlooked the balcony outside the library. She stood staring out them with her arms folded around her.

"Attiyeh Charah is capable of holding his magic much more easily than I am," Amara said, "which means we will be able to wean him off the drug."

The woman in braids smiled, but the friendliness of the expression was suspect, with those little flashes of lightning in her eyes. She was a conundrum, small and unintimidating, yet bristling with weapons and magic. Cassian took a step back, and Peio followed.

The library doors opened, admitting a man who walked as if trying to get away from something. That something appeared to be Danel, who moved as fast as Cassian had ever seen him. Danel grabbed for the other man, but stopped mid-reach when he saw everyone else. The stranger continued on, bowed to Amara, and the Sultana. That wasn't the prince? Was it? Cassian shoved his hands in his pockets. The last thing he wanted to do was meet or shake hands with the man who had almost taken Amara from him.

This new man's irritation, or distraction, was easy enough to identify. His shoulders were set stiffly, and his gaze darted in every direction except back at Danel. When that gaze finally landed on Cassian it stayed, taking in his Republic clothes and pistol belt with a raised eyebrow. Cassian set his water glass on the table and moved to Amara's side. The other man's assessment continued.

"Blue," he said. "How delightful."

"I told you." Amara offered a secretive smile. The man tipped his head and smiled back. Cassian scowled. He wasn't wearing anything blue.

"Cassian, this is Mathei Attiyeh, Master of the Sultana's libraries." Amara twined her fingers through his. Cassian reveled in the touch, and squeezed her hand in return. "Mathei, this is Cassian Haydar. Whom I mentioned to you during our coffee."

"Well, well, well," Mathei said. "I've come seeking answers and what should I find, but exactly the person who can answer them. The Wheel turns for knowledge." He offered his hand. Cassian gripped it. Perhaps a bit too firmly because he was relieved it was not the prince. "Do you know much about tattoos?" Mathei asked.

Mirari spun away from the window, drawing everyone's attention. She looked past them to her brother, where he stood scowling by the library doors, as if he had betrayed her.

Confused, Cassian returned his attention to Mathei. "Do you mean Republic tattoos?"

"Of course. We'd never do something so barbaric here," Mathei sniffed.

"*You didn't tell me everyone here was so full of themselves,*" he said in Meneian. Amara would have replied, but Mathei beat her to it, in what sounded like flawless Meneian. At least to Cassian.

"*The magical ability to kill on sight, or when someone annoys you, does tend to make one pompous. Back to my question?*" Mathei smiled.

Cassian flushed. "The Republic tattoos their soldiers."

"I see. And if I describe a mark to you, might you tell me what his function was?"

Cassian shrugged. Mirari took a few quick steps closer, tugging at fistfuls of the shirt she wore and darting another desperate look at her brother.

"A blade, I think," Mathei began, and Cassian's stomach plummeted. "With an eye at the tip."

Peio looked at Cassian, his face twisting with disbelief before he looked at Mirari. If Mathei had seen such a tattoo, there was only one likely person to be marked with it.

Cassian rounded on Mirari. "What have you done?"

"Please," she said, "it isn't—"

Peio breathed a prayer to the Wanderer.

"What is it?" Amara asked. The Sultana had stood, moving to stand beside Mathei.

"The black blade is the mark of the Vexillae," Cassian said. "And the eye, the mark of their hounds."

"Perhaps you could elaborate." Mathei aimed an accusatory look at Mirari.

"Amara knows." Cassian looked at her because her breath came in short.

"They are magic users that can sense others with power." Her voice was soft, and tremored. "And they hunt down magic users for the Republic."

"They are betrayers. Most of them have Suloi blood," Cassian added.

"Where did you see this, Mat?" the Sultana asked. But Cassian only needed to see the fear and shame on Mirari's face to confirm what he already suspected.

"On the Charah, Benat. Along his back," Mathei answered.

Everyone looked at Mirari, and she shook her head. "Those roles were forced on him, he isn't—"

"Did you not see what he did to Amara?" Cassian snapped. "You've delivered an obscenely powerful mage and spy into the heart of Tamar!"

"He has been nothing but a friend to us, Cassian." Danel finally joined them, to stand beside Amara. "Fought for us, sacrificed himself in an attempt to save us. He was in hiding from the Vexillae when we met him. He left them."

"You do not leave the Vex," Cassian scoffed. "That man has been broken and remade into their animal. He is here to murder mages. I would bet my name." Bitterness ate away at his temper, as he looked to Peio. "And since when do the Suloi believe in second chances?"

"Not to be prudishly attached to logic," Mathei said, "but I cannot see how you would allow that man to remain here in Narfour, Sultana? He has proven to be unstable. Dangerous. And now we know he might also be a spy."

"Mutar Charah," the Sultana said, "you have had a unique interaction with him. And I trust your judgment. Can you speak to this?"

"Please." Mirari came a few steps forward. "He didn't mean to hurt you, he—"

"*You've said enough, Sister*," Danel said, harshly. Mirari stopped, dropping her gaze and folding her hands.

"I am not certain you should trust my judgment, Efendim," Amara said, softly, her expression pained. "They are not lying. He is...conflicted. But I do not know if he is salvageable, and his uncontrolled magic is a great danger to this city. I must admit"—she took an unsteady inhale and straightened—"that I fear him."

Mirari lifted her gaze to the ceiling, tears gathering in the corners of her eyes.

Cassian thought Amara shouldn't have had to say it. Of course she feared him. Benat had attacked her. But Cassian was a stranger, and despite his rusty grasp of social niceties, he knew now was not the time to erupt into a diatribe aimed at a foreign ruler.

"If he was unwilling to do their work, how did the Republic control him?" The Sultana directed a bone-chilling look at Mirari. She gave that same feeling as Amara had, from the moment he'd first seen her, something other. More than a woman, more than a human. Something powerful, and frightening. Cassian shuddered, watching the Sultana and Mirari look at each other.

Soft fingers stroked the inside of his wrist, sending tingles across his palm. Cassian chanced a look at Amara. She also focused on the other two women, but glanced sideways at him, flashing a tiny smile. Not alone, it said. He hadn't thought he'd ever need a woman protector, but now that he had one, who had saved him once already, he didn't think he minded it.

"With poppy," Mirari finally spat. "They drugged him until they could control him with pain, like an animal. Just like you are doing." There was a bit of that steel he knew was in there. Suloi women were deceivingly compliant around strangers. But they were the heart and backbone of their people, and when something they cared for was threatened, they were a force to be reckoned with. At least in his experience. "If this is how the roadborn are treated here, it is no wonder they fled this place."

"Mirari," Danel warned. A burning look was her only response.

"I will protect my people and my city by whatever means are necessary," the Sultana said, meeting steel for steel, but hers was backed with a wintery stare and composure like a marble statue while Mirari's was less honed. "Though you may rest assured it is not in my interest to harm him. Do you understand what a Charah is?"

"I don't care," Mirari said.

"You care for him but you don't care what he is?" Mathei said, his tone thorny and dismissive. "You cannot profess to care for someone without knowing who and what they are."

"May I suggest we calm ourselves?" Amara said, in a tone like she was talking to children. Cassian repressed a smile. "No one here is interested in using or harming Benat. Mirari, you must trust us. And if you cannot, then you must consider who is in a better position to help a mage who cannot control his powers or himself." That water song was in her voice again. He could feel it like a cool drink on a hot day, threading his limbs with calm. And it made Cassian wonder. She had not used it so much in Haenna. Had repressed it. Did she feel safer here, to use her powers?

"I trust you," Mirari said to Amara.

"We need Benat, but I will give him no less choice than I have given any of the Charah. If you wish to know more about this, and the Circle, you may ask Attiyeh Charah or Mutar Charah," the Sultana said. Mirari looked at the floor. "Our doctors are trying to heal him, in the meantime. They have informed me it is unwise to wake him until his body is recovered, because lingering pain will only aggravate his lack of control. Until we have weaned him further from the poppy, we cannot chance him waking under its influence."

"Sitting idle never helped anyone." Cassian looked from the Sultana to Amara, uncertain if he should address her directly. "Mirari and Danel can come with me and Peio to track down the remaining Suloi clans."

"Yes," Danel said. If the prospect of more lengthy travel troubled him, with his leg, he did not let on.

"No!" Mirari shouted. "I am not leaving Benat here with these"—she cut a look between the Sultana and Mathei, who raised an eyebrow in challenge—"people." Mathei's mouth thinned at the insult.

"You have forgotten, Mirari, that this one"—Danel indicated Amara with a tilt of his chin—"saved your life. What she demands of you is yours to do."

"That is what you would do?" Amara asked Cassian when Mirari gave Amara a pleading look. "Leave again? And take these with you, to convince the clans to come here?" Her large, dark eyes were wide and sad, searching his face. He hadn't spent the time he should have, telling her about his internal revelations. He would remedy that the moment they were alone. So that she knew he would come back. But for now...

"I planned to bring them back. Maybe earn myself a place to stay? I am...currently on the outs with several people in Haenna." He scratched his jaw.

"You do not need to put yourself in more danger to prove yourself to anyone. I will vouch for you. You are welcome here," Amara said.

"If you do this thing, Master Haydar, Tamar will be eternally grateful," the Sultana said. Amara shifted, her eyes narrowing a fraction, but she didn't say anything.

"Just Cassian," he said. "I burned my fancy titles before I came here."

"I will send Attiyeh Charah with you. You will have to return via Golge, and to do so someone will have to speak for you."

"I would be honored, Sultana," the petite woman finally spoke, "but I think I would be better put to use in controlling the new Charah, if he wakes. I have a fine replacement in mind though." She gave a vulpine grin and looked at Mathei. His nostrils flared.

"I have work," Mathei said.

"All the work I've seen you doing lately is bellyaching about that missing page."

"Still?" the Sultana sighed. "You are like a boarhound over that single page, considering the other knowledge that awaits you." She waved a hand to indicate the books arrayed about them. Cassian, an untalented but practiced gambler, knew a misdirection when he saw one. Even from a stranger. Or rather, especially from a stranger, since he was not blinded by his knowledge of a person. Everyone else missed the transient smile, the darting gaze. They laughed. But he wondered. "Attiyeh Charah makes a very good point," she conceded, guiding them further from the subject.

Mathei scowled displeasure.

"You?" Danel said, showing disdain the only way Cassian had ever seen a Suloi show disdain, by looking the other man directly in the eyes. "You live a life in stale rooms surrounded by dead words. You will not survive the road."

"You seem to have managed," Mathei retorted. Mirari made a sound of protest, and Amara clicked her tongue.

"*Roadless son of a—*"

"He'll be fine, Pathfinder," Cassian said, quickly, to cut off Danel's curse. This one had a feeling about him like magic. Wasn't everyone in Tamar a mage? Cassian would take any help he could get if he had to cross back through the Republic lines, and the Tamar armies with half a dozen clans. "And Peio."

Mathei glanced at him, then quickly back to Danel. "Wonderful. Just the kind of company I would want on a jaunt into enemy territory."

The Sultana released a little breath. "Mathei and I will draft a message to the Agassi to send forces as escort from Golge." She bowed to Amara. Only slightly, but it seemed to please Amara, from the small smile on her face. There were too many titles and people to process, and Cassian's hunger suddenly sank fangs into his belly. Surely a palace of this size had food somewhere. His stomach growled its agreement, loudly enough that everyone turned to look at him.

"That seems a good point to end on." Humor sparked in the Sultana's gaze. "We'll have food arranged for you, in the breakfast hall. Mistress and Master Garai, shall we go and see Benat?"

After a flurry of exchanged bows and head nods, the Sultana, Danel, and Mirari left, with the petite Charah close on their trail.

"That's better," Mathei sighed, plopping onto a couch and stretching his arms along the back of it. He assessed Cassian, then cast a curious look at Peio. "When would you like to depart?"

"He's just arrived," Amara said in exasperation.

"Well, things move fast here at the palace. Sink or swim, my friend." Mathei smiled apologetically to Cassian.

"I have found I have an affinity for water," Cassian said.

Peio snorted softly, lowering his gaze from the dome to Cassian's. Amara rewarded him with a smile.

"Great Wheel," Mathei groaned, "the innuendo in here is suffocating." He popped up from the couch. "Why am I always subjected to this torture? My prince, my sister, and now my tailor." He gave Amara a quick wink before he headed for the library doors. He stopped when he reached them, and glanced back. "Are you coming? At least allow me the sanctuary of a solid meal if I have to be forced to watch you make eyes at each other."

Amara's smile broadened and she laughed, tugging Cassian after her. Peio came too, behind Cassian and Amara. When Mathei checked to make certain they were following, he saw Peio behind and dropped back. He draped an arm over Peio's shoulders.

"Peio, was it?" he said. "We'll have a chat, you and I."

"About what?" Peio asked, bewildered, to say the least. In the Republic he'd been ignored by almost everyone. Republic citizens and his own people alike. No one ever touched him, except Cassian.

"Everything about the Suloi," Mathei said.

"That will take a great deal of time," Peio said, warily. Mathei patted his shoulder and unslung his arm.

"Yes, I was hoping so."

A BRIGHT SHAFT OF sunlight irritated Cassian from the half-sleep where he lingered, enjoying the small, warm hand that was closed possessively over his wide-awake member. He squinted at the ceiling, white plaster that positively blazed down at him with the reflected sunlight. If Amara was awake, she wasn't indicating it, which made him smile, forgetting the irritation. He didn't want to wake her, he wasn't ready to face the day, and whatever else this new reality had in store for him.

So he lay exactly as he was, only turning his head to take in the room. It had her obvious touch in every corner, every decoration. It was not cluttered, but what was there had been chosen carefully. Soft, cool colors that brought water to mind. Curtains gathered on the floor like rippled pools, rugs masterfully woven with brilliant patterns to keep her feet off the cold stone of the floor. The bed had piles of blankets, suggesting to him that she did not enjoy being cold. That was all right. He could keep her warm. Happily. There were art pieces. Sculptures. Pretty, handcrafted pottery and vases.

He saw it on his third visual trip around the room, hung on the wall above them, between the windows. His painting of her.

Amara shifted, to his utter heartbreak releasing her grip on him. He was soothed when she slid her silken body up his to kiss him in greeting.

"Hello, pretty girl," he murmured in Trade, sweeping her hair away from her lovely face with his hands. He'd have to learn Tamaran. It felt strange to speak the language of the Republic here. She draped herself across him, smiling sleepily. Yes. Poor thing. He'd been unable to stop touching her and kissing her for most of the night. He'd lost count of their trysts when his exhausted body slapped him into sleep.

"Have you been awake long?" she said in a sleepy whisper.

"You like having all this sunlight in here?" he asked. She scrunched her nose, and he rubbed his thumb over her freckles, rejoicing in the simple pleasure of being able to look at her. She was beautiful the way the ocean was beautiful. In a new way every time one looked.

"It is much preferable to that dank cave you called a house."

"Oh, I think you liked my house just fine," Cassian said.

"I liked seeing you where you were comfortable. I liked the idea of…" She hesitated, her gaze darting to his face and away. "…keeping you." She sighed, a pucker furrowing her brow. "You want to leave again."

"I don't want to." He tucked her hair behind her ear. "I can make a difference this way."

"That's what you want, to make a difference?"

"What I want"—he shifted, circling her fully with his arms—"is for you to sing for me."

Her lashes lowered. "For a trade."

"Hmm. And what is it you want?"

She rolled to her back beside him, her head pillowed in the crook of his outstretched arm, and pointed at the painting. "I'd like you to finish it."

"But the subject of that painting is very complicated," he said. "It could take me a very long time, were I to do it properly."

She turned her head toward him. "How long?"

It was his turn to falter, a cold lump lodging in his throat and blocking the words. Fear of her rejection making him want to snatch her up in his arms and distract her from his heart with more physical affection. But she saw through him, mirror that she was. His truth reflected in the dark, fathomless depths of her eyes.

She sat up, leaning on her hip, her feet tucked up close, her hands close together as she dipped her head forward to look down at him. And he held the pose in his thoughts, as the next painting, or sculpture. The second in a never-ending supply of inspiration he was certain she would be for him. His muse.

"A lifetime," he said. Amara tried to smile, but was only able to take a shaky inhale, her eyes brightening as she nodded.

"That's what I want," she said. "A lifetime." She shoved her fingers into his hair and dropped on top of him. "I love you."

"Thank the gods for that." He felt like laughing, and crying relief, and he pushed her curls away from her face so he could kiss her. "I love you too."

"You said no one in the Republic would be your patron," she said, when he released her from the kiss. "I want to be. I want your art in the world."

Emotion filled his throat and stole his voice. All he could do was stare at her. Perhaps she could tell he was overcome, because she softened the emotional firebomb with light touches of her fingers against his mouth.

"Of course all your pieces will have to be for me or of me," she said. The tension went out of him, and he laughed.

"As long as they can all be naked."

She clicked her tongue in admonishment. "Of course."

A series of crashes sounded downstairs.

"Amara! Look who we found!" Kiya's singsong drifted up the stairs. Amara slid off Cassian as he lunged for the floor, where his clothes were piled. She shrugged into her robe with far less alarm than he managed as he fought into his pants and shirt, though she seemed amused by his hurry.

A stampede of steps battered the stairs, and Cassian had only just finished tugging his shirt into place when he was assaulted. Wiry arms and a choking cloud of hair, then another bear hug from behind that squeezed the breath out of him.

"I knew it! I knew it! Peio said he came without you." Kiya jumped up and down when she released him.

Peio mounted the last stair, grinning slyly. Cassian scowled at him and Peio tapped a finger against his brow, a Suloi sign for 'I got you.'

Cassian managed to sling an arm around Kiya's shoulders, and one around Bek's when Kiya calmed herself enough to hold still. He squeezed them both. "It's good you're here," he said. "Peio and I need guides around the city. And Amara has told me she's too busy." He steered them toward the stairs, hoping to give her time to get dressed.

"Peio said you stowed away on a ship," Bek said as they wrangled their way down the narrow, spiral staircase.

"No. We paid."

Bek made a disappointed sound. They led Cassian into a tiny kitchen, which opened to a tinier courtyard where Djar was starting a fire in an outdoor oven. He straightened when Cassian stepped outside. His eye had healed, or rather, the wound had. There was a knotted mass of scar where the eye should have been.

"You aren't any better looking here than you were in Haenna," Cassian said. Djar glowered at him for an intense, long moment. Then his mouth split in a grin and he clapped a hard hand on Cassian's shoulder, steering him to the fire and the grate over it.

"Come, my friend. If you're going to live in Tamar, then you need to learn to make coffee."

Peio took a perch on the low wall that surrounded the patio where they gathered, and the twins leaned to either side of him. Djar showed Cassian how to measure the coffee into the little copper pot. Bek critiqued his technique. And it felt...good. Warm, and too chaotic. As his home had once been. Before Paulus Hirtius stole it all. But this...

He glanced over his shoulder. Amara leaned in the doorway, her head tipped against the frame, watching their laughter and teasing in silence. She blinked rapidly when he looked at her, and a tear slid down her cheek. But she smiled and nodded him back to his lesson with Djar. This was better. As he gazed at her, he could see that she thought that too. Better than any palace. Better than any position of power in a Senate. He'd finally found the right path to follow.

The Suloi might think following the river was a bad choice. But Cassian thought following his river was the best choice he'd ever made.

THE END

Author's Note

THANK YOU FOR READING. *Siren & Scion* was the hardest to write so far. I wanted so badly to get Amara and Cassian's story right, and I hope my efforts paid off in your eyes.

Are you ready for book four?

> *The Wheel spun, from darkness into light,*
> *and washed the world in water.*
> *And lightning in the sea awoke,*
> *Wheel's spirit, humble daughter,*
> *Green and bright, and tertian spoke*
> *Womb to life and laughter*

Be first to know about upcoming releases, extras, and all the fun times—sign up for the newsletter!

https://www.subscribepage.com/motw

Find Me Online:
Author's Website: **https://www.jdevansbooks.com**
Facebook: **https://www.facebook.com/jdevansauthor**
Twitter: **https://twitter.com/jdevansbooks**
Instagram: **https://www.instagram.com/jdevansbooks**

I would love it if you left a review on Amazon. I love the feedback, and it is my soul fuel to keep writing.

And don't forget—your honest review helps other readers know what to expect, and it gives my books visibility, which means I can keep writing them! That's good all around, right?

Easy Peasy—just follow this link:

http://www.amazon.com/review/
create-review?&asin=B0888388LN

Acknowledgments

I THINK, AT BOOK three, we can officially say that this has transformed from hobby to…career? I hope so. I have been writing since I was eight or nine. My first stories were a weird mash-up of Babysitter's Club and…animals. The characters were high school animals. I don't know, don't ask me. I'm sure it had something to do with all the sentient animals in kids' cartoons. There were Westerns too. I was a weird kid, all right? I didn't learn to read until, what some would consider, quite late. My parents had me in a Waldorf school, and in that particular methodology, you allow the child to come to reading when they're ready. So I didn't learn to read until the second grade. Once I learned, I made up for lost time. I read all my dad's Louis L'Amour books. I read The Babysitter's Club. And then the stories started in my head. And the rest is history, I suppose. Or will be, eventually.

But this section isn't about me, it's about other people. Because books don't come to life by the effort of one. Making a book is, honestly, a bit like having a baby. I incubate this little thing, from tiny spark of an idea to small infant. I write the words, bring it into the world, and then it makes its way through the hands of all the people that will shape it.

My lovely editor, Michelle, who, like a doctor, takes its measure and ensures it's quite healthy before cleaning it up and handing it back.

My sister, loyal and steadfast writing partner, who reads from conception to end product, and tells me when maybe I am spoiling my characters a bit too much.

My friend Kate, who like a school teacher, helps me spot problems I am probably blind to because it's MY book and how could it possibly have any flaws?

Terry Roy, who takes my disheveled mess of a book child, gives it a haircut and a good cleanup, and makes it presentable to the world.

Tatiana Anor and Eric C. Wilder, who together have made beautiful book covers, so the rest of the world can see on the outside what I tried to create on the inside.

And of course, you, the reader. Without you, there would be no reason to go to all this effort. You make everything worth it, sharing in my world and characters and, I hope, loving it all as much as I do. Thank you.

Are you hooked on Tamar? Would you be interested in receiving advanced review copies of the next in the series? Consider signing up to be part of my ARC team!

https://forms.gle/v2uxm1DL2KCd1fgg7

Books by J. D. Evans

MAGES OF THE WHEEL SERIES

Prequel (Summer 2020)
Reign & Ruin
Storm & Shield
Siren & Scion
Ice & Ivy (Winter 2020)

ABOUT THE AUTHOR

J. D. EVANS WRITES fantasy and science fiction romance. After earning her degree in linguistics, J. D. served a decade as an army officer. She once spent her hours putting together briefings for helicopter pilots and generals. Now she writes stories, tends to a tiny human, knits, sews badly, gardens, and cultivates Pinterest Fails. After a stint in Beirut, J. D. fell in love with the Levant, which inspired the setting for her debut series, *Mages of the Wheel*.

Originally hailing from Montana, J. D. now resides in North Carolina with her husband, small human almost-clone, aging canine, and too many stories in her head.

Made in the USA
Las Vegas, NV
06 September 2024

94876053R00263